The Q QUEST

Frank P. Araujo

- Quartet Global -

Published by Quartet Global
Seattle, WA
Contact: quartetglobal@gmail.com

Cover painting by permission of Ruth Coelho
Cover design by M. Anne Sweet
Author photo by Frank Araujo

ISBN-13:978-0-9870493-8-7 (Trade Paper)
ISBN-13:978-0-9840493-9-4 (e-Book)

Printed in the United States of America

DEDICATION

For Red.

ACKNOWLEDGMENTS

For all the people who helped me get here—especially, Cat and Roberto.

ONE

DESTRUCTION

The Old Mosque in Kansu, 5 miles SE of Anatakya (Antioch), Turkey
Late summer, 1997, Friday, just before noon

The Bomber stood on the crest of the hill looking down at the large patches of the brown stucco undercoat that showed through the dirty white walls of the peeling exterior of the Old Mosque.

The Bomber surveyed the foyer of the building where men in traditional dress, others in modern clothing mingled and talked in loud Turkish.

He felt strong, brave– powerful. He was The Bomber.

Today the Turks will feel my wrath.

The Bomber wheezed, asthma tightening his chest. Walking away, he turned into an alley behind a row of two-storied, whitewashed houses where he stumbled from a spasm of coughing, thrust out his hand against the side of the building.

When his rattled breathing settled, he looked up, saw where his hand print had stained the white wall with the blackened residue of gun powder.

Still gasping for breath, The Bomber stepped away, glanced down the dirt street beyond the alley, then turned, looked back once more at the mark of his black hand.

At the sound of footsteps, he jerked around, dropped his hand to the dagger in his sash, then relaxed when he recognized the five men who came up to join him.

All of the bearded men wore brimless *taqia,* like his. Two men wore sandals, two wore gym shoes, one wore slippers. All five wore coats, vests or long shirts covering their cotton robes.

The Bomber greeted the men in Kurdish, embraced, kissed each of them, then caught his breath.

"These Turks must die," The Bomber said. "Our deaths will announce to the land that the Kurdish nation must live."

"Belé!" a man in gym shoes said. "Yes!"

"*Xas*!" the slippered one said. "Good!"

"You all now wear the packets," The Bomber said. "The cord tied to the toggle in your right hand sets off the charge."

"When do we act, my brother?" a sandaled man said.

"When the Imam declares the *takbir*, we all pull the toggles."

"As one?" a man in gym shoes said.

"Yes, my brother."

The Bomber stepped to the nearest man, looked into his face, straightened his long shirt, pulled down his vest, buttoned up his jacket. He checked the men's packs, their firing mechanisms, arming each one in turn. With tears in his eyes, he smiled, patted each man's sweating, frightened face.

"Allaah uhbarik fiik," The Bomber said. "God's blessings be upon you."

After giving each man the same blessing, The Bomber stepped back.

"No fears," The Bomber said. "Allaah guides our path."

They separated, each one walking alone toward the Old Mosque.

~*~~*~

At the mosque, The Bomber plopped down on a bench at the entrance, took off his shoes, washed his hands, his feet, his face. The Bomber watched his five Kurds mix in with the crowd. He smiled, knowing they all wore clean underwear.

Near the door two boys selling tea lined up shoes. One offered to clean the bomber's shoes for a tip.

Thinking again of his black handprint on the white wall of the house in the alleyway, The Bomber nodded, dried his hands on a towel, then dropped all of his money in the boy's palm.

The boy's eyes widened. He gasped,

"This is too much, Effendi."

Rising to his feet, the Bomber melded into the crowd entering the mosque.

Inside, he sat cross-legged in a row in the center of the congregation, then looked to the front of the large windowless room sheltered by a domed roof with blue walls split by two support columns.

Out of the corner of his eye, the bomber watched his five other Kurds take up their positions.

One in the front center.

Two on either side.

Two in the middle, next to the support columns.

The Bomber took a deep, wheezy breath that hurt his chest. Peeking back, again, he was proud of his Kurds.

The Bomber raised his eyes from the faded blue wall bordered with Egyptian Koranic designs at the front of the assembly room, to the carpeted podium where a microphone poked up in the center, then to the painted blue door on the left wall.

The scratchy recording of the muezzin's call to prayer ended. The assembly quieted as the Imam with his attendants entered through the side door, moved to the center in front of the raised dais, turned their backs to the audience facing the wall SE, toward Mecca.

Behind them, The Bomber scrambled to his feet with the assembly, straightened, stiffened with his hands at his side.

The Imam intoned,

"*ALLAAH U AKBAR*!'

The Bomber yanked the toggle.

News on TV

Guest room 321, Wilford Dorms, Princeton University, Princeton, NJ
Late summer, 1997, Saturday, 9:25 AM, EDT

Checking herself in the mirror, Colene Mooney ran her hand over her blond hair, straightened her jacket, touched the small string of pearls at her throat. Glancing at her hands, she looked for snags on her clear polished short finger nails.

Satisfied, she stepped back, dropped a monogrammed white linen handkerchief in her purse.

Then, she heard the TV announce a terrorist bombing of a mosque in Anatakya, Turkey. Colene froze.

That's Antioch!

She turned, sat on the edge of the bed, looked at the TV.

A BBC reporter with mike in hand walked in front of his camera man through a chaotic swath of collapsed walls, ambulances with flashing lights, white uniformed attendants carting away bloody bodies, workers moving rubble around the bombed-out mosque.

"The Old Mosque was the scene of destruction today," the reporter said. "The explosion, likely the work of suicide bombers, occurred shortly after the noon hour when large numbers of people were gathered for their Friday Prayers."

Damn. I saw that old Mosque when I was in Antioch three years ago.

"We're asking Captain Attila Akin, Chief of State Security for an assessment of the situation," the reporter said.

The camera cut to the face of a tall man in sunglasses perched on a prominent nose over a thick black moustache, dressed in khaki with the epaulets of a senior officer.

"Can you tell us what happened?" the reporter said.

"It was unspeakable," Captain Akin said. "Witnesses report that the blast ripped the mosque to pieces. Apparently, when the interior supports collapsed, the domed roof crumpled and imploded, then the minarets collapsed."

"Casualties?"

"Too early to be certain. We estimate over 200 victims. But, you can see the carnage for yourself."

"Any idea who did this?"

"We're interested in a Kurdish separatist cell– we found a hand print on the wall of a house nearby that we suspect might be a terrorist center."

"Is this a significant lead?"

"Yes. One of the few survivors, a boy– a tea seller– tells of a man who gave him all his money before going in to pray. We're comparing the bills for fingerprints."

"This is indeed tragic."

"We will rebuild the mosque undeterred by these terrorist efforts," Captain Akin said.

Huh! Wonder what they'll find when they do?

Colene looked at her watch. Time to go.

She had a conference paper to give.

A Conference Paper

Albert Einstein Memorial Auditorium, Princeton Campus
same day, 25 minutes later

Stepping behind the speaker's podium at the table in the center of the stage, the moderator, Professor Jake Ryan made his brief introductions.

Colene watched Robert Jacobson, his head shaved, a black turtleneck under a tweed jacket, a brass stud in his left earlobe, amble up to the speaker's podium.

Nice ass.

Jacobsen paused, waited until the applause died down, cleared his throat, then launched into the details of the physical, social, cultural evidence relating to the dating of the Aramaic papyri found in a grave site 10 years ago in Eastern Syria.

When he'd finished, Jacobsen winked at Colene, took his seat.

Dressed in a blowzy blue suit draped over a faded once-white shirt with a thin, paisley faded green tie, Benjamin Simon lurched to the podium.

He droned on about textual aspects for a half hour, arguing that the papyri were "... either forgeries or revisionist texts of later versions of the Gospel of St. Mark."

Colene leaned over to Jacobsen. She whispered,

"Did you hear about the bombing at the Old Antioch mosque?"

"Yes," Jacobson said. "I'd like to be on the excavation before they rebuild it."

"Think they'll find anything worthwhile?

"Very likely," Jacobson said. "It'll be a rich site."

At the podium, Simon stopped, then spoke in a stage whisper,

"Of particular attention is the Aramaic *ĥswy* 'forgiveness' which in Koine is *aphesis*. This construct makes no sense in the larger context of what are widely accepted texts."

Colene's eyebrows shot up. Simon paused, scowled, swept the audience with his wrinkled brows.

"No sense," he said. "None whatsoever."

Mild applause, louder whispers. Simon scooped up his notes, sat down.

Colene marched to the podium, gripped the lectern with both hands, looked over the crowded large semi-circular hall, paused.

Several late comers came in, looking for seats. The auditorium hummed with murmurs.

Colene smiled, then said,

"You heard the discussions today on the differing Greek texts in the light of these recently discovered papyri. Let's look at the facts."

She noticed people in the front row leaning forward, eyes fixed on her face. She went on,

"The form *ĥswy* is a misreading of the Aramaic *slĥw* which is best translated as *metanoia* 'redemption' in Koine. Now, this makes more sense contextually than does the Greek *sumbibasis* in the text that was used to translate the King James Version."

She turned, glanced over at the glaring Simon.

"This is, by the way," she said. "The same questionable text that our colleague Professor Simon used to construct his argument."

The audience broke into applause.

When Colene sat down, Simon pushed past her to the podium to counter that he was "... certainly justified in using that Greek text as it had been the standard for Greek Gospels for years. I can only conclude Dr. Mooney is mounting a personal attack here."

A burst of boos, catcalls, whistles erupted from several sections of the audience when Simon took his seat. He left the podium, brushing past Colene with a glare as she rose, came to the center.

"Thanks for sharing, Professor Simon," Colene said.

The audience broke out in howls of laughter, cheers and whistles. They clapped for a minute before quieting down.

"You heard it right from our colleague's own lips," Colene said. "We can reject the hypothesis that the papyri are forgeries."

She took her seat to a standing ovation.

The moderator closed the session.

The audience leapt up, cheered, then broke into small knots of people discussing the issues in loud voices. Several people came up on stage, congratulated Colene.

She shook hands with well-wishers, friends.

Retreating nearby to a circle of friends, Simon protested "... an obvious bias of the audience."

Turning to go, Colene bumped into a big man in his early 50s.

Gray-blue eyes glowed beneath a jagged scar over his left eyebrow. His mouth was drawn in a smile. His face reflected approval, admiration, respect.

Her father used to look at her that way.

"I wondered for years if anyone would ever catch that glitch in the KJV," he said.

His voice was in a deep, mellow Southern English. His big hand took hers, warmed, comforted.

Colene's fingers tingled. She stammered,

"I don't know of anybody ever having noticed that text before."

She smelled a faint odor of tobacco through the light hint of his cologne.

"Oh, I wasn't the first," he said. "As a student at Oxford years ago, I found the Reverend Alan Satherthwaite had noted it back in 1707."

"Satherthwaite! Where?" she said.

"In the Cambridge Annals of Theology."

"But, of course! Those articles were repressed for years—because by then, the KJV was held to be inviolate."

Colene jotted down the reference on the face of her program.

"I'd planned to turn that bit of trivia into a dissertation topic but never did," he said.

"I'm certainly impressed."

"I'm Lane Daniels. Do you have plans for lunch?"

"I'd planned to have lunch with some girlfriends. What do you have in mind?"

"We can get something to eat downtown. The dining on campus is God-awful."

"That it is," Colene said. "Lead on."

Daniels took her arm, led her out of the auditorium, hailed a taxi, had the driver take them to downtown Princeton to the Maharani's Palace, a small restaurant standing on a corner next to a used clothing store.

Inside, Colene saw walls painted with classical Indian women dancing in front of four men in colorful turbans seated on cushions, curved swords at their sides. The hostess in a green and gold sari, a prominent red dot centered over her eyebrows, assured Daniels they would be seated in a moment.

A large TV over the small bar caught Colene's attention. A CNN news program was flashing pictures of the mosque bombed the day before in Antioch, Turkey.

Colene shook her head.

"Political and religious ideology is such crap," she said.

Daniels stood, mouth open, staring at the images of destruction. He blinked, turned and smiled at her.

"I'm sorry?" he said

"Never mind." Colene said. "Our table is ready."

Colene studied the man across from her. Healthy, fit, in a tailored gray tweed suit. His face expressive. His conversation witty, interesting.

Saying nothing about himself, Daniels probed her for details of her past from the beginning.

"From the last name and Boston Brahmin speech, I'd say you're Boston Irish."

"Does it show?"

"Then there's that curved nose and bright blue eyes."

Colene reddened, lowered her eyes.

"And, you?" she said.

"As I said, that old article was going to be the centerpiece of a dissertation that I never got around to pursuing."

"You're not in academics?"

"No–just a stuffy art dealer who dabbles in biblical studies."

He raised his eyes, met hers.

"Forgive me if I sound trite but you so remind me of my late wife. She would have loved the way you jumped on that pompous ass, Simon."

He glanced back at the TV, watched it for a few seconds, then back to her.

"Tell me about Colene Mooney," he said.

"Colene Mooney? Boring. Undergrad in classics at Wellesley. Grad school in biblical lit at Harvard. A two year postdoc in Rome studying Aramaic– absolutely boring. "

"And yet James Corbett at Yale hired this boring Colene Mooney."

"Jim's like a father to me. I learned more working with him in a year than in all my previous years of study."

"And your book's been well received too."

"Have you read my book, Lane Daniels?"

He looked at her, a smile on her face. Colene felt like she was melting. She stammered,

"What about the secrets of Lane Daniels?"

"Secrets? None to tell. Started out in biblical studies at Oxford. Got interested in art and starting buying and selling it– talk about boring."

"You mentioned your late wife."

He looked away. The suggestion of a smile died on his lips.

"She was a very special woman."

"Tell me about her– if it's not too painful."

Daniels leaned back.

"Like you—no pretension, totally self-deprecating," he said. "She wanted me to retire, spend more time together. I was willing but I had some things to finish and then..."

"What happened? "

Daniels pursed his lips, hardening his face. He drummed his fingers on the table.

"Hadley's sarcoma," he said.

"O, my God. I'm so sorry"

"I was away for 3 months. When I returned, she was already in stage 4. She died within the year."

"Oh no! How long ago was that?"

"8 years this last December."

Colene put her hand on his.

"I understand," Colene said. "Losing my dad was hard."

"How did he die?"

"Iraq. In the Gulf War," Colene said.

She paused. "Broke my heart."

Lane pressed his hand, sandwiching hers between his.

"We're both scarred."

Colene felt something new–flashes of memory, images of a big smiling man, feelings of being held.

"If what I say next sounds offensive, Colene" Daniels said. "Tell me to go to hell. But, I want to be with you. Now. Alone."

"Go on." Colene said.

"I've never come on to anyone before in my life but I ..."

"You want to make love to me?"

"Yes."

"Now?"

"Yes, now."

The waiter came to the table.

"Have you decided?" he said

Without smiling, Colene said,

"We're sorry to have bothered you but we've changed our minds."

Lane dropped a hundred dollar bill on the table, drew back Colene's chair, taking her arm, he led her out the door.

Morning After

Guest room 321, Wilford Dorms, Princeton University, Princeton, NJ
The next morning, Sunday, 4:15 AM, EDT

He awoke before sunrise.

Glancing over at the sleeping woman next to him, he picked up his clothes, slipped into the bathroom noiseless as a rat.

Stepping out of the bathroom dressed, he sat down at the table, took a pen, wrote a quick note.

Seeing the woman's open purse on the small table, he reached in, drew out a white linen handkerchief bordered with purple stitching, her initials, *CJM*, in the center.

He sniffed it–unperfumed, feminine. Dropping it in his coat pocket, he picked up his shoes, made his way to the door.

He paused, Looked back at the sleeping woman on the bed where they made love last night. He stepped out, easing the door shut. Then, slipping on his shoes, he strode down the back stairwell.

~*~~*~

Colene awoke. She sat up, looked around the dorm room. The bathroom door hung open.

She called out, "Lane?"

Wrapping the top sheet around herself, she slid out of bed.

Looking over at the table, she spotted the note.

Lovely Colene:

I'm afraid I've a plane to catch. I didn't bring business cards but I have yours. I'll contact you. Wish I wasn't in such a rush, but, we'll see each other again. Count on it.

LD

Colene read the note again. Then, a third time.

She looked into the wall mirror, brought her hand to her face, rubbed her lips. Then, in slow, careful motions, Colene tore the note into little strips, let them flutter to the floor.

A Round of Golf

The Green Pines Country Club, Columbia, SC
Early April, present day, 1:15 PM

Hamilton "Ham" Morris drove the white golf cart ahead of Republican Congressman for the 12th district, Damian Styles's blue one to the foot of the fairway. Lurching to a stop, Morris leapt onto the green from behind the wheel like a cat jumping off a couch, snatched his golf bag to his shoulder with an easy, effortless motion, then glanced over at the other man in the golf cart.

Greg Steele, at 5'8'– thick-muscled, in dark slacks, blue polo shirt– wore a blue ball cap with the stenciled double silver bars of an army captain. Steele gripped the top of the cart, swung out onto his feet, turned, spun the heavy bag to his shoulder by the strap, then walked in step beside Morris over to the bag stands at the rear of the tee box.

Looking out over the manicured green, Morris checked out the 10th hole, noting a 364 yard long fairway with a sharp dogleg to the right, a sand trap nestled in the crook before the green.

Taking a deep breath, Morris looked behind him at the sound of the Congressman stumbling out of the other cart.

Pudgy, at 5'6,"the Congressman wore cream-colored slacks, a lime green short sleeve shirt, a yellow ball cap with a nylon mesh front lettered, *"14th Annual Congressional Golf Tournament."*

Congressman Styles hauled out his golf bag, lugged it over to the bag stand, selected a wood, then wiped it with a towel.

Steele plopped his bag into the upright support, whipped out a wood, stepped over to the end of the tee box, took a couple of quick practice swings.

"Gregg," Styles said. "Remember, there are limits to the number of practice swings you get."

"I'll keep that in mind, Congressman," Steele said.

Morris pulled out a wood.

"Too bad your father-in-law couldn't join us," The Congressman said.

"Pap doesn't golf," Morris said. "Says it just ruins a good walk."

"We'll miss his ever-present wit," Styles said.

"It's kinda funny the first few dozen times you hear it," Morris said.

"And, that's when he ain't preaching," Steele said.

Morris gave Steele a dirty look.

The Congressman put on his sunglasses, gripped the wood in his hand, took a leisurely practice swing.

"He does pack the stadiums when he comes to town," Styles said.

Morris looked down the fairway.

"This is a par four," he said.

"I'm off first," the Congressman said.

Congressman Styles stuck a tee in the ground at the edge of the green, adjusted his sunglasses, took one more long, slow practice swing. He addressed the ball, drew back the club, then froze at the sound of Steele's voice.

"What do we have here?"

Morris turned to see a young man drive a green golf cart up and bump the Congressman's cart. The young driver smiled, nodded but stayed put as an older man climbed out, then came striding over to them.

Morris knew K.D. Rogers, executive producer, host of the Christian Family Daily radio network, CEO of the Rapture Network and his father-in-law, JR Hammond's TV show. A thin 5'8", he wore a worn black suit, white shirt, thin black rayon tie, scuffed black wing tipped shoes. Close trimmed light brown and gray hair bordered his pale bald pate. A narrow, neat-trimmed pencil dark brown mustache marked his upper lip. Dark brown ferret-like eyes darted behind rimless oval glasses.

"Where's your golf bag, Dr. Rogers?" Steele said.

Without smiling, Rogers shook hands with Morris, said Hello to Styles, then nodded at Steele.

"I'm sorry to disturb your game," Rogers said.

"What's up, KD?" Styles said.

"We have a problem," Rogers said.

"What problem?" Morris said.

"A leak."

"What kinda leak?"

"Somebody's writing about us."

"Writing what?" Styles said.

Rogers folded his hands behind his back, shifted his weight to one foot like a witness testifying in a courtroom.

"That blasphemer, James Corbett at Yale is writing that our movement is trying to take over the country."

"That's a leak?" Morris said.

Rogers squinted, bobbed his head affirmative.

"He's accusing us in print of trying to start a revolution," Rogers said.

"Sonfabitch," Steele said.

Rogers's face reddened. He scowled at Steele.

"KD's referring to a series of articles in a liberal publication where Jim Corbett at Yale labeled our movement as being outright subversive," the Congressman said.

Steele burst out laughing.

"Oh hell, Dr. Rogers," he said. "Don't nobody but liberals and faggots read that shit anyway."

Rogers glared at him again. Steele lowered his eyes, murmured, "Sorry."

"But howzat ..." Morris said.

Styles inserted.

"I think KD means a link," he said.

Roger's pale face turned baboon-ass red.

"Link, leak. What's the difference? He's exposing us to ridicule and spreading lies and false accusations."

"So, what do you want us to do, KD?" Morris said. "Sue him?"

Rogers spoke through gritted teeth, "I want it stopped."

"Hard to stop rumors, KD," Morris said.

"You're the doer—the man who gets things done," Rogers said. "We count on you to do just that."

"I'll look into it." Morris said

Rogers raised his eyes.

"Finally," he said.

"What exactly do you want us to do," Steele said.

"Keep him under surveillance so that we know what he's up to next," Rogers said.

"That can run into big money," Steele said

"Do it. Send me the bill."

"OK," Morris said.

"This goes much deeper than just mere accusations, Ham," Rogers said. "The man is a blasphemer, an atheist attacking the Word of God. He's Satan's instrument. Sitting in his big chair at Yale he spreads doubt and dissension among our young people."

"I get it, KD," Morris said. "You got my word."

Rogers glared at the three of them.

"Y'all don't believe the clear and present danger here," Rogers said. "When y'all delve into this mess, y'all will see."

Styles locked his arm around Roger's.

"I'll look into it too, KD."

Shaking Styles's arm off, Rogers took Morris aside.

"You do know," Rogers whispered. "Corbett has damaging information on your father-in-law."

"What?" Morris said.

"I can't get in to it now," Rogers said. "I'm still investigating it."

Rogers looked over his shoulder.

"I've got to get back now," he said.

Rogers turned, gave Steele a final frown, made his way back to the golf cart, climbed in and the young man drove him away.

Morris watched the cart disappear beyond a stand of trees on the back green.

"Was he serious?" Steele said.

"Damn serious," Styles said.

"But, the cost of a full surveillance ..."

"We'll do it." Morris said.

"Say what?" Steele said.

"Roger's radio and TV network has revenue streams of over 150 million a year," the Congressman said. "He can bankroll a tail on the FBI with the stroke of a pen."

Morris stood, still staring at the spot where Rogers disappeared.

"I want you on this, Gregg," he said. "Eyes on this guy Corbett–full scale covert surveillance. Start tomorrow."

Steele blinked, then stared at Morris.

"Do you buy all that blaspheme shit, Sir?"

"Not a fucking word," Morris said. "But, we'll do it. We'll charge the bastards. And, they'll pay."

Discovery

Old Mosque ruins, Kansu, Turkey
Late October, present time, 4:22 PM

Mübeccel Zarakolu, head salvage archeologist at the excavation, walked outside the three angles of the corner wall framing the floor site of the remains of the mosque. Checking the quadrants marked off with surveyor's twine fastened to wooden stakes where the walls had stood, she looked for any sign of intrusion.

The five archaeologists– Mübeccel and her four men– wore khaki work shirts, pants, straw hats and boots while she oversaw the site and the eight laborers assigned to various jobs.

Satisfied the integrity of the site was intact, Mübeccel turned back to the tent at the northeast end of the site where her team had pitched the assemblage station. Through the open front flap, she saw the two work tables, desk, boxes, plastic containers and cases for artifacts.

She inspected the exposed dirt underneath the old cement floor. Her team had divided each sector into grids, marked with color-coded ribbons tied to the strings. At the west end of the site, Mübeccel watched the hired workers dumping dirt and sand from the digging into mounds.

In front of the mound, a laborer in baggy clothes wearing a dirty turban scooped dirt, then tossed it against a tiler's screen. After separating out the remains, another worker marked and set the screens with the contents aside for the archaeologists' inspection.

The first archaeologist, Sunay, was on hands and knees digging in a trench quadrant with a trowel. A tall laborer stood near shoveling the residue into a bucket.

The second archaeologist, Cengiz, was walking around the site taking notes.

The third archaeologist, Yunus was in another section overseeing two laborers shovel dirt into buckets and then examining the tiler's screens' remainders.

The fourth archeologist, Bekir was inside the tent, spreading materials on the 2 tables to mark with a white paint stripe to write catalog sorting numbers on them later in black ink.

Coming into the tent, Mübeccel looked over the array of material on the table.

"More pottery sherds?" she said.

"This place is a gold mine" Bekir said. "How much longer do we have on this site?"

"Hard to say," Mübeccel said. "The locals want a thorough excavation before any scheduled construction."

Cengiz came in, dropped his clip board on the end of the table, plopped down in a canvas chair.

"I could use a cold beer," he said.

"Well, don't wish for just one," Mübeccel said. "See that ice chest?"

"Some?" Bekir said.

"Hell yes," Mübeccel said. "Beer doesn't come in bottles of one around here."

Bekir took out three bottles from the ice chest, pried off the tops with a digging trowel, handed one to each of his two friends.

"Who in the hell would've expected we'd find an old synagogue?" Bekir said.

"I imagine the Moslem Brotherhood will shit gravel at that bit of news," Cengiz said.

"Piss on the Brotherhood," Mübeccel said. "Worry about the bean counters in Ankara."

Cengiz got up, looked again at the pottery pieces on the table. "Damn," he said. "These sherds gotta be late first century."

Bekir began,

"Yeah, I've never seen a ..."

"Hey, chicken thieves!" Sunay yelled from outside. "I've found Aladdin's lost lamp. Need some help."

The archaeologists ran to the pit.

Cengiz and Yunus grabbed trowels, jumped in to help dig.

Bekir seized a camera, stood ready to photograph the extraction.

Sunay dug around a sealed pottery jar buried in the hard dried mud clay of the trench floor.

Mübeccel grabbed a clipboard and tool box, leaned over to watch.

Cengiz and Yunus chipped and scraped at the hard dirt with dental picks, being careful not to damage its surface.

Mübeccel tossed Cengiz a brush. He whisked off the dried clay as the jar emerged.

Mübeccel wrote down the site specifics in her notebook. When the jar was exposed and uncovered from the clay matrix, Bekir snapped several shots, then rushed into the tent, swept the table-top clear of material, dropping and scooping the artifacts in boxes.

The three men removed the jar from the pit, carried it to the table and eased it down.

Mübeccel brushed it off with a camel's hair brush. Bekir photographed it from several angles.

Mübeccel looked up at the four of them standing there, looking down at the jar. She traced her hand over the exterior design.

"First century Jewish." she said.

"Do we dare open it?" Sunay said.

Mübeccel looked around at her colleagues, picked up a set of latex gloves.

"A cautious person would open it under strict laboratory conditions," she said. "But, I've never been known for being cautious or prudent."

Taking a deep breath, she slipped on latex gloves, broke the jar's seals with a scalpel, moved the top and worked it open. She reached in, then took out a leather-bound document packed tight in dried palm fronds and a stiff, hardened leather bag. Prizing open the stiff leather, she poured out a dozen or so coins into her hand. Picking a camel hair brush, Mübeccel dusted off the hard dried leather pages, then opened the binder.

Two facing pages of different writing divided the parchment leaves. Mübeccel pointed to one side.

"Greek," she said. "Majuscule Koine."

Looking at the other side, she puzzled for a moment.

Sunay pointed at the writing on the other side.

"That's not Hebrew," he said.

"It's some form of Aramaic," Mübeccel said

"First century Jews writing cultic texts in Aramaic?" Cengiz said.

Mübeccel read some of the Greek portion, then looked up.

"Ready for this?" she said. "The Greek text is a collection of Christian aphorisms."

"Christian?" Yunus said.

"Definitely Christian– New Testament stuff," Mübeccel said.

"What about the Aramaic?" Sunay said.

Mübeccel shrugged her shoulders.

"Damned if I know," she said. "Don't read Aramaic."

The four men stared at her, stunned, silent. Then, all four burst into laughter.

"Let's get this find packed up," Mübeccel said. "I'll take it to Ankara tomorrow. We can enclose the parchment pages in mylar protectors back at the lab."

Mübeccel and Bekir prepared an aluminum case with a foam rubber insert which they cut out and molded to hold the binder. They placed the leather bag with the coins in a heavy plastic folder.

~*~~*~

The laborers stood outside watching the archaeologists unveil the jar's contents. One tall laborer, shifted to one side out of view, slipped his camera phone out of his pocket, then took several photographs of the archeologists, the leather binder and the coins. Moving closer, he zeroed in on the leather binder with the parchment pages.

Then, turning his back to the flurry of activity in the tent, he downloaded the photos, texted a quick message, then sent it. After finishing that task, he returned to the work of closing the site down for the day.

Message Received

Outside of Alexandria, Egypt. An office in the Big House
2 hours later, that same day

The phone on the African blackwood desk rang. Hydra looked at the phone monitor. Text message. He forwarded it to his computer, read it.

"Ur hunch pd off. Pics fllw.
Thy tkng ths 2 Ankara tmrw. Advs nxt mve.
IiN."

Hydra opened the attachments, studied the photos for a moment, then picked up the phone.

"Have the chopper ready to leave in ten minutes," he said.

Delivery

Turkish Military Airport, Ankara Turkey
The following day

Inside the light military transport that dropped out of the clouds onto a rain-slicked tarmac, bled off its airspeed, taxied up to the terminal. Feeling the ground beneath the plane's wheels Mübeccel Zarakolu relaxed.

Looking out the window she saw the accommodation ladder in the area where the civilian government officials deplaned.

She frowned. *Shit. Getting off in the rain, again ...*

Going straight to the desk in the building, she handed the receiving officer the paperwork listing the containers and packages under her supervision. Papers were signed, stamped. Her driver was waiting for her.

When she arrived at the University, Mübeccel headed straight to her supervisor's office, nodded to the two secretaries, went through, knocked at the director's door.

Hearing, "Come in," Mübeccel went inside.

Smiling, Fahir Casamli, the Department head, rose to greet her.

"Mübeccel. So good to see you. I got your message."

He directed her to a table flanked by stuffed chairs.

"Will you have tea?" he said.

"I'd kill for tea."

He laughed, poured the tea into a cup, indicated a bowl of honey and pitcher of cream. Mübeccel took them both, stirred her cup, sat back, patted the aluminum case at her knee.

"I brought the parchments with me," Mübeccel said. "They've not been out of my sight since we recovered them."

Fahir adjusted his glasses. "Let's have a look at them."

Setting aside her teacup, she opened the case, took the pages from the gray foam rubber insert.

Nodding his head, Dr. Casamli looked them over.

"Are they sturdy enough to be examined by hand?" he said.

After a swig of tea, Mübeccel said,

"They were packed in the jar in palm fronds which kept the moisture at a remarkable minimum."

"Any ideas about the dating?"

Mübeccel took another deep drink of tea.

"Could be a codex from the early Christian era."

Fahir frowned.

"But, this site was excavated before the Mosque was built," he said.

"Yes," Mübeccel said. "In the late 20's and early 30's. But, Turkish archaeology was hardly at its zenith at that time."

"Still," Fahir said. "As I recall from reading the original site report, there was nothing uncovered that would suggest anything of a cultic connection, let alone something Christian."

"Well, the text is in Greek and Aramaic."

Fahir blinked, adjusted his glasses again. "Aramaic?"

"The codex is likely Jewish."

Fahir reached out, touched the worn leather binder in the case before him.

He whispered, "Aramaic."

"This puts it in Foucault's arena," Fahir said. "You must take it to him."

Mübeccel rolled her eyes.

"Why was I dreading you'd say that?" she said.

Mübeccel crossed her arms. "You know he's difficult," she said.

"So's life, Mübeccel."

~*~~*~

Stopping outside Professor Foucault's office, Mübeccel took a deep breath and rapped on the door.

"Entrez."

Mübeccel opened the door.

Foucault sat at his desk, bent over a papyrus manuscript, looking through a desk magnifier. He did not look up until Mübeccel came in and closed the door behind her. Raising his head, Foucault scowled at her.

"Yes?" he said.

Mübeccel took a deep breath.

"Professor Foucault," she said. "So nice to see you again. I have something of interest for you."

"Dr. Zarakolu, how would anything you managed to come up with be of any possible interest to me?"

Mübeccel set the open aluminum case on his desk.

"In a recent excavation near Antioch," she said. "We found a number of pages that were written in Greek and Aramaic ..."

Foucault interrupted,

"Aramaic? Which one? Old Syriac? Peshitta? Philoxenian or Palestinian? You're sure it's not early Hebrew? They look the same to the untrained eye."

Mübeccel took out the binder, opened it to reveal the parchment pages.

"See for yourself," she said.

Foucault took it from her, dropped it on his desk and adjusted the magnifier– his frown, a mask of intensity– his voice, a mutter.

"Interesant, très interesant."

He looked up at Mübeccel.

"These writings are definitely late First Century."

He sorted through the pages.

"Palestinian, I'd say..."

He frowned– then froze.

His lips tightened. His body tensed.

He leaned forward, adjusted his glasses, glared at the pages, his eyes widening.

"*Quoi*?" he murmured.

His bony finger traced the Greek text, then shifted to the Aramaic.

He rifled through the pages, reading them in bits and pieces, mumbling and muttering.

Mübeccel cleared her throat.

"Is this indeed Aramaic?" she said.

Foucault looked up, stared at her as if she had just entered the room, dropped his eyes once more to the stack of encased pages on his desk.

His muttering continued.

He rubbed his eyes, took a page, held it up to the light while going from the Greek to the Aramaic text.

Mübeccel cleared her throat again.

"Interesting?" she said.

Foucault's head snapped up. He stared at her.

"What?" he said.

"I merely asked if it were interesting," Mübeccel said.

Foucault scowled, looked back to the writing, read for a few minutes in mumbling reverie. Then he stopped, collapsed back into his chair, put his hand to his chin and sat for a moment blinking his eyes. Then, the frown returned and he looked up at Mübeccel.

"Where did you find this?" he said.

"A town outside of Antioch," Mübeccel said. "We were excavating a bombed-out mosque. The blast exposed a sublayer and this was buried beneath the remains of an old flooring."

"What's the cultural setting of this flooring?" he said.

Mübeccel looked around, saw a chair, pulled it up and sat down.

"Pottery sherds and the corner markings are consistent with Jewish synagogues of that period," she said.

"Any other artifacts?"

"We did find some coins in the pottery container holding the binder and parchment. They are typical of Roman coins from that period, but we're still determining what they are."

Foucault, thrust his chin forward, moved it up and down in a slow nod.

"Can you bring me the coins?"

Mübeccel looked Foucault in the eye.

"What do think this is, Clement?" she said.

He flinched at hearing her use his first name. Once more, he looked at the pages.

"I'm not ... I can't be sure." he said.

"Clement, what's on your mind? You left the planet the second you started looking at this writing. Don't play games with me–we're on the same team here."

Foucault stammered,

"I can't be sure."

Mübeccel raised her voice.

"Well speculate, damn it! There's no one here but you and me. If you're wrong, who in hell will care tomorrow?"

Foucault glanced down at the codex again, choked and swallowed.

"The Greek text is majuscule Koine," he said. "At first glance it looks much like other Jewish texts from that period. The Aramaic is almost certainly Palestinian."

"So, what does all this mean?" Mübeccel said.

Foucault wrinkled his face, looked at her on the verge of tears. He whispered,

"The text is Christian aphorisms—not Jewish.

"That was my impression, too."

"But these collected aphorisms do not appear in this form until they're included in the Christian synoptic gospels Matthew and Luke."

"Are you saying...?"

"This text could be the most significant find of the last 1,000 years of Levantine history. If I'm right, this could be the lost or missing gospel of Q."

Mübeccel's eyebrows shot up.

"Q?" She said.

Foucault went on.

"At the end of the 19th century, German biblical historians had dissected the four gospels of the Christian bible and had determined that two of them, Mark, Matthew and Luke, were elaborations and polemics based on a hypothetical earlier gospel—postulated to be in the form a collection of sayings.

The German scholars referred to this hypothetical text as 'Q,' from the German *Quelle*, 'source.' Since it had likely become obsolete by the time these later works emerged, it was presumed lost as no copies of the Q existed or remained."

Foucault looked down and tapped the codex on the desk.

"Unless I'm very much mistaken, Mübeccel," he said. "That missing document is sitting right here in front of me."

Mübeccel blinked at hearing him use her first name for the first time since she had met him over 10 years ago.

Theft

University of Ankara,
Two days later, 1:15 AM

Dressed in dark gray fatigues, balaclava over head and face, hands in gray leather gloves, gripping a black briefcase, Hydra crept along the unlit hallway in the dim gleam from outside lights. Sweeping along in front of empty offices, he fixed his eyes on a dim glow under a door at the end of the passageway.

At the door, he paused, tried the handle.

Unlocked.

Easing the old wooden door open, he slipped inside, extending the briefcase before him, closed the heavy door without a squeak or creak, then moved into the darkness of the corner.

In the light from a desk lamp, he saw Foucault leaning over an old leather binder gazing at the top sheet of a stack of parchment pages through a round desk magnifier. A pile of old coins sat stacked in front of the leather binder.

Foucault mumbled, his breath coming in excited, wheezy gasps.

"C'est vrai... c'est ça...pas de doute!"

Hydra started to move but froze when Foucault picked up a phone, punched in a number, then sat back. In the quiet Hydra heard the electronic tones, beeps, clicks, then the voice from the speaker-phone on the desk,

"Hello?"

"Jim. It's Clement Foucault."

"Clement! So good to hear you."

"Jim. I've examined it. It's the real thing. The real Macaw, as you Americans say."

"The real McCoy, eh?"

"Jim. This is real, real real."

"You're absolutely sure?"

"Sure? *Bien sûr. Très très bien sûr."*

"This is unbelievable, Clement!"

"It's a Q text, *sans doute.*"

"I'll be damned."

"Jim. Can you come here and see this for yourself?"

"That's like asking a blind man if he wants to see."

"When can you come?'

"It's after 6 here. So, I'll have to make arrangements but I don't see any problem in leaving tomorrow. I can call you then with the details."

"*Excellent*. I can meet you at the airport."

"The drinks are on me."

"Better yet. Good night, old friend."

"*Adieu*, Clement."

From the shadows, Hydra watched Foucault switch off the speaker-phone, move the round magnifier to one side, gather up the ancient codex. When Hydra stepped forward, his case brushed a bookcase.

Foucault's head jerked up.

"*Kimsiniz*?" he said. "*Qui est là*?"

Hydra stepped into the dim light of the desk-lamp, pistol in one hand, briefcase in the other.

"I'll take those coins and the codex," he said.

Foucault stammered, "Who ...?"

"Your past, Foucault."

Clement narrowed his eyes.

"Wait, I know you," he said.

"Now, that's a goddam shame."

Hydra's pistol popped three chirps. Foucault lurched backward over the wooden chair, his outstretched hands convulsed, quivered, then stilled.

Hydra moved behind the desk, kicked Foucault's body to one side, leaned over the leather bound writing, looked at it through the magnifier.

Hydra sucked in his breath. Looked again. Then, closing the old leather binder, he scooped up the pile of coins, dropped them along with the binder and the gun into the brief case.

Turning, Hydra left without a backward glance.

Complications

Halley Hall, Yale University, New London, CN
The next day, 11:35 AM

In a spacious office lit by sunlight streaming in from a wide window overlooking the tree covered campus, Professor James Corbett looked over at his trench-coat draped over two suitcases on the Turkmenian rug with blue, green, yellow and red designs. Having checked his tickets, passport, he was putting books, notes and tablets in his brief case when his phone rang.

"This is Jim Corbett," he said.

An accented voice spoke on the other end.

"We are calling this number as investigation procedures. This is Turkish Police calling from University Ankara. Is this University Yale in United States?"

"Yes" Corbett said. "This is Yale University."

"Who is speaking there, please?"

"Dr. James Corbett."

"Here speaks Inspector Ferhan Ildan. Last night a professor Foucault was murdered here and many national treasures stolen."

"What? Foucault? Murdered?"

"Yes. It seems so. This morning cleaning people find body. Other university people say many artifactures are missing. Must be stolen."

"My God, poor old Clement."

"Yes. Dead. Shot in heart."

"Do you have someone in custody?"

"We yet don't know yet but it looking like thieves. Archeologists say very valuable things and book are taken away."

"Give me a moment. This is a terrible shock."

"Yes," Inspector Ildan said. "Take some moments."

His head reeling, Corbett sat back in his chair, closed his eyes, waited a moment before picking up the phone. He told the investigator all about the previous evening's conversation. He could hear the inspector at the other end writing everything down. After asking him a few more questions, the Turkish policeman hung up.

Staring at the at the open briefcase, items on his desk, then at his suitcases, Corbett leaned his desk with his elbows, and put his head into his hands.

After a few minutes, he picked up the phone, punched in a number.

"Colene. Jim. Could you come over here right now? Thank you."

A knock at the door. Colene came in, wearing gray slacks, light blue blouse, brown athletic shoes. She stopped, looked at Corbett, frowned.

"What's happened, Jim," she said. "You look like hell."

"A call from Turkey. Foucault's been murdered. It looks like the codex and some other artifacts have been stolen."

"O Shit!" Colene said. "Not the Q!"

"It must have happened right after he called me," Corbett said.

"But how in the hell could thieves have known about this?" Colene said. "Right after the man calls you, he's snuffed and robbed?"

"The Turkish authorities just say that valuable documents were stolen," Corbett said. "There are criminal rings that deal in selling valuable artifacts to clandestine collectors."

"So, " Colene said. "Just because some asshole wants bragging, rights we lose the Q. What could we have done with that document?"

Corbett walked to the window, stared out the trees, a passing bicycle rider. Then, he turned back to Colene.

"I wonder ..." he said.

"What?"

"I'm ... Forget it," he said.

"Forget what?"

"Just some suspicions ..."

"Jim!" Colene said. "Something's cooking up there. Out with it."

"I don't want to speculate at this point."

"Speculate about what?"

"I feel this loss as much as anybody, Colene," Corbett said. "After I talked to Clement, I couldn't sleep last night because there are bigger things here than mere academic interests. I've prayed I might be able to help head off a big catastrophe."

"Now, I'm curious," Colene said. "What in the hell do you mean by a 'big catastrophe?' "

"Anything I'd say at this point would just be wild guesses and unsupported conjecture," Corbett said. "We're historians. We don't do things that way. I need to get my facts in order first."

"OK," Colene said. "But don't be cagey. Let me in on your thinking– no matter how wild you think it is."

"Fair enough," Corbett said. "Let me finish what I've started and I'll lay it all out for you. But, I want to have more evidence– hard data."

After Colene left, Corbett sat gazing at the suitcases in front of his desk sitting there like impotent friends.

The Hydra

Ministry of Interior, Ankara, Turkey
Present-day, 10:25 AM

Inside an office in a modern building housing the Ministry of the Interior, Orhan Mehmet, Directing Chief Inspector, Division of Preservation and Protection of Antiquities, stood behind his stained oak desk reading a report, tapping his straight, prominent nose.

Papers stacked in neat piles, an onyx desk set at the head of a large blotter cover, an orderly array of pencils, pens and an 8"curved dagger lay on the desk top. To the right of the desk stood a small table holding a chrome framed picture of a dark eyed, dark haired woman holding a small boy.

The speaker phone to Orhan's right buzzed.

"Yes?"

"Effendi Director," his secretary said. "His Honor, the Inspector General of the Investigative Division sends his apologies and will not be able to join you today for the weekly briefing. He says he will reschedule."

"Thank you, Lila."

Still tapping his nose, Orhan dropped the folder on the desk, walked over, looked out the window at the landscaped garden in the courtyard below.

The speaker phone chirruped again.

"Yes?"

"Effendi Director, it's Chief Inspector Mehmet from Criminal investigations."

At the connection, Orhan said, "Yilmaz, beloved cousin. How are you?"

"So fine, Orhan."

"And your pregnant wife, the lovely Bela and her beautiful children?"

"Bela assures me that they are mine as well, Cousin."

"I don't know how she puts up with you. You must have caught her in a weak moment when you proposed."

"I deny it not."

"Well, you didn't call merely to be insulted. What haunts your mind?"

Yilmaz paused, cleared his throat.

"A name," he said. "Isaak ibn Nur."

"Abdi ibn Nur's kinsman?"

"His brother—this is sensitive but we need to talk."

"We can talk any time about the Hydra network," Orhan said. "Are you free now?"

"By chance, I am. Where?"

"Let's meet for coffee at the Café Blitz. Say, half an hour?"

After clicking off the phone Orhan glanced at the open report on his desk, inserted the file in a locked cabinet. Taking a dark blue suit jacket from its hanger, he brushed the jacket with a camel hair brush.

From a hook in the closet he lifted a holstered 9 MM Glock with blue-black finish. Pulling the Glock from the holster, he checked the magazine, holstered it, snapped it on the belt support at the small of his back, then shrugged into the jacket, straightened his cuffs and tie.

Pausing at the great oak door, Orhan glanced back at the photograph of the woman and the boy, then left.

Confronting the Devil

Rapture Network, Inc., CEO's Office, Columbia, SC
5 days later, 5:30 AM

After reading the posting on the blog at the *Voice of Christianity Today* website, the Reverend Dr. Kenneth Desmond Rogers knit his eyebrows, squeezed his hands at the computer keyboard so tight the fingers turned red, the knuckles white. He glared at the monitor.

Snatching up the phone at his right, he dialed a familiar number.

"Congressman Damian's Styles's offices."

Roberts cleared his throat, announced,

"This is the Reverend Dr. KD Rogers of the Family Values Hour. I need to speak to the congressman."

"One moment, Reverend Rogers."

He was put through immediately.

"What's up, KD?" Damian Styles said.

"Have you seen what your friend and colleague, Corbett, posted on our website?"

"Can't say I have."

"It's libelous, criminal and blasphemous."

"Oh?"

"Not only does he accuse of us of planning a conspiracy to stage a coup and undermine the state, but he goes on to state we constantly misunderstand the Holy Scriptures."

"Really?"

"You're not taking this seriously, Damian. Thousands of people daily see this vicious attack on us."

"What do you propose?"

"May I remind you that we sent you to Congress to deal with this heresy?"

"I'm here, KD. Tell me what you want."

"Corbett doesn't name names. But, he alludes to a ... hold on ... 'an association with a mercenary military group ... to push a religious agenda down the throats of this nation.' "

"Yep," the congressman said. "Sounds like Jim Corbett."

"It gets worse. 'These yokels have little or no understanding of the background or history of the very books upon which they base their misguided motives.' "

"KD. Remember what JR said?"

"JR says a lot of things."

"I quote, 'It's annoying like a mosquito's buzzing but nobody ever pays attention to it.' And, I gotta agree with him."

"The voice of doubt here speaks hidden behind the authority of a powerful university. Vulnerable people of faith can be filled with doubt by such rhetoric."

"It's just that. Rhetoric."

"His ways are clever and powerful to deceive."

"OK," Styles said. "Can't make no promises but I'll put someone on it."

"You're not just saying that ..."

"Word of honor. I got a couple of young eager beavers who graduated from Christian Law Schools. I'm sure they can come up with something. Get back to ya soon."

"You do that."

KD cradled the phone back.

Folding his hands, he rested his elbows on the arms of the chair, then closed the website.

Again, Rogers picked up the phone dialed another number. It rang once.

"Morris."

“Ham? KD.”

“What’s up?”

“Corbett has things on both JR and Styles, and may know about Operation Backfire.”

“I doubt that.”

“Can you afford to take the risk?”

“You worry too much.”

“Have you seen where he mentions a ‘certain son-in-law of a prominent evangelist with connections deep into the defense department?’ ”

“More talk.”

“Don’t forget he has stuff on your father-in-law. Would some snooping reporter pass up a chance to leach information out of somebody as influential as him?”

Morris did not answer.

“Ham?” Rogers said. “You still there?”

“Let me think about.” Morris said.

After Morris hung up, Rogers sat, staring at the phone in his hand.

Cleaning a Revolver

Sword and Shield Security Services, Shanekmandan, SC
The next day, 7:20 AM

From behind the wheel of the black Hummer, Hamilton Morris gazed out at the dense pine forest in the swampy isolated northeastern near the South Carolinian coast. Thirty miles south of the nearest town, Morris came up on the familiar fenced facility with NO TRESPASSING warnings posted every hundred feet apart. At the entrance, the guard raised the barrier, then saluted when Morris drove through.

The Hummer bumped along a broken asphalt road that came to an abrupt, dead-end post near the swampy coastline. Coming to the end, Morris zigzagged around a tangle of kudzu obscuring another road that wound through the swampy woods into a 10 acre clearing where a compound filled with buildings painted in drab dull camouflage came into Morris's view.

Morris drove and parked at a single two-story building next to a sprawling auditorium made from a large Quonset hut with three fresh painted signs identifying the building as a training center and preparation theater.

On the walkway, Morris noticed over a dozen men and a few women dressed in green military cameo fatigues, chatting and circulating around the grounds. Outside the southern perimeter of the compound, his armed guards patrolled the fence line in open humvee vehicles.

On the top floor of the building next door, Morris stepped into his office. There, his metal desk stood by the window flanked by 2 flags– to the right, a draped American flag poled in a round brass disk– to the left, a gray flag with a blue orb in the center, emblazoned with a red, white and blue stars and stripes shield topped with 4 large white runic S letters arranged in the form of a cross in the middle. Behind the shield, a cavalry sabre with a tassel poked through.

Morris brushed at his starched, crisp green fatigues, hung his fatigue hat with the stenciled silver oak leaf on a coat rack, then glared at a stack of paperwork in the inbox on his desk.

After a half hour of reading and signing paperwork, Morris threw his pen down, looked over at the pile of unread papers.

"What a bunch of bullshit," he said aloud.

He shoved the papers to one side, reached into the top desk drawer, took out a revolver swaddled in an oil-spotted cotton cloth. Smelling the oil on the weapon, Morris smiled. He unwrapped the revolver, then laid it on the desk in front of him.

He admired the old 41 magnum Ruger Super Blackhawk with the shortened barrel and unstained walnut grips. It was his first pistol. His father had given it to him on his 12th birthday.

Morris spread out a newspaper in front of him, took a cleaning kit from another drawer, broke the pistol down, extracting the cylinder. Picking up the brass wire barrel brush, he reached for the cleaning solvent when he heard a knock at his door.

Morris looked up, scowled, sat the pistol down and snarled,

"Come."

His adjutant, Carl Rambeau stuck his head in.

"Got your phone turned off, Sir?" he said.

"Goddam right," Morris said.

"Our friend, the Congressman's on the line."

Morris snatched up the phone.

"Damian. Sorry, I was tied up,"

"No sweat, Ham. You called earlier?"

"I checked out what KD said about that Yale bible piss-ant. He's been stirring up real political shit and we do have some sensitive stuff in the works."

"How much clout does an academic have?"

"What about this shit KD says Corbett has on Pap?"

"Innuendo," Styles said. "Dunno how KD got hold of that crap."

"Well, what are these rumors?"

"Ham. We can talk about it *mano a mano* sometime but not now–and not on the phone."

"What if one of those guys at the Post or Times ..." Morris said.

"That's damn remote, Ham."

"Did you hear that stuff on the disc I sent you?"

"The call to Corbett from Turkey? Yes, I did."

"Anything we should be concerned about?"

"Not really. But, it's hot academic stuff."

"Sounded like bullshit to me."

"It's not bullshit, Ham. If this text is what they say it is, it could really shake things up."

"I ain't gonna worry about that."

"One more thing," Styles said.

"What?"

"Don't mention this to KD. Let me handle that."

"I don't tell KD nothing."

Returning to the pistol, Morris reassembled it with slow, deliberate care.

He stopped, looked over at the newspaper on his desk. An article caught his eye.

THE PENTAGON PAPERS IMPACT, NOW OUT IN PAPERBACK.

Morris stared at the headline without reading the book review.

The Pentagon Papers!

He laid the pistol on top of the article, then, picked up the phone, punched in an entry.

It rang once.

"Steele, sir."

"Still on that academic's case?" Morris said.

"Tighter'n a ring around a flea's ass, sir."

"Close out his account."

"Permanently?"

"Quietly. No loose threads."

"Understood, sir."

"One more thing."

"Yessir."

"Hang around down there. Grease a rat, there's nearly always another ready to take his place."

"You got it, Sir."

Morris hung up the phone.

He gripped and stroked the reassembled revolver, then wrapped it in the soft oil cloth, stuck it back in the drawer.

Accident

On a road outside of New Haven, CT
5 days later, 11:52 PM

The dim lights of farmhouses in the rural area blinked from among planted fields set back off the road. A cloudy sky made the moonless night even darker as Professor James Corbett watched his headlights penetrate the night.

Staying within the 60 MPH speed limit, Corbett wore his hat, gloves and overcoat with the heater off, talked into a hand-held recorder dictating notes for a review of a new translation of one of the Dead Sea Scrolls. He came into a wooded area where the surrounding trees cast shadows that reached out, grabbing at the beams of the car lights.

"One notes," Corbett said. "The translator has taken considerable liberties in interpreting the Aramaic texts."

Corbett gave no attention to passing a car parked on a dirt road that switched on its lights, pulled on behind him, then speeded up, overtaking him.

Corbett kept dictating, looking at the road ahead of him.

He heard someone gun their engine behind him, then looked up to see a large black SUV pull alongside him. Corbett glanced over at it, turned back to dictating.

Approaching a curve in the road, Corbett saw the SUV swerve, slam into his Honda, pushing it off the road. He gripped the wheel as he felt his Honda sail over an embankment, then smash into a tree. Inside, Corbett sat stunned behind the inflated air bag.

Pinned against the seat by the air bag and the crushed engine firewall, Corbett tried to open the door but it was jammed shut.

Over the sound of steam escaping from the damaged engine, Corbett heard someone coming. Then, a flashlight from outside the window blinded him. Corbett heard a voice.

"Roll down the window."

Corbett pushed the down button. The window opened part way.

Still blinded by the light, Corbett saw a man reach through the narrow opening with gloved hands. He felt the outsider grab his chin with one hand with a rough jerk, then smash him in the forehead with the heavy flashlight. Dazed, he was aware of the light going from his eyes, and a hand pushing the back of his head. The last thing Corbett was aware of was the numbing sound of the snap of his spinal cord at the top vertebra.

The small digital recorder tumbled to the car floor from Corbett's outstretched, limp hand.

~*~~*~

With his shoes tucked into plastic covers, Greg Steele looked around, then walked back to the still-running SUV, leaving Corbett's body slumped behind the air bag of the Honda.

Ash Shatt Allaah

Café Blitz, Downtown, Ankara
later that afternoon

Eyes shaded by dark aviator's sunglasses, Orhan stepped out of his car. The small plaza echoed with traffic noise and stank of exhaust fumes. Looking over at the wrought iron tables covered with white and red checkered cloths arrayed around the entrance of the café, Orhan studied the faces of the men and women who sat chatting, smoking, drinking coffee, aperitifs and tea.

At the far end of the outdoor café, Orhan spotted his cousin, a husky man with combed back straight hair reading a newspaper. Seated next to an audio speaker, the faint long scar from his forehead to his ear gleamed above his navy-blue blazer.

When Orhan came up to him, Yilmaz kissed him on the cheek.

"I've missed you," Yilmaz said.

"What do you have?" Orhan said.

Yilmaz pulled out a pack of small Spanish cigars and a box of long cigar matches from his inner coat pocket, extended them to his cousin.

"No," Orhan said. "Gave them up."

Yilmaz shrugged, took a cigar out of the pack. Striking the end of a match on the side of the box, he burned the end of the cigar in the flame. Yilmaz spoke without looking at Orhan.

"We broke up a network of Kurdish separatists killing local policemen in drive-by shootings. During the questioning about where they got the weapons, one of them admitted selling artifacts taken from Iraq. That's how Isaak ibn Nur's name popped up."

The waiter arrived, Yilmaz stuck the cigar in his mouth, leaned back, puffed it while Orhan ordered tea and *rakı*. After the waiter left, Yilmaz went on,

"Isaak's part of an artifacts and treasures smuggling ring supplying arms to Kurdish separatists from here to the Iraqi border. They call themselves *Ash Shatt Allaah."*

Orhan listened, his eyes playing over the other clients at the café.

"Does he deal in drugs like his scum of a brother?" he said.

"Seems to be more of a gofer than a wheeler-dealer."

"What's the connection between 'The Bulwark of God' and Hydra?"

"According to our snitch, this Isaak mainly moves the art and stolen artifacts."

The waiter arrived, set down the tea and *rakı*. Yilmaz threw a 20 Lira note on the serving tray. When the waiter reached for his wallet to give change, Yilmaz waved him away. The young man dipped his head, murmured, *"Teşekkür ederim, Effendi,"* and left.

Yilmaz drew deeply on the cigar, blew a puff of smoke, drank the last of his coffee.

"Anyway," he said. "This Isaak was seen in Antioch trying to make arrangements to get to the US."

Congratulations, hello

Colene Mooney's office (formerly James Corbett's) Yale University, New Haven, CT

3 weeks later

Two large poster pictures of Karl Marx and Carl Jung tacked on the wall, replaced the paintings of country-scene landscapes. Clear of clutter, Colene's desk stood near the window. In front of the desk, two red and gold Afghan throw rugs lay on the walkways of the Turkmenian floor carpet.

The shelves in the office were full of different books, the empty table now had a tea service, the former bare walls now held macramé cords suspending hanging spider plants in the corner near the tea table, a small vase with flowers on the table between the couch and stuffed chairs.

Colene leaned over her desk making notes from an open book in Greek when the phone rang– she switched on the speaker phone without stopping.

"Yes?"

"Colene? Damian Styles. How are you?"

She grimaced, closed her eyes before she spoke,

"Fine, Damian."

She wrote *asshole,* in the margin of her note pad.

"How's it feel to be chair of a prestigious department?" Styles said.

"I'd prefer to have Jim Corbett sitting here."

"Poor Jim. I was shocked when I heard about his accident."

"Yes."

"Colene. We've had our differences but I want you to know that you have a friend in congress whenever you need one."

"Let's hope I don't."

She penciled *turd*, next to *asshole*.

"Same old Irish wit. Well, gotta move along. Best wishes for every success and call me if you need me."

"Thank you, Damian."

"Take care, Colene."

She poked off the speaker phone. A knock at the door made her look up.

"Come in."

A sandy-haired young woman stuck her head in.

"Dr. Mooney," she said. "Are you busy?"

"What do you need, Georgina?"

"I was wondering if I could have an extension on the 103 assignment due this week."

"Why?"

"Personal problems."

"Such as?"

Georgina came in, whispered,

"My roommate's pregnant and is considering an abortion."

Colene did not look up.

"Are you pregnant, Georgina?" she said.

"Oh, not me. Her."

"Then there's no problem."

"Huh?"

Colene looked up into the wide eyes of the young woman, and said,

"Isn't not being pregnant much easier than having an assignment due?"

"Well, yeah."

"OK. Worry less about your roommate's bedroom habits and get on your assignment."

Colene shooed Georgina away.

When she left; the phone rang again. Colene dropped her pencil on the pad, muttered, "Damn it," punched the speaker phone button,

"Yes?"

"Professor Mooney?" The speaker was male. His English accented.

"It is."

"Are you interested in looking at some biblical writing?"

She picked up the pencil, wrote

Who is this?

"That's what I do for a living, Sir."

"I have some authentic writings that no one has ever seen before."

"I'm not interested in anything illegal, so, you can ..."

"I've something nobody's seen in 2,000 years."

Colene stared at the speaker phone, her pencil still in hand, paused.

"Are you there?" the man said.

She wrote *STALL.*

"I'd have to examine this ... writing ... first."

"Of course."

"When can you come here?"

"No, you come to me. The Greyhound station in New Haven. Next Monday, 9:00 PM."

"I can find it," Colene said. "Your name?"

The line went dead.

Colene looked at her note pad, scratched

What have I got myself into?

Some Loose Ends

Chief Inspector's Office , Ministry of Interior, Ankara, Turkey
The next day, 8:15 AM

Orhan thumbed through the folder from his principal researcher, noted the names Isaak ibn Nur in artifact smuggling cases and Abdi ibn Nur in drugs and arms files. Scanning the organization section, *Ash Shatt Allah,* most recent entries from the Interpol database showed only spotty data on Isaak. Nothing on Abdi.

His secretary buzzed him.

"Effendi Director, you wanted to be reminded of your meeting with the Head of the Antiquities Department from the University."

"Thank you."

He put the folder away and left.

~*~~*~

The two secretaries stood up when Orhan came in. Fahir came out of his office to shake Orhan's hand.

"Colonel Mehmet," Fahir said. "This is a pleasure."

"What can you tell me about the Foucault murder?"

"A tragedy. We're still in shock."

"What about the stolen artifacts?"

"Irreplaceable loss."

"What can you tell me about them?"

"Very little. Dr. Mübeccel Zarakolu, our head field archaeologist can provide details."

In the chairman's office, Orhan met a woman in her middle 40s with black, gray-streaked curled hair surrounding a chubby, pretty face with round, brass rimmed glasses, her dark eyes, bright, intelligent. She smiled, extended her hand.

"Colonel Mehmet," Mübeccel said. "Your fame precedes you."

"Just Orhan. We're all colleagues."

Fahir ushered Orhan into a chair, told a secretary to bring tea.

Orhan set a small digital voice recorder on the table.

"Tell me everything," he said. "There are always details the police overlook."

Mübeccel told him of the discovery, transport of the artifacts and her encounter with Foucault. Orhan jotted down notes.

"Foucault was taken with the document?" Orhan said.

"Enraptured," Mübeccel said.

"Clement Foucault was not given to emotional displays," Fahir said.

"Truth is he was a real tight-ass," Mübeccel said.

"What about the coins?" Orhan said.

"Late first century, but the codex consumed him," Mübeccel said.

Orhan scribbled a few notes, then snapped off the recorder.

"Was he murdered for the codex?" Mübeccel said.

"Puzzling," Orhan said. "The thief could have just taken the document and coins."

"The police seemed to think he knew the thief," Fahir said.

"May I see his office?" Orhan said.

~*~~*~

The dark room smelled of old books, stale tobacco smoke. Foucault had covered the main window of his office with a bookshelf. The two lights in the room cast shadows into the corners. With a maglite flashlight, Orhan scanned the packed tight shelves filled with texts in Hebrew, Arabic, Latin, Greek, French, German, English and languages he did not recognize. Thin layers of dust covered some sections, some were cleaner.

A book ajar on one shelf caught his eye. Orhan looked at it.

Geschichte Der Aramaische Sprache im Beispielen showed a glow– a greasy smudge on the edge of the cover.

Orhan pulled it. A yellow page marker jutted from the center.

Orhan thumbed through details and descriptions of Palestinian Aramaic orthography from different time periods.

He squinted– pencil underlining marked some entries. Orhan noted the section, *Examples of the First through Third Century Calligraphy.*

The light from his flashlight reflected from the penciled lines– recent marks.

He replaced the book, circled the desk. The chalk outlines where the body was found and bloodstains still marked the floor and wall. On the desk, Orhan found a felt pen without a cap.

He tapped the point on a paper on the desk. Dried out. Orhan spotted the cap tucked in a corner of the blotter pad. Next to it, he spotted a scribbled reminder in the same ink as the dried out pen– a blurred, *"appeler Jim C."*

Orhan jotted down the name and left.

~*~~*~

At Mübeccel's lab, a graduate student in a white lab coat admitted him into a room with artifacts spread out over tables.

"Colleagues, this is the famous Colonel Orhan Mehmet," Mübeccel said.

Students and lab assistants flocked around him. Orhan shook hands, gestured with his eyebrows to Mübeccel toward a corner of the room. She clapped her hands.

"Enough greeting celebrities," she said. "Everyone back to work."

When her staff went back to their stations, Orhan took Mübeccel aside.

"I need a list of the missing artifacts," Orhan said in a low voice. "Also, copies of the site reports, and anything else you can think of."

Mübeccel relayed this to an assistant.

"Does the name "Jim C" mean anything to you?" Orhan said.

Mübeccel shrugged her shoulders. “Nothing.”

A moment later, a very agitated assistant came over, whispered to Mübeccel. They stepped aside, spoke in intense whispers. Mübeccel motioned for Orhan.

“I just found out all of the site photos are gone and all of our site report files have been erased,” she said.

“Oh? “

Mübeccel shook her head.

“We have little or no security here,” she said. “People constantly come and go.”

“I’ll arrange for someone to pick up the hard drive,” Orhan said. “Our forensic lab can recover whatever data were stored earlier.”

“But the photos of the codex are also gone.”

“Were they on film?”

“No,” Mübeccel said. “Everything was on the missing chip.”

~*~~*~

Back in his office, Orhan scanned the forensic report of the murder. Foucault was shot 3 times in the heart at close range with a .765mm pistol. The slugs had gone through his body. One lodged in the back of the chair. Two in the wall.

The angle of entry showed that Foucault was sitting and the assassin standing. The distance from the shooter to the victim was estimated at 2.1 M and the minimum of powder residue on Foucault’s clothes suggested the gun had a silencer.

The grouping of the bullets striking the heart was within a circumference of 4mm.

Damn good shot.

Glancing over the phone logs, Orhan saw the last call was to a number in the US.

Orhan looked at his watch. Coming up on 7 PM. That would be around noon in the Eastern US.

After the series of clicks, he heard the phone pick up.

“Yes.”

A woman’s voice, soft, young.

"I'm Colonel Orhan Mehmet calling from Turkey. I'm following up on an investigation involving a murder and theft of valuable artifacts that occurred here a few weeks ago. Forgive the intrusion, but may I ask with whom I'm speaking?"

"This is Dr. Colene Mooney at Yale University."

"Thank you, Dr. Mooney. Does the name "Jim C" mean anything to you in connection to this telephone number?"

There was a moment of hesitation.

"I know this is just a voice talking to you over the phone," Orhan said. "I can give you my number to call me back collect through the exchange."

"That won't be necessary," Colene said. "My late colleague, Professor James Corbett had this office until recently."

"'The late?' " Orhan said.

"Yes. He was killed in a car wreck a couple of weeks ago."

"I'm so sorry to hear that."

"Thank you. He was a wonderful man."

"Do you know if he talked with Professor Foucault on the night he was murdered?"

"I know for a fact that he did. He was planning to fly to Turkey when he learned Foucault was dead."

"Do you know what this was in regard to?"

"Yes. Foucault had told him he had a rare biblical text and wanted Jim to come see it."

"A rare text?"

"Unique. It could be the only copy of this hypothecated Christian text known to exist."

"Hypothecated?"

"Biblical scholars hypothesize that an earlier version of sayings from the beginning of Christianity existed which provided the basis for later texts that we know as the gospels of Matthew and Luke. But, no existing copies of it had ever been found."

"And, this might have been it?"

"Who knows? The only authority to see it was Foucault and he's dead."

"What's your opinion?"

"Foucault was one of the world's authorities on Aramaic scriptures and first century Judaism. If anyone would know, it would have been him."

"Are there other authorities?"

"The other top scholar in this area was my former boss, Jim Corbett."

"Any idea what he thought about this possible text?"

"He told me that Foucault was convinced it was for real. That's a pretty strong endorsement."

"I'm in charge of the National Security for Turkish antiquities. Are you familiar with the international market in smuggling and selling artifacts?"

"Only that it exists and I wish all those sons of bitches were in jail."

"Are you familiar with a group or an individual known as 'The Hydra?' "

"No. I guess they took the name from the mythical monster."

"Quite. You've been most helpful, Dr. Mooney. May I call again if something else comes up?"

Her heard her hesitate.

"Yes," Colene said. "I might have ... well, something. But, give me your number and I'll contact you if something definite comes up."

"That would be excellent."

He gave her his contact numbers.

After she hung up, Orhan sat with the phone in his hand.

What did she look like, the woman in America with the soft voice and confident answers?

In a Bus Station

Downtown, New Haven, CT
The following evening, 10:15 PM

The older seedier section of the city reeked of exhaust fumes, car grease and danger. Colene glanced around, locked her car, then sped into the Greyhound terminal. She shivered as she pushed her way into a large clean but dingy waiting room.

The cashier's cage huddled at the north end of the room, two rows of metal lockers, stacked 2 high with keys in the locks under a coin and bill money slot flanked the far wall next to a short hall leading to the restrooms.

On the other wall, a trio of glass fronted vending and drink machines invited idle travelers to spend their money on plastic-tasting snack foods.

Chrome pipe chairs with leatherette seats and backs, lined in 4 rows, back to back sprawled throughout the waiting room. Colene cringed at the sight of a panel TV at the south end of the room where a sitcom rolled outlined with a printed dialogue strip.

A dozen or so people sat scattered around in the chairs waiting for bus connections. Colene scanned the room again, sat down, opened a book in front of a woman holding a baby a few chairs away.

Glancing over, she spotted a burly man with a blond buzz-cut come in, stand before the food machines, set down a square metal brief case beside him, then gawk at the items in the vending trays.

Out of the corner of her eye she caught sight of a tall, thin, dark-skinned man with thick black hair and moustache, dressed in a light blue jacket over a light green shirt with dark green buttons and light colored khaki slacks.

He circled the room before he sat one space away from Colene.

She looked up toward him. He set a manila folder on the chair between them. He whispered,

"Look at this."

Colene took the folder, looked inside. A color photocopy of a parchment page written in 2 columns, one in Greek, the other in Classical Aramaic.

Catching her breath, she read as much of the text as she could, her heart racing. The man whispered,

"Six million dollars. Cash."

"I'd have to examine the original first," Colene said.

"Put the folder back."

She set it down. The man snatched it up.

"Noon tomorrow," he said.

The baby behind her let out a scream. Colene snapped around, glanced behind her.

When she turned back, the man was striding out the door, the manila folder under his arm.

Colene sat there, thinking about the photocopy, then picked up her book and left.

~*~~*~

Greg Steele, the man in the buzz cut back by the vending machine watched the transaction in the reflection of the vending machine's glass. He tracked her out the door with his eyes, then picked up his brief case from beside him and followed her.

Son of Light

Chief Inspector's Office , Ministry of Interior, Ankara, Turkey
The next day, 6:25 AM

Orhan opened the email from the Technical Unit of the Investigative Department. The technicians had. recovered most of the missing files from the Archaeology Department's purge hard-drive. Scanning through the lists of artifacts and site reports, Orhan saw the catalog and journal reports.

Nothing there provided any clues.

He cross-checked the names of the archaeologists on the site with a data base of police and investigation reports.

Again, nothing.

He went through the list of employees on the excavation site—a name **'İbrahim Açikoğlu'** caught his attention. Turkish, *açık,* means 'luminous, bright.'

Looking through the Ankara phonebook, Orhan found no such surname in Turkey's second largest city. Going through the Istanbul listings gave the same results.

He thought, *İbrahim. Given name. Common enough—the name of the patriarch, İbrahim, whose son was İsmail, founder of the Arab nation ... father of the Jews too, through his son, Izak Isaak!*

Orhan raised his eyebrows– *nur,* 'light' in Arabic- *oğlu,* 'son' in Turkish.

Isaak– son of the patriarch– son of 'light,'

Isaak ibn Nur.

Orhan clenched his jaw.

This ploy was Hydra's style. Play under the enemy's noses. Have a set of eyes at the site. Laugh at the fools.

Yilmaz's informant placed Isaak ibn Nur in Antioch, trying to get to the US.

Leaning back in his chair, Orhan picked up the ornate Turkish dagger from his desk, ran his fingers over the smooth black onyx handle, the twisted brass guard, the polished knurled pommel. He stroked the 8" curve of the wide blade. Damascus steel. Razor sharp– he used it as a letter opener.

A known terrorist goes into a hotbed of investigation and traps like the US? The payoffs have to exceed the risks. But, both the archaeologists and Dr. Mooney said this stolen document would be priceless.

Dr. Mooney. Her soft, confident voice, her clear, reasonable answers tickled his inner ear.

A Goggle search showed her educational background and picture on the University departmental home page.

Attractive face. Winsome smile.

Scanning her résumé, Orhan saw a long list of published work. No indication of her marital status.

Her personals stated she was interested in gardening, hiking, cycling.

A search through the Interpol site turned up her two brothers. One, an officer in the US Air Force. The other, a lawyer with the FBI. Her deceased father had been a bomber pilot, Col., USAF. KIA ODS, Iraq. Her mother, still living was a Professor Emeritus of Ancient History at Bryn Mawr University.

He dialed Colene's number. She answered on the first ring.

"Hello."

"Hello. Colonel Mehmet from Turkey. I wanted to let you know that we recovered most of the data from the Archaeology Department's computers at the university."

"I'm sorry? Which computers?"

"Ah, I neglected to mention that the files on the stolen artifacts had been purged from the university department's computers."

"Really?"

"I'm afraid we still have no information about the missing documents or artifacts."

"That's regrettable."

Orhan stroked the deep curve of the flat part of the top of the blade.

"Does the name, Isaak ibn Nur, mean anything to you?" Orhan said.

"Not at all."

"I've taken up too much of your time already. You have been most helpful."

He heard her catch her breath.

"One second, Colonel Mehmet."

"Yes?"

"I said before I might be onto something. I'll know more very soon."

"Oh?"

"Can't be more specific now. I'll contact you later."

"Please do," he said.

After ringing off, Orhan sat at his desk running his fingers along the edge of the knife. His dark eyes drifted to the picture of his dead wife and son.

He gripped the handle of the knife, squeezed it– hard.

The Iceman Cometh

Sword and Shield Security Services Training Grounds, Shanekmandan, SC
Later the same day, 11:20 AM

The team leader, R. Brigham Kimball, assembled the assault team poised outside the cement block house. His face daubed in cameo paint, Kimball raised the first two fingers of his right hand, looked around to see his men's eyes locked on his hand movements.

Pointing to each of the five men on his right with a deliberate jerk like firing an imaginary pistol, Kimball then motioned to his right circling his finger, then repeated the procedure on his left. The men nodded, peeled off in a swift, squatted trot.

Turning to the remaining men behind him, Kimball fisted an up-down pumping motion to follow, then led the charge to the block house.

Two men swung a heavy metal ram, smashed in the door. The others poured into the room, blasted manikins spotted with dummy weapons in their hands. Their cylinder-fed AA-14 automatic shot guns with double-aught buckshot ripped the metal manikins to shreds.

Kimball raised his hand, screamed, "Clear!"

The firing stopped.

"Clear 1 red."

"Clear 2 red."

"Clear 1 green."

"Clear 2 green."

Lowering his shotgun in the smell of the cordite filled room, Kimball looked around at his men and grinned.

"Stand down from exercise," he called out.

~*~~*~

On a grassy knoll 300 yards away, Ham Morris and 6 other observers watched the action through field glasses. Morris heard the order to stand down, smelled the waft of cordite from below, then looked from one to another observer, nodding approval.

Morris started to say something when his cell phone rang.

"Morris."

"Steele, Sir."

Morris stepped away, cupped his hand over the cell phone.

"What's up?" he said.

"A gal who's a real slag as bad as the old guy replaced the target."

"Go on."

"Kept the tap on her line when she took over the old dude's job. She got a strange call from some foreign dude wanting to sell her something."

"What?"

"Not sure, so I followed the twat to the bus station. She came in, looked around, plopped her butt down. Couple minutes later, this hajji comes in ..."

"Hajji?"

"Yessir. Got it all on disc."

"This broad's in with towelheads?"

"Playing cutesy-tootsie. Passed a folder back and forth. Then, he split. So'd she. Followed her back to her car. The raghead slipped."

"This is strange."

"Not just your regular hajji, sir. This one's got history."

"Go on."

"Sent the disc to my pal at Langley. Just got back a fix on his camel jockey ass. Name's 'Isaac bin Nur.' Association, 'Shat Allah.' Known terrorist– deals in stolen art and shit."

"Doesn't figure," Morris said.

"Nossir."

"Anything else?"

"That's all I got."

"Her lines still tapped?" Morris said.

"Yessir, office and home."

"When they meet again, be there."

"And?"

"Ice the towelhead."

"And the slag?"

"No. Just him."

"Low profile?"

"No. Make it visible– damn visible."

The Rapture Network

The Rapture Network, Columbia, SC
The same day, 2:20 PM

Wearing a gray, blue and brown checked sport coat over light tan slacks, light green shirt with tiny dark green spots a wide paisley maroon and gold tie, light yellow socks tucked into small shiny cordovan penny loafers, Damian Styles, Congressman representing the district surrounding Columbia, paused before climbing the steps of the Rapture Network building, home of a non-profit organization with a membership of near a million self-declared evangelical Christians.

Covering a full city block, the massive, neo-modern structure with curved windows and covered walls in a gray glossy exterior designed in the appearance of the biblical ark, loomed temple-like over the surrounding buildings.

Well aware that many local residents referred to the building as the "Death Star," Styles made his way up to the Major Conference Room on the 5th floor of the broadcasting complex wing of the building.

Inside the conference room, sunlit from a bank of overarching tinted windows streamed in, lighting a long walnut table with matching chairs on a raised dais in the center surrounded by spectator seats, an overhead projector and a screen at one end.

A 12' painting of a tall, blue-eyed light-skinned Jesus with neatly trimmed light brown hair and beard hung on the wall at the other end of the room.

At the end of the table sat J. Ryle Hammond, the television evangelist, waving his arms as he spoke. At over 6'4", light skin, blue eyes and a pile of long, well-trimmed curly gray hair brushed back over his head, he wore a tailored Armani blue suit, light blue shirt, bright red tie and black western boots with silver toe covers. His trademark red carnation pinned to the boutonniere of his lapel.

To his right K.D. Rogers, executive producer, host of the Christian Family Daily radio network and the CEO of the Rapture Network, Hammond's TV show, leaned on the table with his hands folded in front of him. His folded hands rested on a typed paper showing an agenda for their meeting.

Styles came to the table and shook hands with them.

"Glad to hear you mended fences with that Colene Mooney gal," Hammond said.

"I felt I should," Styles said.

"I know you two ain't always hit it off."

"She's a brainiac bitch."

"Keep praying for her."

"I'll pray she rots in hell," Styles said.

They took their seats, Hammond continued,

"What about this book that Billy Corbett was gonna see?"

"Apparently it's been stolen," Styles said.

"What's it got to do with anything?"

Styles took a drink of water, cleared his throat.

"Possibly a copy of the Q text," he said.

"What in the Lord's name's a 'cue text?' " Hammond said.

"The 'Q hypothesis.' " Styles said. "It holds that two of the four synoptic gospels, Luke and Matthew were taken from an earlier source which they called the 'Q.' "

"So, howcum they call the cue?" Hammond said.

"From German, *Qvelle*, 'source.' German biblical critics came up with the hypothesis."

"Germans, huh?" Hammond said.

With his hand still on the printed agenda, Rogers interjected a hiss.

"Such a document could undermine all of our efforts," he said.

Hammond laughed.

"C'mon, KD," he said.

"I'm serious," Rogers said.

"Ain't none of our folks gonna believe nothing about some dang thing called a 'cue.' " Hammond said. "Shucks, they'd think it was all about a pool game."

"It could be a nuisance– this is a sensitive political time," Styles said.

Hammond sighed.

"Never could get Billy Corbett to see the Bible as God's word," he said. "He'd say it was just a book."

"That's blasphemy," Rogers said.

"Now, poor old guy's dead ..." Hammond said.

Rogers gave Styles a quick rat-like glance.

"The lord moves in mysterious ways ..." Hammond went on.

"You know that's not strictly from the bible," Rogers said.

Hammond stopped, skewered Rogers with his blue eyes, his mouth in a tight smile.

"Not every Christian word has to be a quote from scripture," Hammond said. "And, it ain't blaspheme."

Rogers stared at the paper under his folded hands.

Styles cleared his throat.

"It comes from a 1781 William Cowper poem," he said. "'God moves in a mysterious way his wonder to perform ...' "

Rogers frowned. Hammond smiled.

"Yeah. Poetry," Hammond said. "My son-in-law, old Ham don't care much for poetry."

Styles gave a hasty glance back at Rogers.

"I got some good news for Ham," Styles said. "My colleague on the Defense Committee got 4Sinc another no-bid contract for embassy protection."

"That's nice," Hammond said.

He looked up at the clock on the wall, stood up.

"Well, gotta get moving, gents," Hammond said. "I'm leaving for Topeka, Kansas for a big revival meeting."

Rogers looked down at his agenda.

"Did I mention it's going to be on national TV?" he said.

Hammond grinned, shook Roger's hand with both of his, then turned to Styles.

"We ask the Lord's blessing," he said.

Rogers and Styles bowed their heads, as Hammond put his hands around their shoulders, droned a prayer. That done, he waved, left out the door, the heels of his boots clocking down the passage way.

"That was too close," Styles said.

Rogers stared at Styles, his hands clasped behind his back.

Styles raised his hands, palms up.

"Look," he said. "Where Ham Morris's involved, I don't know anything."

Rogers did not move or change his expression.

Styles stood up, extended his hand.

"I got to get back too, KD," he said. "You know where to get me if you need me."

"That I do," Rogers said.

Rogers watched Styles leave. At the sound of the closing door, he went to a phone in the corner, punched in a number.

"Ham. K.D. Rogers."

"What's up?"

"Just had a meeting with your father-in-law and Damian."

"Better you than me."

"Damian says you got another no-bid contract."

"I was counting on it."

"How real do you think this missing biblical text is?"

"Haven't the foggiest."

"If Mooney got her hands on such a document, we could be in for a lot of trouble."

"You worry too much."

"Well, you know Corbett had some very damaging information on your father-in-law."

Morris voice was like car wheels on gravel.

"Corbett's case is closed, KD."

Shock and Awe

Starbucks coffee shop, Garner shopping complex, New Haven, CT
8:02 AM, Saturday, 3 days later.

In blue jeans, black and white Puma running shoes, a gray hooded sweat shirt with the Yale U. logo, wrap-around shades over her eyes, Colene stepped outside into the patio, latte in hand, the bag with the voice recorder over her shoulder.

The Starbucks coffee house stuck out of a corner of a small shopping center at the southeast side of an intersection. Outside, the small patio of wrought iron tables was set off from the parking lot by redwood planter boxes of variegated bushes and pink and yellow flowers. Colene looked over the area. Across a busy street to the north she saw a health club, a florist and gift store. Across the street from that block of businesses was a Chinese restaurant.

Noticing an abandoned gas station sprawled across the street on the southeast corner of the intersection, Colene glanced over at a broken window at the back, the rear end of a black SUV with tinted windows jutting out from behind the building.

Taking a seat with her back to a planter filled with dwarf camellias, Colene's eyes behind the shades darted over the dozen or so people scattered around the patio. No one glanced her way as she set her bag at her feet, took out a paperback book and sat down not looking at the words, her mind flashing back to the night before.

The man had left the brief message– meet him at 8:00 AM, Saturday morning at that Starbucks.

~*~~*~

Across the street from Starbucks at the back of the abandoned gas station, Steele crawled from the driver's seat on his belly onto the backs of the flattened back seats, scanned the scene through the darkened rear window.

He had a clear view of the patio across the street.

He took up the rifle, chambered a round into the receiver, slid the bolt shut. Steele then slid the weapon through a slot where the SUV's rear door had been drilled into an opening that admitted the rifle's gun barrel and permitted visibility for the scope. A large, diamond-shaped manufacturer's logo covered the hole which Steele now moved to one side.

He had loaded the rifle, a military version of a .222 caliber, with a soft hollow-point round with a thin copper jacket encasing solidified ground beef-bone. The round would expand, then shatter on its initial impact with bone and burst, leaving only minute traces of copper and bone throughout any soft tissue.

~*~~*~

Colene swallowed a mouthful of her latte and glanced over her shoulder at the street and parking lot. Then, she saw the tall, thin man enter the shop from the side entrance. Through the window she saw him order coffee, then step to the condiment bar, pour in several sugars.

Colene started the recorder before he came out and sat next to her.

Wearing light pleated slacks, a long sleeved sport shirt with the tails drooped over his pants tops, sandals without socks, his eyes were shaded with dark sunglasses. Retrieving a newspaper from under his arm, he opened it as if to read.

"When can you get the money?"

"When I get proof what you're selling is authentic."

"You've seen proof."

"A glance at a snatched away photocopy ..."

The man sneered.

"What you ask is impossible," he said.

"Then, we've nothing more to discuss."

Colene reached for her bag.

"Why more proof?" the man said.

"I won't pay a penny for a pig in a poke."

"Pig?" the man said, his voice rising "Now, you insult me?"

~*~~*~

Sighting in the scope, Steele picked out the tall man across the street, centered his target's head within the yellow and green lines of the cross hairs of the visual field of the reticle, concentrating on movement.

The target stood.

~*~~*~

Colene's voice grated,

"Put up or shut up," she said.

"Are you crazy, woman?" the man said.

"You called me. Show me the goods or find someone else."

~*~~*~

Steele took a deep breath, released it, squeezed his hand, eyes never leaving the target. The discharge suppressor mounted on the muzzle of the rifle's shortened barrel jumped with an audible snick.

~*~~*~

The man stood, folded the paper, tucked it under his arm, hissed at Colene though clenched teeth.

"You're a stu ...

The man's shades shattered from his face. The back of his head exploded into a bloody mass.

At that instant, Colene heard a slight cracking sound.

A dark purple space appeared in the man's face where one eye had been.

~*~~*~

Through the scope, Steele saw the target's head explode.

The hit confirmed, he pulled the rifle back and the metal logo cover slipped back into place covering the hole.

He slid off the muzzle attachment, folded the handle, snapped the scope from the receiver mounting, removed the barrel from the stock, stowed all the parts in a fitted case, then clapped the case shut—in less than a minute.

~*~~*~

Blood, bone and brain matter splattered over a heavy woman in shorts slurping a whipped cream drink at the table behind them.

The lifeless body jerked backwards in a staggered collapsing motion, fell, striking the backs of people in 2 chairs into a sprawled bloody heap.

There were seconds of gasping. Then, men and women broke into yells and screams.

"What the fuck ..."

"O my god, o my god!"

"Shit!"

"Call 911!"

Two or three slapped cell phones to their ears. Four or five jumped up, stared at the bleeding body. Seven or eight more poured out of the shop, shoved their way forward to see.

"Shit. Oh shit."

"What happened?"

"Sweet Jesus, what a mess!"

"Did anyone see who did it?"

Shocked, Colene stared down at the prone body, watching blood ebb over the patio tiles, feeling like she was in a movie, watching herself.

She struggled to remain aware of what took place—her presence there, at that time, looking down at the body of a man she was talking to a moment before.

Reaching into her bag, she switched off the digital recorder, then stood frozen, listening to wild and fantastic versions of what had just happened.

~*~~*~

Steele rolled backwards, pushed up the back seats, wedged the case on the floor between the front and back seats, legged over into the driver seat. He started the SUV, drove off at normal speed around the empty station onto the street away from the coffee shop.

Seeing no traffic coming his way, Steele pushed a panel button releasing a license plate in the plate well of the rear bumper, drove away just within the speed limit.

Calm but stoked by the rush of having taken out his target—his nerves, his whole body electrified.

Aftershock

Starbucks coffee shop, Garner shopping complex, New Haven, CT
8:34 AM, Saturday, 22 minutes later

Sinking back in her seat staring at nothing, Colene ignored the press of the bodies of the onlookers. A fire department unit arrived. Then the police came.

Uniformed officers poured in, herding everybody back from around the body. Colene eased out of the chair, said to a nearby uniformed policewoman,

"I saw it all."

The officer told her to sit nearby as the police and firemen cleared the area around the body. About 30 minutes later two detectives, a man and woman arrived. They walked around the body, talking in low voices. The man leaned over the corpse, made several notes, put a cell phone to his ear, requested a Crime Scene team.

The uniformed officer spoke to the woman detective who came over to Colene.

"Detective sergeant Hazel Wilson," she said. "How're you doing?"

Colene took her card without reading it, replied,

"I just saw his head get blown apart."

Colene focused on the detective's face.

Hazel Wilson was around forty, short dark brown hair framed a face with large dark brown eyes, a sloping nose and lips in a tight smile. Dressed in brown slacks, a dark blue shirt under an open dark gray jacket, inside her coat, Wilson wore her badge and sidearm on her belt around her slim waist.

"Let's get outta here and you tell me what happened," Wilson said.

"Where?"

"C'mon. I know a place around the corner."

Colene wobbled, picked up her bag. They walked around the corner to a grocery store.

"We can sit inside and talk," Wilson said.

Coming inside the store, Wilson led Colene up to the counter of a small snack corner with tables.

"Coffee?" she asked Colene.

"Yeah."

They collected their drinks and sat at a table in the corner. Colene just stared at the dark coffee in her paper cup while Wilson poured sugar and powdered creamer in hers.

"Feel like talking now?" she said.

"Sure ... " Colene said. "Gimme just a second."

"Don't see guys get their heads blown off every day?"

"Not this week."

"Take your time."

Wilson took out a note pad.

"Sorry. I didn't get your name?"

Colene took a card from her bag, handed it to the detective.

"Start from the beginning ..." Wilson said.

~*~~*~

When she finished talking, Colene saw Wilson staring at her

"No idea who this guy was?"

"Only that he wanted to sell me a possibly stolen manuscript."

"This manuscript, you say, was likely stolen in Iran a few weeks ago ..."

"Turkey."

"Wow. That's a fast turnaround."

"Would you like to hear the recording?"

"Definitely."

Colene played the scratchy recording of the shooting. Wilson replayed the killing interlude several times. With the man's last words the sound of the bullet's impact, a slight cracking noise sparked, like a chirrup.

"Hear that?" Wilson said. "That's the report of the gun."

"I heard it the moment he was killed."

Wilson brushed her hair back, looked Colene in the eyes.

"Why didn't you inform the legal authorities about this likely illegal solicitation?"

"Maybe it was an unwise decision. But, if I'd called with wild speculations about a missing codex, I doubt anyone would've taken it seriously."

"It's damned serious now."

"I'm not holding anything back."

Wilson looked Colene in the eyes.

"I believe you," she said. "Just from now on, keep us informed of anything new."

"Do you need to take me into custody?"

"Naw. We know where to find you, Colene. If you were gonna bolt, you'd never have waited around for me."

They stood.

Wilson put the tape recorder in her pocket, looked down at Colene's bag.

"Is that a Gucci *Nuovo Mundo*?" Wilson said.

"On a professor's salary? It's a Target *Molto Fako*."

Wilson laughed, shook Colene's hand.

"Go home. Take a shower. Have a drink. Go to bed or go to a movie. Get this shit outta your head. There's gonna be an aftershock. Call me if you need help or have anything to add. We do have counselors available."

"I'm OK. I've got friends."

"Good. I'll call you ... tomorrow. Mind what I say about the emotional hangover."

"I've got a brother with the FBI."

"Your bother's a Feeb? If I'da known that I'da taken you straight down town."

Colene held out her hand again.
"Thanks, Detective."
"It's Hazel. You take care."

PTSD

Colene Moody's home, New Haven, CN.
Same day, Saturday, 2:55 PM

Looking around at the sycamore lined street of old houses she passed every day, Colene shivered, gripped the steering wheel until her knuckles turned white. Turning into the driveway, she hit the garage door opener, then stopped her Honda Accord inside. Killing the engine, she sat, stared for a moment at the instrument cowling, a buzzing feeling in her head, her ears. Then, grabbing her bag, she stepped out, clicked the car door shut with her electronic ignition key, pushed the button by the door to close the garage.

Opening the back door, Colene walked through the kitchen into the living room, stopped, looked around the room. Her gaze drifted to the phone propped up on its charger stand near the glass enclosed dish cupboard. She went over to it, picked it up– then stopped. Looking at the phone in her hand, then at the bag on her arm, she took a deep breath, popped the phone back onto the stand, tossed her bag on the coffee table in front of the sofa.

Plopping down in a brown and yellow stripped chair that matched the sofa, Colene supported her chin with her hands. Glancing back at the phone, she shifted her attention to the bag on the coffee table, grabbed it up, lugged it into the kitchen, dropped it on the small red dinette table. Turning to the refrigerator, she opened it, stared inside.

Taking out a carton of milk, Colene checked it then put it back. She closed the door, then opened it again, reached in, grabbed a quart of orange juice, carried it to the sink. Throwing back the cupboard door, she grabbed a small blue glass, poured it full of juice. She leaned over the counter top, stared at the juice in the glass in her hand. Setting the glass down, she picked up the carton, put it back in the refrigerator, then stood, gawked at the closed door for a few seconds.

Turning back to the sink board, she ran her finger around the rim of the glass of juice, then walked out of the kitchen leaving the glass of juice on the sink board.

She went back to the phone.

Dialed her older brother.

Voice mail.

"Hi, this is Jack and Ros. Sorry but we're out. Leave a message and we'll get back to you."

Colene clicked off, punched in another number.

It rang twice.

"Hello."

"Maureen?"

"Oh, hi, Colene. How're you doing?"

"Is Danny there?"

"No. He's off on a training program and won't be back for a couple of days. Are you OK? Something wrong? You sound awful."

Colene hesitated.

"Well, I need to talk to him."

"I can't .. I mean ... He's outta touch. You know how that FBI shit is. What's going on, kiddo?"

"Well, do you know where Jack is?"

"You know he and Ros went to Grenoble on that ski trip they've been planning."

Colene bit her lip.

"Will you have Danny call me as soon as he checks in? You got my number, right?"

"Wow. You sound stressed, kid. What's wrong?"

"Just some shit in my life."

"Colene. Do I need to worry about you. Do you need help? Would you like to come here?"

"No, sweetie, it's nothing ..."

"Are you sure?"

"I'm sure."

"Well, I'm here if you need to talk or anything ... Colene?"

"Yes ..."

"Stay in touch, please. Promise?"

"Promise. Just have Danny call me. OK?"

Colene went back to the chair, fell in it, fist against her chin. She looked over at the front door. The mail lay on the throw rug in front of the door's drop slot. She got up, gathered it, thumbed through it, then dropped the pile on the coffee table.

Again, she walked over to the phone stand, looked down at the phone, narrowed her eyes, picked up the phone, punched in a number.

It rang twice.

Mick Jagger's "I can't get no satisfaction" came on, followed by the message, "You know what to do."

"Ara," she said. "It's Colene. Call me back. Urgent."

She clicked off, stood there, phone still in her hand. It rang.

"Hello."

"What's urgent?"

"Man, my life's coming apart."

"How so?"

"I just saw a man get his head blown open in front of me."

She heard him pause, catch his breath.

"Where are you?"

"Home."

"Meet me. Now."

"Where?"

"You remember where we had lunch last time?"

"Yeah, it was ..."

"OK. Be there as soon as you can. Bye."

Colene stared at the phone in her hand.

~*~~*~

The Cantonese Garden was in the older part of town. Colene took in the faux green pagoda with the red trim front, curtains across the window, the name in gold letters, Chinese characters beneath. Stepping through the glass door into the entrance foyer set off by tall lacquered mahogany screens, behind the podium at the cash register, a chubby Asian woman with gray spotted black hair pulled back in a bun at the back of her head looked up at her.

The woman was dressed in silk black pants, an embroidered satin jacket closed at the throat, her tiny feet tucked into black slippers with red and yellow needle point across the toes.

She smiled, came forward extending her hand, holding red-covered menus under her arm.

"Doctor Professor. So glad you come have dinner with us."

Colene shook her hand.

"Hello, Mrs. Wing. I'm meeting ... "

"I know. This way, please."

She led Colene through to a closed booth at the rear, next to the kitchen. She seated Colene inside, brought a pot of tea, two small cups, sat them before her, then disappeared behind the kitchen door.

Colene sipped the tea. The curtain parted.

Ara Agajanian slipped in, plunked down across from her.

"Pour me some too," he said.

Colene filled his cup.

Ara took a slurp, looked over at her.

"You look like shit," he said

"Ara. I'm sorry to drag you into this but I just didn't know what to do."

"Talk to me," he said.

Colene looked across the table at a stocky, 5' 7" fireplug of a man, dressed in levis, a black tee shirt, a black leather jacket, short curly coal black hair brushed straight back over his forehead. Large dark brown eyes looked at her through black horn-rimmed glasses, his thick black eyebrows strung below his wrinkled brow like a long, fat ebony earthworm crawling over his eyes, a prominent nose stuck out from under his glasses, over pursed lips.

Colene took a swig of the hot tea, drew a deep breath, then told him everything up to the shooting.

When she finished, he leaned back against the seat, pressed his fist to his lips.

"This is some heavy shit, Colene," he said.

"Second time I heard that today."

He leaned forward.

"We can't talk here," he whispered. "Let's go to my place."

"Shall I follow you?"

"No. I'll bring you back to get your car later."

He seized her by the hand, led her through the kitchen door. Inside, Mrs. Wing handed Ara a large paper bag, smiled again at Colene.

"Come back see us soon, Doctor Professor," she said.

Without letting go of Colene's hand, Ara snatched the bag, went through the back door into the alley. Colene saw his silver gray '72 Mercury, parked at the back.

He opened the door, brushed a pile of candy wrappers and chip bags off the seat for her. Colene looked down, flinched, hesitated. The floor board was piled with a mix of wrappers, bags, refuse. Ara locked her door, came around, put the large bag in the back seat, got in, started the engine.

As soon as the big V-8 kicked over, Ara jammed it in reverse, tore out of the alley, turned onto the main street looking in his rear view mirrors as he moved in and out of traffic.

"Scanning for cops?" Colene said.

"Making sure we ain't followed."

Ara turned, reversed course, stopped, reversed course again looking behind him before driving on to an old residential part of town.

His house sat back in a tree covered lot off the street surrounded by a water run-off drain. When they drove in over the culvert, Ara pushed a module button under his dashboard. A heavy iron gate slammed shut barring entrance to the property. He drove his car up to the house, jumped out, opened her door.

"When are you going to clean this mess out of your car," Colene said.

He shrugged.

"C'mon in," he said.

The sun had set, darkening the surrounding lot from the shade and shadows of pine trees around the perimeter. Next to the brick, two storey square house, a forest of large antennas poked up at one side next to the chimney. A small lawn hugged the front of the house surrounded by a mix of bamboo, sunflower and tall stalked plants planted in rows and beds with pebble laden paths wandering among them that spread over the greater portion of the lot.

Ara opened a steel door at the rear of the house by punching a code into a key pad, then ushered her into a short hallway that opened to the kitchen where a collection of cutlery was arranged around a block cutting board in the middle of the room in front of the stove.

"Howcum your kitchen's so clean and your car so yucky?" Colene said.

"House-cleaner," Ara said.

She followed him into the living room at the front of the house. A couch and three chairs surrounded a coffee table that sat in front of a shaded window near the door way. The walls were covered with bookshelves stacked full of books.

At the back of the living room adjoining the kitchen was a hallway that led to a tiny room in the interior of the house in back of which loomed another steel door with a key pad. Ara opened with a punched-in code.

Colene stepped into another larger room where two large etchings by Escher hung at either end of the room between a long bookcase that stretched along the wal. A stair case led upstairs on the other side of the room. Underneath the soffit of the stair case, she saw an enclosed closet area with another steel door and keypad to one side.

Ara opened this door to a lighted staircase going down into the basement. He motioned for Colene to follow, led her downstairs into a large basement area.

"Welcome to the Batcave," he said.

Colene looked around. The room was huge and extended far beyond the floor plan of the house. At one end was a large computer work station with a 30"monitor screen. Next to that she saw a small laboratory with bottles, beakers and a microscope table.

Next to the work station sat an elaborate electronic array with dials, monitors, speakers. A drafting table stood next to the electronic set-up as more rows of books shelves lined up along the wall.

Ara set down the brown paper bag, took out the containers of Chinese food, set these on a table near the computer station.

"Chopsticks or fork?" he said.

"Fork's fine."

"I can't eat Chinese food with a fork," he said.

They sat on stools at the table. Ara opened the containers, scooped rice into two porcelain rice bowls.

"You've got enough food here to feed the Red Chinese Army," Colene said.

"There's cold brewski in that little icebox by your knee."

Colene took out 2 bottles of Polish lager. Ara popped the tops, prying the lids with the edge of a spatula-like tool, against the top of his hand.

As they ate, he pointed at her with his chopsticks.

"You know this all ties together," he said.

Colene stopped, her fork of food in front of her mouth.

"What do you mean?"

"First, this professor in Turkey gets snuffed and robbed. Then your boss is suddenly killed. Then, you get a call from a Turkish cop who asks you about terrorists. Then some Arab jamoke shows up just a few weeks later wanting to sell you a mysterious manuscript, and then he gets greased– right in front of you."

"Yeah?"

"Ain't just chance, Colene."

Colene wrinkled her brow, put the fork full of food into her mouth, chewed, washed it down with a swig of beer.

"So, what's the connection?"

"This Turkish cop asked about a smuggling network, right?"

"Yeah. But, I didn't know anything about it."

"These nutcase assholes support themselves by stealing and selling anything they can to finance their crazed activities."

"Understood. But, why're they so crazy fanatical?"

Ara looked at her, chewed on a piece of barbecued pork.

"C'mon, Colene. You're in the bible business. You know ideology is worse than drugs."

"Of course. But, that kind of terrorist and religious nutcase shit's out over there, in the Middle East somewhere. This is happening here."

Ara stopped chewing, looked at her, took a deep swallow of his beer.

"It's here too, Colene." he said.

Sad News

Bahtim, North of Cairo, Egypt
3 days later, Tuesday, 6:10 PM

From a wrought iron balcony of a dingy apartment building, Abdi ibn Nur stared at the rutted, dirty pavement circling the worn cobblestones surrounding an old fountain. Stroking his sparse bearded chin, he noted how the brown dust that covered everything north of Cairo had grimed the tiles on the side of the fountain. The fount's basin was dry, cracked from the constant severe water shortages since the English occupation.

Abdi shifted his gaze to a plaster copy of an obelisk in the center of the fountain, faded and pitted from the constant attack of dirt, dust and the arid climate. He found the battering of wind, sand and neglect that had long faded the classical Egyptian symbols on the sides depressing. White, dried splotches of bird dung, flowing Arabic graffiti along with pits and scratches pockmarked the plastered surface of the old fountain, spoke to him further of the deteriorated state of a once great civilization.

The air reeked of diesel and gas fumes. Shreds of paper, discarded plastic shopping bags floated around the square. On one side of the street, Abdi saw paunchy, snake-eyed goats nibbling at bits of grass and acacia shoots.

The recorded voice of Umm Kulthum, the great Egyptian songstress blared from an open window of the first storey of the apartment building, singing about wandering through a moonlit garden. Humming along to the song, Abdi came inside, sat at a large table strewn with papers, maps, drawings, looked from the map to the papers then to a pad of notes as his thin lips murmured the lyrics of the song.

The sound of the door to his apartment opening, caused him to drop his hand onto a nickel-plated revolver near his note pad. He relaxed when he saw his friend, Waleed come in the room.

"*Ya,* Waleed, *salaam*."

"*Ma'a alxeim salaam*," Waleed said.

They embraced, kissed each other lightly on the lips. The burley Waleed, tall as Abdi, wore a light blue loose fitting *gellabya* with a faded maroon rimless *ta'ya* on his head.

"What news?" Abdi said.

"The General Sultan in Burkina Faso can deliver the RPGs as soon as he receives payment."

Abdi reached down for a pack of Egyptian cigarettes, shook one out, handed the pack to Waleed.

"So, all we need is to come up with the money, *mush kiida*?" Abdi said.

"*Ta'aban*, Of course."

Abdi lit his cigarette with a wooden match, held it out for Waleed.

"So, we proceed with the next step," Abdi said.

"How does that look?"

Abdi pointed to the map in front of him.

"Good. This hotel in Peiraias is favored by German tourists. We'll hit it on Sunday night just as the Krauts are getting ready to leave. The Greeks will be busy getting the tour parties ready for the airport and won't pay attention to us coming in."

"What about the Greek cops?" Waleed said.

"Sunday night most of them are drinking coffee, chasing whores and swilling ouzo."

"How much can we expect to get?"

"In cash, maybe a few thousand Euros. But, from the credit cards we lift from the Krauts, we can skim at least a million. More than enough for the RPGs."

Waleed shook his head.

"Credit cards?"

Abdi took a long drag on the cigarette, blew out the smoke, walked to the window, looked out over the noisy plaza.

"The Man can hack into their accounts before the Krauts can cancel them. Once he's located the account, he'll plant an algorithm in the form of a credit. From this, he can acquire the new numbers once they've been changed and bleed funds until they eventually cancel the account. By then, The Man will have the funds creamed off into a Russian bank and we do business."

Waleed, frowned.

"A problem?" Abdi said.

Waleed held up his hands, palms outward.

"It just seems so much bother," he said.

"How so?"

"Why don't we hit a Casino ... say, in Izmir. We get cash ..."

"Cash?"

"You can't beat cash, my brother."

Abdi gestured with a sweep of the cigarette.

"Cash is a problem."

"Problem?"

"You've got to transport it. It can be stolen. It can tempt greedy people to betray you. It's traceable. It's bulky. These days, even our Somali pirate brothers want electronic transfers into Swiss banks."

"But, a casino in Izmir is so easy," Waleed said.

Abdi dropped the cigarette on the tile floor, mashed it underfoot.

"Nothing in Turkey is easy. You have Turks."

Waleed hunched his shoulders, raised his hands, conceding defeat.

"I argue no more."

"Anything else?" Abdi said.

"How do we get the container with the RPGs from Burkina Faso into Palestine?"

"Easy. We bring them into Alexandria by sea and overland into Palestine."

They stopped at the sound of someone coming up the stairs. Abdi stepped to the table, dropped his hand on the pistol. Waleed closed his hand over a gun in his belt inside his robe, turned, faced the doorway.

A knock at the door. A voice called out,

"It's me, Rafi."

The two men relaxed as a small dark stocky man with a bushy mustache stepped in. He strode straight to Abdi, seized him by the hands.

"I bear very bad news," he said.

Abdi's face tightened.

"Tell me."

"Your beloved brother's dead."

Abdi put his hand to his head, sank down in a chair, burst into loud sobs. The two other men came forward, encircled him with their arms, cried with him. He pushed them away, buried his face in his arms on the table, wept alone. His two friends stood over him, embracing, patting, comforting him.

After a few minutes, Abdi raised his wet face to Rafi and choked.

"How?"

Rafi wiped his eyes.

"He was shot in America."

Abdi's body jolted like a shock.

"America!"

Rafi nodded.

"He was sent there by The Man to sell a book to a Christian woman."

Abdi's face trembled. He grit his teeth, snarled,

"What!"

Rafi raised his hands, glanced over at Waleed.

"Apparently the book was very valuable." Rafi said.

"Worth my brother's life?" Abdi screamed.

"Why in America?" Waleed said.

"I know not," Rafi said. "All I'm told is that he was shot while arranging to sell this book."

Abdi clasped his hands together on the table, his face a mask of anger, hatred. His lips curled, his voice choked.

"So, The Man sends my precious brother to his death because of a fucking book."

Waleed and Rafi stared at each other, then back at Abdi.

He looked up at them, eyes narrowed into slits.

"Jews," Abdi said. "Has to be Jews."

Waleed and Rafi both nodded affirmative.

Abdi's body shook.

"Fucking Israel scum," he said.

"It's likely," Rafi whispered.

"It's certain!" Abdi yelled.

He came to his feet, doubled his fist, shook it in their faces.

"Think. Who else could do this? He goes to America to sell a book to Christians– a woman, at that!. The Americans don't know him."

"How can you be so sure of that?" Waleed said.

"Isaak studied art history," Abdi said. "He didn't work with us on arms or drug deals. The Man only had him work on the art things. Who else but the Jews could know that?"

"But, the fingers of the American CIA are long and in every plate," Rafi said.

"I can't accept that," Abdi said.

Waleed looked at Rafi, shrugged his shoulders.

"It could have been the Jews," Waleed said.

Abdi smacked the table with the bottom of his fist.

"We'll make that fucking Jew pig sow bleed well and long before she dies."

Abdi grabbed the phone, dialed a number.

After the third ring, a voice mail message come on.

"It's Abdi. I've learned of Isaak's death. Call me immediately."

He slammed the receiver onto the cradle.

"Who did you call?" Waleed said.

Abdi looked at him and then at Rafi.

"The Man." Abdi said.

The phone rang. Abdi snatched it up.

"Abdi."

The voice spoke in Egyptian Arabic.

"I extend my heartfelt condolences, my brother."

"Why?"

"You ask 'why?' "

"Why was he there?"

"I sent him there in the interests of the cause we all embrace."

"That means nothing to me."

"That matters not. He didn't die in vain."

"He's dead just the same."

"He likely looks down on us from Paradise, eating lamb with the Prophet and the heroes of the past, wishing us well."

"Words, words. He was killed by the Jews."

"Perhaps."

"I'm going after them. I'll make those whelps of ..."

"No. You will not."

"I want revenge. My family has bled. I want them to bleed five times as much."

"True. But, you must be patient."

"Blood calls for blood!"

"And so shall it be. But, in good time."

"That's not enough. I want ..."

The voice that interrupted was calm, slow. Abdi froze at the tone.

"Hear me! I feel your pain, your passion for the loss of your beloved brother. But, you cannot endanger what we're doing. Not now, not tomorrow– not ever! You will continue as before. You have work to do. Put your energy into doing what you have to do. That is the greatest gift your brother would ask of you."

Abdi held the phone in one hand, sobbed on his other arm.

"I have heard you," he said.

"*Allaah ubarik fiik,* may God bless you," the voice replied, then clicked off.

Rafi and Waleed watched with open mouths. Abdi replaced the phone in the cradle, wiped his eyes, looked over at them.

"Bring the map," he said. "We've work to do."

A CD

Colene Moody's Office, Yale U.
Monday, 9:25 AM

Colene threw her bag and coat on the couch, poured water into her electric kettle, dropped a teabag into her teapot, then stepped over, stared out the window at the groundsman driving a motorized grass mower. When the kettle sounded, she poured water in the pot, dunked the bag up and down.

A knock at the door made her jump.

"Come in," Colene said.

Gloria Farnsworth, the department administrator poked her head inside.

"Hi, Colene. You busy?"

"Just woolgathering."

Gloria held out a newspaper.

"Did you hear about the shooting at a Starbucks?"

Colene flinched.

"Yes," she said.

Gloria thrust the newspaper under Colene's nose, then said, "There's an article in this morning's paper."

Colene scanned the article. Her name was not there.

"I can't handle more bad news right now," she said.

Gloria handed her a disk envelope.

"I meant to give you this before," she said.

"What is it?'

"Dr. Corbett hated to type up his notes, so he'd dictate on a recorder for us. He gave me this the week before he ... died."

Colene's face softened.

"Thank you, Gloria."

After Gloria left, Colene opened the disk on her computer. Short sentences of fragmented notes, thoughts and impressions on works read, reminders to check out sources, comments on reviews sped past her eyes. Scanning down to the latest entries, Colene saw the comments change.

8/3

More crap from RR. They're training constitutional lawyers in private religious law schools. For what? A takeover? Save us all from wickedness?

8/6

Read about JRH's sil. Congress now looking at that shootout. Innocent people gunned down in Iraq by "Security people." Stinking Nazis. Bet nothing comes of it.

8/8

Another diatribe by JRH's partner about Jerry Johnson's "heretical"review in the NYT Critiques. Heresy. Is this the 21st century? JRH's partner reminds me of Dostoevsky's Grand Inq.

8/12

JRH's thick with congr. DS. No surprise. The showman & the pseudo-scholar. Heavenly match. DS, ever politico– now on National Def committee. No wonder the great evangelist's sil loves him. Damn mercs.

9/2

JJ's review of the New Testament translation got RR worked up. Called him "Satanist."These guys are out of the Middle Ages. JRH's just riding the wave. More TV and radio time. It's going to be hard to get research money next year.

10/15

God. Foucault dead. The work gone. Stolen. Was it the Q? He'd have known. Can't believe it. No facts ... just a feeling LD's hand here.

10/17

No news on Foucault's death or the missing codex. Talked with F Casamli. Nice chap. They found the ms. in Antioch. No idea of what they might have had. Gone now

10/22

JRH's buddy calls me a Satanist. Self-righteous twerp. DS received an award from these nutcases. 2nd rate scholar makes a 1st rate ideologue politico.

10/30

Tomorrow night Halloween. Few kids these days. Scared? Saw where case against JRH's sil thrown out. Politics and religion. Nitric acid and glycerine. Some brilliant minds make the worse villains. LD?

11/10

Read in the Political View of the active role of RR noodle heads and their growing political influence. DS now a ringleader. No surprise. JRH's sil got big DOD contract. DS again. My head tells me these are only loose pieces but my gut tells me they connect.

Colene sat back, reflected.

JJ, Jerry Johnson from Harvard. His book discussed historical Greek texts used to translate the gospels and showed that later texts showed additions not present in earlier ones. The Fundamentalist news media attacked him as a revisionist heretic.

She downloaded the contents of the CD and sent it to Ara, adding a note,

Maybe you can use some of this. I'll send more details when I've gone through them again.

Her phone rang.

"Dr. Mooney. There are 2 people here who wish to see you."

Colene caught her breath– Gloria was using her serious voice.

"Have them come in," Colene said.

Naqmat 'Revenge'

Bahtim, North of Cairo, Egypt
Tuesday, 6:38 PM

Rafi sat beside Abdi at the table, stared at the tear-streaked face staring in front of him. Waleed brought the map over, spread it before Abdi, then sat beside him on the other side. Abdi looked up at Rafi.

"Who are the ones who told you of my brother?" Abdi said.

"Three of our brethren from the *Ash Shatt Allaah*," Rafi said.

"They're in the US now?"

Rafi nodded.

"They operate out of New York and were in touch with Isaak when he landed. They helped him conduct the business with the woman about the book."

"Do you think they can catch this Israeli bitch-whore?"

"What?" Waleed said.

Rafi choked, his eyes now wide.

"I said, can they arrange a snatch?" Abdi said.

Waleed grabbed Abdi's hand.

"My brother," Waleed said. "The Man said not to do this."

Abdi's head snapped toward Waleed, his face a mask of anger, hate.

"He said for me not to kill her. Nothing was said about grabbing her."

Waleed and Rafi stared at each other, then looked back at Abdi.

"Is this wise?" Waleed said.

Abdi pushed back from the table, came to his feet. He loomed over them, his hand doubled into a fist.

"Wise?" Abdi said. "Since when do we obey a stinking white man like cringing dogs?"

"But," Rafi said. "We've agreed to help and cooperate for our common interests ..."

"WE'RE NOT STINKING SLAVES!" Abdi screamed.

He strode around the table.

"The time has come for us to take charge. We've been the messenger boys for too long. We need to act on our own ..."

Waleed raised, shook his hands to Abdi.

"But we need these people. They supply us with the money and guns we need."

"Listen to me," Abdi said. "I know they are going to be bringing in a big supply of weapons very soon. When we get hold of these, they will have to dance to the tune we play."

Waleed and Rafi were both staring at him now. Abdi came over, sat beside them.

"This is what we must do," he said. "Complete this simple operation and we'll have the money. Rafi, contact the brothers in the US and have them snatch the Jew whore-bitch. Then when the weapons arrive, we'll be in Alexandria."

"Do you know for certain when and how they'll arrive?" Waleed said.

"I know for certain The Man will have us do his dirty work and transport them."

Rafi looked at Waleed, nodded. Then both men looked back at Abdi.

"Makes sense," Waleed said.

"Rafi, can you contact the brothers in the US today?" Abdi said.

Rafi grinned, shook Abdi's hand.

"Consider it done," Rafi said.

Interviews

Colene Moody's Office, Yale U
Monday, 9:55 AM

Colene opened the door to detective sergeant Hazel Wilson followed by a 5' 3" well-built African American woman dressed in a dark blue pants suit, her dark brown eyes fixed on Colene, a half-smile on her lips. Wilson smiled, shook hands.

"This is Agent Mary Rich, FBI," she said.

Colene ushered them to the couch, asked if they'd like tea. Wilson frowned.

"Not for me," she said

"Tea would be nice," Rich said.

Wilson stretched out on the couch, looked up at Colene.

"The FBI's taken over this case, Colene," she said. "And since you're our principle witness, Agent Rich's here to talk to you."

"How can I help, Agent Rich?" Colene said.

Rich took out a recorder.

"Mary, please. May I record this?"

"Please do."

"Tell me everything you told Hazel," Rich said. "Start at the beginning when you first got the phone call and take us up to now."

Rich sat the recorder in the table. Wilson whipped out her notebook like a traffic cop. Colene told them everything from the first conversation up to her talking to Wilson. Rich made notes, asked a few questions while Wilson followed with her notes.

"We IDed the deceased," Rich said. "Name's Isaak ibn Nur. Interpol lists him as a smuggler in international illegal artifacts. He musta got into the country using forged documents."

Rich closed her notebook.

"So, our information corroborates your end of the story."

"Who killed him?" Colene said.

"Rivals?" Rich said. "Dissatisfied customer? We did find ashes in his hotel room of what may've been the color photocopy you mention. Sent these to the lab but I doubt there's anything useful."

"Sorry you had to go through this, Colene," Wilson said.

"Am I in trouble?" Colene said.

Rich shook her head.

"Nothing criminal. But, your involvement's another matter."

Colene looked down.

"Have you heard anything else?" Wilson said.

"No. But, I did talk to an investigator from Turkey."

"Who?" Rich said.

Colene went to her desk.

"Here's his name and number."

"I'll check this out," Rich said.

Wilson looked over at Rich.

"Anything else?"

"Not now," Rich said.

"Well, that was easy enough," Wilson said.

They stood. Wilson and Rich shook Colene's hand, started for the door.

"I don't know what it's worth," Colene said. "But I was just looking through some notes written by my former colleague."

"Former colleague?" Wilson said.

"My boss, Jim Corbett. He was killed in an accident a few weeks back."

Rich paused, eye brows knit, eyes fixed on Colene's face, then said,

"Oh?"

"Jim Corbett was the one that the professor in Turkey had called about the codex."

"Go on," Rich said.

"Before he was killed," Colene said, "Jim told me that there might be some connection between the codex and something going on here."

"What specifically?" Rich said.

"That's it. He didn't say any more."

"Really. Why not?" Rich said.

"Jim Corbett was a scholar. He didn't gossip, said he'd elaborate later."

"Did he?" Wilson said.

"No. He was dead the next day."

Rich shook her head.

"OK. If anything else comes up ..."

"Today I got a disk of his last memos. In it, he talks about personal attacks from religious fundamentalist groups, shootouts overseas by mercenaries and right wing politics ..."

Mary Rich stopped, blinked, her eyes narrowed. She looked down at her watch.

"Hazel, we gotta move," she said.

Rich looked back to Colene.

"I'll be in touch, Dr. Mooney. Thank you so much for your help."

Rich took Wilson's arm, escorted her out the door.

Open-mouthed, Colene watched them hurry though the door.

Was it something I said?

Colene noticed Orhan's number on the table. She looked at the time, late afternoon in Turkey.

She called.

"Alo."

"Colonel Mehmet?"

"Professor Mooney?"

"Something has happened."

"Yes?"

Colene recounted the story from the beginning to the interview with the FBI agent.

"What did you say the name of the murdered man was?" Orhan said.

"Hold on ... Isaac ben Nor, I believe."

Colene heard Orhan gasp.

"Isaak ibn Nur?"

"That was it," Colene said.

"Do you recall my asking you earlier if you'd heard that name before?"

Colene blinked.

"Now, I do."

"He was a person of interest in this theft and murder."

"So how'd he get here?"

"Network connections." Orhan said.

"Who killed him?"

"Too many possibilities."

Colene caught her breath.

"Do you think I'm in danger?"

"Likely not," Orhan said. "But, please stay in contact with the police and the FBI."

"I don't know what to do. I've never been in a situation like this."

"Look," Orhan said. "You're familiar with analytic methods."

"Yes."

"Make a list-chart. Break it down into major headings."

"Headings?"

"Like associates, authorities, international, groups."

Colene picked up a pad and pencil.

"OK"

"Then, write down all the names of everyone you know involved."

"Involved in what?"

"Everything. Put each name in each category under the heading where it's pertinent."

"Pertinent to what?"

"Pertinent to any aspect of this case."

"OK. Got it."

"Once you have a list of a names, look for connections."

"What kind of connections?"

"Do they know each other. Who has access to who. Who's interested in what another's interest might be. Seek the links–always the links"

"That's doable."

"Stay in contact. Let me know if I can help and feel free to have the authorities contact me if need be."

"Thank you, Colonel."

"Call me Orhan."

"Thanks, I'm Colene."

She started to write on the yellow pad when her phone rang.

"Colene Mooney."

"It's Mary Rich."

"Yes, agent Rich."

"Sorry to be so mysterious back there but I couldn't talk in front of Hazel."

"I'm not sure I understand."

"We need to talk. Can you come here tomorrow?"

"Where's 'here?' "

"I'll give you the address."

Colene wrote it down.

"I can come down later in the week," Colene said.

"That'll work," Rich said.

"Time?"

"Is 9 AM too early?"

"No. I can be there."

"Very important. Bring the disc you mentioned."

"I can send you the file with the contents."

"That's fine but bring the disc," Rich said. 'It's potential evidence."

"I'll do that."

"Also, that name you gave me, Orhan Mehmet?"

Colene caught her breath.

"Yes?"

"He's genuine, very high up in the Turkish department of Antiquities."

"That's the first good news of the day."

~*~~*~

Colene wrote down the categories– *Codex, Religious, Unknowns*. Then, she penciled in names she could think of. She went back to the list on the disc.

JRH? Context. *RR*.

RR? In Corbett's lexicon, 'Rabid Right.' She googled 'Right Wing fundamentalists.' Several million hits showed up. Scanning through the first page, a website caught her eye. The Rapture Network. It was linked to the Family Values Radio Network.

Colene logged on.

"Aha!" she said.

The facing picture was that of Jamison Ryle Hammond, Televangelist, TV star of the Rapture Network. *JRH*.

She erased, *Religious,* wrote down *RR* and put *JRH* under it.

JRH's partner, buddy. Context. *RR*. She noted that the CEO of the Rapture network was the Reverend Dr. Kenneth David Rogers.

She Googled him. His bio listed him as "KD." She wrote *KDR* down under *RR* along with *JRH*.

JRH's sil? Context. Murder. Overseas. Nazi. Nothing came to mind. She wrote down a new category *Overseas* and put down *sil*.

LD. Context. Terrorists? A google search revealed nothing significant. She put it under *Overseas*, under *sil*.

DS. Context. *RR*. This was a no-brainer. Damian Styles, ideologue politico, bright but a "true believer,"and not an objective biblical scholar. Hired as an assistant professor fresh out of grad school at Trinity College and Seminary, he quit before being denied tenure. She wrote his name under *RR*. But, there was a connection to the unknown *sil*. She wrote it under *Overseas* too.

Jim Corbett. Where to put it? *RR* and *Overseas*

Anyone else? She looked it over her list of names, organized into 3 columns, *Overseas, RR*. She added another, *Cops*.

Isaac ibn Nur. *Overseas, Codex*.

Cops was easy. Rich and Wilson. How about Orhan? OK. He was in *Cops* and *Overseas*.

She hesitated, thought. *Was Orhan really a cop? Had to be. He investigated, fitted the list heading structurally.*

She looked up, eyes wide.

A connection:

Structurally, as a national politician, Damian Styles fit in the cop category too. He had the same access to all the important information and knowledge. She added his name to *Cops*. But, he was also on National Defense committee, she put him under *Overseas* too. She looked over the list again.

Damian Styles was the common link.

TWO

Doc Nerd

Colene Mooney's bedroom, New Haven, CT
5:01 AM, the next day

Colene's bedside phone chirruped. She groped for it. The digital clock on her night table read 5:02 AM.

"Hello."

"It's me."

"Ara. It's five-fucking AM."

"We gotta talk."

"I'm not awake."

"I'll be there in half an hour. Be ready."

He hung up. Colene rubbed her eyes.

"Shit," she said.

~*~~*~

Colene heard his car before it screeched to a halt in front of her house. She opened the car door, saw the fresh snack wrappers on the floor, closed her eyes, climbed in.

"Buckle up," Ara said.

"Damn it, Ara," she said. "You're a doctor. You can't live on junk food."

He scanned the mirrors, looked around, roared off.

"Yeah," he said.

"Don't 'yeah' me. This is a stinking mess."

He ignored her, eyes pinned to the mirrors.

"What're you looking at?" she said.

"We're being followed."

His dark eyebrows pinched together, gaze fixed on the black car behind him, he turned left and headed down the street, keeping within the speed limit down the boulevard toward the turnpike. Two blocks away from the turnpike feeder lane, an 18 wheeler truck and trailer swept by in the opposite lane. Ara gunned the Mercury's V-8, spun in behind the semi, then tore off in the opposite direction.

Colene grabbed onto the passenger handle over the window.

"Are you fucking crazy?" she said.

He kept his eyes glued to the mirrors.

"Naw. Just a mild form of Asperger's," he said.

Ara whipped the Mercury into a side street, mashed the foot feed, whipped the car to the left into an alley way, wheeled behind a dumpster, braked to a sudden stop. Colene clung to the handle glaring at him.

After a short wait, he put the car in gear, drove down to the other end of the alley, lurched across the street into another alley, screamed down to its end. Glancing around, he turned back toward the neighborhood where Colene lived.

"Now, where're you going," she said.

"Isn't there a big park near your place?"

"Yes. About 5 blocks to your right."

"Cool."

He found the park, pulled into the parking lot, braked in the corner. Colene let go of the handle, eased back in her seat.

"What in the hell's going on?" she said.

Ara swept the surrounding street with his gaze.

"Tellya when we get to my place."

"Why not now?"

"Got stuff to show you there."

He looked across at her.

"This is some deep shit, Colene."

"Why do I keep hearing that again and again?" she said.

Ara punched the gas pedal and the big V-8 engine roared.

Hanjar 'a long curved Arabian knife'

Queens, New York City
7:43 PM, the same day

Signs and advertisements in Arabic script in the windows of the shops around the neighborhood advertising Middle Eastern products and services reflected the cultural tastes of the residents. Bearded men in long blowsy shirts over slacks, feet in sandals, strolled along the street speaking in Arabic, Farsi, Urdu and other Middle Eastern languages. Women with heads covered in scarves, wearing long, loose-fitting dresses, hurried along the streets, scolding and herding their children along in the same languages. At a small café, men sat at sidewalk tables drinking tea, talking in loud voices, waving their hands.

Inside a dingy apartment on the third floor of one of the buildings looking out over the busy, noisy street, Saleem Duhani sat at the kitchen table near an open window writing a letter. In the living room two men sat on a ragged couch in front of a TV, playing a video game.

Saleem's cell phone jangled a carillon-like sound. Seeing the call was international, he put it to his ear.

"Sallaam aleikum," he said.

"Axi. Ma'a alekum as ..," came the reply.

"U abarikatu," he interrupted.

"Allaah kareem"

Saleem smiled.

The recognition code matched his cousin's voice.

"*Ya*, Rafi," Saleem said in Arabic. "How goes it?"

"I informed Abdi of the tragic death of our brother, Isaak."

Saleem reached for a pack of cigarettes, stuck one in his mouth, lit it.

"We had no idea he was in the US," Saleem said. "A friend who works in a lab near the university in Connecticut told us. We called The Man in Egypt, then I called you."

There was a long pause. Saleem said, "Are you still there?"

"I'm here, my brother."

"Trouble?"

"The Man told Abdi to do nothing."

Saleem took a long drag on the cigarette, exhaled the smoke.

"That seems strange."

"What do you know of this woman who lured Isaak to his death?"

"Some kind of professor. You know Americans. Their women do anything they want."

"Is she an Israeli spy?"

Saleem shrugged his shoulders, waved his cigarette.

"Well, we know this woman was there when he was shot," he said.

"Doesn't that speak of Jews to you?"

Saleem stuck the butt of the cigarette in his mouth, narrowed his eyes, looked out the window at the street scene below.

"Perhaps," he said.

"The Man told Abdi to take no action. But, he didn't tell *us* not to."

Phone in hand, Saleem stepped into the front room where two men were playing and laughing at the video game.

"Turn that damn thing off and come in here," Saleem said.

He pushed the speaker phone button on the cell phone as the two came in, stood beside him.

"Hear me," Rafi said. "Why not capture her and take care of her in a way that lets the Americans and Jews know that they can't kill our warriors unavenged?"

"The Man has us handle money transfers and run messages," Saleem said. "We're not set up to ..."

"Think, Saleem. Your names could be on the lips of every true believer throughout our holy world."

"But, Rafi ..." Saleem said.

"Capture this Jew twat, cut her head off and film it, like the brothers did in Iraq and Pakistan."

Saleem shook his head.

"But, there are only three of us," he said.

"In Allaah's name, she's only a woman. They won't be expecting it."

Kassim, the man at Saleem's right, nodded, looked at the other man, Mekki.

"We can do it," Kassim said.

Mekki stuck up his thumb in approval.

"I like it," he said.

Saleem frowned, shook his head.

"I don't know ..." he said.

"I have a long, curved and sharp *hanjar* I bought years ago when I was on *hajj* in Mecca," Mekki said. "A holy dagger that has never tasted infidel blood."

Saleem looked up at the two men grinning on either side of him.

"It seems I'm out-voted," Saleem said.

"I'll get you the funds to do it," Rafi said. "Make the arrangements tonight."

"Rafi," Saleem said. "What will The Man think of this?"

"The Man doesn't need to know until after the fact."

"Will he approve?"

Rafi's voice came as a growl,

"Once the deed is done, there's not a fucking thing he can do about it."

Double Take

Ara Agajanian's House, New Haven, CT
later that same day,

The smell from Ara cooking omelets reminded Colene she was hungry. She sipped a latte Ara had made at his professional espresso machine. He peered over at her from the stainless steel gas stove in his kitchen.

"Be done in a second," Ara said.

"Smells lethal."

He rolled the omelet onto a plate, shoveled a scoop of potatoes fried with green onions, brown mushrooms and pieces of dark sausage.

"Come get it, before I throw it to the dogs," he said.

Colene took the plate.

"Ara," she said. "You don't have a dog."

He took a dish with a larger omelet, piled high with potatoes and sausage, drowned it in catsup and hot sauce.

Colene scowled.

"Hey, you're ruining your own masterpiece."

"Can't stand the taste of eggs," Ara said.

They ate without talking. Finished, Ara stacked her dish, knife and fork, rinsed, then washed them in the sink.

"So," Colene said. "What's so frigging mysterious that you had to have me here to talk about it?"

Ara shook water from his hands, wiped them on his shirt, motioned for Colene to follow him, led her downstairs into his underground office, went to the computer station at the other end of the room, then motioned for her to take a chair next to him.

"Your former boss was a gadfly buzzing the ass of some very nasty people," Ara said.

He pulled up a photo on the screen of a handsome man in his fifties with a broad smile, a mass of gray curly hair in a dark blue silk suit. Colene recognized the face of the Televangelist, J. Ryle Hammond.

"He and Corbett went to high school together before going on to a Baptist seminary outside of Atlanta," Ara said.

"I knew Jim had been in seminary but this connection's news to me."

"Hammond became a TV personality and preacher. He's a showman who survived the big flap over TV preachers in the late 80s because he kept his skirts clean."

"What's this got to do with Jim and the rest of this mess."

"Getting there. Hammond's spokesman for a growing movement of fundamental Christians who want to turn this country into one huge religious congregation."

Ara brought up the face of a balding, severe looking man, with a thin moustache, in a dark suit.

"KD Rogers's successful radio program, 'Family Values,' paired with Hammond in a new Christian Crusade, called the 'Rapture Network.' "

Ara brought up another photo of a chubby faced man with a pompadour hair piece.

"Damian Styles," Colene said.

"Your former colleague at Yale."

"He wasn't much of a historian," Colene said. "He tweaked all his work to fit in with his own religious leanings."

"That's why he went into politics."

"He's a back-stabbing worm," Colene said.

Ara brought up a the face of a man with buzz-cut hair, intense narrow blue eyes in a Green Beret Army officer's uniform.

"Who's this?" Colene said.

"Hamilton Morris, son of a career military sergeant. He won a scholarship to the Citadel and went into the army's Green Beret Special Forces division. He was indirectly involved in the Iran-Contra scandal and left the military. "

"What's he got to do with any of this?" Colene said.

"He formed a private security company with an infusion of right-wing capital called 'Sword, Shield Security Services, Inc.,' AKA *4Sinc*. They provide private security to embassies and private companies working in dangerous places, like the Middle East– all through political connections."

"What's their tie-in to the rest of these right-wing goons?"

"He's married to JR Hammond 's daughter, Judy."

Colene grabbed her purse, dug out the list she had made, spread it on the table next to the monitor.

"The Turkish cop told me to make a list and look for a common link," she said. "There was one from Jim Corbett's list I couldn't figure out. "

She pointed to the *sil* entry.

Ara looked at where she was pointing.

"*'S-i-l,'* son-in-law," he said.

"Now, this makes sense." Colene said.

Ara brought up Styles's profile again.

"As a congressman Styles has wormed his way into several key defense committees which have awarded huge no-bid contracts to 4Sinc."

"How does this fit in with the guy I saw murdered?"

Ara turned in his chair, looked her in the eyes.

"They've had you under surveillance," he said.

"Me? Why?"

"James Corbett posted several critiques on Fundamentalist websites which prompted angry personal attacks."

"All biblical historians get these. We just ignore them."

"Corbett accused them– in print– of planning an ideological *coup d'état*."

Colene's mouth popped open. She stared over at Ara.

"A coup?" she said.

Ara pulled up a blog-site. On the wall postings, he opened a entry earlier that year by J. Corbett. He pointed to the last paragraph of the posting.

"Note, he says he can give names of a cabal out to enact fundamental policies as the law of the land."

After reading the postings, Colene said, "This clears any doubt of what he was thinking."

"He was exposing the connection between the Rapture Network and the 4Sinc mercenaries," Ara said. "I think they're the ones who snuffed your Arab contact."

"Why?" Colene said. "He was just a delivery boy."

Ara turned back to the monitor, brought up the Corbett file Colene had sent earlier.

"You're being tailed," Ara said. "Probably have your lines tapped too."

"Should I go to the police?"

"Where's the hard evidence? This is all circumstantial."

"What should I do?"

"Know you're a germ in a petri dish. Don't say or do anything they can see."

"That sucks."

"It does, but we can play a trick or two ourselves."

"Like what?"

Ara grinned.

"We can tap their lines too," he said.

Phone Outage

Rapture Network Building, Columbia, SC,
9:43 AM, Friday

Mrs. Beulah Leathergate, Administrative Assistant to the Reverend Dr. K.D. Rogers, CEO of the Rapture Network, had been talking on the phone with her daughter for over a half-hour. From time to time she would glance over the two secretaries at their desks across from hers in the large anteroom leading into the main chamber of the her boss's office. Satisfied that her staff were staying busy, she turned her attention back to her daughter's comments.

"She said what?" Beulah said.

"Well, she said that ..."

A crackling sound popped in Beulah's ear– static noise. Then, the line went dead.

"Darlene?" Beulah said. "Darlene. You there?"

Trying to reconnect, Beulah pushed the receiver cradle, clicked the connection, then hit the reset buttons.

Nothing.

"Oh, shoot," she said.

Marsha Littlewood, a heavy set woman in her late 30s with a pile of long combed back brown hair looked over at her.

"What is it, Mrs. Leathergate?" she said.

"My phone's dead. Try yours."

Marsha and Agnes Wright, the other secretaries, picked up their phones.

The lines were all dead.

The two secretaries looked first at each other, then over at Beulah, shook their heads.

"Just what we need on a busy Friday," Beulah said

She dug in her purse for her cell phone, pulled up a menu, punched in the number.

"I can't see why people have to go through this voicemail monkey business just to get an answer to a simple question why our phones quit," Beulah said.

A moment later she heard a recording come on reporting the outage, then announcing that repairmen had been dispatched.

Beulah cut off the call to the phone company, went to her cell phone's contact directory, punched in her daughter's number.

~*~~*~

Sitting in a van three blocks away, Ara Agajanian picked up the call from Beulah Leathergate, closed the electronic interception program on his laptop, took a bite from a rye roll thick with pastrami, sliced kosher pickle, wiped the mustard from his mouth.

He logged onto the New York Times crossword puzzle website, clicked on the advanced user button. Finishing it in less than five minutes, he did three more crosswords before he left for the Rapture Net office.

~*~~*~

Beulah Leathergate looked up, scowled at the dark-eyed man in the Southern Bell uniform who came into the office with a clattering string of tools hanging from his belt.

"Well, it took you long enough to get here," she said.

Ara smiled, touched the brim of the ball cap with the Southern Bell logo.

"Sorry," he said. "Came as soon as I could. What seems to be the trouble?"

"All of our office phones have quit working."

Ara picked up her phone, punched in numbers, tapped the ear piece.

"When did they quit?" he said.

"Just before I called your office."

"Been having problems?"

"No. They've been working perfectly fine."

"How did they quit?"

She frowned, narrowed her eyes.

"What do you mean?" she said.

"Did they poop out slowly? Just go dead? What?"

"They made a crackling sound and kind of a pop."

"Then?"

Beulah snorted.

"Then, nothing," she said.

Ara shrugged.

"Sounds like a power surge," he said.

"Can you fix it?"

"No sweat. But, I'll need to check all the lines."

"How long will that take?"

"Less than an hour."

Beulah rolled her eyes. "Be my guest."

Ara went from handset to handset, plugged a connecter to each one, tested it on a red hand-held computer. He turned to Beulah.

"I'll need to check the internet connections too."

She looked up, gave him a dirty look, waved toward the desktops.

Ara mumbled an apology, inserted a UBC connector into each computer, checked the readings on his hand-held receiver.

Turning to the scowling Mrs. Leathergate, he pointed at the door to the CEO's office.

"Is this office locked?" he said.

She rolled her eyes, heaved her heavy body to her feet, took keys from her desk drawer, opened the office door.

"Try not to disturb anything," Beulah said.

"I'll try," Ara said.

Ara came in, looked around the big office. Two flags, a US flag on the right, one with a white field and blue border with a gold cross in the middle, stood in stands on either side of the window. A file cabinet stood in the corner, a glass table with 4 chrome pipe and leatherette chairs occupied the middle of the room.

Rogers's massive desk crouched under a painting of an Anglo-Saxon looking Jesus Christ, with neatly trimmed light brown beard and hair, staring off into the distance. Below that a number of photos of Rogers and others in stiff postured poses hung in frames on the wall.

Ara moved to the phone, unscrewed the receiver, inserted a tiny bug, then plugged into the desk top beside the seat, found a lap top sitting on the side table. After inserting the probes into them, he glanced up at the closed office door, pressed a small electronic receiver the size of a thumb tack into the side of the sliding door for the computer keyboard. Then he went over, placed one under each of the leatherette chairs, turned, jangled his way to the door.

Coming out, he looked over at Beulah

"Are there any other outlets?" he said.

She rolled her eyes again.

"Yes," she said. "The conference room down the hall."

She got up, led Ara down the long hall, unlocked the door for him.

"Do you need me here?" she said.

"No," Ara said. "Just be a few minutes."

When she walked out the door, Ara bugged the table phones, another one in the recess by the back wall, then snapped tiny receivers under every other chair. Looking around, he walked around the room checking reception on the monitor of his hand-held, then added two more receivers at the center spots of the table.

Coming out in to the reception room, he filled out a worksheet, showed it to Beulah.

"A power surge caused the outage. I've checked all the phones and computers on these lines. Doesn't seem to be any damage."

"How long before we get our phones back?"

"I'll reboot the system before I leave."

Ara set an aluminum clipboard with an invoice in front of her.

"All I need is a signature."

"How much is this going to cost us?"

"No charge," Ara said. "Your maintenance plan covers it."

She smiled for the first time.

"Well, that's a relief," she said.

Beulah signed the invoice. Ara tore off a copy, gave it to her, clanked out the door, tools rattling.

A minute later, Beulah picked up the phone, heard the dial tone.

"Well, that's over," she said.

Marsha, the secretary, looked over at her.

"That man gave me the willies," she said. "Did you notice how dark he is?"

"He did have real dark eyes and hair," Agnes, the other secretary said.

"I just hope he wasn't one of those *Moslems*," Beulah said.

Windshear

Canton Municipal Airpark, Canton, OH
2:22 AM, the next morning

On a moonless night, 4Sinc operative, R. Brigham Kimball rode his black Honda RC212V motorcycle along a connecting road running through fenced-off industrial locations toward the airpark in Canton, Ohio located on the outskirts of town tucked into an industrial zone of small refineries, factories and warehouses.

Kimball rolled his motorcycle into a clump of trees to the east of the airfield, then stood in the shadows scanning the scene with infra-red binoculars for the security patrols. Dressed in a dark gray form-fitting body suit, he peered out from the dark gray balaclava made from the same nylon velveteen material pulled down over his face.

The night was still. Kimball swept the glasses over the buildings, the small commuter terminal, the tarmac parking lot located in the front, the three hangers by the terminal where parked aircraft lined up in rows.

The interior of the buildings lurked dark, deserted, only exterior light bled from the security lamps surrounding the area. The hanger crews had long gone home– the only activity on the site was the security patrol roving around the airfield.

Satisfied, he slipped on a small back pack, moved out along the opposite side of the well-lit cyclone fence surrounding the airfield, edged around the parking lot, then dashed to the corner of the building where the fence attached to the edge of the structure.

Checking his surroundings again, Kimball shinnied up the fence, dropped onto the pavement on the other side with only a whisper of noise.

He moved his tall, slender 6'3"body cat-like along the darkened edges of the structures, staying away from the sporadic splotches of light. Coming to the end of the small buildings, he dropped to a crouch, looked around. Seeing nothing, he sprinted the hundred yards to the hanger area, paused in the darkness at the edge, put on, adjusted his night vision apparatus, scanned the rows of aircraft lined up in front of the hangers.

Finding the line he was looking for, he ran forward, in a bent-kneed dash until he came to the first one in line.

A bank of security lamps from the hanger flooded the area with yellow light. Kimball removed the night vision goggles, slid between parked planes, dashed from shadow to shadow, dropping into a squat each time, surveying his surroundings. Then, at the end of the line of aircraft, he spotted the blue and white Lear Jet he was looking for. He double-checked the hull number against the one written in black marker across his hand.

Looking around once more, he made his way to the plane. At the sound of a vehicle approaching, he dropped to the ground by the chocked wheels of the aircraft next to it, froze as a hand-held searchlight brushed over the shadows darkened by the flood of the overhead lights.

The beam swept over the non-reflective material of his body suit without pausing. Kimball stayed still until he heard the sound of the vehicle moving away.

Moving over into the shadow cast by the blue and white Lear jet, he removed his pack, took out a roll-pack instrument case, laid it out, selected two thin picks, then inserted them into the key hole at the base of the cabin door. Jimmying them until he felt a slight click, he twisted until the door popped free. Extracting the picks, he replaced them in his side pocket, took out a short pry-rod, inserted it into the slightly open door. Running his finger along the edge of the door jamb, he found the trigger button to activate the interior cabin light, depressed it with the tool, then opened the door. Grabbing his back pack, he scrambled up the accommodation ladder built into the door, raised, closed the door by the suspension lanyards.

Inside the darkened cabin, he let his eyes adjust to the available light streaming through the porthole windows of the aircraft. He made his way to the cockpit, sat himself in the pilot's seat, took out a multi-tool from his back pack, selected a phillips head screwdriver.

Clicking on a red beam from his night vision headlight, he removed the instrument cowling, found the connections for the steering controls, inserted a small plastic electronic device between the male and female connections, then replaced the instrument cowling.

Removing his forehead light, he checked through the cockpit windows for security guards. Seeing none, he stepped out, looked back over the control area, making sure he had left nothing disturbed.

Making his way to the back of the main cabin, he crawled back into the tail section, wriggled into the rear baggage bin. There, he removed the flooring cover, fixed a noodle-like attachment over the guy wires controlling the tail and rudder, then replaced the floor paneling, crept back to the door.

Keeping the cabin light button depressed, he dropped to the ground, eased the door closed. Fishing the picks from his side pocket, he relocked the door, wiped the keyhole clean with powdered graphite, stowed the pics in the roll-pack along with the rest of his gear into the backpack, moved out back into the shadows.

Coming up to the fence, he heard a growl, then a dog barking. He stepped over near the entrance of a small building, took a red spray can out of his bag, sprayed the jamb of the door, then dove back behind two metal fuel barrels as a security guard came up with a German shepherd on a leash.

The dog barked, peering into the shadows, stopped for a second, sniffed the door, whined, then barked at the shadows again. The guard shined his light in the direction of the barrels where Kimball had curled up into a fetal ball in the corner by the fence. The guard swept the light over the area– the dog kept barking.

The guard jerked back on the leash, silenced the dog.

"C'mon girl," he said. "Just a rat."

Kimball stayed frozen until the guard took the barking dog away. Then, he climbed the fence, dropped to the other side, sprinted across the road back to his motorcycle. Stowing his back pack, he checked in on his cell phone.

"Home, this is dark cloud," Kimball said.

"Go on, dark cloud. I read you five."

"Detail's done."

"Any problemos?"

"Only one."

"What was that?"

"That dog spray with the bitch in heat scent didn't work."

"Wonder why not?"

"'Cause the guard dog was a bitch."

A Plot Thickens

CEO's Office, WKJC Radio, Columbia, SC
Three days later, 10:45 AM

The knock at the door made KD Rogers jump.

"Come in," he said.

He relaxed when he saw Congressman Damian Styles's chubby figure dressed in his usual gray suit, today in a powder blue tie over a cream-colored shirt.

"I got your call," Styles said.

Rogers straightened, assumed a serious pose, pulled his lips into a scowl-smile hybrid.

"Senator Northridge." Roger said.

Styles rolled his eyes.

"He's a pain in the ass."

"I wish you wouldn't use profanity, Damian."

"It's not profanity, KD. It's a mere obscenity."

"Regardless."

Styles took a seat at the front of Rogers's desk.

"Sam Northridge's got a lot of backing from some of the left-leaning members of our party that could block our version of the defense contractor bill in the Senate."

"Can't you do something?"

"I've got a solid block of votes line up in the House but the Senate's another story."

Rogers smirked.

"Well, we won't have to worry about it," he said.

"What do you mean?"

"It can be taken care of."

Styles's mouth dropped open.

"You can't be serious!" he said.

Rogers's face lost all expression.

"There's more than one way to skin a cat, Damian."

"You're not suggesting violence ..."

"I'm suggesting nothing," Rogers said. "I'm merely saying the matter is being taken care of."

Rogers waved his open hand.

"I do have more real concerns, however."

"KD, look. This is deadly serious, I ... "

"You've said it yourself. We're in a war. Wars are terrible. Let it go at that."

Styles gasped, stared.

"Let it go?" he said.

Rogers waved his hand, dismissing Styles.

"I'm more concerned about this supposed scholarly undermining of our beliefs," he said.

"What do you mean?"

"You were one of them. I'm talking about these pagan attacks on our Holy Scriptures."

"You mean secular biblical studies?"

"You can call them that. I prefer conspirators in a Satanist war on truth."

Styles closed his eyes, shook his head. A smile came to his lips.

"Academics are no more concerned with us than we should be concerned with them," he said. "Our people don't read their canned tripe. And, as JR said the other day, even if they did, they wouldn't accept it."

Rogers scowled at him.

"It's a festering boil on the face of the entire Christian movement. A bright young man in our seminary became so obsessed with trying to find the original word of God, he studied Greek and Hebrew and became so enthralled with these studies, he fell into Satan's trap. He eventually went to a secular university, left our faith and is now a self-confessed atheist."

"That's too bad, KD. But, the work of academic historians in ivory towers doesn't reach the rank and file ..."

Rogers raged.

"But it does! Look."

He shoved a copy of *News Weekly* into Styles's face. The cover showed the picture of Jerry Johnson, Harvard biblical historian with the story caption, '*HOW ACCURATE IS THE BIBLE?*'

"See how they mock the word of God?" Rogers said.

Styles looked at the magazine.

"The editors are just sensationalizing this kind of stuff to sell more magazines," he said.

"Something has to be done about this assault on our basic beliefs."

Styles thumbed through the magazine, stopped, scanned an article on the popular daytime TV hostess, Emma Pearl. He chuckled.

Rogers scowled.

"What do you find so amusing?"

Styles's smile blossomed into a broad grin.

"You may have stumbled onto something here, KD," he said.

"What do you mean."

Styles folded back the magazine showing the picture of Emma Pearl, microphone in hand in front of her TV audience.

Her classic molded African-American features reflected a simple basic beauty enhanced by a sculpted hair style that framed her attractive face. Her figure, the product of many years of dieting, gym work, cosmetic surgery, stood out clad in a bright red designer dress. Her perfect whitened teeth, product of the efforts of the best orthodontists sparkled through her painted red lips shown bright against her dark brown skin.

"All I see is a picture of a popular Negro entertainer," Rogers said.

Styles sat the magazine down, tapped the picture.

"I was on her show and that appearance brought in contributions way outside our district. Lots of people saw me that day."

"So?"

"Lots of people, KD. Lots."

"Am I missing something here, Damian?"

"What I'm proposing is that we get Colene Mooney from Yale, to come on Pearl's show to give her spiel about missing biblical texts."

"That's extremely dangerous," Rogers said.

Styles shook his head, wagged his finger.

"But, we'll have a surprise."

"What?"

"We'll have JR on the same program."

Rogers's eyes snapped up, stared.

"JR?" he said.

"Yes. Colene does her thing and JR comes in for the kill."

Rogers looked back to the photo of Emma Pearl.

"I don't know," he said.

"Emma will set her up" Styles said. "Colene does her scholarly bit, baits the trap with herself."

"This woman's program stands at the edge of heresy," Rogers said. "The content of her show is always about sinful events, uncensored sexual exploits, drinking and drug stories. This is pure Godlessness ..."

"Give the devil his due, KD. We can use this against him."

"Then too, there's this woman speaking of the Holy Scriptures as mere works of man. That's outright blaspheme."

"Right. But, that's the point, KD. JR will be on the show to point out how it's blaspheme."

Rogers sat back in his chair, struck his serious pose once more with hands folded tight, stared at Styles.

"I've not always been completely comfortable with JR's style. It borders on the theatrical.. ."

"Well, doesn't it gather sheep into the fold?"

"I freely admit that JR is a great voice and at times has acted as God's right hand fist."

"So, what's the problem?"

"The problem, Damian, is that there are always vulnerable and impressionable individuals out there who may be swayed by Satan's power."

"That's why it is so important to have JR there to counter that possible effect."

Rogers pursed his lips, spoke in a low voice.

"I always fear the devil's power."

"As do I. But, look at it this way. Colene will talk about scripture in a detached, irreverent way that JR will tear apart. The overall effect will be that people will find their faith rekindled by JR and Colene's work will be discredited."

Rogers put his hand to his lips.

"It just might work," he said.

Styles laughed, slapped his knee.

"It will work. JR will eat her for lunch."

"You think so?"

"I know so. He'll not only make her look ridiculous, think of all that free air-time exposure we'll get."

Rogers rubbed his chin.

"I guess I have to agree," he said.

Feebs and Spooks

Federal Building, Yonkers, NY
next day, Friday 1:15 PM

Colene came into the building, dropped her purse on the belt trailing into the security station's X-ray machine, stepped through the frame of the metal detector, retrieved her bag, then found the elevators.

Office workers returning from lunch crowded inside the small interior, pushed Colene to the rear. Then a ride to the 12th floor jerked, punctuated with stops letting employees off, until the elevator reached the highest floor.

Colene stepped out alone, spotted the number 1204 on the opaque glass office window, checked it against the scribbled note with Mary Rich's instructions. Stepping into the office, she found a short counter, behind it 2 women and a man sat working at desks. One of the women stood, greeted her.

"I've an appointment with Agent Mary Rich," Colene said.

"She's expecting you," the woman said. "This way please."

Colene followed the woman through a hall into an inner office. Mary Rich opened the door at the woman's knock.

"Come in, Dr. Mooney," Rich said.

"Hi, it's Colene, remember."

Rich smiled, shook Colene's hand.

"Of course," Rich said. "I'm having someone join us."

Colene sat on a couch in front of a glass topped coffee table while Rich buzzed someone on her office phone.

"Coffee, Colene?" she said.

"Thanks, no. Just finished lunch."

Rich came over, took a chair beside her.

"Sorry to make you come all this way but I think you should hear this from one of my colleagues in another federal department."

A rap at the door. It opened. Colene was struck by a deluge of casual brown. A tall young man with big brown eyes standing out under thick brown eyebrows and a mop of dark brown hair, dressed in brown slacks, sweater, penny loafers stepped in.

He came over to Colene, grinned, pumped her hand.

"Hi," he said. "Will Johnson."

Rich chuckled when he plopped down in the chair next to Colene.

"Overlook the frat rat appearance, Colene. Willy can give you the lowdown on this man you saw killed."

"Sorry you were exposed to that violence," Johnson said. "Lucky you weren't hurt."

"Thanks," Colene said. "It was traumatic."

"This crook– Isaak ibn Nur– had a fat Interpol file," Johnson said. "He dealt in international smuggling, selling various kinds of artifacts through an underground network of collectors and traders. We've linked him to his brother, Abdi, who smuggles everything from arms to drugs and murder."

"Who killed this Isaak?" Colene asked.

Johnson shrugged his large shoulders.

"No idea," he said. "But, it's interesting that he contacted you."

"That's no surprise," Rich said. "You're in a place of interest, do high profile studies that would interest someone wanting to sell something like a stolen artifact."

Colene shook her head.

"But," she said. "Academics don't have that kind of money."

"Still, you might have access to someone who does," Johnson said.

"This Isaac guy was insistent– seemed to think I could just take a few million outta petty cash and give it to him."

"Male Arabs usually expect a woman to do what she's told and not argue," Rich said.

"In your tape you mentioned a 'pig in the poke,' " Johnson said. "To a devout Moslem, even to mention a pig is an insult. Coming from a woman made it made it worse."

Colene looked from Johnson to Rich.

"So, what's with the mysterious call back?" Colene said. "You said you didn't want to go on about anything in front of Hazel Wilson."

Rich glanced at Johnson.

"Something you said about your former boss's notes," Rich said.

"Go on." Colene said.

"You said that Professor Corbett mentioned certain connections between a religious network and a paramilitary group– even listed names," Rich said. "What do you know about that?"

"Not much," Colene said. "I listed all the people involved from Jim's list, broke it down into several categories looking to see who was involved where and with whom."

"Do you still have this list?" Johnson said.

"I'll send you a copy," Colene said

"What did you come up with?" Rich said.

"One name, Damian Styles, fit in all the categories."

On hearing the name, Johnson and Rich turned, stared at each other for a few seconds.

"Hot damn," Johnson said.

"What's going on?" Colene said.

Rich took a deep breath, stood, paced around the area.

"We've been looking into a few connections with Congressman Styles," she said.

"What kind of connections?" Colene said.

"Let's just say we have an on-going investigation where the Congressman is a definite person of interest," Rich said.

"We'd appreciate you're keeping this to yourself," Johnson said.

Colene rolled her eyes.

"Damian and I have never been, shall we say, close."

"I understand Styles was in your department for a while," Rich said.

"He was too doctrinaire for a good historian," Colene said. "After a few years he went home and got into politics."

"How well do you know him?" Rich said.

"Well enough to know he's a first class creep."

Colene took the disk out of her bag, handed it to Rich.

"Here's the original of the download I sent you,"

Rich took it.

"So, I guess you can take the tail off me now," Colene said.

Johnson's head snapped up. Rich's face wrinkled into a frown. They both stared at Colene.

"Tail?" Rich said.

"Yeah," Colene said. "The tail you've put on me."

Rich and Johnson gawked at each other for a moment.

Colene," Rich said. "We don't have any kind of surveillance on you."

"Someone's been following me," Colene said.

"How do you know?" Johnson said.

"My friend Ara spotted them."

Rich pulled her chair up.

"Talk to us," she said.

"After the shooting," Colene said, "I called a close friend for help."

"Who's this friend?" Rich said.

"Ara Agajanian."

"Is this a longtime friend?" Johnson said.

"When I was a grad student at Harvard, we lived in an old Victorian. Ara had the up-stairs loft."

"Go on," Rich said.

"He has a mild form of Asperger's syndrome– mentally brilliant but socially very eccentric. Emotionally, he was kind of a lost puppy and all us girls in the house kind of adopted him as a kid brother."

"You trust him?" Rich said.

"Completely. We've been close friends since graduation, nearly 8 years or so."

"What does he do?" Johnson said.

"He comes from a very wealthy family, has doctorates in medicine, mathematics, computer and electronic engineering– he's rather reclusive, stays home, studies and invents things."

"So, he spotted this tail," Rich said.

"Mr. Johnson?" Colene said.

"Everyone calls me Willy."

"You're with the FBI too?" Colene said.

Johnson glanced over at Rich.

"Actually, I'm with another government agency," he said,

"CIA?" Colene asked.

He shrugged.

"Something like that."

"Have you ever heard of an international network called 'The Hydra?' " Colene said.

Willy's big dark brown eyes darted to her face.

"I've heard of a hypothetical group or person called 'The Hydra.' "

"Do they exist?"

"Don't know." Johnson said. "That's why I said 'hypothetical.' "

"What's your gut feeling?"

Johnson grinned.

"I'm a fed. We don't get paid for feelings, gut or otherwise."

He shook Colene's hand.

"Be careful out there," Johnson said. "We'll check on who might be shadowing you."

He waved at Rich, strode out the door.

Rich sat there, her arms still folded across her chest.

"Colene," she said. "You stay in constant contact with me– and one more thing."

"Yeah?"

"Don't you or this pal of yours do anything illegal."

An Invitation

Colene's office, Yale University
the following Monday, 9:30 AM

With her arms full of bags, books and her hands full of mail, Colene unlocked the door to her office, pushed the door open with her butt, dumped the bags on the small sofa, carried the mail to her desk, then dumped the pile of notices, letters, fliers on top. She then performed her morning tea ritual. When the pot boiled. Colene dropped the tea-filled porous infusion spoon into her cup. She carried it her desk, set the cup on a round glass coaster.

She plopped down in her desk chair to organize the pile of mail. Pulling the wastebasket close to her desk, she tossed in the fliers, advertisements, notices after a glance. She stopped when she came to a long violet envelope with her name written with green ink in a florid hand. The return address jumped out at her,

From the personal desk of
EMMA PEARL

She tore open the envelope with her fingernail, pulled out the letter, flicked open the folded page. She blinked at an ornate invitation to appear as a guest on the daytime TV show, 'Emma's Hour' to talk about her recent book, *An Inquiry into the Four Gospels*.

Her interoffice phone rang.

"Yes."

Gloria, her department secretary's excited, staccato voice spoke in a stage whisper.

"Colene. Some woman from NBS television wants to talk to you. I think they want you to be on national TV."

"You're kidding."

"Seriously," Gloria said. "I've heard this woman's voice on TV before."

"So, let's see what she has to say."

A click later, Colene heard the soft lilt of an African-American woman's voice.

"Professor Colene Mooney?"

"Yes."

"Dr. Mooney. So good to talk to you. I'm Shondrah Bell, program director for the Emma Pearl show. How are you today?"

"Fine, thanks."

"We sent you an invitation some time ago. Did you receive it?"

"Just got it today."

"Wonderful. We would love for you to come on our show and tell us about your exciting book."

"Have you read it?"

"Not yet. But, I'm looking forward to it."

"Do you know if Ms. Pearl's read it?"

"As a matter of fact, I do. Emma never leaves things to chance and reads all the books she recommends on air."

"Impressive."

"Dr. Mooney, as I said, we'd love to have you tell our audience about the work that has gone into making this exciting book."

"Are you sure you've got the right person? That book was written for biblical historians. Most mainstream readers would not likely appreciate it."

"Dr. Mooney. If Emma wants you– and this requests comes straight from her– she knows that she has the right person."

"Well, I'm caught a bit flat-footed. I've never been in the public eye."

"That'll change. Once our audience gets a chance to hear from you about your work, you'll be very surprised."

"To coin a cliché, this is kinda sudden."

"Of course it is, but Emma really wants you on her show."

"When would this be?"

"We'd like to tape it in 3 weeks. It will air the following day. We pay a very nice honorarium of $3,000.00."

"You know how to tempt."

"We sure do. Oh please, say you'll do it."

"I'd like to consider it."

"That's understandable. But, we are under a time constraint. Can you call me back with your decision by tomorrow morning?"

"Sounds reasonable enough."

Colene took down the program director's direct number.

She looked down at the written invitation. The attractive font made the letter look suitable for framing.

How many other people would kill to have a chance like this?

When the word 'kill' passed through her mind, she gave a chilled quiver.

She dialed Ara's number. When he came on, she gave a quick recap of her conversation with the TV program director.

"Wow. National TV," Ara said.

"Why me?"

"Guess they wantcha."

"Get serious. I'm not famous."

"Not yet."

"Damn it, Ara. I'm not joking."

"Me either."

"So, why would they want me?"

"Look. The whole bible scene is hot right now. Her sponsors want to sell stuff and you're a platform they can use."

"I dunno."

"If you're not comfortable, don't."

"The money's good."

"Piss on that. Go with your guts."

"By the way. I went to see the FBI lady."

"And?"

"She said they weren't tailing me.

"Really?"

"That's what they said."

"They?"

"Yeah. There was a kid– I mean a young guy from the CIA there too."

"Interesting."

"They both acted surprised when I told them we were being tailed."

"We?"

"I told them about you. Is that a problem?"

"Shouldn't be. I'm not surprised, by the way."

"That I told about you?"

"No. That you weren't tailing you."

Colene stopped.

"Well then, who the hell is it?"

"Not sure but it's gotta do with this nutcase religious group."

"Ara. Am I in danger?"

"I don't think so. But, stay fully visible in public view as much as possible."

"So, what do you think about this show thing?"

"I say, do it."

~*~~*~

Colene dumped out the cold cup of tea in the sink, put the kettle on to make herself another. She looked over again at the invitation on her desk, then snatched up the phone, called the program director.

"Hi, this is Shondrah."

"Colene Mooney. I'll do it."

"Splendid! I'll be in touch in a few days to iron out all the details. Emma will be thrilled."

"Me too."

She cradled the receiver and glanced at the invitation once more. Her phone rang.

"Colene Mooney."

"Hello, Dr. Mooney. This is Orhan."

"How are you?"

"More importantly, how are you doing?"

"Well, it's gotten complicated."

"How so?"

"I met with the FBI and even a guy from the CIA. They told me they knew about this Isaac guy from Interpol."

"Yes."

"I've also been followed."

"Followed?"

"I told the authorities somebody has been tailing me. They said it wasn't them."

"Whom do you suspect?"

"I honestly don't know. A close friend of mine thinks it might be some religious group."

"What kind of a religious group?"

"We do have right-wing Christian fundamentalists here."

"We have them here too—only they're not Christians."

"They're a pain in the ass."

"As are these here."

"Also, when I made a list of all the people involved, as you suggested, I broke it down by categories, one name did crop up across the board."

"Oh?"

"A politician and former colleague I don't trust."

"Do you need police protection?"

"No, but it's damn scary having to look over your shoulder all the time."

"I understand. Please be very careful."

"My friend suggested I keep in public view as much as possible."

"An excellent suggestion. Please let me know if there's anything I can do to help."

"I'll do that. Thanks for checking in."

After she hung up, she sat looking at the ornate violet invitation in front of her on the desk.

Switch in Time

Orhan's home, Ankara, Turkey
Monday, 9:40 PM

A riot of color of books with titles in French, English, Turkish, Arabic lined the shelved cases that ringed the living room of Orhan's house. An overstuffed sofa, chairs surrounded a low, flat coffee table perched on a red, gold, green Turkmenian rug near an unlit fireplace where Orhan took down a copy of Pamuk's *Kara Kitap*, 'The Black Book,' threw it on top of the packed clothes in his open suitcase.

He took a sip from the glass of *rakı* then set it on the small table next to the chair holding his travel case. The doorbell rang.

Looking through the front door peephole, he saw his cousin, Yilmaz, then opened the door to him.

"Are you ready?" Yilmaz said.

"Are you sure I can handle this?" Orhan said.

"You know the Americans. They want face to face intel."

"Fuck them."

"Too late. They're already fucking us."

Yilmaz handed Orhan a black hard plastic suitcase with a file in a manila folder.

"You can familiarize yourself with the details on the flight over."

Yilmaz handed Orhan an encased ID card on a lanyard.

"You're on a US military flight leaving at midnight," he said. "You'll be there tomorrow morning."

Yilmaz looked at his cousin's face.

"You know I'd be on this flight myself ..."

Orhan finished his cousin's statement.

"If my wife wasn't having a baby."

~*~~*~

On the flight, Orhan finished reading through the file for the third time, glanced down at the black case at his feet, turned to a US marine major sitting next to him.

"Major," Orhan said. "Would you know how far it is from Washington to New Haven, Connecticut?"

"Right at 275 miles."

Orhan translated the distance in his head, "About 450 kilometers."

"Your first time in the US, Colonel?" the Major said.

"No, but, I've never been to Connecticut."

The major grinned.

"Do you have a lady up there?" he said.

Orhan gave a start.

"Do you live in the Washington area?" Orhan said.

"Maryland. Outside the Beltway."

Orhan nodded.

"Beltway. I forgot they call it that."

"So, have you been to DC before?" the Major said.

Orhan looked at the Major, assessing him.

"I'm working on an investigation ..."

"Investigating, huh? Still, nothing wrong in mixing a little business with pleasure, Colonel."

"Is that what you're doing, Major?"

The Major flinched.

"No, no. I meant ...," he said. "My wife's a Yalie."

Orhan smiled, nodded.

"That's why you know the road so well," he said.

Limelight

Suite 4137, Sheraton Hilton Central, Chicago, Il
The following Monday, 8:16 AM

Colene laid out the suit she had brought on the bed. She looked it over. Basic black. Nice cut to the jacket with matching pants and a short skirt.

She then placed the jacket over a hanger supporting a polished Egyptian cotton blouse in a light lemon yellow with lime green buttons, took out a string of pearls from a case, set them over the blouse's collar, laid it out on the bed.

She stepped back, inspected it again.

OK. Now, which: the pants or the skirt?

She frowned. The skirt was kind of short.

"Fuck it," she muttered, then grabbed, folded, hung up the pants.

She set the black shoes on the floor by the bed beneath the draped the jacket and skirt. Again, she stood back, surveyed the array, hand under her chin. The shoes were polished ebony Moroccan leather in a smooth finish, heels not too high, blunted toes. Colene took in a deep breath, smiled.

OK.

A knock at the door made Colene grab for her robe. She opened it to a tall attractive African American woman in a designer blue dress, smiling at Colene with perfect teeth.

"Hi, Dr. Mooney," she said. "Shandy Bell. Welcome to the Windy City. Sorry I wasn't able to meet you at the airport last night."

Colene gasped.

"Oh shit!" she said. "Am I late?'

"Heavens no. I came by early to go over today's program and take you to the studio."

Colene motioned her inside.

"Hey," Colene said. "Last night was the first time I was ever met by a capped driver in a black uniform and taken to a swanky hotel in a limo."

"I hope everything's met your satisfaction," Shondrah said.

"You kidding? I'm just a small town military brat with two older brothers."

Shondrah laughed, threw her Gucci designer bag in a chair. Colene directed her attention to the outfit laid out on the bed.

"Is this OK?" Colene said.

"Perfect."

Shondrah plopped down in a brocade covered chair.

"Go ahead and get dressed. I'm taking you to breakfast first and then on to the studio."

"Are we going in a limo?"

Shondrah chuckled.

"Emma wouldn't have it any other way."

~*~~*~

Walman Exhibition Center Studio, Chicago, Il
Same day, 11:05 AM

Trailing Shondrah through the studio, Colene felt like Dante following Virgil through Hell. A jungle of wires, outlets, speakers, cameras, banks of lights, sound booms, hurrying people stalked her passing.

Colene flashed back to an image of the interior of a bee hive she once saw on PBS. Everyone rushed about in purposed motion, fixed on some little activity that coordinated with someone else.

The tall figure of Shondrah breezed through this bustle of organized energy, chaos, noise, showing a smile, giving a nod to every one she encountered. Colene followed Shondrah off the staging area into the back hall where a line of rooms stood hidden behind closed doors, then walked to the end of the hall, where Shondrah turned to Colene.

"This is the green room where we'll get you ready to meet your soon to be adoring public," she said.

Colene raised her eyebrows.

"Get me ready?"

Dangling diamonds hanging from Shondrah's ears flashed like tiny strobes as she laughed, opened the door, showed Colene in.

"If we didn't touch you up a bit, you'd look like Marley's ghost on TV."

Colene sighed, took a seat as a male attendant with multiple face piercings topped off with an orange and purple pomade stand-up Mohawk, dressed in a black outfit covered with sparkly sequins flicked a cover over her suit, leaned her back in the chair, spoke in a silky voice.

"Don't be concerned, sweetiekins," the make-up tech said. "We're just gonna touch you up to look absolutely fab in front of the camera. Won't hurt a thing."

Colene forced herself to relax for the half hour the tech applied the basic make-up in quick, precise strokes. Uncomfortable with 'face paint,' she gripped the arms of the chair.

Shondrah reappeared at that moment.

"You look just great," she said.

Colene looked at herself in the mirror.

"I look like shit," she said.

The make-up tech giggled. Shondrah smiled, then said,

"It's *showtime*, Colene."

~*~~*~

Shondrah led Colene down the hall into the staging venue. Colene saw a recessed area behind the camera, sound blocks that consisted of tiers of seats in staggered rows, now filled with murmuring people. Shondrah pointed to the lighted area in front of the stage where a shimmering curtained reflected flashes of light behind a brown leather couch with two matching chairs at either end. She whispered,

"Emma will come out and do her intro monologue. When she's done, I'll walk you to the edge of the stage, then she'll introduce you, sit you on the couch and go from there."

Colene took a deep breath.

"OK," she said.

In the shadows in front of the stage, Colene saw a technician wearing a headset hold up his hands for quiet. The noisy scene became still– even the low chatter, mutters, murmurs, mumbles of the audience hushed, as he held up his ten fingers, then counted down. With the last finger erect, he dropped in a point to the corner of the stage. A spotlight lit up an announcer standing at a mike.

"Ladies and gentlemen," he said. "Honored guests present and at home, welcome to EMMA'S HOUR!"

Colene flinched at the burst of taped music, shouts, hoots, loud applause as the spot light whipped over to focus on the hostess, Emma Pearl.

Emma stepped onto the stage wearing a bright red dress with a flashing diamond necklace. Standing slightly over 5', she was smaller than Colene had imagined. She moved with an athlete's ease to the center stage, bowed, brought up the cordless traveling mike in her hand.

"Thank you, thank you. I love you all. Each and every one. Thank you and thank you again."

As the noise faded, Colene watched Emma pace around waving her free hand as she told of a recent trip to Italy and an encounter with a Roman taxi driver. After a round of laughter from the audience, she paused.

"Suddenly, I knew what a kamikaze pilot musta felt like. I mean, this guy kept turning around talking to me with both of his hands going 65 miles an hour and, man, the traffic was not only bumper to bumper but everyone seemed to be honking and waving, rolling down their windows and hollering at each other."

As the audience laughed, she looked around, hand on hip, said, "I bet that dude was responsible for more born-again converts than the whole Hammond Crusade."

As the roar of laughter begin to quiet down, Shondrah took Colene's arm, led her to the edge of the stage, pinned a tiny mike on her lapel, released her with a stage whisper.

"You're on, kid."

Nodding as the laughter died down, Emma raised her eyes.

"Speaking of Christian Crusades, my next guest is an expert."

Shit, Colene thought. *I don't know anything about Crusades!*

With the mike in her hand like a fairy queen's wand, Emma moved to the edge of the stage looking into the camera in an up close and personal pose.

Her smile faded. She spoke in a soft, serious voice.

"My dear friend, Dr. Taleisha Dawn, professor of African American Religious History at Morgan State recommended a book to me a month or so ago. Now, I want you to know, I read my bible–read it every night. So when Dr. Dawn told me it was a real eye-opener, I went right out and bought a copy of *An Inquiry into the Four Gospels* by Dr. Colene Mooney."

She turned back to the coffee table center stage in front of the couch, snatched, then held up a copy of the book with its brown dust jacket. The camera zoomed in on the faceplate showing the title, cover art, author's name.

Emma went on,

"Friends. I could not put this book down until I had devoured every word on every page."

She set the book on the coffee table, turned back to the audience.

"Ladies and Gentlemen, here and at home, welcome Dr. Colene Mooney, Professor of Biblical History at Yale University, to *Emma's Hour*."

Shondrah gave Colene a little nudge to walk on the stage. Emma met her at the center, wrapped Colene's hand in both of hers, kissed her on the cheek, sat her down at the end of the couch, then plopped her tiny frame into the big chair at the end.

"Dr. Mooney. Thank you so much for coming here."

"Call me Colene," she said. "I'm more than a bit surprised to be here."

Emma's face lit up.

"Really? Why's that?"

"Well, my book hardly fits into the popular market. It's an analysis of the history of the early Greeks texts and codices that were used to form the four canonic gospels of the New Testament."

"Ah Colene. don't you think that us rank and file Christians want and need to know about our sacred Bible?"

"Well, Emma. It's just that ... I didn't write it for a popular audience and am just danged surprised anyone but another historian would read it."

"Maybe not, but I honestly had a hard time putting it down."

Colene felt an emotional thud– a jab, like being out on the far end of a thin limb of a tall tree, and someone just handing her a saw. But, she recovered.

"Well, I'm delighted that you liked it," Colene said.

She heard some of the audience laugh.

Emma went on.

"I was surprised to learn that all of the gospels were written years after the death of Christ."

Colene heard a murmur from the audience.

"Actually, most were written several decades after."

"How do we know this?" Emma said.

Colene gave a short summary of the background of where the oldest texts remained, then spoke of the wide variation of different texts from different periods. As she went on to explain how some texts contradicted others and showed later additions and changes, she picked up on mutters from the audience.

Emma pressed the point home.

"But, how did they know which texts to use when they translated the bible?"

"Some texts were more popular than others and more in line with the thinking of the influential decision makers– they had no way of knowing as we do now which texts were older."

"Is that a problem?" Emma said.

"Could be, where you have texts that differ and in some cases, contradict each other."

At this remark, louder murmurs, voices bled out from the audience. Emma turned her head, gave them a quick scowl.

"So," she said. "Which ones were the right ones?"

"Right ones?" Colene said. "Which ones were more 'right' than others came down to a matter of opinion."

More rumbles spilled in from the audience. In clear enjoyment of the controversy, Emma leaned back in the big chair. The camera, the audience's attention reflected in the bright-eyed, brown-skinned woman in the bright red dress with the smile on her face.

"You also mention certain 'lost gospels,' " Emma said. "What about them?"

"Nearly every different Christian sect had their own set of gospels."

"Really? How many were there?"

"Several that we know of. Very likely dozens more that we don't know about."

"So, howcum we only got four gospels in the Bible now?"

"The choice of which gospels to include was made by a committee of bishops at the Nicene Council in 325."

"So, what happened to the ones they didn't like?"

"Most were destroyed."

"Destroyed?"

"Yes."

"Then, how did we come to find out about them?"

"Several early theologians mention and cite them. Later in the middle of the last century, two important discoveries were made. One, where we found out how people were living in the Holy Land and their thinking around the time of Christ. And the other, where many of these purged documents surfaced again."

"What were these discoveries?"

"The scrolls of the Essene cult in Qumran near the Dead Sea in Israel in 1946 and the Nag Hammadi texts found in a jar in Egypt in 1945."

"What about the Q text?"

Colene flinched, then forced herself to relax. She had mentioned this topic in her book. She took a breath and explained the hypothesis.

Emma homed in for the kill.

"Does such a text exist?"

Colene shifted in her seat.

"Until recently, scholars thought it was likely only an oral tradition," she said. "But, who knows? There might be one out there."

Emma jumped on her remark like a hen on a junebug.

"There might be? You mean, there is one?"

"All I can say for certain is that I've never seen such a text."

Emma narrowed her eyes at Colene.

"Do people just blow this Q text idea off as some academic fantasy?"

"People pretty much believe what suits them but we historians relay on hard evidence," Colene said. "As it stands, I've not seen any solid evidence of the existence of a discrete text."

Emma caught Colene's eyes again. "What about 'faith?"

Colene answered her gaze.

"Never touch it. I'm like Jack Webb's Sergeant Friday on the old Dragnet show. When questioning a witness, he'd say, 'Just the facts, ma'am.' "

"What about the sanctity of the Bible?"

Colene did not hesitate. "Which bible are we talking about?"

Emma smiled as more murmurs leaked out from the audience. She turned, faced the camera, smiled.

"We'll be right back, folks."

During the commercial break Emma leaned over, patted Colene's hand.

"This is great, Colene. You're doing just fantastic."

A line from Virgil's Aeneid streamed through Colene's inner vision, *"Timeo dona et dona ferrentes,* 'I fear Greeks bearing gifts.' "feel like a guy who's just been asked," Colene said. ' 'Answer yes or no: Do you still beat your wife?'

Conference call

Sword and Shield Security Services, Shanekmandan, SC
Same day, 12:05 PM

"Ham"Morris raised his head at the knock at his office door.

"Come," he said.

Dressed in khaki slacks, dark gray polo shirt and brown Red Wing work boots, Gregg Steele stepped into the room, closed the door, came to stiff attention.

"I'm here as requested, sir," he said.

Morris rose, reached across his desk, shook his hand, then pointed to a chair.

"Glad you could come down, Gregg," Morris said.

"The Mooney broad's on TV, so this works out fine."

"No sweat," Morris said. "I wanted to go over some things that have come up with you."

"Yessir."

"Brig Kimball will be joining us too."

Steele bristled at hearing Kimball's name.

"So, how is the big Mormon ex-Jarhead?" he said.

Morris shot him a frown.

"See for yourself. He'll be here in a minute." he said.

Steele just looked at Morris without smiling.

A rap at the door broke the tension.

"That's him now," Morris said. "Come."

Brigham Kimball stepped through the door, dressed in green fatigues with the 4Sinc logo on his left shoulder, he stood at a stiff attention.

"Good morning, gentlemen," he said.

Morris shook hands with him. After looking into Steele's eyes, Kimball gave him a brief bob of his head, a tight lipped smile, then sat down beside him.

"Look," Morris said. "I know you two ain't always seen things eye to eye but fuck that. I called you both here because I have intel to share and need you both."

Kimball and Morris stared straight ahead at Morris.

"As you know," Morris said. "We have a 'silent partner' in Egypt. He's reported to me that there's movement by the militant Hamas group in Gaza to attack nearby Israeli farms."

"Shouldn't we advise the Mossad about this?" Kimball said.

Steele snorted. Morris gave him a scowl.

"No, Brig," Morris said. "That's not in our best interests."

"Yessir," Kimball said.

"We've been waiting for something like this to happen to implement Operation Backfire," Morris said. "In the face of what amounts to an armed invasion, we can mobilize the US to intervene and impose martial law, neutralizing the liberal factions."

"What are the obstacles?" Kimball said.

"The Hamas hajjis need guns to pull it off," Steele said.

"Getting guns into the Middle East never has been a problem," Kimball said.

"It has lately," Morris said. "Most weapons come in from Iran through Syria but Israeli security forces recently blew up the ship carrying the Iranian arms they'd planned to use."

"So now, our plan is about to flounder because we can't arm these jihadists because our Israeli allies intercepted their arms?" Kimball said.

"Looks that way," Morris said.

Steele put his hand to his chin, frowned in thought for a moment.

"Ya know, I might have a connection that could help," he said.

Kimball sneered.

"What connection?" he said.

Ignoring him, Steele folded his arms across his chest, looked straight at Morris.

"I got an old army buddy who's on the NSA inner circle. I've done him a couple of favors and I can call them in."

"Just don't let on about Backfire," Morris said.

"No sweat," Steele said. "I'll just ask for a connection—he won't want to get in any deeper than that."

Morris looked over at Kimball, for a second, then pushed the desk phone to Steele.

"Call him," Morris said.

Steele whipped out his cell phone, punched in a number.

"Joe? Gregg Steele," he said. "Can we talk."

"Call you back," the voice on the cell phone's speaker said.

Steele set his cell phone on the edge of the desk. When it rang, he answered, activating the speaker.

"Joe?" Steele said.

"What's up?"

"If I wanted– and I ain't saying I do– to get my hands on some hot military assets, where would I go?"

"We talking small arms?"

"Yeah."

"I dunno but "Red" Bax in the ATF would. You know him?"

Morris's eye opened wide at mention of the name. He looked at Steele, pursed his lips, then nodded.

"Thanks, Joe," Steele said. "You've been a help."

"OK, Gregg," Joe said. "By the way..."

"Yeah."

"This squares us, asshole."

Joe cut off.

Morris leaned back in his chair as Steele picked up his cell phone.

"You know this guy, Bax, Sir?" Kimball said.

"I know Red Bax," Morris said. "But, I'd never have brought him to mind. He might be just the one who's able to supply the spark to kick start Operation Backfire."

Emma's Hour

Suite 4137, Sheraton Hilton Central, Chicago, Il
Monday, 11:56 AM

The technician in the head set caught Emma's attention by holding up ten fingers, then counted down. The red light on the side of the camera lens turned from red to green.

"Welcome back folks," Emma said. "We've been chatting with historian Colene Mooney from Yale University."

She turned her beaming smile back at Colene.

"Now, we heard Dr. Mooney express certain reservations about the role of faith in her biblical studies in the need to be objective. And, that makes sense. However, our next guest has no such reservations.

Will you all give a big welcome to the Reverend Dr. Jefferson Ryle Hammond, leader and director of Christians International United."

The spot light spun to the edge of the stage where J. Ryle Hammond stepped out, faced the audience, raised both his arms above his head with his hands clasped like a prize-winning boxer.

The audience broke into loud whistles, hoots, cheers as if he were a rock star. Bowing, nodding like a showman, Hammond strode to center stage. Standing 6'4", he towered over the tiny Emma as he took her hand, leaned over, hugged and kissed her on the cheek.

Dressed in a dark blue suit with his signature red carnation pinned to his lapel, his thick curly gray hanging in trimmed locks above his bright blue eyes, he smiled his perfect white teeth, waved to the cheering audience.

"Praise the Lord, Sister Emma," Hammond said.

Emma extended her hand to Colene.

"Reverend Hammond, this is our other guest, Dr. Colene Mooney from Yale."

Hammond reached over, took Colene's hands in both of his, kissed her on the cheek, plopped down next to her on the couch, reached over, patted her hand again.

"So nice to meet you, Colene," he said. "I've heard so much about you."

Emma asked Colene,

"Have you met Dr. Hammond before?"

"No," Colene said. "But I've certainly heard of him."

Emma got right to the point.

"Reverend, have you read Dr. Mooney's book?"

"No. I haven't, but I'm always delighted to hear about anybody reading the Holy Bible, whether I agree with them or not."

Emma picked up on this comment.

"Are you saying that you don't agree with Dr. Mooney?"

Hammond laughed.

"Well darlin', how can I disagree if I haven't read her book?"

A round of clapping, howls, approving cheers came from the audience.

"What's your view on her argument that there is a lot of confusion and misunderstanding about how the Bible's been put together?"

"Ain't no confusion, Sister Emma," Hammond said. "The Holy Bible's God's Holy word revealed through the prophets. Ain't nothin' more to it."

More cheers and applause came from the audience.

"Dr. Mooney. Would you respond to that?"

Colene folded her arms across her chest.

"I'll repeat what I said earlier, which Bible?" she said.

Hammond didn't hesitate.

"The Holy Bible, Darlin'. Ain't but one."

"Now when you say that there's only one, I find that confusing," Colene said.

"How so, sweetheart?" Hammond said.

"In English alone, we've the King James Version of 1611, which replaced the *Great Bible*, commissioned by Henry VIII in 1539, which was then replaced by the *Bishop's Bible* of 1568– all of these, by the way, were versions of the earlier translation of William Tyndale in 1525, which was largely based on Luther's translation into German in 1522."

"Really don't make no difference, Colene. They all say the same blessed thing."

At his remark, the audience burst into cheers, whistles, applause. Hammond smiled, waved approval.

"True in part, Reverend Hammond," Colene said. "But these translations were made from a series of Greek, Hebrew and even Aramaic texts, many of which were revised and at odds with each other and, in many cases, were mistranslated."

"Still don't make no difference, Colene," Hammond said. "It's all the word of God."

Emma moved in quickly.

"Now, Dr. Mooney has been very circumspect on the issue of approaching her studies with faith. How do you view that, Reverend Hammond?"

Hammond grinned, like a great white shark spotting a fat seal.

"That's all it is, Sister Emma. Faith. Faith in the love of Jesus Christ. Faith in the truth of His holy word. Faith that he died for you, for me and everyone else on this planet. Faith that if you accept him and let his wondrous spirit enter into your sinful heart, you can share eternity in his kingdom when he comes again. And, most important, faith that he's gonna come again."

He turned toward the audience, faced into the camera.

"And soon!" he said.

At this response the audience clapped, cheered, whistled their approval. Emma looked around, wrinkled her brow.

"Hmm," she said. "Sounds like you brought your own cheering section here with you today, Rev."

Hammond slapped his knee, laughed out loud.

"Just good honest Christian folks out there. I don't need to bring no cheering section. Got one wherever I go."

More cheers, applause rumbled through the studio.

Emma went on the attack.

"But Reverend, how can you just dismiss an important study like Dr. Mooney's without giving it the consideration of examining it?"

"Don't need do, Sister. Got God's word at hand. Everything else is just opinion."

Colene snorted, her eyebrows shot up.

"'Just opinion?' " she said. "Do you have any idea how many centuries and decades it's taken just to come to a basic understanding of how these old texts were made? Or do you have an inkling of the years of preparation it requires to read these works in their original?"

Hammond dipped his head in agreement.

"Oh, I hear you, Colene. I got the greatest respect for y'all that look back on these earlier works for us preachers. Y'all do a great job. But, the simple fact is that the revealed word of God is there for all to see, read and believe."

"But Reverend," Colene said. "Many of these early writings are laden with anecdotes and myths. As a historian, I prefer the facts to the myths."

"That's nice, Colene. But I prefer the truth to the facts."

Another burst of applause ripped through the studio.

Colene shook her head at that last remark.

"I find that statement to be a myth," she said.

Boos, cat calls, whistles erupted, prompting Emma to scowl at the audience. She growled,

"Courtesy, please. We're all adults here."

Emma turned back to Colene.

"So you're saying there's no place for faith in your historical studies, Colene ..."

Hammond interrupted.

"Ya know, Sister Emma, I was in seminary with Colene's former department head, Jimmy Corbett. I can't help but feel that he, a really sweet, wonderful man, was misguided. We had many long hours of discussion on this very topic and that's why I know where Colene's coming from."

He turned to Colene, patted her shoulder.

"It's wonderful to study the word o'God," he said. "Jimmy was a great friend, a great scholar and a great person. We all miss him and I can say how proud and happy I am to see this lovely young woman continue on doing this wonderful work."

"I certainly agree," Colene said. "Professor James Corbett was my teacher, my mentor and my dear friend. However, when it comes to reading texts that can have such a dramatic impact on one's life, I hope that people can come to understand the difference between what scripture is based on evidence and what is based on wishful thinking."

Emma glanced over, getting cues from the technician with the headset. She came to her feet, picked up the hand mike from the table, strode to center stage.

"This has just been wonderful today. What a treat to have such great people here with us today like Dr. Mooney from Yale and the Reverend Hammond."

Emma ended on that note.

Hammond came to his feet, kissed Emma and Colene, blessed them both, looked into the camera.

"This has been an inspired and inspirational time for me to be here with y'all today."

Colene thanked Emma.

"Well," she said. "It's certainly been educational for me too."

~*~~*~

Delta Airlines VIP Lounge, O'Hare Airport, Chicago, IL
7:59 PM, that evening

Colene had enjoyed the steak and lobster dinner with Emma. The ride to the airport in the limo was pleasant. The driver had checked her bag, handed her the boarding pass for first class, then she made her way up the escalator through the crowd of busy travelers, past the noisy venues. An airline representative met her before she made her way through security, took her through a separate station, then to the VIP lounge.

Seated in a comfortable chair, the attendant asked if she'd like something to drink. Colene, full from her dinner, said,

"A glass of cold water would nice."

When the glass was set before her, Colene leaned back, looked up at the TV. A CNN news flash was showing the outdoor scene of a blazing crash in the background. Colene heard the reporter declare,

"We are all still in a state of shock over the plane crash that has killed Senator Sam Northridge, his family, and the crew of the private jet outside of Canton, Ohio. The crash occurred shortly after takeoff and at first indication, it is attributed to pilot error and windshear, due to the continuing meteorological conditions outside the airport. More information will be given as it becomes available. Wolf, back to you."

Colene suspended the glass of water at her lips, aware of the shock that came from fulfilled anticipation. Somehow, she had expected this.

Crocodile Tears

On the way to the Trade Winds Motel and Lodge, outside of Richmond, VA,

the following Monday, 4:40 PM, Early April

KD Rogers spotted the artificial palm trees and bright signage of the Trade Winds Motel and Lodge looming off the highway. He turned his silver Lincoln Continental into the motel lot, parked, got out of the car with beads of sweat on his face, his bald head, then pinched, pulled loose the white shirt clinging to his sweated body, brushed at the wrinkles in his faded black suit. He wiped a few drops of sweat from his cheeks with his sleeve as he entered, brushed his way to a small conference room in the rear of the building.

A door with a brass plate caught his attention. He checked the name– Philip Morris Memorial Conference Auditorium. A faux mahogany table, 12 chairs adorned with orange leatherette seats and backs lining the sides caught his eye when he entered. A water color of the famous tobacco factory hung on one end of the room over a folded serving buffet made from the same faux wood as the table and chairs.

Rogers pushed his way into the room, plopped the black cordura messenger pack on the table, then took a handkerchief from his pocket, wiped his damp brow and bald head. He turned at the noise of the door opening, saw Damian Styles come into the room.

"Well, I see you've arrived," Rogers said.

Styles wore light yellow cream colored slacks, a light gray cotton sport coat over a light orange shirt, open at the throat.

"Howcum you're sweating, KD?" Styles said.

"Danged AC in my car went out."

Styles looked around the small room.

"We're early." he said.

"Good," Rogers said. "It'll give me a chance to get set up."

Rogers took out his Dell computer, unwound the power cord, searched for an outlet.

"Peeyew, " he said. "This place stinks of smokers."

"Tobacco owns this state, KD," Styles said.

Rogers found the outlet, plugged in the cord.

"Don't think I don't know that," he said "But the use of tobacco is still a sin."

"Morris is bringing his second in command."

"I thought Steele was watching that Mooney woman."

"He is," Styles said. " Kimball's actually Ham's second in command."

"I thought Steele was."

"No. And, I get the feeling Steele doesn't like taking orders from Kimball," Styles said. "He's an ex-Marine officer and very right on."

"Christian?"

"Mormon."

"Devout?"

"So I'm told."

"Mormons aren't true Christians."

"C'mon, KD. This guy's a straight shooter."

"There could be a problem here."

"Howzat?"

"Mormons take their orders straight out of Salt Lake City."

"Maybe. They're on our side."

"You can't trust them. Look how the Catholics turned on us."

"Let it go for now, KD. I hear someone coming."

The door opened. Ham Morris walked in, dressed in green slacks and a green polo shirt. He came to the table, shook hands with both men.

"Brig Kimball will be joining us," Morris said.

Styles patted Morris on the shoulder.

"Howz the family, Ham."

"OK."

Morris turned. "I hear Brig coming now."

He raised his voice.

"Brig. In here."

Rogers saw a tall, slender man with, deep blue eyes step in the room, dressed in green military fatigues, a buzz cut, holding a black ball cap with the 4Sinc logo in his hand. Rogers glanced at his feet encased in spit-shined cordovan paratrooper boots.

"Gentlemen," Morris said, "Brig Kimball. My back-up quarter-back."

Without losing eye contact, Kimball gave a stiff slight bow, shook hands with Styles.

"Congressman," he said.

"The Reverend KD Rogers," Morris said.

"A pleasure, Reverend."

Squinting, Rogers gripped Kimball's hand in a limp press.

Kimball's dark blue eyes did not change expression when he made the same curt nod.

"Let's get down to business," Morris said.

"Just a second," Rogers said. "I'm about set up."

Kimball shot a glance at Roger's computer.

"Is that clean, Reverend Rogers?" he said.

"Of course, it's clean," Rogers said. "I wipe it off every time I take it out."

"Brig's asking if it's been debugged," Morris said.

Roger's eyes snapped behind his horn-rim glasses, eyebrows knit, mouth in tight pucker.

"How can bugs get in it if I have it with me all the time?"

"Not insects, KD ," Styles said. "Electronic bugs"

"Impossible. I keep it under constant lock and key."

"You'd best let us check it out, Reverend," Kimball said .

"We can do that later," Rogers said, his face turning red.

Morris rolled his eyes.

"OK," he said. "We'll take your word for it."

"What do you got, Ham?" Styles said.

Ham took a flash drive from his pocket, inserted it in the USB drive of Roger's computer, opened up a file.

"Here's the outlay," he said.

Morris brought up an organization tree.

"This has been cleared with Jackson at State and Bob Lehman at Defense. The whole structure kicks in as soon as they impose martial law."

"Doesn't that mean congress, Sir?" Kimball said.

"No," Styles said. "We can give the President emergency powers in the event of an attack with clear mass destruction intent by an outside power or group."

"Will that get by Congress?" Kimball said.

"Well, it was facilitated by the removal of an obstacle," Morris said.

"Yes," Rogers said. "Senator Northridge."

"Congress is under control," Styles said. "We can deliver it straight to the President within an hour."

"So, once the Hajjis cross the lines," Morris said. "Everything kicks in from the top down."

"Why didn't they do that after 9-11?" Rogers said.

"They weren't prepared," Morris said.

"But we'll be," Styles said. "Go on, Ham."

"The plan is pure stainless steel," Morris said. "We've been waiting for the green light but Northridge was a stumbling block."

"Nasty break, him dying in that plane crash," Styles said.

"Damn nasty," Morris said.

Kimball stood without a twitch, both hands folded at his back.

"Let's not start the victory dance too early, gentlemen," Rogers said.

"No worries, KD," Styles said. "Once the National Media pricks are under our control, martial law's a cinch."

"What about the military?" Rogers said.

"No sweat," Morris said. "When we jam it down the public's throats, the Pentagon Hall walkers will let us take the heat."

"Affirmative, Sir," Kimball said. "They won't want to get their hands dirty."

"I've things lined up in Congress so we can use the sedition act to clap the lid on the liberals," Styles said.

"We're in the driver's seat," Morris said.

"What about the Godless outliers?" Rogers said.

"They'll be too scared to make any noise," Styles said.

"Plus, we got the guns," Kimball said.

Rogers knit his eyebrows at Kimball.

"What about your co-religionists?" he said.

Kimball's head snapped around. He returned the look to Rogers.

"My co-religionists, Sir?" he said.

"Yeah, KD," Morris said. "What in the hell do you mean by that?"

"My question is," Rogers said, "Can we trust the Utah crowd?"

Blue eyes blazing, tan face reddening, Kimball growled.

"That's insulting, Reverend Rogers," he said.

"Take my word, KD," Morris said. "There *is* no problem."

"I'll hold you personally responsible," Rogers said.

Morris stood to his full 6'4"height, glared down at Rogers.

"What in the fuck does that mean?" he said.

Rogers looked away, changed his tone of voice.

"What I meant is," he said. "I'll take you at your word."

"Let's get back to the agenda," Styles said. "We gotta call Hammond and let him know to have his message ready for the Christian Alert."

Back at the computer, Rogers took out Morris's memory stick, went online, typed in an address. A phone signal hummed, the image of J. Ryle Hammond came on the screen.

Dressed in a dark blue suit, a light blue shirt and solid red tie, the red carnation in his lapel, Hammond smiled.

"Well, howdy. Pleasure to see y'all out there. How're things, boys?"

Styles leaned forward.

"JR. Did you get the speech?"

"I did, Damian. Pray to the Blessed Lord I never have to give it."

"We all pray for that," Styles said. "But, please familiarize yourself with the text."

Spotting his son-in-law, Hammond said,

"Ham, how'ya doing boy?

"Fine, Pap. You?"

'What's the story on this, Ham?" Hammond said. "This piece you sent me is right full of scare talk. You planning something?"

"Never can tell, Pap. Gotta be prepared."

"Well, I gotta say I don't like it. Not one dang part of it."

"What's the matter with it, JR?" Styles said.

"It's all hate talk. It's all about fighting and killing and scaring people. The only thing in it I see about Jesus is when we ask everyone to pray we're victorious."

"But, we are at war, JR," Rogers said.

"KD. My personal feeling is that we'd be better off asking everybody to pray for peace, just like I do on my show every time I speak. Didn't see much about praying for peace in what you sent me."

Styles stepped in.

"I understand exactly what you're saying, JR. I'm delighted to hear that you agree with me."

"Agree with you? Shucks, Damian, ain't you the very same guy who wrote this bag o'goat tripe?"

"I am indeed, JR. Don't forget it's just an emergency plan. We all share your hopes and prayers that we'll never have to use it."

"Dang funny, didn't sound that way when I read it. But, in the interests of brotherly love and in adoration of our Blessed Lord Jesus Christ who died on the cross for you and me and for the continuing love and fear of our Father in Heaven, I'll look at it again."

"Bless you, JR."

"See ya boys."

Hammond's image faded. Kimball stared at Morris.

"My God, Sir," Kimball said. "Reverend Hammond sounded outright hostile."

Shaking his head, Morris waved his hand.

"When the chickens come home to roost," he said. "Old Pap'll do it and everyone will fall into line."

Styles wiped his face with a handkerchief.

"No doubt he'll do it," he said. "But I didn't like his suspicions."

Rogers stood listening, hands folded behind his back.

"It makes no difference," he said. "What he doesn't know can't hurt him."

New Friends

Colene's Office, Yale U., New Haven, CT
The next day, 3:40 PM

Colene snatched up her desk phone at the first ring "Colene Mooney."

"Dr. Mooney, it's Orhan Mehmet."

"How are you?"

"Thank you, well. I'm in Washington, DC hoping that I can come up to see you today."

"Fantastic. When would you be arriving?"

"I can be there around 1800, that's 6:00 PM your time."

"Do you need someone to come get you?"

"No need to bother. I can meet you somewhere."

"There's a good French restaurant close to the airport. When would you be returning?"

"Tonight. I have a flight to Turkey scheduled for tomorrow afternoon."

"That's no problem. We can have dinner and a great visit before your return flight."

"Splendid."

"I'd like to bring a friend, if that's not a problem."

"Your friend and you both will be my guests for the evening."

"That's great. The name of the place is the *La Tricouleur* on Manx Avenue."

"I'll find it and meet you there."

Colene called Ara as soon as she hung up.

"Yeah," he said.

"Remember that Turkish policeman that I mentioned?"

"Sort of."

"Well, he's coming here tonight. I really want you to be there too."

"This guy's a Turk, right?"

"Yes."

"You know about us Armenians and Turks."

"He'll meet us at the *Tricouleur*."

"I'll pick you up."

"Make it 6."

"Cool."

~*~~*~

On a side street, the other side of the Yale campus
Same day, same time

Steele lounged behind the wheel of the black SUV. The red light on the phone monitor next to him blinked off. He leaned over and pushed the play button. Colene and Orhan's voices came on. Steele jotted down the name and address of the restaurant.

When Colene called Ara, a buzzing chirruping noise came on, Steele switched it off.

"Smart sonofabitch," he said.

Steele smiled—he knew where to go next.

~*~~*~

Ronald Reagan Washington National Airport, Arlington, VA
Same day, same time

Orhan jotted down the name of the restaurant in his note pad, walked over to the Delta Airlines counter, made arrangements for a flight to New Haven. After giving the counterperson all the details, documents, he stepped to the window, set his briefcase down on the floor, gazed out at the airplanes landing, taking off, moving over the airfield like giant toys.

Why am I so hyped up by this visit? I feel like a teenager, meeting a girl for the first time?

He reflected.

Was this jaunt all business?

Was the time taken for this detour justifiable?

Where would this lead?

For a moment, he stared at the landing field, then raised his eyes to gaze at the city beyond. He tried to concentrate on the movement of the cars along the thoroughfare on the edge of the river.

The simple truth is, he decided, *I'm going because I want to go.*

~*~~*~

Outside Colene's office building, Yale Campus, New Haven, CT
same day, same time

Sitting on a bench in the shade of a tree, Saleem Duhani tore up the bread from his sandwich into small pieces, tossed it to the squirrels scampering around his feet. He had tried to coax one close enough to take the crumb from his hand, but the rodent flashed its tail, dashed out of reach when he reached out, looked back at him, chattered a scold, then popped to one side, waiting for another piece of bread.

Placing a small hunk of the bread on the edge of the bench, Saleem glanced back at the window in the building where he knew the female Professor had her office. From his bench spot, Saleem could see both the rear and side doors. He made a visual sweep of both exits, then glanced up at the office. He had been on that bench since before noon. After arriving, finding her name on the hall directory, walking by her office, he had made sure she was there.

The squirrel jumped on the end of the bench. Saleem smiled, watched it out of the corner of his eye as it snatched up the bread chunk, jumped off a yard or so away, held the crumb in both paws, ate it looking up at Saleem.

Saleem sat another crumb out on the bench, this time closer to him. Then looked back at the two exits of the building. His cell phone chirruped, scaring off the squirrel from the bench.

"Yes?" he said.

"Anything?" Mekki said.

"Nothing. Keep waiting."

Mekki hung up.

Saleem saw the squirrel had snatched the bread crumb while he was talking.

He set out another chunk. This time just an inch or so away from him.

Then, he sat very still, waited.

Encounter

Café Tricouleur, Corner of Manx Avenue and Dexter Blvd., New Haven, CT
The same day, 5:40 PM

Orhan spotted Colene and Ara from the restaurant's front window as they came walking around the corner from the parking lot. He looked Colene over– this was the woman with the confident voice and impressive speech. He matched what he saw with the image he had made of her in his memory, liking the reality. Then, he noticed the short, thick man walking beside her.

He sighed, feeling some disappointment but stood to greet them as soon as they stepped into the foyer of the restaurant. He came forward, extended his hand.

"Dr. Mooney, I presume."

"Hi," Colene said. "This is my dear friend, Dr. Ara Agajanian"

Orhan shook Ara's hand with a slight bow.

"I'm honored."

"Cool," Ara said.

"Let's go in," Colene said. "I'm starved."

The hostess showed them to a table at the end of the dining room, seated Ara across from Colene, Orhan to her right, gave them menus.

"Anyone for a drink?" Colene said.

"I rarely drink," Orhan said.

"Oh, sorry," Colene said. "Forgot you're Moslem."

"Secular," Orhan said. "I just try to keep a clear head."

"Good," Colene said "Because, I need a glass of wine."

"And, I'll join you," Orhan said.

He turned to Ara.

"Dr. Agajanian. You're Armenian?"

"Yes."

"I hope my being Turkish presents no discomfort for you."

Ara started.

"Not for me," he said.

"Gentlemen," Colene said. "The menu. I'm starved."

They ordered, Colene turned to Orhan.

"What a surprise having you call today."

"When did you arrive stateside?" Ara asked.

"The day before yesterday. My cousin's wife was having a baby and he asked me to step in to hand carry some sensitive information to Washington."

"Police business?" Colene said.

"Something like that."

"Must be hot stuff," Ara said.

Orhan turned to Colene.

"I wanted the chance to talk."

"It's a wonderful surprise."

Orhan looked over at Colene.

"I was shocked to hear you witnessed an assassination."

"It was quite a jolt," Colene said. "I'm just now getting over it."

"Do you see a connection between the murder and the guy trying to sell the religious document?" Ara said.

"We speculate it could be the same one stolen from Professor Foucault," Orhan said.

"That's not much to go on," Ara said.

"What is your doctorate in, Dr. Agajanian?" Orhan said.

"Which one?" Colene said.

Orhan blinked.

"I beg your pardon?"

"He's got four," Colene said.

"Four?"

Colene went on.

"Medicine, mathematics, electronic engineering and anthropology."

"That's incredible," Orhan said.

"No biggie," Ara said. "How're you gonna track down this Hydra gang?"

"They seem to be a network of smaller organizations that smuggles everything from art to arms which they sell to bankroll political and religious terrorism."

"I asked a government man about Hydra. He was very closed mouth about their existence," Colene said.

"They exist," Orhan said. "We've traced individuals to definite cases."

"Are they all religious fanatics?" Ara said.

"I can't say. But the smuggling profits end up with arms in the hands of insurrectionists."

"Religious ideology is such bullshit," Colene said.

"You should know," Orhan said. "You're in the eye of the hurricane with your bible studies."

"I don't care about the religious angles."

The waitress arrived with the food. The salads were tasty. The conversation turned to favorite foods until the main course arrived.

Ara looked over the chateaubriand.

"This looks decent," he said. "I hope it's not too rare for you,'

"I've spent time in Paris," Orhan said. "Unlike many of my Turkish compatriots, I like rare beef."

"Do you cook?" Ara said.

"I'm quite fond of cooking," Orhan said.

"What else do you do for fun?" Ara said.

"I'm a bit of a film fan."

"Really?" Ara said. "What's your liking?"

"The French expressionists, American realists. I especially like the modern people like Altman and the Coen brothers."

"What about Hitchcock?" Ara said.

"I love everything he did," Orhan said.

"Even *Psycho*?" Colene said.

"Especially *Psycho*."

"I couldn't take a shower alone for years after I saw that movie," Colene said.

"Me either," Orhan said.

"What about your family?" Colene said.

Orhan lowered his eyes, pursed his lips in a little tight smile.

"I'm afraid it's just me right now," he said

" 'Right now?' " Ara said.

"I'm widowed."

"O, my," Colene said.

When the waiter arrived with the check, Orhan scooped it up.

Colene looked at her watch.

"We should be going," she said. "You got a plane to catch."

They stood, Orhan stepped to the front, paid the bill, then followed Colene and Ara outside.

"Let us take you to the airport," Colene said.

"If it's not inconvenient."

They strolled out to the parking lot around the corner of the restaurant into the shadowy glare of a pair of flood lights lighting the area.

"Here's the car," Ara said.

"It looks like a racing stock car," Orhan said.

"Ara takes his driving very seriously," Colene said.

As Ara stepped up to the door of his car, a faded gray Chevrolet station wagon screeched up behind them. Orhan saw three men jump out.

Kassim, wearing a green ball cap ran over, shoved an automatic pistol gun in Ara's face.

"Move, I'll kill you," he said.

Mekki, a tall man whipped out a long curved knife grabbed Colene, dragged her towards the old Ford.

"Get in, stupid bitch," he said.

The third, short, stocky Saleem thrust a pistol into Orhan's face.

"On your knees, dog," he screamed.

Ara shouted at Mekki dragging Colene.

"Sonofabitch! Let her go."

Colene spun, kicked Mekki in the knee.

Orhan raised his hands, gave a quick glance to his left when Saleem shoved the pistol into his face.

"On your knees," Saleem said. "I'll blow your head off."

Orhan shot another oblique glance.

"Over here!" he shouted,

Saleem turned, looked. Orhan grabbed his wrist, twisted it, pointed the gun at Kassim in the green hat in front of Ara, jerked Saleem's wrist holding the pistol.

The pistol discharged. Kassim's green hat flew off when the slug hit his head– he jerked forward, fell.

Orhan spun, throwing the stocky Saleem over his hip, twisting his wrist, jerking the gun free. Orhan felt the wrist snap. Saleem jerked back his broken hand, grabbed it with his free hand and ripped the pistol from Orhan's grip.

Saleem fumbled the handgun, jammed his thumb against the trigger.

The pistol fired. The shot went through Saleem's eye.

Ara lunged at the tall Mekki just as he slashed down with the knife at Colene's head. Ara slammed his shoulder into the taller man, causing the blow to glance off the side of Colene's scalp, opening a gash. Mekki recovered, drew back to strike again.

A gun report.

Mekki sprawled back, fell dead from a shot through the temple. Orhan stood, holding Saleem's pistol.

Ara, Orhan ran over, knelt beside Colene.

"Her scalp's cut– looks superficial," Ara said. "There's a hospital just a few blocks from here."

"Go ahead with her," Orhan said. "Call in. I'll wait here until the police come."

Orhan scooped up Colene, carried her to Ara's car. Ara opened the rear door. Orhan set her in the back seat. Ara leapt behind the wheel, fired up the engine, backed out, then tore out of the parking lot.

Orhan watched the car disappear down the street, then turned back to look at the three bodies. He became aware of motion, a noise behind him—too late. Then, pain– blackness ...

~*~~*~

Orhan came to with a jerk. He tried to sit up. His head hurt, his vision blurred. Thoughts spun through his head.

He remembered– the attack, the noise, the blood– Colene's blood– the bodies ... then, a voice piercing the surrounding, dizzying fog ...

"Hi, partner. Coming around?"

Awareness flooded Orhan. He was on a stretcher. An emergency medical technician bent over him. Orhan looked around.

"Colene!" he said. "Where is she?"

"Someone gave you a nasty lick."

Orhan looked up into the face of a woman. A badge hung from a chain around her neck. His eyes focused on her name tag, *Sgt. Hazel Wilson*.

"Where am I?" Orhan said.

"We got the call from the guy on his way to the hospital," Wilson said.

Orhan struggled to get up.

"Whoa, easy," the EMT said.

Orhan looked around.

"Where are the bodies?"

"What bodies?" Wilson said .

"There were three bodies," Orhan said.

Wilson looked around the area.

"That's the question of the year."

"Arabs, I think," Orhan said. "They attacked Dr. Mooney, Dr. Agajanian and me... Where's Colene?"

Wilson walked over to the gray Ford.

"There's blood everywhere," she said. " Spent cartridges..., Colene's in the hospital. Agajanian has a cut sleeve. And, we found you out cold ..."

She turned around, faced Orhan.

"...But, there just ain't no bodies," she said.

"Whoever slugged me must have carried them off," Orhan said.

Scrambling to his feet Orhan stumbled over to Wilson and pulled out his diplomatic passport, his Interpol ID.

"I'm Colonel Orhan Mehmet from the Turkish government. I was here with Dr. Mooney when we were attacked."

Wilson waved her hand.

"No need. Colonel," she said. "We checked you out with the feds before you came back from dreamland. Looks like you saved their asses tonight."

"They're all right?"

"Aside from a nasty cut on Colene's scalp."

Orhan leaned against the side of the old gray Ford, placed his hand on his head.

"I don't understand why they took the bodies?" he said.

Wilson shrugged.

"More important question is 'Who took the bodies?' " she said.

~*~~*~

Sgt. Wilson led Orhan through the ER to the back where in one of the clinical stations Colene sat on the edge of the bed with a gauze bandage wrapped around her scalp. The antiseptic smell of the clinic bit Orhan's nostrils.

Colene looked up, smiled when Orhan came in.

"Our hero," she said.

Ara standing next to the bed wearing a white lab coat, looked over to him.

"You were awesome, buddy."

Orhan went up to Colene.

"Are you all right?" he said,

"Aside from my ruined hair-do and Indian princess headdress, I'm fine."

Colene turned to Sgt. Wilson.

"Hazel. It's been weeks."

"Never a dull moment with you around, Colene," Wilson said.

"You know each other?" Orhan said.

"The locals tapped me when they got your call," Wilson said. "When I came on scene, our Turkish friend here was out cold in a bloody mess."

"Where were the attackers?" Colene said.

"Well, the bodies were gone," Orhan said.

"They were dead," Ara said. "I can attest to that."

"Someone hauled them off– fast," Wilson said.

"Why?" Colene said.

"To avoid identification," Orhan said.

"We'll get prints off of the car," Wilson said.

"Then, who did it?" Colene said.

"My guess is whoever's been tailing us," Ara said.

"Tailing you?" Wilson said.

"We don't know but I mentioned it to the FBI ..." Colene said.

Wilson rolled her eyes.

"O shit," she said. "This is a feeb thing. I'm outta here."

"Hazel," Colene said. "You're not abandoning us?"

"No, and I ain't getting caught in any turf wars either. The feebs don't like us pissing on their trees."

"Just the bodies were gone?" Ara said.

"Aside from the mess around the attack scene, no weapons were found. Just the car and a few spent shell casings," Wilson said.

"What's the next step?" Orhan said.

"It's up to the feebs," Wilson said. "I'll call Mary Rich tonight. She knows Colene."

Wilson turned to Orhan.

"As far as we're concerned here, Colonel. You're free to go."

Wilson strode to the door of the room, then stopped, turned back.

"Goodnight all," she said. "We really must do this again soon."

"Wow. This has been some shit," Ara said.

Colene looked at Orhan.

"You look terrible," she said.

Ara came over, took a small flashlight from his lab coat pocket, looked in Orhan's eyes.

"I don't want you to go back to DC tonight," he said. "You have a slight concussion and need bed rest."

"But, I must... " Orhan said.

"Absolutely not," Colene said. "You're staying at my place tonight."

Orhan blinked, caught his breath.

"I don't want to impose– this is complicated... I'm not sure ..."

Colene interrupted him.

"Leave it," she said. "We can sort it out in the morning."

"Colene's right," Ara said. "Tomorrow will take care of itself."

Orhan threw up his hands.

"Americans," he said. "You amaze me."

Follow-up

Colene's House, New Haven, CT.
Later that evening, 10:46 PM

Colene opened the back door, led Orhan into her house, threw her things on the couch, went back into the kitchen, switched on the light.

"Is it too late for coffee for you?" she said.

"Do you have any brandy?"

She stepped to a cupboard, opened a door, took down a bottle of Courvoisier.

"I thought you didn't drink," she said.

"I do now."

She poured a glass of brandy for him, another for herself.

"This is very good brandy," he said.

"You saved our lives tonight."

"I suppose."

"I was too mad to be scared..."

"That's good."

"... until that son of a bitch cut me with that knife."

"It's good that Ara deflected the blow."

"If it weren't for you," she said, "we'd all be dead."

He turned his eyes to the glass in his hand, swirled the brandy, then looked up at her.

"Are you and Ara ..." he said. "I mean ..."

"Involved?"

"I guess that's how you say it."

Colene threw back her head, laughed.

"He's like my kid brother," she said. "We met at Harvard."

"I'm very impressed by him."

"He has a mild form of Asperger's."

"Asperger's?"

"It's a syndrome– a form of autism. His condition's very mild and controlled by medication. Asperger's guys are usually super-brilliant, but often have zero social skills."

"Social skills?"

"Ara's never aware of what's going on around him unless he's directly observing it."

"But, he's so bright, witty."

"That's also part of the syndrome. Ara's completely incapable of telling you a personal lie but can't always read interpersonal social clues."

"I found him fascinating."

"Probably your police training– you saw beyond the outer shell."

Orhan paused again.

"Then, you're not ..."

"Lovers?" she said.

"Lovers."

Colene chuckled.

"That thought has never entered either of our heads."

Orhan dropped his eyes, stared into the glass in his hand.

"I'm sorry. I had no right to intrude ..."

"No offense taken."

"Is there someone in your life?"

He set the glass down on the table with a thump, rolled his eyes, looking around the ceiling.

"What's wrong with me?" he said. "I'm sorry. It must be that knock on the head."

"I had a very brief schoolgirl crush on an older guy but that went nowhere—and won't. So, I just keep busy."

"My apologies."

"Stop apologizing. What about you?"

"What about me?"

"Do you have a social life?"

"You mean a love life?"

"Yeah. A sex life?"

"Like you. I just keep busy."

"Why not? You're widowed, you're young..."

"Like you, I stay busy."

Orhan stared at his glass, Colene stared at him.

"Tell me about your loss," she said.

He looked away.

"I don't think I can."

"Too painful?"

He paused, pursed his lips, raised his eyes.

"My wife and son were blown up by a car bomb ... that was meant for me."

"O God, no!"

"I'd been investigating an art smuggling ring connected to an arms and drug network. I took down the central figure... They came after me. My family paid the price."

Colene stared at her glass of brandy, picked up it up, swirled it.

"This has to do with the Hydra business, right?"

"I'll not quit until I've taken every one of them down."

She reached out, touched his cheek, brushed a tear from his jaw-clenched face.

"Makes my problems seem petty."

His eyes flashed, his face hard.

"No pity, please."

"No pity, dear man," she said.

She stared at him. When he looked up at her, she set her glass down.

"I need you," she said.

She came to him, put her arms around him, kissed him on the lips. She felt him soften. He kissed her back.

~*~~*~

Colene's kitchen, New Haven, CT
next morning, 7:44 AM

Colene had cooked scrambled eggs, a ham steak, whole wheat toast, then it laid out on a plate. She picked up the coffee pot just as Orhan walked in.

"O shit," she said. "I forgot about the ham."

"Ham's fine," he said. "I'm especially fond of pork sausages."

She handed him the coffee, he looked at it, smelled it, tasted it, then set it aside.

"How are you?" she said.

"Conflicted."

"How so?"

"I'm happier than I've been in years. I'm walking into a fine English breakfast. I made love to a beautiful, clever woman long into the night but, feeling shame for taking advantage of a sensitive situation."

Pouring herself more coffee, she shrugged her shoulders,

"No way you could've taken advantage of me. You got into my bed last night because I wanted you there."

"I'm also conflicted with fear."

"Of what?"

"I'm me. I live in Turkey. I chase art thieves. You're you. You live here. You study bibles. That who we are. That's what we do."

"You're asking what happens next?"

"That's the large part of it."

"Do you think you're falling in love with me?" she said.

He turned, sought her eyes.

"I believe I've been in love with you from the first time I heard your voice."

"Now, I'm getting scared," she said.

"No demands. We live in our own worlds. Like dolphins, we emerge from the deep of the sea, flash in the sun for seconds, then return to our own worlds."

"That's very poetic," she said. "Where do we go from here?"

Colene lowered her eyes before the tears came.

"I think it unfair to both of us to build hopes or expectations on mere dreams," Orhan said.

Choking back tears, Colene put her hand to her mouth.

"I can't ... can't say how I feel at this point ..."

"You don't have to ..."

He took her in his arms.

~*~~*~

Colene called FBI Agent, Mary Rich, arranged to meet with her during the next week.

She passed the phone to Orhan.

Rich and Orhan both agreed Orhan could return to Turkey.

~*~~*~

New London International Airport,
That next afternoon, 2:43 PM

Colene moved into the slowing traffic in front of the lower deck of the airport terminal. "Just leave me off at the curb. No need to stop," Orhan said.

"I don't want you to go."

"Then, it's better this way."

She turned, touched his cheek, then brushed her tearing eyes.

"Kind of a brusque goodbye," she said.

"It's not really goodbye."

"I hope not."

She leaned over, kissed him on the lips. Afterwards, he leaned back, his mouth in a slight smile.

"I'll stay in touch," he said.

"Please do," Colene said.

When he stepped out, she drove away, tears clouding her eyes, not daring to look back in the mirror at the man standing there, watching her leave.

The Heirloom

An office in a large house, Outside of Alexandria, Egypt
Next day, 2:45 PM. April

Hydra stepped up to the door of his office wearing light cream-colored slacks, an open neck short sleeve lime-green cotton shirt, his feet in tan leather sandals. He ran his hand over his thick gray hair, unlocked the steel door to his office, stepped into the room, then stopped to gaze at the light from the window glinting off the brass frame of a large painting hung in a nook surrounded by book shelves along the long wall.

A low African blackwood table sat on a black and white camel-hair rug surrounded by 4 red low chairs in front of a desk made from the same African blackwood that crouched near the window.

He stepped over, looked at some papers on his desk, then dropped them into a stack- box. Then stepping to the frame of the painting, he unlocked a catch in the side, swung the frame out to reveal a safe built into the wall. He twirled the two dials on the locks until he heard the safe click open, reached in, took out a worn leather binder covering weathered parchment manuscript pages, then carried it to his desk. He eased his lean body into the polished blackwood desk chair, set the binder in front of him, stared at it for a moment.

A knock at the door caused him to jerk his head up. Sweeping the binder into the front desk drawer, he slid open another drawer to his right, dropped his hand on a pistol.

"Come in," he said.

Ahmed, his servant poked his head in, bowed.

"Ya Sayidi," he said. "Would you wish coffee or tea this morning?"

Hydra relaxed.

"Tea would be fine, Ahmed."

When Ahmed closed the door, Hydra slid the gun drawer shut, removed the binder with a box of latex gloves. Poking his hands into the gloves, he stared at the binder for a full minute, his eyes wandering over its aged, worn cover. Ritual-like, he reached to the binder, opened it, hesitated, extracted a magnifying glass from the open drawer, then scanned over the first page.

The binder was about 17" long, 12"wide. The cracked, dry parchment pages showed through the transparent thick mylar covers. Hydra squinted at the continuous writing squeezed together in Greek block letters that took up half the page, then at the curved Aramaic script on the other half. The Greek writing was clearer than the faded Aramaic side.

Lips pursed tight, his breathing shallow, he focused his eyes, scanning first one side, then jumping to the other. At one point, he stopped, reread one section, then compared the other side, set the glass down, shook his head, rubbed his chin.

Hydra opened left side drawer of his desk, took a linen handkerchief out of a dark brown hand-tooled Moroccan leather folder, held it in his hands. He smiled, let his eyes play over the simple white linen bordered in purple with the monogram, ***JCM.***

He brought it to his nose, drew a deep breath, whiffed the faint odor. He then dropped the handkerchief on the open codex lying in the center of his desk, leaned back in his chair, folded his hands behind his head, chuckled with a quiet clicking of his throat, all the time, staring down at the white linen cloth in the ancient binder.

Sitting erect, he picked up the handkerchief, placed it back into the ornate leather folder, stowed in the drawer, closed it, then brought his hands together in front of his face, pressing them to his mouth.

A knock at the door jolted him back into consciousness. He swept the binder and glass into the center drawer, again slid open the gun drawer, his right hand resting on the edge.

"Come in."

Ahmed came in with a tea service which he set on the table with a cup, a plate of sweet breads and cheese.

"Does Sayedi require anything else?"

"No, Thank you, Ahmed."

The servant left without looking back.

Hydra closed the gun drawer, took out the codex, the magnifying glass. He read some more, put down the glass, looked again at the pile of notes in front of him.

After scanning his comments, he reached down, closed the binder in a slow, controlled movement, stroked the closed ancient leather binder like it were a cat, then rose, picked up the binder, replaced it in the safe, shut the door, spun both sets of locks.

Stepping over to the table, he poured a cup of tea, looked up at a knock at the door.

"Yes."

Ahmed entered with a bundle of letters, magazines.

"Your mail, Sayidi."

"*Shokran,*" Hydra said.

After Ahmed left, Hydra sorted through the pile of letters, spotted the cover of *Soldier of Fortune* magazine, a color photo of men in military garb approaching and surrounding a house in a rain forest setting, then picked it up.

Hydra opened the magazine to the Personal Section in the back pages, scanned through the *Positions Sought* section, focused in on a personal note.

A small blurb read, "Michael's gone deer hunting. Hold all calls and letters."

Hydra's eyebrows knit, his mouth twisted into a tight smile. He closed the magazine, threw it to one side, took a bite of the sweet bread, chased it with a swig of tea, gazed over at his massive desk.

New Revelations

On road home, New Haven, CT
Same day, 6:00 PM

Colene's cell phone chimed *Für Elise*. She glanced at the faceplate.

Ara.

Flipping the phone open, she put it to her ear.

"Yes," she said.

"Where are you?"

"Heading home from the airport."

"Meet me at The Coffee Station, off Fulton on Brand."

"When?"

"Now?"

"Now works. Be there in 5."

When she pulled into the lot, she saw Ara's car in the slot near the door. He was sitting at a table in the patio looking at a magazine. After parking next to his car, she stepped out, called over to him.

"Did you get me a latte?"

He pointed to the paper cup across from him, without looking up. When she joined him he asked without taking his eyes off the magazine.

"Dropped him off OK?"

"Yeah."

Still not looking at her, Ara frowned at the magazine.

"That was some shit last night," he said.

"I'm still worn out from it."

Ara raised his eyes, lowered the magazine.

"Orhan spent the night OK?" he said,

"Whadya mean?"

"There's something chemical between you. Saw it from the start."

Colene lowered her eyes, sipped her latte.

"He's interesting," she said.

"The guy saves our lives and 'he's *interesting*?"

"OK. He's special."

"My grandfather would be shocked if he knew that a Turk saved my life."

"He's not that way," she said.

"Right. He's on top of it."

Colene shot him a frown, sipped her coffee.

"Who took those bodies?" she said.

"Probably the Mercs."

"Mercs?"

"Mercenaries. The 4Sinc guys are set up like a private army. Don't forget, the head of this outfit is the son-in-law of the megapreacher Hammond."

"How can I forget him?"

"You guys are buds now, after your TV stint."

"Why take the bodies?"

"Cover any links back to them."

"That doesn't make sense."

"Yeah, it does. Their agenda is to take control of our military and police force and put it all into a private sector basis."

"Like in *Robocop*?"

"They've come damn close to that already."

"What's their connection with these rightwing fundamentalists?"

"Congruent agendas and the family connection."

"Yeah, but those animals that attacked us last night were Jihadists."

"That's a loose end," Ara said. "For now, we need to concentrate on what we got."

"Just what do we got?" Colene said.

Ara leaned over, rubbed under his nose covering the top of his upper lip.

"I got into the Rapture network main offices," he said. "Bugged the CEO's computer, then sprinkled bugs all over the place. I've been monitoring everything they say."

"O shit."

"Last night, I came home and listened to some of the output from this surveillance. What I picked up from a meeting of the CEO with some others is very heavy shit."

"I'm not even going to ask how or when."

"You're gonna meet with the Feebs tomorrow and I have something I want you to give them."

He handed her a disc. She took it, stuffed it in her purse.

"Dare I ask what's on this?"

"A goldmine of intel. The fruits of my labors will give these guys a good picture of what's going on behind the curtain."

"Picture of what?"

"There's enough there to feed a shopping mall full of conspiracy theorists– but, the bastards are clever. They say things only suggestively."

"Whadda you mean?"

"Ever since the Nixon tapes debacle, these yokels never implicate themselves directly or declare anything that can be used as direct evidence."

"When did you burn this disc?"

"This morning. Make sure it gets to the Feebs."

"Do you think we were watched?" Colene said.

"Yes."

"Really?'

"Fuck'em. We can bug them too, remember?"

"That's comforting," Colene said.

Festering Conspiracies

FBI Office, Federal Building, Yonkers, NY
The next day, 2:00 PM.

The smell of cleaning fluid burned Colene's eyes when she opened the door to the FBI office. She wrinkled her nose at the ammonia odor before she spotted agent Mary Rich talking to her secretary.

Dressed in her dark blue pants suit with low heeled shoes, Rich looked up, saw Colene, stepped over, took Colene's hand in both of hers.

"Colene," she said. "Please forgive me for not coming up last night."

"Not much point to it," Colene said. "By the time you heard about, it was all over and done."

"Come on in," Rich said. "Can I get you some coffee?"

"Water would be fine," Colene said.

Rich ushered Colene to a chair, poured water from a pitcher into a glass, set it before Colene, sat down next to her.

"Look at that cut," Rich said.

"We're lucky to be alive."

"We?"

Colene told her about the call from Orhan, dinner with Ara, the attack in the parking lot.

"And, the three bodies were gone?" Rich said.

"Yes, when Hazel and the other officers found Orhan, he was out cold."

"Orhan is Col. Mehmet?"

"Yes. He saved our lives."

"Any ideas who removed the bodies?"

"Ara thinks it was the Mercs."

"Ara–that's Dr. Agajanian–suggested it was Mercs?" Rich said. "What 'Mercs?' "

"Some kind of paramilitary group that does government security contracts."

"O God," Rich said. "4Sinc."

"For what?"

"Four S, incorporated. They're known by the acronym '4Sinc.' "

"I've heard that somewhere..." Colene said. "Yes. Ara mentioned it."

Colene took the disc from her purse, handed it to Rich.

"Ara bugged the right wing guys' offices," she said. "He got into their CEO's computer and asked me to give you this."

Rich's jaw dropped. She blinked, looked at the disc in her hand, then passed it back to Colene.

"O shit," she said. "I didn't hear this."

"I said..."

"I know what you said," Rich said. "But, I told you not to do anything illegal."

"Hey," Colene said. "It's our asses on the line here. A man got his head blown apart in front of me and I damn near got killed night before last. Ara's been there with me every step of the way and if it hadn't of been for Orhan, you'd be reading my obit right now."

"That's not what I meant..."

"This may not be evidence but it can be useful."

Rich turned over the disc in her hand, pursed her lips, looked up at Colene.

"OK," she said. "We're off the record."

She picked up her phone.

"I'm gonna call Willy," she said.

While waiting for Johnson, Rich played part of the conversation at the motel.

Johnson knocked once, came in, leaned against the wall, listened to the voices on the disc. When the conversation finished, he said,

"Holy shit. Where'd you get that, Mair?'

"Colene's cracked 4Sinc," Rich said.

"You're shitting me?"

"Nope. This clearly implicates 4Sinc," Rich said.

Willy strode over near the couch, dropped his tall body in a chair, draped his leg over the arm rest, looked over at Colene.

"We couldn't say much before," he said. "But, let's say we've been tracking an ... internal set of events."

"What he's hemming and hawing about is that we suspect 4Sinc to be tangled in a potential coup," Rich said.

"A coup?" Colene said. "In our country? The US?"

"Yeah," Johnson said.

"And, you're not blowing the whistle on these guys?"

"Very complicated," Rich said.

"What the fuck does that mean?" Colene said.

Johnson got up, leaned against the door, looking Colene in the eyes.

"What were gonna say can't leave this room," he said.

"A few months ago we were looking at another case," Rich said. "We stumbled across convincing intel suggesting a group action to take control of national defense and major police functions."

"That comes off a bit strong," Johnson said. "On the surface, it looks more like a national crack-down."

"The result of which would be a suspension of individual rights," Rich said.

"So why aren't you guys doing anything about it?" Colene said.

"Because it looks wired from near the top," Johnson said.

"This is very political, Colene," Rich said. "We've only been able to bring in a few people. The whole damn bureau is divided into political factions– there are guys here who'd actively support such a move!"

"It's not only political," Johnson said. "Some of these guys are waist deep in our present administration."

"I'm sorry," Colene said. "But aren't government officials supposed to support and defend the constitution?"

"Depends on how you define 'support and defend,'" Johnson said.

Rich stood up, folded her arms, paced back and forth.

"All we can do is gather data–solid, hard evidence," she said. "How'll the intel on this disc allow us to make a case?"

"If we act too soon," Johnson said. "We'll be slapped down hard."

Rich looked over at Johnson.

"Willy what you heard came from Colene's friend. He tapped into the RapNet."

"Sounds like it's a go for Operation White Knight," Johnson said.

"These data are illegal," Rich said. "We can't use them."

Johnson grinned.

"We can still use the intel," he said.

Rich shook her head.

"Too many loose ends," she said.

"No," Johnson said. "There are some real connections shown on this disc."

"What about those goons that tried to kill Colene?" Rich said. "Col. Mehmet thinks they're Arabs."

"Col. Mehmet?" Johnson said.

"Colonel Orhan Mehmet from Turkey," Rich said. "Remember, you checked him out earlier?"

"Now, I remember," said Johnson. "But, this is a blind side, I don't get the connection."

"We got the car," Rich said. "Maybe we'll get some prints."

"What about me?" Colene said. "My ass is stuck out here."

"It's not clear why these guys attacked you," Rich said.

"Also," Johnson said. "I don't see any connection with them and the RapNet-4Sinc business."

"Well, why would these mercenary cowboys haul the bodies away if there wasn't some connection?" Colene said.

"We're all just guessing," Rich said. "But what we do know is that somebody's tailed, attacked you and disappeared the bodies."

"Another fact is that getting rid of bodies breaks any connection back to the RapNet," Johnson said.

"Where would these RapNet clowns get the resources to pull that off?" Rich said.

"Maybe it was the same cowboys that killed the guy in front of me," Colene said.

"Could be," Johnson said.

"Am I in danger?" Colene said.

"Don't think so," Johnson said. "If they're the same guys, they could have taken you out any time."

"That's my feeling too, Colene," Rich said. "Keep a low profile until we vet their car."

"So, I'm to keep a low profile to keep a bunch of nutcases from chasing and shooting at me?" Colene said.

"I'll contact Hazel Wilson to get you some 24-7 protection," Rich said.

"I can't tell you how reassuring that is," Colene said.

Guns, Guns, Guns

Dante's DC Lounge, Rosslyn, MD
5 days later, 11:15 PM, early May

Ham Morris tugged the collar of his trench coat up around his ears. The moonless evening was cold and damp. He glanced around, checked over his shoulder to both sides, pushed a tan brimmed hat down to his ears to cover his buzz cut, then hurried along the dark street. Coming to the corner, he paused, looked around once more, scanned the bar across the street.

He took in the line of closed shops and stores leading to an all-night Pizza Barn. Seeing no movement, he peered back across the street running like a black, still river, at the grayish building with neon beer signs showing through dirty windows with faded brown frames with a door that had once been red but looked like the color of dried blood. Taking dark sunglasses from his hard leather case, Morris checked out the area one last time, crossed the street, pushed his way through the gore-colored door.

He paused inside the bar. Dim overhead lights cast shadows on the few customers that sat at the scattered tables. No one looked up when Morris walked in. Smoke hung in the air in a dim interior. The smell of burnt tobacco, spilled liquor, cheap perfume bit Morris's nostrils. Seated on a stool behind the bar, a lone bartender with a purple birth mark on his forehead, in a white shirt and black vest glanced at Morris, gave him a blank look, then went back to watching an old movie. At the bar a young black sailor was talking in rapid, rhythmic phrases to an older woman in a short skirt who kept dabbing ashes from her cigarette onto the floor. At a corner table, a couple argued in loud whispers, gesturing with hand motions flicking ashes from their cigarettes like flitting bats. Next to them, a man and woman in their late 70s, dressed in worn shabby, clothing, turned, stared at him.

Morris spotted the balding red headed man sitting in the back at a table next to an old jukebox. Morris paused before going over to him, checking to see if there were other people within listening range.

The redheaded man was short, round with a solid build. Short auburn red hair circled his bald head, a neatly trimmed mustache covered his upper lip, his greenish blue eyes swept the room. He looked up, saw Morris standing at the doorway, kept his blue-green eyes on him, gave a little smile.

Dressed in a dark brown tweed jacket, shirt but no tie, the redhead man held a burning cigarette in his left hand, his right on a half-full glass of watered whiskey in front of him. He leaned on his elbows on the table, with the cigarette in his fingers. When Morris came over, made no move to stand or shake hands.

"Hello, Bax," Morris said.

"Ham," Red Bax said.

"You wanted to see me?"

"Oh? I heard it the other way around."

"Howzzat?"

"I wuz told you wanna see me?"

"OK," Morris said. "So, we wanna see each other."

"Charming, ain't it?"

"Can we cut the bullshit?"

Bax crushed his cigarette in a tin ashtray.

"Forgot you're a busy man."

"So it's gonna be more bullshit."

Red shook another cigarette from the pack, looked up at Morris.

"Smoke?" he said

"No."

"Mind if I do?"

"Make any difference?"

"Naw."

"So, whadya got, Bax?"

"Might have something."

"Go on."

Bax lit the cigarette, sucked in the smoke, leaned against the back of his chair.

"When they took Noriega down in Panama, the Army seized a bunch of containers of unstamped cigarettes. And, a bunch of weapons from the Ukraine. But, before they could be impounded, they went missing."

"Didn't know that."

"Lots of things you don't know, soldier boy."

"Can we keep it civil?"

Bax blew out a cloud of smoke.

"We were on the lookout for these items for a long time but nothing ever happened and pretty soon everybody forgot about it."

Bax paused, scanned around the room, leaned forward, whispered,

"Last month we get a buzz from a snitch about three containers of unstamped Marlboros located in a yard outside of Charleston."

"And?"

"We moved on it, came in like gang-busters and grabbed 6 cans of unstamped ciggies and the three containers of guns–Kloshies to Soviet RPGs."

"Good shit?"

"Hell yes. One can is even half full of ammo."

"What kind of shape are the pieces in?"

"Like new. The cans were sealed airtight and the pieces packed in cosmoline."

"So," Morris said. "You wanna make a deal."

"You said that. I'm just telling what I heard."

"How much?"

"12 mil."

"Dream on."

"OK. Since we ain't got nothing to talk about, I'm outta here."

Neither Bax or Morris moved. After a few seconds, Morris said,

"Don't see you moving."

"Just being polite. I was here first, remember?"

"Give me a real number."

"I could work with 8."

"So could I, but I said a real number."

"OK, bright boy. Speak up."

"I can go 2"

Bax laughed.

"Now, who's the joker. Get real."

"Maybe 4."

Morris heard a noise behind him. He tensed, Out of the corner of his eye Morris saw the bartender standing at his elbow.

"Can I getcha something?" he said in a raspy voice.

Morris looked at Bax with a hard glance. Bax didn't move.

"Bring me a beer," Morris said.

"What kind?"

"Just pour me a glass of whatever's coming outta that tap."

"Coming up," the bartender said.

Morris tilted his head, watched the bartender walk back to the bar. He motioned to Bax to keep quiet until the bartender came back with the beer glass on a cardboard coaster on a serving tray.

"That'll be two fifty," he said.

Morris fished a five out of his coat pocket, chucked on the tray.

"Keep it," he said.

The bartender nodded, walked back behind the bar, punched a cash register, then went back to watching the old movie.

Morris turned back to Bax.

"We were saying..." he said.

Bax leaned forward, whispered,

"We're talking 3 long cans– not 20 but 40 footers. So cut the crap. I'm busy too."

"Red," Morris said. "There are a lot of Soviet guns out there."

"But none as sweet as these."

"Suppose I talk to some people and come up with 2 each. That's a decent payday."

"We're getting close, John Wayne. Seven and a half takes the lot."

"OK. Lucky seven it is. When can you deliver?"

Bax hesitated, cleaned the tip of his cigarette in the ash tray.

"Tiny problem," he said.

"Here it comes," Morris said. "What is it?"

"I can't make the delivery."

"Say again?"

"An interagency investigative unit's got a half dozen cameras on me every time I unzip my fly."

"Whadda you saying, Bax?"

"Look, soldier man. I know you're screwing me. But I can give you the bargain basement price. The cans are stored at a private security contractor's facility and I happen to know that these guys hire cheap dumb labor and on Sunday nights, there are only a couple of guards on the grounds."

"You mean you want my guys to move in and steal the cans."

"Otherwise, we're gonna have to cut someone else in. That's risky and expensive."

"I don't like this," Morris said. "We don't steal."

"Take it or walk away. Your choice, Ham. All I'm doing is telling how we can work this thing. "

"Lemme think on this. I'll get back to you."

"When?"

"Tomorrow night. Latest."

"And the money?"

"Once we're happy with the merchandise, we'll settle. You know where to find me."

"That I do, soldier boy, " Bax said.

A Possible Connection

Colene's house, New Haven, CT,
3 days later, 7:45 AM, mid May

Colene got out of bed, stretched, then peeked out the window at the two cops in the parked black and white, already in sunglasses from the morning sun, sipping coffee from paper cups.

Turning to look at herself in the mirror over her bureau, Colene ruffled her hair then thumped downstairs to the kitchen.

When she filled the kettle in the sink, the brandy bottle sitting on the end of the sink board caught her eye. The gold writing on the bottle stood out like a small beacon. When she put the kettle on the stove, she noticed the empty unwashed tumbler next to the bottle.

Colene picked up the glass. The smell of stale brandy teased her nostrils. She caressed the glass in her hand for a second, then squirted the inside with soap from a dispenser, turned on the water, left it soaking in the sink.

Pouring hot water through the coffee grounds, Colene stole another glance at the brandy bottle. She poured her coffee, went over to the little kitchen table by the window. As she sipped her coffee, she raised her eyes again to look at the bottle at the end of the counter.

She set her cup down hard on the table, pulled her cell phone from the pocket of her robe, punched in Ara's number.

He answered at the first ring.

"Yeah?"

"Where are you?"

"In the car."

"Can you come by?"

"When?"

"You busy now?"

"Not too. Be there in 20."

She finished drinking her coffee staring at the single bottle on the sink board. Leaving the kitchen, Colene went to her laptop in the corner of the living room, popped open the cover, logged onto her emails. Scrolling through the long list of cybershadows, Colene closed the email window, went to google earth. Bringing up Turkey, she looked first at Ankara. Then Istanbul. Finally, Izmir. She closed the landscapes and urban centers, logged off, went back into the kitchen.

Her phone lay on the table next to her empty coffee cup. Colene pulled Orhan's card from her robe pocket and dialed in the number.

A woman's voice answered,

"Alo, Araştırma Soruşturma Departmanı."

"Hello, I'm Dr. Colene Mooney from the US. Do you speak English."

"I am."

"Is Col. Mehmet in today."

"Regretfully, Director Mehmet is out of office for rest of week. May I take message?"

"No message. Could you just tell him I called?"

"I can, Doctor. He calls you back?"

"If it's convenient."

"He has your number?"

"Yes. He does."

"I'm being sure he knows you call, Dr. Mooney."

"Thank you."

"You are most quite welcome."

Colene took the phone with her back into her computer. She googled Col. Orhan Mehmet. Over 10,000 hits popped up. Leafing through them, she saw a military profile in Turkish showing a picture of a younger Orhan in an officer's uniform. Using the Babylon translation software, Colene read about Orhan's education in the National Turkish Military Academy, his military career. She saw his posting in counterinsurgency units, his graduation from the FBI academy for foreign investigators in Rochester, Virginia.

Seeing nothing in the files about his personal life Colene closed the google window at the knock at the front door.

She called out.

"It's open,"

Ara let himself in.

"Howcum?" he said.

"Howcum what"

"The door's open?"

"There're cops outside."

Ara shrugged.

"What's up?"

"There's coffee."

Ara rolled his nose.

"What you call coffee is coffee-flavored water."

"Go in and make your own."

"Cool."

Ara went into the kitchen. Looking over her computer monitor, Colene saw him frown at her selection of coffee beans. She watched him pour a handful in her Krupp grinder, then pour in another handful before pressing the top, making a swirly-grindy noise as the beans became grounds. When the water made boiling sounds, Ara reached for the filters.

He picked up the bottle of Courvoisier.

"Been drinking?" he said.

"I had it out the night Orhan was here."

Ara poured a cup of water through the grounds into a large cup.

"You got cream?"

"Skim milk."

"Forget it. I'll take it black"

Colene poured herself another cup from her pot. Ara brought his cup of black, muddy brew to the table. He took a long noisy slurp, then reached over, touched, looked at her head.

"That cut's healing nicely."

He caught her eyes with his.

"You like him, doncha?"

Colene lowered her eyes, stared into her cup.

"Yes."

"He's a neat guy."

She slammed the cup down. A brown line of coffee ringed her hand.

"Shit," she said.

"Shit?"

"Damn it, Ara," she said. "I'm feeling something I've never felt before."

"Yeah?"

"I don't know how to handle it."

Ara took another noisy slurp of coffee.

"What'd he say?" he said.

"He said he feels the same way."

"And?"

"And, we've got different lives and can't just jump into an affair."

"He said that?"

"In so many words."

"Intense," Ara said. "As long as I've known you, you've always been heavy into the career thing."

"My work's important to me."

"So's your life."

Her eyebrows knit, her mouth pursed.

"Look who's talking?" she snapped. "Mr. Solitaire Singleman himself."

Ara raised his hands, palm out.

"Hey, old buddy. I'm not giving advice to the lovelorn. Only replaying your own tune back to you."

Colene lowered her eyes.

"Sorry. That was a low blow. All I'm saying is ... I'm..."

"Confused."

Colene looked up at him.

"You never get confused?"

"Sure," Ara said. "I just don't do those kind of emotions."

Colene looked away.

"What a gift."

"I just keep busy."

"That's it," Colene said. "I'll keep busy."

Ara drained the last of the coffee from his cup, rose to his feet.

"I got a short errand to run. Be back in about a half hour."

"Go for it."

After closing the door for Ara, Colene turned back to her computer, opened her emails, scrolled through them, skimming and deleting. Then, she stopped at a flyer with an attachment announcing an international conference in Alexandria, Egypt.

She scanned through the program on Biblical Texts, opened the section on Biblical and Near Eastern Archaeology– one session jumped out at her.

Recent findings in the Levant showing Original Testament connections to the New Testament. The session was chaired by Naom Feldstein from the U. of Tel Aviv.

The name was familiar to her.

Why?

Colene raked her memory.

Nothing.

She opened her address book, then dialed Robert Jacobsen at U. of Texas.

He answered after a couple of rings.

"Bob Jacobsen."

"Bobby, it's Colene Mooney."

"Hi, Sweets," he said. "How's my favorite bible hound?"

"Hey, you going to that conference in Alexandria next month?"

"Not this year, Doll. I'm up to my ass in alligators working on our Ein Tamar collection."

"I saw a session that might be fun. Old and New Testament connections.

"Huh? Didn't know historians ever got that close to us in the dirty finger nail crowd."

"Well," said Colene, "I'm still putting some stuff together on the Q document ..."

"The Q? Wow. There's a coincidence?"

"What's a coincidence?"

"Well, Ari Feldstein's chairing that session."

"Ari? I thought the program said Naom Feldstein."

"He's Naom's brother. Ari's the big cheese at Hebrew National U. Anyway, I heard a wild rumor about the discovery of a Q text."

Colene froze, then choked.

"What kind of a rumor?"

"The kicker is someone–maybe Ari Feldstein himself–told Joel Sampierre that Ari's not only heard of it, but that he knows people who've seen it."

"That sounds like bullshit."

"Ari's a wild guy but not really a bullshitter."

"You know him?"

"Yeah. We dug together 4 summers ago in the Negev around Beersheba."

"Can you contact him?"

"It'd be impossible to get this time of year. But, he'll be chairing that session for sure."

After she cut off, Colene stared at the flyer on her monitor. It came back to her.

Ari Feldstein– one of Israel's foremost biblical archaeologists whose book on Sinai prehistory laid out conclusive evidence that the Jewish migration depicted in Exodus was likely a myth.

What did he know about the missing Q text?

Colene looked back at the flyer. She had to go.

Filing her registration and paying her fees on line, she rang another number. It rang once. A woman with a thick German accent answered,

"E and J travel."

"Heidi. This is Colene Mooney."

"Hello, Dr. Mooney."

"Is Demitria in?"

"One moment and I ring."

A pair of clicks later, a woman answered.

"Colene! It's been sooo long. How are you?

"I'm fine, Dimi. And, you?"

"Splendid. Wonderful."

"How's that handsome husband of yours?"

"O, did you hear? Kostos is Chief of Staff at New Haven Central."

"How're the boys?

"OmyGod. Yani is on the all-city soccer team."

"Fantastic."

"Oh yeah. Yorgi is doing great in his music. By the way, he's giving his senior recital at St. Joseph's Episcopal Cathedral next month. Do I send the invitation to your home or to your office?"

"Home's fine."

"So, how's your love life? When are you going to let me find some nice rich handsome Greek for you?"

"Thanks, but no, Dimi."

"OK. So, to what do I owe this wonderful call?"

"Need some travel arrangements."

"Where?"

"Alexandria."

"Alexandria! Romantic Egypt. Cool. When?"

"Early next month. First week in June."

"Fares may be a bit pricey but lemme see what I can do. All right?"

"What do you need from me?"

"Fax or email me your schedule and I'll get back to you with some numbers."

"Sounds great. How's your folks?"

"Just fine. They spoil the boys."

"Grandparents are supposed to do that."

"Well, it happens in spades with Greek grandparents."

"You were one of my best students." Colene said.

"O Colene. I was not."

"Dunno if I'll ever forgive that good looking, slick talking Greek doctor for getting you to run away with him."

"Wasn't my fault he was so sexy."

"You're forgiven."

"I'll get right back to you with the ticket info, OK?"

"Sounds great. Love you, Dimi."

"Love you too, Colene."

Colene heard the rap on the door. She opened it to Ara.

"I'm back."

"I'm going to Alexandria."

"Egypt?"

"That's where it is?"

"Why?"

"There's a conference I want to hit."

"That's dangerous."

"I've got a lead."

"Lead. Shmeed. Your ass is hanging out on this one."

"It's my ass."

"We've been through some deep shit recently..."

"I've a reliable source that might be a connection to the Q text."

"That's not worth risking your life for."

"It's what I do, Ara."

"Can we talk about this?"

"Won't change my mind but good ideas are always welcome."

Ara sighed, raised his hands, shrugged his shoulders.

"Gotta run," he said.

Colene grabbed the short, thick man, hugged him.

"Thanks for being there little brother."

"Call me anytime."

After he left, she walked back into the kitchen, her cellphone still in her hand, looked over at the lone brandy bottle at the end of the counter. Dropping the cell phone in her robe pocket, she picked up the 2 dirty cups, plopped them in the sink, filled them with tap water.

Drying her hands on a dishtowel, she turned, picked up the brandy bottle, put the clear bottle with gold writing into the cupboard, then closed the door.

No Slip-ups

Hamilton Morris's Bedroom, Charleston, SC.
1:32 AM, the next morning

The cell phone on the night stand by his bed beeped three sharp tones. Ham Morris awoke, sat up, glanced over at his sleeping pretty, blond wife next to him, snatched the phone off the receiver.

"Morris."

He heard Bax's wheezy voice.

"Sorry for the early morning reveille, soldier boy but I told you they're all over my ass."

Morris eased out of bed, tiptoed into the bathroom, eased the door shut.

"Whadya got?" he said.

"Three blue Matson containers in a commercial security facility in Portsmouth, Virginia. You ready for the reg numbers?"

Morris opened the drawer on his wife's side of the counter, took out an eyebrow liner, tore off a tissue from a dispenser, laid it out on the counter, wrote down the three numbers.

"This is vital," Bax said. "All three cans will have a handmade circle with an X in the center under the reg number. If that ain't there, the deal's queer."

"Anything else?"

"Day after tomorrow's Saturday and Sunday night they'll be down to a minimum security staff of 3. These guys won't be pros–

likely just above minimum wage rent-a-cops. Best time to show up is around 4:00 AM when they're finishing the shift."

"What about paperwork to get in?"

"I've faxed you the removal authorizations. They should just sign off and you'll be on your way."

"What about follow up inquiries?"

"It'll take at least 3 weeks just for the paperwork to go through the system. By the time the shit turns up missing, everybody'll be so busy covering their own asses, it'll get buried."

"What about the paperwork you're sending me?"

"Legal and righteous looking but total bullshit with no comebacks."

"OK, anything else pops up, get back to me fast," Morris said.

"Hey, it's your playground now," Bax said before he cut off.

Morris copied the numbers into the phone's memory, dropped the tissue into the toilet bowl, then urinated on it before he flushed it down the drain.

Slip-ups

Chesapeake Bay Security Depot, Portsmouth, VA.
3:47AM, Monday Morning.

The moonless night was warm, humid as the inside of a panting lap dog's mouth. Brigham Kimball looked out the open window of the container truck at the dark patches of weeds that swept by in the lights. Ahead, the lights of the security depot loomed out of the gloom beyond dark rows of bushy salt grass. Squinting, Kimball made out the entrance. Dim florescent lights sprayed bluish glow over a closed gate. Behind it, to his right, he spotted the guard station.

When the three trucks pulled up to the gate, Kimball stepped down, gripping a covered aluminum clipboard with the phony paperwork, walked over to the entrance. Rattling on the gate, he called out,

"Anybody there?"

Kimball saw a uniformed guard step out of the small guard shack, switch on a flashlight, peer over in his direction. Looking through the glare of the light, Kimball caught sight of a young African American in his early 30s or late 20s wearing a windbreaker with a stenciled badge over his uniform, a sidearm, a portable radio on his guard belt approach the gate.

"Yessir?" the guard said.

Kimball flashed a forged ID.

"Morning," he said. "I'm from Federal Central Authority, Norfolk. I've got orders to remove three containers deposited here to another facility."

The young man shined the light on the laminated ID Kimball held out, looked it over, then back to Kimball's face, then unlatched a portal in the gate, slid it back.

Kimball opened the clipboard, took out the papers, handed them to the guard through the opening.

The young guard scanned the papers with his light, looked back at Kimball.

"Kinda unusual making a transfer on a Sunday night."

"They call, I haul," Kimball said. "I had to get these guys outta bed to get here on time."

The guard shined his light over the 3 waiting trucks, turned back to Kimball.

"I'll have to call my central office before I can let you in."

"No problem," said Kimball. "You got any coffee in there?"

The guard glanced back at Kimball, clicked the portal shut.

"I'll be right back," he said.

From outside the gate, Kimball watched the guard call through the window of the small guard shack in the dim light of the interior. After a short exchange on the phone, the guard came back over to the gate.

"Any problems?" Kimball said

"No sir, not as long you have signed papers with the proper release codes– which you seem to have," the guard said.

Kimball signaled the 3 drivers, then watched the guard go inside to push a control button. The heavy stainless steel gate rolled back, the 3 trucks drove in.

The guard motioned Kimball to come into the guard shack. He pointed out to Kimball on a map of the facility under a plexiglass cover on the counter where they were.

"Proceed down this lane, turn right past the first building marked 10-D. Keep going past the next two buildings and you'll see a stack of containers. You'll have to find the ones you want but all the numbers are visible and the cans're all accessible," the guard said.

"Sounds easy enough," Kimball said.

"There's a roving patrol," he said. "I've already let them know you're in the area."

Signaling the drivers, Kimball climbed in the passenger side of the first truck. The three rigs moved out down the lane through a warren of long single storey tin buildings where insects hovered in the cyanic glare of the ubiquitous arc lights set at each corner.

Kimball's nose stung from the acrid stink of ozone emitted by the lamps, his eyes adjusting to the dark lane as the trucks' headlights probed the shadows of the predawn night.

When they passed the third long building, the first driver spotted the stacked containers back by an enclosed area. Kimball along with his team of three drivers and two assistants, got out, checked the reg numbers on the sea containers.

"Never mind the 20 footers," Kimball said. "We're looking for 3 40s"

They went up row after row but none of the numbers on the few 16 foot containers they found matched.

One of the relief drivers, a tall man named Harris came up to Kimball.

"Is this all of 'em, Sir?" he said.

"Don't know," Kimball said. "Hope to hell we're not on a fool's errand."

They walked around, shined their lights on each one, checked the numbers against their list.

"Shit," Harris said. "I think we got sold one."

Kimball walked over to the separate enclosure behind the stacks of containers. Seeing the swing gate was secured with a lock, he shined his light into the compound. At the back of a building, he spotted the dull paint of 3 large ocean containers. He turned to Harris.

"I think I've found 'em."

"So howcum they got'em locked up" Harris said.

Kimball didn't answer. He reached down, looked at the massive chain and lock made from high test, alloyed steel.

"Should I go back and get that guard to open this up?" Harris said .

"That'd be a waste of both our time," Kimball said "Get the torch outta the cab."

While Harris ran to the truck to get the portable acetylene torch, Kimball called out to the others.

"Fan out. Keep an eye out for that roving patrol."

Harris lit the torch, adjusted the flame, cut the lock, pulled open the gate. The trucks drove through, backed up to the three containers. Kimball checked out the numbers, saw the hand-painted circles with Xs in them. Everything matched.

The drivers had all three containers loaded up in less than 15 minutes, then rolled back out. Kimball closed the gate, rearranged the chain, hooked the stub of the cut lock through the links, making it appear like a secure closure.

When they rolled up to the main gate, the young guard walked to the first truck, shined his light on the container, turned back to Kimball.

"You're not authorized to remove those containers," he said.

Kimball climbed down from the cab with the papers, showed them to the guard.

"I have complete authorization to remove these containers. It's all right here in the paper work."

He pointed to the numbers.

"See these are the bin numbers and my orders are to remove these containers tonight. This is a priority ..."

"No way," the guard said.

Pulling up his clipboard, he showed Kimball a paper with a blue stamp.

"My orders are not to release these containers without confirmation from my headquarters."

"Hold on," Kimball said. "I've already given you the authorized release forms ..."

"No," the guard said. "You only showed me standard release forms. These containers require a special ATF form which you don't have. You'll have to wait until I get authorization from my supervisor."

A pick-up with more security guards pulled up at that moment. Kimball saw one had a radio in his hand when he bailed out of the pick-up, rushed over to the younger guard.

"Hold those guys right there, Mike," the guard said. "They cut a lock and entered the high security zone. I called in and Central said to hold these guys here until the military police team arrives."

The young guard, Mike stepped back, dropped his hand to his side arm.

Kimball shook his head, raised his hands, turned around.

"More damn delays," he said. "Now, how long is this gonna take?"

The guard Mike dropped the clipboard, drew his side arm, leveled it at Kimball.

"As long as necessary," he said. "Now, show me your hands."

Motioning with the palms of his hands extended in front of him, Kimball, stepped forward.

"OK, officer Mike. I know you're just doing your job and we're gonna cooperate. This is obviously just a simple misunderstanding. Some bureaucrat didn't sign a paper he shoulda and ..."

Kimball spun, lashed his foot out in a side kick, his heel catching Mike just below the sternum. Kimball watched him fall to the ground clutching his stomach. The two other guards grabbed for their sidearms but Kimball's team had piled out of the cabs of the trucks with automatic weapons.

"Drop 'em!" Harris yelled. "On your knees. Hands on heads."

Both of the guards dropped their pistols, fell to their knees, laced their fingers behind their heads.

Kicking the young guard's pistol away out of his reach, Kimball shook his head.

"Rent-a-cops," he said. "Go home and play some more paintball."

Harris with two other men jerked the 2 guards from their knees, shoved them into the guard shack. Still clutching his belly, Mike stumbled toward his kicked-away pistol. Kimball spun again, kicked him in the ribs with the instep of his boot– the young guard fell, groaned, rolled over on his side. Kimball kicked the pistol into the weeds along the fence.

Pointing out the switch for the gate to Harris, Kimball hollered,

"Get it open."

Harris opened the gate, Kimball waved him through. When the third truck cleared the gate, he turned to go.

Kimball heard the pop of two shots, felt a stabbing hot pain, lost his breath, fell to his knees. Two more reports—he felt two other hot bolts of pain strike him in the back, as he looked back. The young guard, Mike crouched behind the fence, the cuff of his pant leg still stuck on the edge of his ankle holster.

Kimball heard a burst of automatic fire, then saw Mike jerk, fall backward, sprawl motionless on the ground. Then, Kimball felt himself being dragged, loaded into the truck by Harris and someone else.

Kimball felt his chest—looked at his hands. They were red, wet.

Everything faded to black.

Aftershock

Hamilton Morris's home, Charleston, SC
10:05 AM, Sunday morning.

When he pulled his bleeping iPhone from the stand on his desk, Morris saw the call from a secure number in his 4Sinc network.

"Morris."

"Sir, Harris. Third mobile unit."

"Where's Brig?"

"We have a problem, Sir."

"Go on."

"Col. Kimball's down, Sir."

Morris froze.

"Down?" he said.

"Yessir. Lost him in this morning's operation."

"How in the hell.... wait. You're sure he's ..."

"Yessir. Died in my arms."

"Fuck."

Morris set the phone down, looked around the room, rubbed his head before he picked it up.

"What's the present situation?"

"All secure, Sir. The colonel was the only casualty. We're in route with the containers to the deployment area now."

"Did you have to shoot your fucking way outta there?"

"No Sir. A red-hot rent-a-cop got a lucky shot and took out the Colonel."

"OK, Harris. You know the drill. See it gets done."

"Wilco, Sir."

Morris stared at the iPhone in his hand, resisting the urge to hurl it against the wall. It went off again.

"Morris."

Bax's wheezing voice came on.

"What kind of a cluster fuck operation are you running?"

"What do you mean?"

"I give you a piece of cake removal and you send in a bunch of cowboys who shoot up the place."

"I don't have the details but I lost a damn good man,"

"Man, this whole operation has turned to shit. Those cans are on a high alert list now."

"Don't worry about that. Where I got 'em, they'll never find 'em."

"Don't be so fucking sure."

"They'll be out of the country before the end of the week."

"You'd better hope so. If they grab my ass, yours is next."

"Keep your fucking shirt on, Bax. I said I got it under control.

"That ain't too comforting coming after the way you bungled this one."

Morris squeezed the iPhone after Bax clicked off. He stepped over to the window, crossed his arms across his chest, looked down on his yard.

After staring out at the trees surrounding his lawn for a while, he punched a number in the iPhone.

It rang.

"Steele, Sir."

"I need you. Shut down what you're doing and get back here immediately."

"Problems, Sir?"

"Yeah, Kimball's gone."

"He left, Sir?"

"No. He's dead."

"Dead!"

"That's what I said."

"How ..."

"Don't wanna go into it now, Gregg. Shut down and get back here, now.

"Yessir."

"Any kickback on those hajjis?"

"As I said, I hauled off the meat when the cop guy took 'em out. He was slick."

"OK. Close it up and get back."

"What about the twat?"

"Fuck her."

"Love to."

"Get your ass back here now, Gregg."

Morris clicked off the iPhone again, tossed it on the table and sat down behind his desk.

A Rare Coin

Orhan's house, Ankara, Turkey
The next day, 9:15 AM

The connections on Orhan's laptop dragged across the monitor. He glanced at his watch. His meeting with the Minister was in an hour.

His email box popped up online. Scanning through the received traffic, a message in Arabic jumped into view.

Salim Habib, his counterpart in Syria, had collared a fence with a trove of coins– one, a first century rarity. Alerted by Orhan's report of the theft and murder at the University, Salim wondered if this coin might be part of the stolen collection.

Orhan popped his cell phone open, punched in a number.

"This is Col. Mehmet. May I be connected to Dr. Zarakolu?"

A moment later, Mübeccel's voice came on.

"Col. Mehmet. To what honor do I owe for this call?"

"A possible lead," Orhan replied. "My colleague in Syria came across a suspicious coin. Is there any way to find out if it could be one of those stolen at the time of the murder?"

"Yes. We know lots more about the coins than the text– which is why I went to Foucault in the first place."

"Can you give me some idea about what to look for?"

"Camila Ogan on our faculty's an amazing artist and a leading authority on that period's coinage. She made sketches of the collection."

"Would she have anything she could lend me to verify these coins in Syria?"

"I'd be astonished if she didn't. She'll be in this afternoon. Can you come by then?"

"Perfect. Thank you, Dr. Zarakolu."

"It's Mübeccel, Colonel."

"Of course."

~*~~*~

The meeting with the Minister went well. The feedback from the debriefing Orhan had given the CIA was very positive. Pleased with the results, the Minister hung on every word when Orhan recounted the attack by the Arabs in Connecticut.

"I've news on that," His Excellency said. "Our American friends inform me they recovered three bodies dumped in a 'landfill,' whatever in the hell that is, and have identified them from their terrorist watch list."

Orhan shook his head. "So, why did whoever removed the bodies leave me alive?"

The Minister shrugged.

"Allaah knows but doesn't reveal."

"It doesn't make sense," Orhan told the Minister.

"I'm also informed the postmortem on the bodies reveals you acquitted yourself as a true son of Turkey."

"More luck than skill."

The Minister rose.

"You're too modest, Orhan. We're proud of you."

~*~~*~

Orhan found the office of Dr. Camila Organ, the archaeological artist at the University. His knock at the door prompted a mumbled response.

"Don't break it down. It's not locked."

Stepping into a well-lit office, a panoply of sketches, renderings and drawings assaulted his vision. Drawings of skulls, tools, coins, baskets, pottery lined every available wall space of the office. Even more sketches sprawled over a table-top in the center of the room.

Behind the table to one side, a tall sketch board on an easel loomed up in front of a wide, uncurtained sunlit window. A woman poked her head from behind the sketch board, gawked at Orhan, then raised her eyebrows.

"Well, the famous Col. Mehmet comes to call," she said.

The speaker's large dark brown eyes, raven black hair were framed in a face with a large, well-formed nose, prominent cheekbones. She dropped her brush into a tray, stood, wiped her hands on a cloth, looking Orhan over with a slight smile.

An unbuttoned, open, much paint-stained lab coat revealed a dark purple silk blouse open at the throat. A gold coin dangled from a ring on a thin gold chain in the cleft of her décolletage.

She motioned to a chair at one end of the table.

"Sit," she said. "I'll make tea."

Orhan made a conscious effort not to stare at the attractive woman. But, she made no such effort, kept looking back at him.

Orhan cleared his throat, said, "Dr. Zarakolu said you might be able to show me some examples of first century coins, as I. ..."

She interrupted.

"Mübeccel's already explained."

"Could you possibly ...?"

She cut him off again.

"I did see the coins and have made sketches. I'll show you what I have."

She filled an electric water kettle at a sink at one end of her office. She tilted her head, looked back at Orhan. The same small smile hung on her lips.

"I'm Camila, by the way," she said.

Orhan stood, extended his hand.

"Please call me Orhan."

She stepped over, took his hand, looked into his eyes, murmured,

"A pleasure."

She then turned, picked up a pile of sketches, looked through them, brought some of them to Orhan.

"There were 12 coins in the collection," she said. "These sketches are what they looked like."

"Did you make these sketches from a photograph?" Orhan said.

"The one in my mind and inner eye," she replied. "I have a rather photographic memory."

Orhan sucked in his breath at the detail of the sketches.

"These are amazing."

She leaned over, her face next to his.

"As you can see, there were three types. The large one is a *stater* with an impression of Athena on one side and the owl on the other. It was common to that region. Likely minted from a mold created in Athens. Coins of this type were still in wide use in various forms up into the third and fourth centuries. The 5 smaller ones are *tetradrachm* with the head of the governor of a local *polis*, or political region. The other 6 are *decadrachm*."

"Valuable?"

Camila stood up, shook her long hair.

"Quite. Collectors would go for the *stater*, as it's the rarest of the bunch."

"What would be the going price?"

She shrugged, then leaned over next to Orhan, her face nearly touching his..

"It's in fairly decent condition," she said. "Maybe $50,000 US."

"And, the rest?"

"My guess would about $16 to $18 thousand US for the rest."

She remained close, her cheek only a few inches from Orhan's face. He smelled her perfume, heard her breathing. He cleared his throat again.

"May I take these to have copies made?"

She looked over at him as he stared at the sketches.

"Take them. The originals are in my head."

The tea kettle whistled. She swung back to the little table by the sink at the end of the room, poured hot water into two small glasses with tea leaves. She looked back at him again, the same small smile playing on her mouth.

"What do you take in your tea?" she said. "I've honey, sugar or mint."

"Mint would be fine."

She raised her eyebrows.

"No sweetness?"

"Just mint."

She stirred the tea, then brought the glasses over in cup holders.

"How long have you been a policeman?" she said.

"I try not to think of myself as a policeman—more of a coordinator."

She drew a chair up near him, then sat, her knee touching his.

"Your reputation precedes you, Orhan."

"Whatever that means," Orhan said.

He frowned at the glass, watching the leaves swirl, clot, then settle at the bottom of the glass.

She sipped from her glass.

"I read of your tragedy."

"I try not to think of it."

"But, that's impossible, isn't it?"

"Only if you let it haunt your thoughts."

"Does it bother you for me to talk to you this way?"

Orhan raised his eyes, met hers.

"I don't let much bother me these days," he said.

She sipped her tea without taking her eyes from his face.

"You're an amazing man, Col. Mehmet."

Orhan shook his head, sipped his tea.

"Not really. This tea is excellent, by the way."

She leaned back, propped her head against her hand, the small smile broadening.

"I'm glad it pleases you."

Orhan drained the tea from the glass, sat it on the table, picked up the sketches, then stood.

"Thank you, Dr. Ogan for the loan of these sketches. I will return them when I'm back."

She stood too, took his extended hand.

"I look forward to it," she said.

~*~~*~

Returning to his office, Orhan found the note that Colene had called.

He looked at his watch. 5:00PM.

He called Colene's office number.

She answered at the first ring.

"Colene Mooney."

"It's Orhan."

"I'm so glad you called. I've made a decision."

"A decision?"

"I'm going to a conference in Alexandria."

"What? Whatever for?"

"I've learned there'll be a guy there who just might know something about the codex."

"Colene. That's not worth risking your life for."

"I'm not worried. I'll be at the main convention center near the University."

"Egypt's dangerous. And, Alexandria's damned dangerous."

"I'll be OK. I can take care of myself."

Orhan pressed his lips together, said nothing.

A long pause, then she spoke,

"Are you still there?"

"Colene. Please don't go."

"I have to."

"You don't."

"I knew you'd say that. That's what Ara said too."

"He's right."

"I understand your concerns– but, this is something that I have to do."

Orhan drew a deep breath.

"I can't argue with you. But, this proposed adventure sets off every alarm in my head."

"I understand, Orhan. I do. I wish I could tell you how I feel about you but I'm not sure. Whatever I'd say would certainly be wrong."

"I know how I feel about you, Colene. I've been denying it to myself ever since I left you. I've lost those I've loved before. I don't think I could go through it again."

"I can't tell you how much it means to me. But, I've got to do this. All I can promise is to be extra careful."

"I wish in my heart of hearts that you not go. But, call me and I'll come. No matter where you are."

"I will, sweet man. Thanks for not trying to lay a guilt trip on me."

"I would, if I thought it would have even a small chance of success."

Roses have Thorns

Colene's House, New Haven, CT
The next day, 9:25 PM

After pulling on levis, a sweat shirt, running shoes, Colene drew aside the curtain in her bedroom, peered out the window.

The street light reflected off the window of the unmarked police car parked across the street like a black stone on an expensive onyx cufflink in the moonless night. Spotting the headlights of Ara's car coming down the street, she ran downstairs.

Colene stepped out, locked the door, then flinched when she climbed into Ara's car.

"Why're all these potato chip bags all over the floor?" she said.

Ignoring the remark, Ara pulled away from the curb.

"Delighted to see you too, Dr. Mooney. I'm cooking dinner tonight."

Ara kept looking back in the mirror as they drove down the street.

"Whatcha looking for?" Colene said.

"Our friend that's been tailing us for months."

Colene looked back.

"I don't see anybody," she said.

"'Cause whoever it was isn't there anymore."

She wrinkled her eyebrows at him.

"Are you sure?"

"Sometimes I'd see a shadow of a van or an SUV hanging back, just out of sight," Ara said. "It'd be there, for a second, then, poof! Gone."

"You're not imagining it?"

"You forget. I don't imagine."

Colene didn't say another word until they arrived at Ara's "Batcave."

~*~~*~

Plopped in a comfortable chair, her foot dangling over the arm, Colene sipped a glass of Spanish Rioja *vino tinto* from a deep, stemmed glass, watched Ira cooking steaks on a small Weber barbecue kettle. He had arranged two sirloin tips over the coals and the smoke exuded meaty, garlicky smells from the vent holes. Two russet potatoes sat beside the steaks, baking their hearts out.

Ara put the finishing touches to a salad of cherry tomatoes, baby spinach leaves and artichoke hearts, sprinkled with a tiny bit of garlic feta, garnished with Spanish Olive oil, a tiny bit of crushed lemon mint, topped with juice from a blood orange.

"How do you come up with all these fancy meals?"

"Just basic food– the way us Armenians eat."

"Hah."

"You should see my mother. Now, there's someone who can cook."

"I know your mother, Ara."

He raised his eyes, looked over at her.

"Dinner's ready," he said.

After they'd eaten, Ara served a small scoop of frozen sweet cream speckled with vanilla bits on top of a lemon cookie. He'd swirled a thin string of dark chocolate and Armagnac on top, then poured three fingers of Champagne cognac into a snifter.

Colene took hers to the big overstuffed chair as Ara put on Rodrigo's *Aranjuez*, then slid in next to her.

"OK. Out with it," Colene said.

Ara shrugged.

"From where I sit, you're going to Egypt's a done deal."

Colene squinted her eyes at him.

"Hey, Dr. Agajanian. I know you. You don't give up that easy."

"Not a question of giving up, Colene. More like acceptance."

"You and Orhan don't approve."

"Orhan and I don't live your life."

"But, you don't approve."

"Here. Let me freshen your cognac," he said

Ara poured about a half inch into her snifter. She took a deep sniff, followed it with a slurpy sip.

"This stuff is amazing. It's kinda bitter but it still grows on you."

Ara laughed.

"Yeah. All we need now is a good cigar to finish it off."

Colene made a face then looked over at him.

"You know, I'm getting to like that Orhan."

"I've noticed."

"Doesn't bother you, does it. I mean, me talking about him?"

"Why should it bother me? I like the guy."

"Well, I just like the guy... he's very sexy... and ..."

She leaned back, closed her eyes. A feeling, a want to curl up and sleep, come over her. Conscious, she fought the curtain closing around her.

I can't just doze off.

An awareness of Ara reaching over, taking the snifter from her hand, arranging her on the chair.

Then, some funny business with her pants– like the time when she was 6, she showed her genitalia to her little brother, his eyes wide, his saying,

"Where'd it go,' Leen?' "

He always called her "Leen."

Still did.

But, Ara?

It made her smile.

Ara was like her little brother. Serious, but so sweet.

The other girls in the house teased him, but always lined up to have him help with their homework.

Some scratchy feeling.

Ara.

Socially, a robot.

That's what the other girls called him—not her.

Ara had a heart of Gold.

Like her brothers.

The Mooney Mob.

That's what their neighbor old Mrs. Shagrew called them.

Colene, the ring leader.

Her family— old Uncle Tom Moran.

So severe, so argumentative.

Was he the one who got her interested in bible studies?

Yes. An outspoken atheist, defrocked Jesuit priest– a communist, some said– but, always challenging her to think.

Thomas Francis Moran. From Northern Ireland.

A shadowing curtain was sliding around her. Thoughts, thinking wandered, tangled up in convoluted dreams.

~*~~*~

Colene woke with a start, caught her breath, looked around.

She was curled up like a cat in the overstuffed chair.

Ara was wiping dishes and putting them away.

"Oh, shit," she said. "I musta fell asleep."

"So, you did."

"Ara. I'm sorry..."

"For what? Taking a nap? No biggie."

"What time is it?"

"About 2:30."

"In the morning?"

"Damn sure ain't afternoon."

She stumbled to her feet.

"Ara. I gotta go. I got things... oh, crap. Tomorrow, I've got all kinds of ..."

Ara tossed the dishtowel to one side. He picked up his keys.

"Let's go," he said.

~*~~*~

When they approached the house, Colene put her hand on Ara's arm.

"I don't want those cops to see me staggering to the door."

"I'll walk you to the door."

"That's just as bad," she snapped. "Come up the alleyway. I'll go in through the back."

"Did you forget that you chain-locked your back gate?"

"Rat's ass. I did."

"Do you have the keys?"

"No. But, hey. I know what. I can step over my neighbor's fence. There's a low spot where I can climb over into my yard."

"Doesn't sound too good to me."

"Here. Let me out."

Colene climbed out, staggered to her neighbor's fence, belly-rolled over, landing on the pebble-covered walkway that ran around their back yard. She stood up, wove side to side, then waved at Ara.

He waved back at her but didn't move.

Colene turned to the low spot in the fence into her yard, stepped on the horizontal brace board, heaved herself over into her yard, tumbled down butt-first into a rose bush.

"Shit!" she said. "Forgot about that damn rosebush."

Ara got out of his car, came over, stood on the runner of her neighbor's side of the fence, looking down at her.

"You OK?" he said.

Colene twisted herself to her feet out of the rose bush, glared back at him.

"I'm alright. Just scratched from asshole to appetite."

"Need help?"

"No I'm fine."

She stumbled toward her back door, picking thorns out of her butt, back, arms, got to the back door, fumbled with her key. When she opened it, she turned, glared at Ara still watching over the fence.

"Go home, Ara. I'm going in and take a bath."

Another Link

Ministry of Interior Affairs, Damascus, Syria
A week later, 9:40 AM

The long halls and tall ceilings of the old building echoed the clock-clock of Orhan's shoe heels on the tile floor as he headed toward the offices of the Investigative Division of the Syrian Secretariat of Antiquities and National Treasures. Entering the office, he saw a dark, dour woman in a hejjab sitting at her desk behind the counter who looked up, shot him a scowl.

"Yes?" she said,

Orhan smiled at her Druze accent, showed her his Interpol carnet.

"Col. Orhan Mehmet," he said. "I believe Minister Habib's expecting me."

Without changing her expression, the Druze woman nodded, motioned for Orhan to sit, then disappeared into a rabbit's warren of glassed-in offices behind her.

Less than a minute when the unsmiling woman came back with Salim Habib right behind her. Her duty done, she ignored both men, went back to her desk.

Habib stepped through the counter doors, grasped Orhan's hand, kissed him on the side of his mouth.

"Welcome, welcome back to Damascus," he said.

"Glad to be here, Salim."

"Come," Salim said. "First some tea and then on to business."

He turned to the scowling woman.

"Fatma. I'll be tied up all morning. Call me on my cell, if I'm needed."

She nodded, without looking up.

When they walked out the door, Salim laughed.

"She's a talker, that one."

"Friendly as a hyena too," Orhan said.

Salim, a big man, Orhan's height but with bright blue eyes, graying blond and reddish skin that bespoke his Circassian Caucasus mountains origins. Dressed in a bright blue, white-pinstriped suit with a rose bud tacked to his lapel, a long red scar ran down the left side of his face, from his hair line to his close-shaved chin.

He patted Orhan's back.

"You old Turkish dog," he said. "I've missed you, you know."

"How so?"

"The old days. Chasing thieves down alleyways like in the movies. Hours spent going over files. Beating your butt out on the shooting range..."

"Now, that part, I don't remember," Orhan said.

"It's a lie. But, that's how I prefer to remember it."

They left the building, walked to a tea shop a few blocks away, took an outside table.

Salim signaled the waiter, took out a small silver cigar case, offered one to Orhan.

After Orhan refused with a wave of his hand, Salim selected one, returned the case to his inner pocket, extracted a long match, he spoke in a low voice while doing a lighting ritual.

"A few days ago, one of my snitches turned a big buy of early Levantine coins," he said. "I remembered your wire about the theft at the University and I gaveit a bit of extra attention. There's a ring we've been tracking for some time and this snatch looked especially good."

"Is this the Lebanese network?"

"No. It's an Israeli group working out of Cairo."

"Ah, the stolen cartouches from the Luxor depository."

"The same bastards. So, we set up a fake buy and *voilà*! We land a fat one."

"Oh?"

"A Persian. He's a long timer on the scene. Came across his tracks but we never seemed to get a glimpse of him, but when he went in for the buy, we nailed his ass."

"Iranian?"

"Turns out, he's not part of the Cairo group. Strictly freelance."

"So, where'd he get the coins?"

"Won't say. He's been very cagey about protecting his sources. Too, he knows we've not got a lot to nail him with so he's looking to walk away with a fine and stay in business."

"Do you have the coins?"

Salim reached for the inner pocket of his suit, took out a leather wallet, opened it, took out a large coin then handed it to Orhan.

"This is it."

Orhan held it, looked at it, then put it away when an attendant appeared with two glasses of tea and sweet pastries. The two men turned their attention the tea with the Syrian version of baklava in a circular nest of paper thin filo dough with crushed pistachios, almonds, walnuts and honey, seasoned with powdered cardamom, cinnamon and ginger.

When the attendant cleared the plates, Orhan took out the coin along with a copy of Camila's drawing of the stolen coins.

He pointed it out to Salim.

"See, it's the *stater.* The archaeologist who made this drawing told me it could be worth up to 50K US."

Salim gave a small whistle.

"Damn. Honesty sucks, my brother. Think how we could dispose of 50K split two ways."

Orhan didn't take his eyes from the coin.

"Just evidence, Salim," he said.

Salim took another puff on his cigar, smashed it in the ashtray, looked up at Orhan.

"How do you want to handle this?" Salim said.

Putting the drawing back in his pocket, Orhan handed the coin back to Salim.

"Let me talk to him," he said.

"Be my guest," Salim said.

~*~~*~

Orhan sat at a able in the center of an interview room in the National Prison. He placed the coin and the drawing on the table top in front of him.

He looked up when a burly uniformed guard brought a man in to the table, told him to sit, then took a chair by the door.

The man was in his late thirties with large eyes, smooth olive skin. He glanced at the coin, then at the drawing before looking straight at Orhan with no fear.

Orhan spoke to him in Farsi.

"I'm Orhan, Mr. Hoshkar."

Parvez Hoshkar flinched, then blinked. The Farsi was unexpected.

"You speak Farsi," he said.

"A lot of people do," Orhan said.

Parvez nodded, not taking his eyes from Orhan's face.

"No games, Parvez," Orhan said. "Tell me where you got this coin and I'll do what I can to get you off with a minimum of loss."

"What coin?"

Orhan tapped the *stater*.

"This one."

Hoshkar shrugged.

"They were part of a lot I got from a dealer in Cairo."

Orhan looked at him without blinking for nearly a full minute.

"Bullshit," he said.

Hoshkar closed his eyes, raised his hands, shrugged his shoulders, said,

"Look, you may not..."

Orhan interrupted.

"I said no games. I meant no games. You're a businessman. I'm a businessman. Let's talk business and cut the bullshit."

Hoshkar sat back, folded his arms, stared at Orhan.

"So, talk business."

"This coin is just so much capital to you. However, to me, it's a connection. A connection to a theft and a murder which connects to the sale of drugs, firearms and international terrorism. You're a businessman—apolitical. So am I. I'm a cop. We're in the same business. You sell things people want. I capture bad guys. Since what you sell involves bad guys, our interests overlap We really don't much give a shit about each other, now do we?"

Hoshkar listened, tapping his finger on his arm.

"Go on," he said.

Orhan tapped the *stater* again.

"Where did you get this?"

Hoshkar stared at the coin, then looked back at the unblinking Orhan.

"Cairo."

"Who from?"

"This goes no further?"

Orhan nodded.

"Name's Ali. Operates outta Dubai."

"Ali what?"

"All I know him as is "Ali, from Dubai."

"How'd you contact him?"

Hoshkar stared at Orhan.

"You know, my Turkish friend. I've been doing all the talking. I'm also aware that when you're done asking me questions, that rock ape by the door is going to take me back to the same cell where I was before you came in."

"Business involves expenses, risks. You invest, try to make a little profit."

"I don't spend without some assurances of the risks. And, I don't invest without some collateral backing me up."

Orhan folded his hands, leaned forward, his elbows at the table.

"I told you, no games," he said. "You tell me where I can find this Ali and you walk today."

"In the classic literature, not of your culture or mine, they call it *quid pro quo.*"

Orhan pulled his cell phone from his pocket, punched in a number.

"Salim," he said. "I'm making an agreement with Mr. Hoshkar. He'll give me some interesting tourist information about Dubai and you'll accommodate him with a one-way trip to Tehran. That agreeable? Fine. I'll pass him the phone and you can share the good news."

Orhan handed the cell to Hoshkar who took it.

"Hello. OK. Agreed. When? Your word is good enough, Mr. Minister."

Hoshkar handed the cell phone back to Orhan.

"In Dubai there's a night club called 'The Pasha's Paradise,' " he said. "There's a corner at one end of the hall, near a small bar where they play cards. Ali's always there on Thursday nights."

"What's he look like?"

"Yemenite. Small, dark. Always wears a cream yellow panama, a white suit and a bright yellow bow tie."

"Anything else?"

"A Rolex Oyster the size of a clam shell and a diamond ring with a stone the size of my fingernail."

~*~~*~

Salim sat beside Orhan in the United Emirate Airline's VIP departure lounge waiting for the call for the flight to Dubai. Salim jiggled the ice in his scotch.

"I wish I could get you to stay over for a day or so."

"Duty calls," Orhan said.

Salim shook his head.

"How'd you get that damn rug merchant to turn around so fast?"

"I just told him, I don't play games."

"The guard told me you talked to him in Farsi."

"True."

"Where in the hell did you learn Farsi?"

"I worked in Iran for a year and a half."

"I remember now. You were on some international wrestling team."

"That was my connection. I was in the military at the time and was supposed to keep my eyes open."

Salim laughed.

"A bloody spy. Orhan, you'll never stop surprising me."

"Not a spy, Salim. Just an observant student of the art of grappling."

An attractive woman in a UEA uniform came over and spoke to Orhan in Turkish,

"Effendi Colonel. They are ready to board first class now."

Orhan and Salim stood and embraced each other.

"My thanks for the upgrade," Orhan said. "I usually fly steerage."

"Our grateful response for ridding our jails of Persian undesirables."

Orhan followed the flight attendant to the exit, then looked back, waved at Salim.

"I'll be in touch," he said.

A Change of Plans

Starbucks, 5th Avenue and Jefferson Davis Boulevard, Columbia, SC
Thursday, A week later, 3:30 PM

After collecting his cappuccino at the counter, Morris took a chair at a small table in the back near the restrooms. A door to the side entrance separated his table from the others, giving some privacy.

Having shed his shooting glasses for a pair of dark wrap-around shades, Morris appeared to gawk at an advertising newspaper print hand-out while peering from the corner of his eyes, scanning the customers.

A man in a maroon beret with a dark blue and white stripped tee shirt sat at a table at the other end of the dining area poking at his iPad.

Two older men sat nearby chatting in what Morris guessed to be Romanian.

A heavy-set woman in a tight dress flopped down on an overstuffed chair nearby the two men, talking on her cellphone, waving her bright-red fingernail polished hand holding a large, whipped cream topped mocha.

Then, Morris spotted Gregg Steele breeze in through the door. He shot a glance at Morris, strode to the counter, ordered a "regular coffee," then came over, sat down at Morris's table.

"What's up, Sir?" Steele said.

"As I told you, Brig Kimball bought it."

Steele blinked, stared at Morris.

"How'd he buy it?" he said.

"Some paintball playing rent-a-cop got a lucky shot."

Steele made a noisy slurp.

"No body armor?"

Morris snarled.

"It wasn't a fucking combat zone, Gregg. It was supposed to be a low profile removal."

Steele sucked in a deep slurp.

"That's too bad."

Morris shot him a glance through the dark shades.

"I see it breaks your fucking heart."

Steele stared over his cup at him.

"Why're you on my case, sir? I wasn't there."

"You hated Brig."

"We weren't close..."

Morris rustled the paper, dropped his head, murmured,

"He was good, Gregg. A great logistics and operations man."

Steele set down the paper cup down on the table, looked up at Morris.

"If he was so fucking good howcum he's so fucking dead?" he said. "And how did he get his ass nailed by an amateur?"

Morris turned his head, looked out the window.

"Let's drop it."

He changed his tone.

"You did some fine work on the girl, Gregg."

"Just doin' my job, sir."

"So, how'd we leave it?"

"I've got a local guy monitoring the phone bugs. She's no threat. She's got a crazy boyfriend with a wild car that gave me the slip a few times but, he's no worry either."

"So, what happened with the hajjis?"

"Strange. The chick and her burley boyfriend meet some big dark guy in a suit at a restaurant. When they go out to their car, these 3 sheet-caps jump out, throw down on the 2 guys and grab her."

Steele leaned closer, lowered his voice, went on,

"The suit had the moves– pounds a towelhead holding a pistol in his face, turns the guy's hand, shoots the other camel jockey pounding on the boyfriend then takes out the 3rd dude– all with the first guy's gun."

"Sounds like a pro."

"All the fucking way. He 'tween-the-eyeballed the one holding the gal while he was holding a blade to her throat with no hesitation. Gotta be a cop or military."

"What happened then?"

"Well, the chick got cut. The boyfriend takes her off in his car, leaving the suit with the dead hajjis. Now, I don't want this to get international, so I slipped up, popped the suit with a sap, tossed the hajji-trash in the back of the van, took 'em to the dump."

"What happened then?"

"Dunno, sir. When I get back, there were cops all over the place, so I backed off."

"Smart. So, who's this suit?"

"Not clear. Think he's from Turkey."

"Turkey?"

"Yeah. Picked that up from her phone tap."

Morris shook his head.

"OK," he said. "I'm sure the Network's got their money's worth outta this. Sounds like a royal gang-bang to me."

"What's next, Sir."

"I want you in Egypt when the cans arrive."

"You call and I haul, sir."

"Check in with me tomorrow. I'll have all the necessary shit together for you."

Steele stood, drained the coffee, crinkled the cup in his hand.

"I am sorry about Kimball," he said.

Morris didn't look up from the paper in his hand.

"Right," he said. "I know how you love Mormons and marines."

The Panic Button

New London, CT, on the way to the Airport
The next week, 4:15 AM

The old Mercury's big V-8 growled as it ripped along the turnpike dodging in and out of clusters of spotted early morning commute traffic. Behind the wheel, Ara Khachatur Agajanian, MD, Sc.D, Ph.D., and several master's degrees, scanned the extra wide rear view mirrors for tails or cops. Beside him in the passenger seat, Colene leaned over, tapped the speedometer.

"Slow down, Ara," she said. "It's going to be close enough making this flight without getting your butt hauled over for speeding."

Seeing her little speech had no effect, Colene scowled at Ara's smile.

"I'm watching for cops," he said.

"Right."

Colene looked away, out the window.

"I called Mary Rich," she said.

"Who?"

"The FBI agent I told you about. She'd called my brother Danny."

Ara gave a quiet snort through a tight-lipped smile, squeezed the noisy Merc between a blue commuter van full of staring people, then passed a cabbie wearing a Sikh's turban.

"Don't say it, Ara."

"Say what?"

"You know."

Turning her head, she frowned out the window until they rolled into the airport's entrance.

Ara wheeled up to an empty space at American Airline's drop-off, scrambled out, leaving the Mercury idling, stepped back, drug out her suitcase from the trunk of his car.

Ignoring her objections, Ara carried it to the sidewalk, dropped it, yanked up the handle.

When Colene stepped up to hug him, he thrust a cell phone into her hand.

"A phone?" she said.

"A satellite phone."

"I don't need this. I have my ..."

Ara interrupted.

"This is a new Thuraya. I've programmed it to stay in constant contact. Now before you get all protesty, I want to show you something. This phone can call from anywhere in the world and be on my screen in nanoseconds. Very important. If you push the 1 and the 4 buttons together twice, it sends an alarm. I forwarded the codes to the consular office and the embassy."

"Kind of an international 911."

"You could say that."

"You think of everything. I love you, Ara."

"The feelings are reciprocated."

She hugged him, kissed him on the cheek, then grabbed the handle of her suitcase, swung her purse, along with her laptop case over her shoulder, walked to the terminal entrance. As she turned to step through the automatic doors, Colene saw Ara's reflection in the window, standing on the curb, watching her go inside.

She got in line at the international flights check-in, then looked back.

Ara was gone.

Now, just an empty space loomed at the curb where he had parked to drop her off.

She stared at it until a car pulled in to drop off passengers.

The Alexandria Connection

Dubai, UAE, International Airport
The next day, 2:15 PM

A steaming hot wool blanket of humid heat wrapped itself over Orhan like a wet, sticky net as he exited the air conditioned airport to find a cab. Inside the new Mercedes, air conditioning gushed welcome relief.

The Pakistani driver asked in Urdu-laced Arabic for the destination. Orhan told him to go to the Ministry of Internal Affairs, then settled back in the plush seat as the cabbie made a honking entrance into the stream of traffic.

"*Ya Sayed*, you're from Syria?" the driver said.

"Turkey."

"Ah, yes. Turkey. I've a cousin in Istanbul. Perhaps you've heard of him: Abdulkadir Ali Lamna."

"Sorry, no."

"He's a very big businessman and can get anything for you. I'd be delighted to provide his phone number and address for you."

"I'm a policeman," Orhan said.

The driver glanced back over his shoulder at Orhan.

"A policeman," he said. "Most interesting."

The driver said nothing more on the route to the Ministry.

Upon arriving, Orhan paid him, stared at his face a few seconds, then climbed the steps into the building,

As the heat, humidity, smell of car fumes bore down on him, Orhan felt like he was pressing his way through a column of warm water– even dragging his suitcase up the marble steps drained him. Pushing through the huge doors, into the building's cool cave interior with its subdued light, fresh air, clean smell brought immediate relief.

Finding the Dalmatian marble-fronted elevator, Orhan got in, zipped up with no noise to the top floor. The door popped open into a plush carpeted area with three office fronts. Stepping out, Orhan found the office of the Directorate of Internal Security to the left.

Inside, a man in a red-checked kafiyya draped over a white gellabya greeted him from behind a large Finnish birch wood desk.

"*Salaam aleikum,*" he said.

When Orhan presented his credentials, the man took them from him, held them, looked from the identity cards to Orhan's face before handing them back.

"Is the Director available?" Orhan said.

"I'll ring him immediately," the man said.

Orhan sat down in a blue upholstered Finnish chair. A minute later, a short portly man in a navy-blue double-breasted pinstripe suit breezed into the room.

"Colonel Mehmet," the Director said. "We are honored. Hassan, see that we have tea."

The Director ushered Orhan into a massive office to a glass table where two matching love seats alongside two plush chairs lounged on opposite sides, then indicated that Orhan sit down.

A knock at the door.

The Director called out,

"*Ta'al.* Enter."

A white-robed dark-skinned servant with a red cotton turban, a wide red sash glided in, settled a tray on the table with two tea glasses in metal holders, a matching glass tea urn, metal handled sugar bowl with spoons.

When the servant left, the Director poured tea into a glass, then heaped several teaspoons of sugar which he passed to Orhan before serving himself.

"How may I be of service?" the Director said.

"A fence," Orhan said. "Antiquities, jewelry, collectibles. All I have is a name, Ali, and a description. Yemeni, small, dark. Natty dresser, wears yellow bowties, a large diamond ring, panama hats."

The Director smiled, sipped his tea.

"Ali bin Yussef," he said. "A slippery one."

"I was told he shows up on Thursdays at a club, The Pasha's Paradise."

The Director sat back in the chair, sipping his tea.

"Ali's one of the smarter ones," he said. "He deals through a web of middlemen and stooges."

"So, I won't be able to bring him in?"

"If you do, like in America, his lawyers will have him out in less than an hour. He's very generous with the local constabulary and has friends who are friends and relatives of friends."

"I see."

"Please don't misunderstand, Colonel. We will cooperate with you in every way we can. But, our laws are such that certain citizens and visitors of influence enjoy, shall we say, certain rights."

"So, all have rights but some have more rights than others," Orhan said.

The director took a long sip of his sweet tea.

"One thing," he said.

"Yes?"

"Ali loves to gamble. As I've heard, he's not always wise about paying his debts which has made him a number of enemies."

"So, his long-term tenure on this planet is not that secure."

"Quite so."

~*~~*~

After checking into a hotel, Orhan stepped back into the heat, caught a cab to the Pasha's Paradise Tea Room. Along the way, he gazed out at the gaudy skyline of Dubai with its flashy malls, luxury hotels with vending machines that sold gold bars in ingots, exclusive expensive "private"clubs.

The *Burj Khalifa*, the current world's tallest building thrust out on an palm shapped islet in the Persian Gulf poked its pointed nose above the skyline.

The cabby took Orhan to the outer, seedy central district on the inland side of the city. He pulled up to a white-washed club front advertising itself as a Tea and Entertainment Center along a busy street cluttered with vendors selling cheap goods imported from China, Singapore, Pakistan.

Orhan got out, glanced up at the cheap neon sign, *The Pasha's Paradise* written in Latin letters, then went inside to a smoky, noisy coffee and tea bar.

The club had three bars stationed around grimy plastic tables where working class men sat drinking tea. The rear bar offered patrons illegal, forbidden alcoholic drinks.

Nearby, six men sat around a table playing cards. Several poorer patrons hung around watching the players look at their hands, at each other, make bets.

Orhan spotted Ali. He stood out with his dark skin contrasting with his cream-colored panama, white suit, a shirt fastened with a bright yellow bow-tie with pink polka-dots.

Sitting down at a nearby table, Orhan ordered tea, watched Ali bin Yussef out of the corner of his eye.

A small dark man with quick, ferret eyes, Ali shot furtive glances around himself as he scooped up his cards, took in the faces of his fellow players. A ring with a large stone on his finger crackled in the refractions of the florescent light as Ali sorted cards in his hand.

Orhan sipped his tea, watched. After a few rounds of betting, Ali threw in his hand, mumbled something to the other players, got up, made his way to the bathroom.

Orhan followed him inside.

Standing at a basin washing his hands, Orhan looked up in the mirror at the door of the stall Ali had gone in. Then hearing a flush, he saw Ali step out, rearrange his suit, push his way out of the door without washing his hands.

Shaking the water from his hands, Orhan took a towel from the bathroom attendant, dropped some coins in the dish, dried his hands, then stepped out, slipping up behind Ali.

"We need to talk," Orhan said.

The little man spun around, his weasel eyes darted, caught Orhan's face.

"I don't talk to people I don't know," he said.

Orhan popped out his Interpol ID.

"Now you know me," he said.

Ali looked from the ID to Orhan's face, then back at the ID.

"I've done nothing wrong."

"Didn't said you have," Orhan said. "I just want to talk."

"What about?"

Orhan pointed to an empty table. They sat. Ali took an Italian cigar from a pack from his pocket, lit it, glared over at Orhan.

"So, talk." Ali said.

"Parvez Hoshkar," Orhan said.

"That's supposed to mean something to me?"

"Cairo."

"A city in Egypt."

"A first century *stater*."

"What's that?"

"Can we cut the bullshit?" Orhan said

"You're the one spewing nonsense. I'm just listening."

Orhan signaled a waiter.

"Something to drink?" he asked.

"You're buying?"

"I asked."

"Scotch."

A young Pakistani or Bangladeshi waiter came over. "Do you have rakı?" Orhan asked him

"We have everything," the boy answered.

"Scotch and a rakı with two coffees."

"Immediately, Sayedi," said the boy and sped away through the maze of tables.

Ali blew smoke in Orhan's direction.

"Cheap scotch won't buy anything from me, Turk."

Orhan folded his hands in front of him on the table.

"Where and from whom did you get the coin you sold Parvez Hoshkar?"

"I don't know what you're talking about."

"We can go downtown and refresh your memory."

"I've been downtown many times. Can't say it ever did my memory much good."

Orhan leaned back in his chair.

"You're awfully confident in your influence," he said.

"Certain friends one makes are important."

"You have such friends?"

"I do. And, they don't come cheap."

"Are you asking for baksheesh?"

"Talk is cheap, Turk. Information is expensive."

The young waiter came back, set the drinks down, reached for his change purse. Orhan dropped a large bill on the tray, waved him away.

Ali downed the scotch in one swallow, dropped a handful of sugar cubes into the demitasse of dark coffee, stirred it.

"I got nothing to say," he said. "We both know there's nothing you can do to me here. So let's say your modest investment of a shot of cheap scotch and a rather decent coffee only represents a tiny loss in any enterprise you're seeking to create."

Ali downed the coffee, got up, strolled back to the poker table without looking back.

Orhan took a sip of the rakı watching the little Yemenite gather up his cards at the table.

So, what's the next step?

Orhan drained the rakı, swigged the thick coffee, avoiding the sediment in the bottom. In a habit from his old police surveillance days, he scanned the room. A familiar face seized his attention.

Pausing, dropping his eyes, Orhan took in the man's frontal appearance in his peripheral vision.

Round face.

Short black hair, parted in the middle, framing the pie face.

The mouth– small, thin red lips.

The brows black, thin, sketched over deep brown charcoal colored eyes with an Asian cast.

Orhan's height– more slender, wiry, strong.

He wore a cheap, dark blue suit, a white shirt buttoned at the throat with no tie.

Wrinkling his brow, Orhan pumped his memory, grasped for a name.

The face bespoke violence. Murder.

A name ... It wouldn't pop up.

Orhan adjusted his neck, stealing glances at the face.

The man's gaze didn't waver. But, it was not on him. He didn't even glance Orhan's way—just sat like a predator– a leopard, perhaps– eyes never leaving his prey.

Orhan searched around to see who the pie-faced man was tracking.

It was someone at the card table. Orhan watched the players shift their weight, move around in the motion of play. Then he saw the man was focused on Ali.

The name popped into his mind the instant Orhan made the connection.

Fahir Muz.

A Turk. Freelance assassin. Trade name, *Bıçak Ağzi*, Knife-edge.

Muz's gaze did not waver. He tracked Ali like a cat marks a bird. Muz's glare was intense– a small tight-lipped smile hovered under his thin, fine nose. His skin was pale. His hands folded on the table in front of him, small, rodent-like.

Ali's luck with cards was not running well. Orhan saw him throw in the hand, get up, relight the Italian cigar. With a careless glance back at Orhan, Ali moved toward the door.

Orhan ignored him, turning his attention to an entertainer who had just sat down to play the oud.

Out of the corner of his eye, Orhan watched Muz track Ali. When Ali stepped to the door, Muz slipped to his feet, eased his way through the tables after him.

Orhan rose, followed both men out the door.

Outside, Orhan stepped up to a vendor, pretended to look at the wares while tracking the two men walking down the street. Ahead, careless, Ali strolled, glancing at the vendors, their items for sale along the way.

The Turk, Muz, followed close behind, throwing quick glances behind him, scanning for anyone following.

Marking the two men, Orhan crossed the busy street.

Ali stopped, went into a tobacco store.

Muz stopped, pretended to gaze in a neighboring shop window.

Up ahead about 200 meters beyond the store, Orhan spotted an alleyway.

A logical place for an attack.

Orhan sprinted ahead, crossed back across the busy street, came into the alleyway well ahead of the Turk, who stayed in front of the shop window next to the tobacco shop.

The alley was empty. Two steel trash containers hugged the walls of the building on one side. Orhan ducked behind the first dumpster, crouched, peered around it.

About two or three minutes later, Orhan saw Ali stroll by. An instant later, he saw Ali swept back into the alley in a dark blue flash of the Turk's cheap suit.

Orhan saw Muz was a pro. He clapped his hand over Ali's mouth, pulled a knife to cut his throat.

Orhan sprang forward, struck Muz's slashing arm, causing his cut to slice off a piece of Ali's bow-tie. Before Muz could regain his balance to slash again, Orhan struck him over his ear with his open hand, drove him to the ground with his knee against his kidney, pinning him on top of the stunned Ali.

Muz shook his head, blinked, tried to turn for another swipe with the knife. Orhan grabbed his wrist, twisted the arm back until he heard it snap.

Muz opened his hand, gasped a strangled cry. The knife fell in a clatter to the ground. Orhan shoved Muz's head into the metal side of the dumpster. Once. Twice. The third time, Orhan felt him pass out but kept on top of him pinning him and Ali to the ground.

Hearing the commotion from the street, people came poking in the alley. Ali yelled for someone to call the police.

"Let me up," Ali screamed.

"As soon as the cops get here," Orhan said

~*~~*~

It took over a half hour for the police to get there. Orhan stayed on top of the dazed Muz while Ali protested until the police arrived.

Showing them his Interpol ID, Orhan told the policemen what he had seen.

The police handcuffed the still groggy Muz, picked up the knife, took a statement from Ali. As they hauled the bloody-headed Turk off, Ali looked over at Orhan.

"You saved my life," he said.

"You're lucky I recognized him. Somebody wants you dead and is willing to pay to get the best to do the job."

Ali flinched, his tiny eyes wrinkled.

"I gotta get outta here for a while," he said.

"I may be able to help you," Orhan said.

Ali shot him a glance.

"I can help myself."

"Good. Next time I won't be there."

Ali stopped, lowered his eyes, motioned for Orhan to come closer.

"The coin came from a seller in Alexandria."

"Name?"

"No idea. It was a one-time buy. The guy's not Egyptian. He's Palestinian."

"How'd you contact him?"

"Didn't. He contacted me. Told me it could bring up to 22 or 25 K."

"Dollars?"

"Euros. They're harder to trace than dollars."

"How'd he get your name?"

"Through the trade"

Ali paused, looked around like a weasel.

"Do you think it's him who put out the hit on me?" he said.

"No idea."

"Then who?"

"When you run with the dogs, Ali, you're going to step in dogshit."

Ali looked around, bit his lip.

"What can you do for me?"

"A word from the Director of Interior Affairs can get you off the radar. Screw it up and you'll meet another of Muz's colleagues."

"I've heard of this director. Can you get me a favor from him?"

"You gotta do better than the Palestinian with no name in Alexandria."

Ali frowned, dropped his eyes and muttered,

"The Alexandria part's right. There's a guy there– an archaeologist, I think. I got the coins from him."

"Including the *stater*?"

Ali nodded.

"All of 'em."

"What's his name."

"Sheffield. Raymund Sheffield."

"American?"

"Brit."

"How's he moving stuff?" Orhan said. "The Egyptians are on artifact smugglers like stink on shit."

Ali shot Orhan a sneer.

"Cash greases the tightest squeeze," he said.

THREE

Surprise

Montaz Receiving Center, Port of Alexandria, Egypt
3 days later, 11:20 AM

Mountainous masses of machinery– cranes, derricks, offloading turrets of huge ocean containers sprawled over the port dockside. On the edge of the landing, tractors and mechanized lifts shifted the steel boxes from ship to shore then to dockside designated for delivery stations. There, high lattices of steel girders rolled on rails, shifting these heavy metal packages of trade into organized stacks to be plundered by lines of growling, diesel fume-spewing trucks. Inside all of these vehicles, humans dwarfed, tiny in the shadows of the monstrous structures maneuvered them into their positions.

Torrents of tractor-trucks honked and snorted diesel smoke in chaotic assembly pushing to enter the receiving area to retrieve their designated cargo. At the gated portals, the drivers presented paperwork to pass through a maze of clerks, custom officers and sentries. With much shouting, waving of hands, showing angry faces, the drivers slunk off to various venues to wait in queues to have the monolithic “shipping cans” loaded on their empty trailers. Once having taken possession of their precious prizes, a noisy network of mechanical caterpillars oozed out to a huge steel cage of a gate, where a horde of armed uniformed guards rechecked their magical passage papers, then threatened, bullied and lobbied them for bribes to make their exit easier.

At the head of three of these trucks loaded with shipping containers, Gregg Steele, bare-headed, dressed in chocolate military fatigues thrust his papers under the nose of a sweating customs guard, pointed to the official stamps pressed on the page in curlicued Arabic. The mustachioed guard scowled at the papers, searched for some irregularity, and finding none, smashed his rubber stamp on the pages, ripped off the front copies and indicated clearance with a glare and jerk of his peaked-capped head.

Sorting the papers at the desk in slow, deliberate motions, Steele gave the guard a smug grin before climbing up on the side rail of the first truck and waving for the two trucks behind to follow. Opening the cabin door, he slide into the passenger seat and pointed his finger straight ahead. The tall Arab driver with dark intense eyes, nodded, put the truck in gear and rolled out the gate with the two others in tow behind him.

Giving the papers a final look, Steele smiled.

It felt good.

Nothing better'n bullying bullies.

He turned to the driver.

"You speak English, Abdi?" he said.

Surprise flashed in the man's dark eyes for an instant. Then, his face panned into a toothy grin.

"May I ask, Sir?" he said. "How you know my name?"

"Ain't all you guys named 'Abdi?' " Steele said.

The smile did not falter.

"Ah, I see," Abdi said. "It's a joke,"

"Glad you got a sense of humor," Steele said.

"I do, sir."

"You from here?"

"Do you mean *Alek-san-dreeya*, sir?"

Abdi used the Egyptian pronunciation of the name of the city.

"Yeah."

"No, sir. I'm from Palestine."

"You mean Israel?"

"Nearby to that place, sir."

Steele smirked, looked out the window into the side mirror at the other two container trucks rolling right behind him.

"You Palesteenos don't like them Israelis too much, do yah?" Steele said.

The smile returned. "We try to get along with them, sir."

"Is it hard because those guys kick your butts all the time?"

"There have been difficult times," Abdi said.

Steele rolled down the window and spit. Rolling it back up, he reached over and twisted the knob on the air conditioning controls.

"Crank up the AC. It's too fucking hot."

Abdi swatted the instrument cowling with his open hand.

"It appears to not be functioning," he said.

"Shit!"

"It seems a bit warm," Abdi said.

"Warm, shit. It's fucking hot."

Abdi nodded. The smile broadened.

Steele rolled down the window, leaned his elbow out, then slipped on a pair of wire framed sunglasses from his shirt pocket. He shifted his feet, felt something underneath– an oily rag. A brown blotch of grease marked his boot.

"Crap," Steele said.

"A problem, sir?" Abdi said.

"Fucking dirty oily rag."

"I'm sorry, sir."

"Goddam it. These are new boots."

"I can have your shoe cleaned when we get to the drop-off."

"It's gonna look like shit. Fucking browns are sweated, now my boots are greased."

"You are military, sir?"

"Used to be, Jocko. Fought your cousins in Desert Storm."

"Oh?" Abdi said.

"I was lead shooter on a Ranger sniper team."

"You shot many men?"

Steele sneered.

"Lots," he said.

Abdi nodded.

"In fact," Steele said. "Just recently, I popped one in the States."

Abdi flinched. His eyes' narrowed, his knuckles tightened white on the steering wheel. His face did not change.

"In the States?" he said.

"Helluva shot," Steele said. "If I say so myself."

A tear crossed Abdi's cheek. He made a small choke.

Steele looked over at him.

"Something wrong?" he said.

"Perhaps some dust in my eye," Abdi said.

Leaving the port area, Steele saw the road now ran along fenced off buildings and warehouses in a more commercial area of the city. Ahead, a cross road branched off into a deserted, undeveloped section. When they came to the corner, Abdi turned the truck into the cross road.

"Hey," Steele said. "This ain't the fucking way."

Abdi pulled over along the side of the deserted road and turned off the engine. Steele's face turned beet red.

"What the fuck you doing, asshole?" he bellowed. "We got a goddam schedule to keep."

A nickel-plated revolver appeared in Abdi's hand. He thrust it under Steele's chin.

"You killed my brother, you son of a Jew whore," he said.

Steele grabbed for the gun.

Abdi squeezed the trigger.

The blast of the discharge blew away the right side of Steele's head. Blood, brains and bits of bone blew out the open cab window. Steele's sunglasses spun through the air.

Abdi reached over with his free left hand, opened the door, kicked Steele's body out onto the oily dirt of the shoulder of the road, then stepped out on the side rail. The driver from the truck behind ran up, stared at Steele's twisted body oozing blood over the side of the road.

Abdi pointed, fired again and again until he emptied the chamber. Steele's body twitched and jerked from the impact of the bullets.

"He killed Isaak!" Abdi screamed.

The driver of the third truck came up to join his colleague.

"Abdi," he said. "We must leave here, now."

"Yes," the first driver said. "There'll be police."

Abdi jumped down on the ground, spat on Steele's body and kicked it.

"My great regret," he said. "I've not got time to shit on this Israeli dog."

"I'll get his billfold," the first driver said.

The second driver pleaded. "Let's go."

Abdi nodded, spat again, crawled into the cab, started the truck. The second driver ran back to his truck. But, the first one, after lifting Steele's wallet spotted his sunglasses on the ground.

He scooped them up, put them on, then sprinted back to climb in his truck's cab to follow Abdi.

More Complications

Congressman Damian Styles Office, Capitol Office Building, Washington, DC
The next day, 10:45 AM

Stepping into the office, Ham Morris took in the framed awards and letters that splashed the walls of the office interior of Congressman Damian Styles, Republican, 12th district, South Carolina. The Congressman's great gunmetal gray desk sat before a blurry window looking out over the blotched paint exterior of the older building revealing the wear and tear of pollution of the atmosphere of the capital city.

Styles shut the door after showing Ham Morris to a table in front of the Congressman's desk.

"You got my message," he said.

"That's why I'm here," Morris said.

"OK," Styles said. "Here's what's shaping up. The Christian Caucus's all on board. We've lined up all the fence straddlers in the Conservative bloc. The liberals are so disorganized they'll not know what hit them."

"You're damn confident."

"Confidence comes with doing your homework, Ham."

"So, you think these guys will fall into line on privatizing more of our National Defense."

"My libertarian colleagues would support privatizing the constitution."

"Really?"

"This new crop of freshmen have come in on a promise to cut spending, reduce taxes and advance the war on terrorism."

"So, what does Pap and that jerk, Rogers, have to do with this?"

Styles pulled a coffee service to him, poured coffee into a cup, poured two teaspoons of sugar, then cream, stirred it.

"Ham," he said. "I know how some folks can get irritated at KD."

"He's a self-righteous little prick."

"He can be difficult," Styles said. "But his influence on voters in certain key districts is the main reason we're looking at this lot of bright, young and new sunny faces in this Congress."

"So, he knows how to sell a product."

"He does. Do I have to mention the income streams his radio network generates?"

Morris folded his arms across his chest.

"What's he got on Pap, Damian?"

Styles choked on his coffee.

"Ham," he said. "Do you really want to open a barrel of rattlesnakes?"

Morris's narrow blue eyes did not blink when he nodded.

"OK," Styles said. "Just remember, you asked."

He set the coffee cup back in the saucer.

"Recall how KD's was on your ass about the late professor Corbett having 'something damaging' on your father-in-law?"

"Rogers only said it'd ruin Pap."

"And, you never asked."

"Fuck yes, I asked!" Morris said. "But, he'd only smirk and say shit like 'career devastating.' "

Styles stared into the coffee cup in his hand. After a long pause, he said,

"Jim Corbett and your father-in-law were once lovers when they were young men."

Morris blinked, his mouth fell open. Then, he exploded.

"Pap?" he said. "A faggot!"

Styles reached over and set the empty cup on the tray.

"I was even briefly involved with Corbett myself," he said.

"You telling me, you're queer?" Morris said.

Styles did not waver.

"We all make our own way through life, Ham," he said. "Jim Corbett was a wonderful human being and a first rate scholar."

"But, Pap..."

" 'Pap,' " Styles sneered. "He admitted it to me one night while in his cups."

"I don't fucking believe it."

"Your father-in-law admired Jim Corbett and considered him his friend all his life."

Morris put his hands to his face, sat back in his chair.

"I thought it was those black hookers Pap's so fond of."

"Oh, there've been lots of hookers," said Styles. "Black, yellow, white and every color."

"So, how'd Rogers know to put the squeeze on me to take Corbett out?"

Styles rose, walked over to the window behind his desk. Putting his hands behind his back, he stared out for a moment looking at the passing traffic, then turned back to Morris.

"I made the mistake of telling him," he said.

Morris frowned.

"Is Pap aware Rogers knows this?" he said.

Styles shook his head.

"I doubt it." he said.

"Then, Roger's never brought it up to him."

"KD Rogers is scared shitless of your father-in-law."

"So, that's why that little Hitler-looking fuck pushed me to lean on Corbett."

Styles stared out the window again.

"Don't tell me anything about that."

Morris's Blackberry went off.

"Sorry, Damian," Morris said. "Priority text message. "

Digging the phone from his pocket, he looked at the small screen, then muttered,

"Jesus fucking Christ!"

Styles stepped back to the table, sat down and poured himself another coffee.

"Problems?" he said.

"Egypt," Morris mumbled. "Gregg Steele and three containers of assets fucking gone."

"Steele? Gone?"

"Found his body with his head blown off."

Morris jumped to his feet, stalked through the door.

"Gotta handle this," he said. "Get back to you."

He strode out growling and thumbing his blackberry, unaware of the stares of the lobbyists, petitioners and admiring congressional constituents grouped in the outer office.

Convention Encounters

The Royal Hilton Hotel and Convention Center, Alexandria, Egypt
A week later, 3:15 PM

Still shaking off the jet lagged tired, sleepy and groggy feeling, Colene lumbered onto the escalator, rode up to the mezzanine of the convention center, then at the top, stalled, stared into the large hall adjusting to the noise, bustle and activity in the foyer. She spotted a placard on a tripod with announcements of the day's presentation program at the end of the room, shouldered her way through the filled conference room to the posted list of sessions and locations, found

LEVANTINE PRE-IRON AGE CONSIDERATION

to be presented in the King Rameses II Ballroom.

A voice from behind gave her a start.

"Colene. Colene Mooney."

Colene turned, recognized Middle East historian, Fran Healy's freckled face and red hair.

"Frannie," Colene said. "How're things at Haahvahd?"

Fran, tall and dressed in a black pants suit, gave Colene a rib cracking hug, then led her to the side of the room, away from the press of the crowd.

"Didn't expect to see you here," Fran said.

"Didn't expect it myself," Colene said.

"Isn't this a bit off your beaten path?"

"I'm here to hear a paper that might link some texts that I'm looking at."

"Oh? Who's giving it?"

"Avi Feldstein."

Fran rolled her eyes.

"What?" Colene said.

"Feldstein's a megacreep."

"How so?"

"Smart– brilliant, even– but ..."

"But?"

"A classic 100 kilogram turd predator."

Colene shook her head.

"I'm not here for romance– strictly business."

"No matter. He'll hit on you because you're female and sexy."

Colene laughed, hugged her friend and after agreeing to get together later for drinks, she found the King Rameses II room, went in, took a seat near the back.

There were several unfilled chairs in the room. Colene heard loud murmurs, soft conversations in French, Arabic, German, even languages she didn't recognize. At the table at the front of the room, speakers shuffled papers, greeted each other, took their seats. Then, Colene caught sight of a standout.

He wore a light-gray cotton suit over a black polo shirt, tall, broad-shouldered, bronze skinned and clean shaven– the dark shade of his beard gave his face a 5 o'clock shadow. Large dark-brown eyes were set in a handsome, careless face with prominent lips, crowned by a pile of black curly hair. His gaze wandered around the room while he spoke and listened to his colleagues.

This has to be Feldstein.

The chairperson rapped the conference to order. Feldstein sat, still glancing around the room.

The conference papers were tangential to Colene's interest. She stared at Feldstein.

He sat, rubbed his chin, scanned the audience, listened without comment. When his turn came to speak, he rose. He lounged behind the podium one hand in his pocket, spoke to notes on a

PowerPoint slideshow, described his recent results from digging in the Negev where he had found pottery shards with pre-Canaanite inscriptions.

In his summation, he leaned one hand on the podium, then caught sight of Colene in the back row. He raised eyebrows, brightened his face, grinned his wide mouth as he fixed eyes and smiled at her, his voice now a loud purr.

"These bits and pieces," he said, "confirm the findings of Palestinian, Jordanian and Lebanese colleagues in dating this site as a major find representing this critical pre-Iron age period."

Feldstein took his seat to mild applause, leaned back in his chair and smiled at Colene.

At the end of the session, Colene met Feldstein at his table where he stood to greet her, his large eyes fixed on her face.

"Dr. Feldstein," Colene said.

"Just Avi."

"I've heard you might have some information on the possible existence of a codex of the Q document."

"You heard that where?" he asked.

"Bob Jacobsen."

"Really?"

"Is there any truth to this?"

"Could be. What are you doing for dinner tonight?'

"Busy," Colene said. "But, we could get together for coffee ..."

"How about we meet downstairs in the Queen Nefertiti lounge at 9 tonight? I'm tied up right now but would love to talk to you about it."

Colene hesitated, then smiled.

"That works for me," she said.

~*~~*~

Colene fought off jet lag weariness, glanced up at the clock behind the bar. Feldstein was late. A few seats away, a fat, middle-aged Egyptian leered at her from behind gold rimmed glasses. He raised his glass to her.

"May I invite you for a drink?" he said.

Resisting the temptation to tell him to stuff it, Colene smiled. "Thanks. I'm expecting someone."

"Some other time, perhaps," he said.

Colene made a tight lipped smile.

Feldstein strolled up, took Colene's hand, kissed it, then motioned to a table in a round booth near the end of the bar.

"Shall we enjoy some privacy?" he said.

Colene followed him to the booth, scooted in on one side. Feldstein slid in next to her.

"What are you drinking?" he said.

"White wine."

Feldstein signaled a bar maid, gave her explicit instructions how he wanted a large single malt scotch along with Colene's order, then turned back to Colene.

"You know you're a beautiful woman," he said.

"Let's talk about the codex," Colene said.

"Not only beautiful but tough too."

"Tough enough to be just interested in this codex."

Feldstein shrugged his shoulders. The waitress, a dark-eyed Greek, stepped up, glanced at Colene as she sat the glasses in front of them.

"Do you want this on your hotel bill, M'sieur?" she said.

"Yes," Feldstein said. He signed the bill.

When she left, he turned back to Colene.

"So, where did Bob get the idea I know anything about a codex... Q or otherwise?"

"Because you likely told him."

"He must've misunderstood."

"What?"

"Rumors."

Colene sought his eyes, her face expressionless.

"Rumors you exaggerated?"

Feldstein took a long, noisy sip of his drink than leaned toward her.

"What's it worth to you?'

"Depends on the quality of the data."

"We have a deal?"

"I'm listening."

Feldstein looked around the room.

"This stays here."

"Go on."

"A guy asked me to authenticate some First Century coins."

"And?'

"He told me about the text."

"Name?"

"This can't get back to me."

"Cut the crap. His name?"

"Raymund Sheffield. He's here in Alexandria."

"This smells fecal."

"The coins were genuine. The guy's real. Brit. Cambridge trained."

"Never heard of him."

Avi dropped his eyes, looked around again.

"He doesn't publish. Went rogue. Deals under the table."

"So," Colene said. "The great Israeli archewog deals in pilfered artifacts."

Feldstein scowled, then, softened his expression.

"You've no idea how much you could mean to me," he said. "I've exposed myself to you. You could ruin me."

Colene took a sip of wine.

"All I've heard so far is bullshit," she said.

Feldstein pulled a pen and slip of paper from his pocket, wrote down a number, then looked over at her.

"Come up and see me. You won't be sorry."

He slid the note with his door key card across to her. Colene didn't look at him or the note.

"21136," Feldstein said. "It's on the card.

He slipped out from the booth, smiled back at her and walked out of the bar.

Colene looked at the note, pulled out her cellphone and punched in the number. It rang twice. A request for voicemail came on in Arabic, French and then English.

"Dr. Sheffield," she said. "This is Colene Mooney from Yale University. I'm interested in information about a codex of the Q document. Call me back earliest."

She clicked off. Before she could get the phone back in her bag, it buzzed. She answered,

"Colene Mooney."

"Sheffield, here. Can we meet?"

"When?"

"Tomorrow?"

"Where?"

"My office ..."

Colene pushed back her grogginess, her desire for sleep, wrote down the address on the same slip of paper.

He rang off.

Colene rolled her head, loosening her neck, went to put the pen and paper along with her phone back in her bag, then caught sight of the room key on the table.

Raising what felt like lead coated eyelids, she looked over at the bar.

The heavy Egyptian still sat there. He turned, smiled at her.

Picking up her bag, Colene walked past the Egyptian, dropped Feldstein's door key in front of him, walked to the end of the bar, looked back, smiled at him before she left.

Complications

Department of Police and Security Services,
Alexandria, Egypt, next day, 8:15 AM.

The ceiling fan inside the office of the Superintendent of Police and Security Service wheezed, squeaked, jiggled on its axis. Sitting beneath the soft stir of the breeze, turning the tattered pages of an old worn issue of the International Edition of Time magazine, Orhan pushed the grating sound out of his mind, shoved impatience back, scanned over out-of-date pictures of riots in India. Then, out of the corner of his eye, he caught sight of a female secretary with a beehive hairdo behind a scarred, scuffed counter motioning him to come over.

"Colonel Mehmet," she said. "His Excellency, the Chief Superintendent will see you now."

She pointed to a big scratched door at the back of the room.

Orhan went into a large office where the Chief Superintendent, Farouk Hagg, short, heavy set, in his late 50s with a pile of gray hair, thick moustache, dressed in a stained, worn old fashioned gray double breasted suit sat at a large wooden desk. Seeing Orhan enter, Hagg rose, extended his hand.

"My dear Colonel Mehmet," he said. "What brings you to Alexandria?"

"International concerns, Your Excellency," Orhan said.

Hagg came from behind his desk, indicated some easy chairs around a table.

"Let's discuss it over tea," he said, then paused. "Unless, you'd prefer something stronger?"

"Tea will be excellent."

Hagg served Orhan from a brass tea set on his desk. Then he stirred several spoons of sugar in a glass, took a noisy slurp, sat back, looked over at his guest.

"What are these international concerns?" he said.

"I've traced some stolen ancient coins back to here."

After another noisy swig of tea, Hagg wiped his mouth with a paper napkin, shook his head.

"Most alarming," he said. "I'll ask the Director of Drug and Illegal Trade Control to join us."

The short man heaved himself to his feet, walked to the door, called out to his secretary.

"Ala'ata," he said. "Request Director al Mehandi join us at his earliest convenience."

Hagg turned back to Orhan, folded his hands behind his back, paced in front of his desk.

"This news distresses me greatly," he said. "I was informed these activities have been stamped out here in Alexandria."

"There are always rats in the woodwork," Orhan said.

"Perhaps this is just a minor incident," Hagg said.

A short rap at the door caused him to turn.

"Ah, that will be Mahmoud."

Hagg opened the door to a tall, slender man with short, brushed back, thinning black hair. His dark brown, narrow eyes sat over a prominent nose and pencil moustache. His tailor-made suit, a dark blue pinstripe draped his frame over a light blue shirt and dark blue tie. When Orhan shook his hand, he saw the Director's hair, eyebrows and moustache were dyed.

Hagg ushered al Mehandi to a chair, said to him,

"Colonel Mehmet has information of trade in stolen coins here in Alexandria."

Al Mehandi's dark narrow eyes wrinkled into a squint.

"Stolen coins?" he said.

"Syrian authorities apprehended the seller in Damascus," Orhan said. "I picked up the source in Dubai."

Without taking his eyes off Orhan, al Mehandi closed his hands, brought them together in front of his large nose.

Orhan noticed a large diamond ring on the pinkie of his left hand.

"What were these coins?" Al Mehandi said.

"First century Roman. Worth over 25 thousand US."

"Roman coins, you say?" Al Mehandi said.

"They've been authenticated," Orhan said.

Al Mehandi smiled, opened his hands, looked from Orhan to the Superintendent.

"Well," he said. "There you have it."

"Did I miss something?" Orhan said.

"We've never had a problem with Roman coins here in Alexandria," al Mehandi said. "And, the few cases we've encountered of artifact smuggling have been exclusively our own Egyptian treasures."

Orhan nodded, sat up straight in his chair, laced his fingers together in front of him, took in al Mehandi again.

The suit was fine Italian wool, the shirt French linen, the tie Syrian silk. Scanning down, Orhan noted Al Mehandi's long narrow feet encased in navy blue Italian silk socks, tucked in hand-tooled Italian shoes. Orhan peeked over at Hagg's worn, droopy faded cotton socks in scuffed cheap shoes poking out from under the trouser legs of a cheap, threadbare suit over a faded once-pink shirt, frayed at the collar and cuffs.

Hagg nodded at Al Mehandi's explanation.

"You're telling me there is no traffic in Levantine artifacts here in Alexandria?" Orhan said.

"Some," Al Mehandi said. "But, nothing of any significance, Colonel."

"That's a relief," Hagg said.

"You doubt my sources?" Orhan said.

"Only expressing my reservations, my Colonel," Al Mehandi said. "But certainly not your judgment. Please forgive me if I've offended ..."

"No offense taken, Director," Orhan said. "After all, this is your beat."

Al Mehandi reached into his inner coat, drew out, opened a silver cigarette case, offered one to Orhan.

"Cigarette, Colonel?"

"Thank you, no," Orhan replied. He noticed the cigarettes were French Gitanes with a gold ring around the end of the filter.

Al Mehandi leaned back in the chair, looked over at Orhan, exhaling a puff of smoke.

"While I cannot say 'no' definitively," he said. "I highly suspect this source to be based on rumors."

"Rumors?" Orhan said.

"Do you have a name for this source here in Alexandria?"

"I was hoping you might be able to provide that," Orhan said.

"Precisely my point, Colonel," al Mehandi said.

Orhan smiled at both men, stood and presented his hand,

"Colleagues," he said. "I thank you both for your trouble and generosity in sharing your time."

~*~~*~

Orhan left the building, caught a cab to the municipal airport where he booked a commuter flight to Cairo. Before the flight, he found a phone bank, dialed a number.

A male voice answered, "Office of Antiquities, Security Section."

"Col. Orhan Mehmet from Turkey, here. Is Director Hamid ad Din available?"

"The Director is presently in a meeting with the Minister, Col. Mehmet. Can I have him call you when he returns?"

"No. I'm in Alexandria, catching a commuter flight to Cairo. I'll see him when I arrive."

"This is Ahmed, Colonel. I'll have a car pick you at the airport."

~*~~*~

The ride from the Cairo municipal airport to the main part of the city was long and slow through noisy, congested midafternoon traffic that snaked along the dusty highway. Orhan leaned back in the front passenger seat, appreciating the air conditioning of the black Mercedes SUV with tinted windows.

The driver in curved, wrap-around dark glasses, ear plug leashed to a spiraled phone cord ascending out the back of his black suit coat like a white curly asp, kept his eyes fixed on the road.

In the back seat, another black-suited agent rested a Beretta M12 machine pistol with an inverse clip taped on in his lap, checking out the surrounding area through the darkened windows.

"It's good to see you again, Col. Mehmet," the driver, Ahmed said.

"It's been some time, Ahmed," Orhan said. "Last time I saw you, you were about to be married."

"I've three children now, my Colonel."

Orhan sighed.

"Yes," he said. "It has been some time."

~*~~*~

A big man, often told he could double for the actor Omar Shariff, Hamid ad Din, the Director of Internal Securities of the Ministry of Antiquities and National Treasures, met Orhan as soon as he stepped through the office doors. He wore a white cotton sport coat, blue and white striped shirt with no tie over tan cotton slacks. His feet were tucked into penny loafers with crepe soles. He grabbed Orhan's hand, snagged him into a big bear hug, kissed him on both cheeks.

"*Merhaba, Effendi,*" Ad Din said. "It's been too goddam long."

"Sallaam, Hamid," Orhan said.

Ad Din pulled Orhan into his office, plopped him down on a large leather sofa, poured a half glass of Glenfiddich single malt scotch from a cut-glass crystal decanter, pushed it to him.

"Let's have it," ad Din said. "You're damn sure not here for the dancing girls."

Orhan took a long sip of the scotch, let the fiery liquid flow down his throat.

"I arrived in Alexandria last night," he said. "This morning I called on Superintendent Hagg. "

"Now, that was a rich source of information," interrupted ad Din.

"He called in his adjutant, Al Mehandi."

"And, you came to the conclusion that Farouk is working for Mahmoud, right?" ad Din said.

Orhan nodded.

"That bastard Al Mehandi is wired straight to the top," ad Din said. "Every pound of anything illegal sold or traded puts at least 10 piasters in his pockets."

Ad Din grabbed the decanter, poured another half glass.

"I've a good lead," Orhan said.

"What good lead?" ad Din said.

"Salim Habib made a collar in Damascus."

"Damn good man, Salim."

"I'd put out a call about Levantine coins stolen a while back at Ankara University."

"I remember that. Murder too, wasn't there?"

"So, Salim nabbed this Persian who's got a real first century *stater*."

"No shit?"

"I got the Persian to talk. He fingered a guy in Dubai named Ali."

"Let me guess, Ali bin Yussef."

"Why's it everyone knows about this rat except me?"

"Doesn't work your side of the street. Go on."

"I saved his ass in Dubai."

"Don't feel too self-righteous," ad Din said. "You did humanity little service."

"Ali told me he picked up the coin in Alexandria."

"He got a *stater* in Alexandria?" ad Din said.

"From an archaeologist."

"Bingo!"

"Bingo?"

Ad Din tossed down the rest of the scotch, smacked his lips, looked over at Orhan.

"Raymund Sheffield," ad Din said.

"Who's he?"

"One slimy Brit bastard. Started out high and mighty—Cambridge Ph.D., former pal of my boss, dug around Luxor. Suddenly, valuable pieces started to go missing. Inquiries didn't turn up shit. But then, one hot item he was responsible for turned up in a sting. So, Sheffield quit, became a consultant to collectors in antiquities and rare collections."

"He's in Alexandria?"

"You didn't mention this to Farouk or Mahmoud."

"Of course not. As soon as al Mehandi opened his mouth, I knew I was in the wrong place."

"You horse's ass," said ad Din. "Shoulda come here first. Those guys will..."

"I know. I know." Orhan said.

"Hey, you wanna cigar? We just got some real nice Havanas in a big bust ..."

"Along with this scotch?"

"Like it? It's better than Haig and Haig Pinch."

"Hamid. I don't need any Cuban cigars, good scotch or ..."

"Keep your damn Turkish underwear on, Sahibi. I'm gonna lay it out for you about this asshole, Sheffield. We've got his address, details, the whole package. What's more.. "

Ad Din went over to his desk, opened it, took out a holstered pistol, passed it over to Orhan. He recognized a Glock 17 with an oversize magazine extending out of the handle.

"What's this for?" Orhan said.

"You just might need it," ad Din said.

Archaeological Expeditions

Old Souq District, Alexandria, Egypt,
The next day, 11:12 AM

The old Mercedes taxi crawled through the thicket of traffic and human congestion, marking its progress and presence with constant honking. From the back seat, Colene peered out through the dirty window past the noisy pack of cars, trucks, motor carriers at the horde of people packed, haggling, buying, selling things to eat, to wear, to use along the street.

The driver pounded on the horn, hummed to a clanging popular song that blared from a ghetto-blaster perched on top of a dashboard covered in pink faux fur.

Coming to an alley, he veered off, pulled up, jolted to a stop in front of a shop set back off the street with curtained glass windows. A sign over the door in Arabic and Latin letters identified the place.

Hamil Akbar and Sons,
Imports and Exports

The diver turned to Colene, pointed to the meter.

"Do you want me to wait for you, Madame?" he said.

"No," Colene said.

She paid him with a tip, got out, went into the shop.

Faded yellow walls peppered with fly specks marked the interior. A buzzing fluorescent lamp spewed bluish shadowed casts of light over a long scratched, scuffed wooden counter. Two men standing at one end looked up when Colene stepped in. One, a young man dressed in a white shirt, dark brown slacks, brown sandals stepped over to Colene. The other, a big man wearing a bright green silk shirt hanging over cream-colored slacks stayed, stared at her.

"May I help you?" the white-shirted young man said.

"I've an appointment with Dr. Sheffield," Colene said.

The young man, stepped to the rear of the room, opened a door, murmured something in Arabic. A moment later, Raymund Sheffield came out, smiled, came around the end of the counter, shook Colene's hand.

Tall, thin, in his late 40s, his brushed back, long thinning light brown hair hung over the back of his cotton light gray jacket, a light brown with dark brown checked shirt underneath, pleated tan slacks draped around his sparse waist caught by a slim brown leather belt with a twisted wire brass buckle. Narrow, small, ovoid light gray eyes stared at her from a prominent boney face, made serpentine when he smiled, parting narrow lips, showing long, straight teeth.

He spoke in an aspirate voice, "Dr. Mooney. A pleasure."

"Thank you for seeing me on such short notice."

"This way, please."

He led her into his office. In contrast to the dingy entrance, the interior was papered with a dull gravel-like texture. Framed photos of important people dotted the walls along with a scattering of hung artifacts. After seating Colene in a wooden chair, Sheffield sat down behind an old wooden desk.

"How may I be of service?" Sheffield said.

"Avi told me he authenticated some first century coins for you."

"Yes, a while back."

"May I ask where you came across them?"

"You may ask. But, much in my business is highly confidential."

"We can dispense with nonsense, Dr. Sheffield. I want some information about a Q documentary codex."

Sheffield hesitated, drew a pack of Benson and Hedges from his desk drawer, lit a cigarette, blew the smoke to the side, looked back at Colene, smiled.

"The Q document's a fiction," he said.

"I don't believe you."

"You think not?"

"I think we're still playing games."

"Well, I've never seen such a codex."

"Avi Feldstein told me you mentioned this codex."

"Avi talks too much. I only deal with what I can substantiate."

"Another source told me about the theft of first century coins and a possible codex."

"Let me guess. One of Feldstein's friends."

"No. Col. Orhan Mehmet in Turkey."

Sheffield tensed. For an instant his face flashed surprise, anger. He relaxed.

Colene smiled, stood, extended her hand.

"Thank you for seeing me on such short notice," she said.

Sheffield blinked, his thin lips pressed together, his eyebrows furled. His small gray eyes never left her face.

"Sorry I've been of such little assistance," he said.

"No problem," Colene said. "I can find my way out."

She rose, walked out of the office, nodded toward the two men, now joined by two others. One, an Egyptian in a faded, dirty light blue gellabya, another, an Englishman in a light tan cotton suit. The Englishman smiled, murmured, "Hullo."

Stepping outside the building onto the alley, Colene took the satellite phone from her bag, pressed a programmed number. It rang twice.

"Colene," Ara's voice came on. "Where'n the hell are you?"

"Alexandria."

"Go on."

"I just met this archaeologist, Sheffield. He knows something. Every alarm bell in my head's gone off."

"Get out of there," Ara said. "Now!"

"Ara, I ..."

A noise from behind made her turn. Sheffield, an automatic pistol in his hand pointed at her abdomen, hissed,

"Give me the phone."

Eyes on the pistol, Colene compressed the 1 and 4 keys, handed the phone to Sheffield.

Snatching it from her hand, he slammed the phone down on the pavement. It bounced without breaking.

Sheffield smashed it twice with the heel of his shoe before it broke, then pushed her inside.

The four men inside stood, stared, said and did nothing as Sheffield shoved her into his office.

~*~~*~

Ara's Den, New London, CT
5:59 AM, same day

"Colene!" Ara screamed. "Answer me!"

The line went dead. An instant later, a red light flashed, a beeping alarm chimed.

Ara stared at the phone's monitor screen. Lines of numbers scrolled across the screen. Then, it stopped flashing, sounding, the numbers remaining.

"Shit," Ara said. "Shit, oh shit!"

He set the phone down on a table top, folded his arms, paced back and forth, then snatched it up again, punched in a number.

It beeped once.

A man's voice answered, "American Embassy, Security Section."

"This is Ara Agajanian in New London, Connecticut. I'd called before about a possible alert on colleague of mine in Alexandria."

"Who did you talk to, Mr. Agajam... I'm sorry..."

"Agajanian. Clarence Wilborn."

"He's out of the office right now. Can I take a message?"

"Hell no. This is an emergency. I've made arrangements to notify him if my colleague's in danger."

"Your colleague?"

"Yes. Colene Mooney. Dr. Colene Mooney ..."

"Is she connected to the embassy?"

"There's no time for 20 questions. Her life's in danger. She needs help, now."

"Now, let me get this straight ..."

"No. You get this straight. You get hold of Wilborn *now*. You tell him Dr. Mooney's life's in danger and that I'm calling Ralph Samuelson, head of the Egypt desk, now."

"Take it easy, Mr. Aganaja ...

"No, stud. Call Wilborn now, or by God, your next posting'll be in Djibouti."

"Does Mr. Wilborn have..."

"Yes. Call him. Now!"

Ara sat the phone on the desktop, plopped down on a stool, put his face into his hands, his body convulsing as if crying– but making no tears.

Then, he picked up the satellite phone, grabbed a connection cable, plugged it into his computer.

~*~~*~

Sheffield pushed Colene into the wooden chair, plopped down on the edge of the desk in front of her, dangled the pistol from his finger.

"What in the hell are you doing?" Colene said through clenched teeth.

"You tell me."

"Look, asshole. I came to ask a few questions. You answered them and I'm going home."

"Not until we clear up a few things."

"Such as?"

"Why all this interest in a codex?"

"That's my business. I'm a biblical historian."

"At Yale. I know. Most impressive. You got my name from that shit, Feldstein."

"So?"

"I said nothing to him about a codex. He asked about it when I showed him the coins."

"That's why you snatch and break my phone, then drag me in here at gunpoint?"

"Let's cut the shit, Mooney. Where'd ..."

A loud noise rumbled in from the outer office, voices shouted in Arabic and English. Sheffield stuffed the pistol in his coat pocket, stepped over, reached for the handle– the door banged open. A tall thin Arab pushed in, shoved Sheffield back to the edge of the desk, thrust a nickel-plated revolver in his face.

"Abdi!" Sheffield said. "Get that bloody revolver out of my face."

"You're part of this Jew scheme too," the man called Abdi said. He glared over at Colene.

"Who's she?" he said.

"Knock this shit off," Sheffield said.

Abdi backhanded Sheffield in the face, throwing him backwards across the desk.

"Are you crazy?" Sheffield screamed. "You'll ruin everything."

"Dog!" Abdi said. "You're in with the Jews like all these Egyptian ass-kissers..."

Sheffield rolled across the desk, pulled the pistol from his pocket, fired at Abdi. The shot went wide.

Abdi swung the revolver, squeezed three shots into Sheffield's chest, knocked him sprawling to the floor– he writhed, twitched, groaned, then his body went limp like a balloon losing its air.

Frozen, shocked, Colene grasped the arms of the chair. Abdi jerked her upright, pointed to Sheffield's bleeding body.

"There's your ally."

Abdi pushed her through the office door.

A half dozen men in the outer office were holding guns on the four men cowering with hands raised at the end of the room.

"Tell The Man his lapdog is dead," Ali yelled at them in English. "I've got the guns. He deals with me now."

Abdi growled in Arabic, shoved Colene to one of his men. The man twisted Colene's hands behind her, lashed them with a thin sisal rope.

Turning back to the four men, Abdi ranted at them in Arabic, pushed Colene through the door to two black SUVs parked in front. He shoved her onto the floor of the back seat of the front one, then climbed into the front seat.

"*Yalla*!" he shouted.

They roared off, blaring engine noise and screeching tires.

Old Friends

Ara's Den, New London, CT
6:18 AM, same day

Ara stared at the clock. Over a half hour. No call back.

His fingers flew at his computer keyboard. Finding the wanted number, he activated it. His speakers beeped twice. A woman's voice answered.

"Director Ralph Samuelson's office."

"This is Dr. Agajanian. I need to speak to Ralph. Priority."

"Call name, please?"

"Blackbird."

After few seconds, the woman's voice chimed back on.

"The director is on the line."

"Ara? It's 6:00 in the goddam morning."

"The woman in Egypt we discussed. I think she's been taken."

"This is the... Got it. The Yale professor."

"I called Wilborn but haven't heard back yet."

"I'll call. But Ara ..., no promises."

"Understood."

Ara's chest fell. He rubbed his mouth.

He stared at the monitor screen.

What to do?

Go to Alexandria!

Back at the keyboard, he scouted flights.

Printing out a list, he grabbed a pad. Things he would need. He scribbled a list.

He booked a flight for that afternoon.

There was more to do.

Help. He'd need help.

Who?

Dan Doyle.

Back at the computer. The name entered, connected.

The speakers sounded—a man's voice.

"Celtic Salvage Services."

"Ara Agajanian. Lemme talk to Dan. Urgent."

"You're a lucky louse, Doc. He's standing but a few feet away."

A shuffle of voices. Laughter.

"Doc," Doyle said. "What's up, laddie?"

"I need your help. Can you meet me in Alexandria tomorrow morning?"

"Alexandria? What in the hell for?"

"I got a friend in deep shit and need some heavyweight back up."

"Hmm. Full crew?"

"This is life or death. I'll cover every expense."

"Worry about that later. I've got some mates working outside of Benghazi. They can be in Alexandria by tomorrow afternoon."

"This could get heavy, Dan."

"I specialize in heavy, Ara."

"You know I'll..."

"Give Jamie your flight details," Doyle said. "Talk slow 'cause he's a Galway man and donna always get the details right."

More Feebs and Spooks

FBI Office, Federal Building, Yonkers, NY
5:20 PM, later the same day

Agent Mary Rich's name had been included as an *info addee* on the Home Security data-line because she was part of a network of interest involving one Professor Colene Mooney of Yale University.

She read the memo from the Director of the Egypt desk for the third time—Colene Mooney reported as missing in Egypt.

Rich shook her head.

Not good news. She liked Colene.

A knock at her office door made her jump. Willy Johnson poked his head in.

"Come on in," Rich said. "I guess you've heard."

Willy slid his long legged body into a chair.

"There's more," he said.

"More? About Colene?"

"Kinda."

"What 'kinda?' "

"We've been eyeballing some dirty people in the ATF. One guy in particular seems to have links to the 4Sinc assholes."

"There's a match made in Hell."

"Three shipping containers of seized Ukraine arms went missing last month. We've just learned they were off-loaded in Alexandria, Egypt."

"Holy shit. That's where Colene's gone missing."

"Gotta be a tie-in, Mary."

"What can we do?"

"Sit tight. Our people in Egypt are on it but who knows where those damn weapons will wind up."

Rich made a face, looked away from Johnson.

"Great," she said.

"This is our first strong tie to 4Sinc and their bible-loving pals with friends in Congress."

"Still, nothing we can take to the bank."

"Nope," Johnson said. "But, something always beats nothing."

Nasty Business

Old Souq District, Alexandria, Egypt
Same day, 11:57 AM

Driving up in his rented car, looking at the map Hamid ad Din had given him in Cairo, Orhan spotted the alleyway a block in front of him off the main street. He wrinkled his face at the sight of clumps of people rushing up, peering down the alley. He slowed almost to a stop.

Two black SUVs burst out of the alley, scattering people, then tore off down the crowded street past Orhan's rented Honda.

Resisting his first impulse to chase after them, Orhan turned into the alley, honking onlookers out of the way, pulled up near the shop where people were pressing in, shoving each other, trying to see through the curtained windows. Orhan got out, pulled out his Interpol ID wallet, pushed his way inside, then shouted in Arabic,

"I'm a policeman."

Moving people aside, Orhan squeezed his way into the building, into the office. Onlookers huddled around the door way, gawking inside at four men bending over a body lying on the floor.

"You haven't touched anything?" Orhan said.

One, an Englishman, shook his head, no. Blood collected in pools around three holes in the dead man's chest.

Orhan bent down, looked at the body, then at the four men.

"Sheffield?" he said.

The four men stared at him with eyes still wide with shock. The Englishman nodded affirmative.

A siren's high-pitched whine penetrated the room. Orhan heard shouting from the outer office.

"Police!"

"Move back!"

"Get out here."

"Stand aside."

The onlookers pulled back from the door. A short, burley police sergeant with narrow dark eyes, a prominent nose over a bushy Joe Stalin moustache, holding a pistol, shoved his way in, came over to the body. He looked back at the crowd, waved his drawn pistol.

"Get back out of here," he shouted.

Other uniformed policemen pushed their way in, herded people back out of the room. The sergeant stared at the body, looked at the four men.

"What happened?" he said.

The young man in the white shirt spoke up, related how "...some people pushed their way in here, ... quarreled with Sheffield, shot him, and took off, taking the girl with them."

"What girl?" Orhan said.

The Police sergeant glared at Orhan.

"Who are you?" he said.

Orhan showed him his Interpol ID.

"What is your interest here?" the sergeant said.

"An international investigation," Orhan said. "The dead man was a person of interest."

"So, now he's dead," the sergeant said. "No more interest. Get outta here."

Taken aback, Orhan blinked.

"This is directly relevant to my investigation, Sergeant," he said.

The sergeant stuck his pistol in Orhan's face.

"Get out, Turk. You're crapping up *my* investigation."

Orhan opened his hands palms out, backed out of the room. The sergeant shouted orders to clear the room. The uniformed officers shoved the four witnesses out. From the outer office, Orhan watched the sergeant walk around the body.

An ambulance pulled up outside. Orhan saw the attendants unload a collapsible gurney. They wheeled it inside to the office. As the medics loaded the body onto the stretcher, Orhan saw the sergeant go through the desk, remove some papers, tuck them in a folder, then follow the body outside. Another uniformed police officer called out to him.

"Sergeant Gamaal," he said. "You're not going to wait for the detectives?"

"Idiot," Gamaal said. "I've important evidence to get back to the office."

Gamaal shouldered his way outside, got into a car, drove away without looking back.

Orhan stepped over to the other police officer, showed him his ID.

"Why no forensic?" Orhan said.

The policeman shrugged his shoulders, rolled his eyes.

The police seated the four witnesses in chairs. Orhan pulled up a chair, sat next to the one in a green shirt.

"Would you like a smoke?" Orhan said.

The green shirted man nodded. Orhan called to a nearby uniform officer to give the man a cigarette. When the man lit up, he looked over at Orhan, spoke in Turkish.

"Turk?"

"Yes," said Orhan.

"I'm Azeri. I worked in Izmir 2 years before I came to Egypt."

"What happened here?" Orhan said.

"Abdi and his goons came in, screamed at the Doctor."

"Abdi?" Orhan said.

"Abdi ibn Noor. Palestinian."

Orhan caught his breath, nodded.

"What happened next," he asked.

"There was shooting," the Azeri said. "Then they left dragging the girl with them."

"What girl?" Orhan said.

"One who came to see the Doctor. American. Never saw her before."

Orhan froze.

O Shit! Colene!

Orhan took a deep breath. Then, he let it out.

“You say Abdi ibn Noor did this?” he said.

“Yes.”

“Where did they take her?”

“Allaah knows.”

“Why did Abdi kill Sheffield?”

“They argued. When he left, Abdi told us to tell The Man that he had the guns now.”

“What ‘Man?’ “

”The Man in the big house.”

The detectives arrived. The chief inspector, a big man with a pock-marked face in a black suit came over to Orhan.

“You a witness?” he asked

Orhan handed him his ID. The detective looked, nodded, handed it back.

“What brings you to Alexandria, Effendi?” he said.

“An important investigation. Sheffield was a person of interest. I arrived just as they drove off. Two black American-made SUVs. I didn’t get close enough to see the plates.”

“Wouldn’t have made any difference,” the detective said.

“I can think of nothing else I can tell you to help your case,” Orhan said.

“Don’t worry, Effendi. It’s already shitted up.”

Orhan turned to the Azeri in the green shirt. “Can you talk to me later?”

“Yes. There’s a coffee house around the corner. I can meet you there in about an hour after the police take our statements.”

Floor Mat

City streets, Alexandria, Egypt
Same day, 12:05 PM

The two vans roared down crowded streets, made screeching turns to the sounds of honking, shaken fists, cursing. In the back, pushed down on the floor, Colene fought panic– events of the past few moments flashed through her mind—a video tape on a short, endless spool.

Everything hurt in a wrong, wrong way.

Coming to that seedy part of town.

The serpentine Sheffield– his gun thrust in her face, smashing her satellite phone, pushing at gunpoint into his office.

Men bursting in– gunfire.

Seeing another man killed right in front of her, then being dragged into the next room.

Her hands being lashed behind her– a smelly, twisted rag stretched across her mouth, its salty taste of dried sweat causing her to gag.

Being hauled outside, shoved onto the floor of the back seat.

Men piling in– holding her down under their stinking, dirty feet.

Feeling body pain, discomfort– humiliation.

Hearing the staccato jabber of their nattering in Arabic.

Then, drifting back to coming up to that damned office in the taxi with the dirty windows—

Colene shook her head, forced herself to listen, look, smell–think in the present.

The man in the front– their leader.

He shot Sheffield.

He shouted directions to the others.

Something about him...

She heard more yelling waves of Arabic.

Arabic. Why didn't I ever study Arabic?

Got to learn Arabic, she told herself. *Arabic– very useful.*

What will they do to me?

She grit her teeth.

Think! Don't give in. Can't be any more scared than I am now.

Don't think about that, damn it.

The buzz of voices between the front and back continued.

Arabic– shouldn't be that hard. I mean, I studied Hebrew, Aramaic. If I knew Arabic, I'd know what these assholes are talking about.

Would that make any difference now?

Colene heard the man in front yelling at the driver.

Directions? Instructions?

Another swerve caused Colene to shift her weight, lurch, roll against a man's feet—a small man, seated at her head. He glared down at her—his thin face, narrow beady eyes, rodent-like.

He kicked her.

"Muffabidd!" she yelled against the gag.

The small rat-like man kicked her in the ribs. Colene howled like a dog.

Her assailant raised his foot.

The man in the front seat, turned, grabbed the kicker, jerked his nose up next to his, shook him, yelled in his rat face, then shoved him back against the seat.

The kicker stopped kicking her.

The man on the other side shifted his feet to avoid hitting her.

The man in the front seat—Sheffield had called him 'Abdi'—looked down at her.

"Sorry," he said.

Abdi gave the little kicker a quick dirty look, then turned his attention out the window.

Colene tried to stretch her legs.

The two men in back had shoved their feet to either side of the floor. Having nowhere to move, she drew her knees up close to her abdomen.

Guy in front killed Sheffield, she thought. *But, he stopped that little asshole from kicking me. Something about that guy. Familiar. What? His nose? Thin face?*

The car hit a bump—jostled her, hurting her rib cage.

Doesn't matter. Can't trust them. What will they do to me?

The panic started to return.

A thought came to her—a game she played as a kid.

Lying on the floor, she'd pretend she was a rug. But, that was then.

Not a rug now. A floor mat.

She concentrated on being a floor mat.

Floor mats don't think. I won't either.

In the ridiculousness of the moment, she felt her fear letting up.

She smiled behind the rag twisted in her mouth like a horse's war bridle.

I'm gonna get outta this shit—somehow.

Ride in the Country

Coffee and Tea shop, Old Souq District, Alexandria, Egypt
Same day, 1:37 PM

The little coffee shop was in an alcove filled with round wire tables and chairs. Male customers in gellabyas, Western clothes, slacks and sandals, sat drinking tea and coffee, talking, laughing, gossiping, waving hands. Out of the corner of his eye, Orhan watched the table next to him, overheard conversations.

"There was an Englishman there."

"He was the one killed?"

"Yes. There was another one too."

"A strange shop. The curtains always closed."

"Weird things took place there."

"Lots of Europeans came there."

"Nobody knew what went on. Must've been some bad business."

"Did you see those black American vans? Organized crime for sure."

"The drivers weren't Egyptian."

"Most likely Americans disguised as Egyptians."

The Azeri in the green shirt came in, saw Orhan, sat at his table, ordered coffee, leaned over, spoke in Turkish in a low voice,

"I'm Abdulatif, accountant. I was the Doctor's fiscal manager."

"What did Sheffield do?" Orhan said.

"Bought and sold artifacts. I just kept the management ledger. I'd calculate expenses, give him the figures. He'd give me a check from a separate corporate account. I'd deposit it and pay the bills."

"You never saw any other transactions?"

"No. The Doctor was closed mouth about those things. At the end of each quarter, I'd prepare a spread sheet to pay the taxes on the revenues and expenses. But, I never saw any invoices beyond what he gave me."

"What was he buying and selling?"

"Mostly trinkets. Cheap jewelry from India and China he'd wholesale to local businesses here and Cairo—phony hieroglyphic cartouches made in Taiwan sold to tourist shops in Luxor and Aswan."

"Any big money items?"

Abdulatif smiled. Orhan took a swig of coffee.

"That trade was done under the table," Adbulatif said.

"So, who's this "Man" you mentioned?"

"A shadow. Only the Doctor knew him."

"Was he bankrolling Sheffield?"

"I never saw any outside financing but a few weeks ago the Doctor and I went to this big house outside of the city. It was like a fortress. I waited in the car. The Doctor went in, then came out later with a small box and said, 'There's a lot of money in here.' "

"What was it?"

"I don't know. The box was small, about 10cm wide, 15cm long and 5cm deep. The Doctor said that he could always depend on 'The Man.' "

"You never saw him?"

"Only the Doctor ever saw him. Even Mr. Robert didn't."

"Who's Mr. Robert?"

"An Englishman. The Doctor's overseas seller and buyer."

Orhan drained the last of his coffee as an old waiter arrived with coffee for the Azeri. Shuffling his cup and saucer onto the waiter's tray, Orhan paid, waved the waiter away to keep the change.

"Can you find this place again?" Orhan said.

“I can,” Abdulatif said.

~*~~*~

They drove west of the city through the outskirts of an industrial area. Abdulatif pointed them on a road back away from the coastal area. It came out onto a small bay, tucked in some rolling hills blocked off from the seashore. A spit of land in the shape of a short-stemmed sunflower extended into the estuary forming a narrow peninsula which fanned out into a large, flat 2 hectare island-like area.

A narrow road ran over the narrow strip up to a large, four-storey flat roofed house that sprawled over the greater portion of the land mass, circled by a 8' high cyclone fence. A large gate framed the entrance cutting off any intrusion from the estuary except for a landing that jutted out from the west side. A motor yacht and a speedboat were docked at the pier.

Scanning through field glasses, Orhan spotted a landing strip behind the house. A helicopter pad stood at one end. Three or four armed guards in desert fatigues roamed the grounds.

Orhan lowered the glasses.

“I don’t see either of the 2 vehicles I saw drive off,” he said.

“Abdi wouldn’t come here,” Abdulatif said.

“Oh?”

“The Doctor didn’t like Abdi– likely The Man didn’t either.”

Orhan looked through the glasses again, spotted a convey of three gray vans tearing down the road, over the strip out to the island structure. Orhan watched two armed guards dressed in desert fatigues, eyes covered in sun glasses open the gate, snap to attention as the vans roared in. Orhan counted 12 people dressed in the same fatigues as the guard get out of the vans.

A big, muscular man wearing dark sunglasses, a black ball cap, a tight fitting tee shirt tucked into fatigue trousers popped out from the front passenger side of the first van, ran up the steps, turned, barked orders to the others.

They stood ramrod straight at attention until the dark capped, tee-shirted leader went inside with 2 others in tow. Then, the remaining men relaxed, greeted the guards, shared smokes, chatted.

"Who are those men?" Abdulatif said.

"I don't know," Orhan said. "But, they're all Americans."

Orhan scanned over the surrounding area once more, shot several pictures with his phone camera of the house, the guards, the roads in and out, the landing, boats in the estuary.

"Let's go back," he said. "This place is impenetrable– for now."

Some Troops land

Al 'ila, The Big House, outside of Alexandria, Egypt
The same day, 4:20 PM

Morris pushed the door open, strode down a hall past walls littered with memorabilia, artifacts, art, his two assistants in step at his heels. At the end of the short hall, he saw a tall man, dressed in fatigues, standing at rigid attention waiting for him.

"Platt," Morris said. "Where's DH?"

A slight inch taller than Morris at 6'5', lanky, wiry muscles stretched over a long, thin frame, Platt's ruddy, freckled skin, the sunburned, outdoors look of a redhead, showed on his hands and face in dark brown blotches. Coarse reddish brown hair combed back, cropped short over sides close-clipped to the skull framed a wrinkled, hound-dog face.

"Ain't here, sir," he said.

Platt's voice, like the sound of gravel driven over at slow speed, was low, musical in its Southern slow, drawn-out pace

"What the fuck's going on?" Morris said.

Platt squinted, snapped his hands behind his back in a parade rest as he spoke,

"Steele came into town. Next day he went out to collect the assets– then, the following day, local cops found Steele's corpse all shot up. A pack of Palestine camel jockeys headed up by an asshole name of Abdi ripped off our assets."

"Who's this Abdi dick?"

"The Big Guy dug him up—had a brother named Isaac who was his gofer. Big guy sent this Isaac to the States where he got his ass sniped in a coffee shop."

Morris started, caught his breath, looked over at his two assistants, shook his head, then muttered, "What a circle jerk."

"Sir?" Platt said.

"Nothing," Morris said. "Let's go in and set down."

A dark skin servant in a white gellabya with a red sash and white turban, came up, whispered to Platt.

"Excuse me, sir," Platt said to Morris. "Phone call."

Platt went over to a large desk at one end of the living room next to a set of glass doors leading outside to a patio surrounded by the lawn.

He picked up a phone, listened, nodded looking at Morris, motioned for him to sit down. The servant came in, set coffee mugs in front of the seated men.

After a short exchange, Platt came over, sat down next to Morris.

"They shot Sheffield," Platt said.

"Who's Sheffield?" Morris said.

"A Limey archeologist the Big Guy was dealing with."

"What's this got to do with recovering our assets?" Morris said.

"It was Abdi that killed the sonofabitch."

"Where's that leave us?" Morris said.

Platt narrowed his eyes, pursed his lips, put three teaspoons of sugar in a white coffee mug, poured in a dollop of milk, stirred it. He looked over his shoulder, called out,

"Honey? Could you come in here for a minute."

A tall, big-boned women dressed in fatigues came in. She wore no make-up, her shoulder length dark brown gray-streaked hair was combed, pulled straight back held by a single black band. Her small narrow brown eyes were set deep in her face over a straight nose, large mouth, square chin. She did not smile.

The men stood.

"This is my wife, Mabel," Platt said. He turned to her, said,

"Sugar, you remember Col. Morris. This is his adjutant, Carly Rambeau and his orderly, Bob Deacon."

"Gentlemen," she said, shook hands without smiling.

"Baby, didn't that Abdi have some relatives around here?" Platt said.

"No," Mabel said. "But the two guys that work on the motor launch are from Palestine."

Platt grinned, patted his wife on her butt.

"That's my girl," Platt said. "Thirty years as an Army supply sergeant, she don't miss a trick."

"I'm confused," Morris said.

"Don't be," Platt said. "We just got a key piece to the puzzle."

They stood up. Morris and his two assistants followed Platt, along with his wife, Mabel, out to the boat house at the end of the dock slip. Platt called to two armed guards who went to the motor boat, grabbed the two Palestinians, brought them into the boathouse, shoved them into chairs.

Platt folded his hands behind his back, walked over to them, leaned over, his face next to theirs.

"Where'd Abdi take them containers he hijacked?" he said.

Yusuf, the taller one said, "We know nothing of Abdi doing."

"We are no see him for over a week," Mekki, the younger one said.

"Boys," Platt said. "I'm gonna ask y'all again real nice. Where'd Abdi take them containers?"

"On my father's grave, we don't know no containers," Yusuf said.

"I'm swear too," Mekki said. "We now know what Abdi do."

Platt back-handed Yusuf across the face.

"Where's Abdi?" Platt said.

Yusuf wiped at the blood dribbling from his nose, scowled at Platt.

"You hit me," he said. "I still don't know what you ask."

Platt turned to Mekki, said,

"Where's Abdi, boy?"

"Please, sir. I know nothing."

Platt sighed, looked around the boat house. A tea tray with two small glasses on a table near a work bench caught his eye. He walked over, set the glasses on the table top, picked up a hammer from the work bench, smashed the two tea glasses into shards.

He picked up a wide-mouth gas funnel off the workbench, took a hacksaw, sawed off the smaller pointed end leaving a nub, then swept the broken glass into the funnel. He turned, nodded to a burley blond guard with a buzz cut, a US Marine Corps emblem tattooed on his neck.

The guard pulled Yusuf's hands behind the back of the chair, slipped a plastic tieband over his wrists, bound them tight with a quick jerk, grabbed Yusuf's hair, forced his head back, pried his mouth open by pulling down on his chin.

Platt shoved the stub end of the funnel into Yusuf's open mouth, shook the shards down, turned to his wife.

"Honey," Platt said. "Could you please hand me some of that roll of duct tape yonder on that bench."

Mabel snatched the roll off the workbench, stretched off an 8" piece, tore it off with her teeth, handed the strip to her husband.

"Thank you, sugar," Platt said.

He stretched the tape over Yusuf's open mouth, looked at Mekki.

"Where's Abdi?"

The other guard, a big African-American wearing shades, a black beret, pushed Mekki down in the chair, pulled his arms back, secured his wrists with a plastic slipband.

"On my soul," Mekki said. "We don't know where this Abdi."

Platt backhanded Yusuf in the face again. His eyes rolled back, he gagged. Blood leaked from his nose. He began to choke.

"Where is he?" Platt said to Mekki.

"Loose him," Mekki screamed. "He chokings on his blood. He don't know Abdi's where is. In Allaah's name, if I know I tell you."

"Where's Abdi hang out?" Platt said.

"He has place at old waterfront."

"Where in the old waterfront?"

"It's big shed on pier along the Jazeera."

"What's the number?"

"81"

"You sure?"

"Yes. Like prayers in left hand. This place is Abdi's sister husband. A policeman."

"Bullshit," Platt said. "Ain't no Palestine policemen here."

"He is Egyptian. Wife Filistiania."

Platt looked over at Morris, winked.

"We got the motherfucker, sir."

Platt turned, pulled an old Colt .45 from a belt holster under his fatigue blouse, fired a round through the choking Yusuf's head, then another above Mekki's wide-eyes, tucked the pistol back in the holster, then turned to his wife.

"Sugarlumps," he said. "Think you could rustle us up some sandwiches. Dunno about these guys but I'm as hungry as a bitch wolf."

On the Way Back

Outside of Alexandria, Egypt
The same day, 4:45 PM

On the way back to Alexandria from the big house on the island in the darkening shadows cast by the descending sun in the foothills near the coastline, Orhan looked over at Abdulatif.

"So, why was Sheffield working with Abdi?" Orhan said.

"Abdi was a donkey," Abdulatif said. "Sometime you need donkeys."

"So, the 'him,' Abdi told you to tell was this 'Man' you mention?"

"Exactly."

"What about that pushy police sergeant, Gamaal?"

"Never seen him before."

"I saw him rifle through Sheffield's desk and take some things."

"I saw that, too."

"Any idea what he took?"

"No. But I know the Doctor didn't keep important papers in his desk."

~*~~*~

After dropping Abdulatif off at his home, Orhan phoned Hamid ad Din, related all that happened that day.

"Any idea who this 'Man' might be?" Orhan said.

"I can only speculate," ad Din said. "Every once in a while, we'd see some big deal pop up and know there's some evidence suggesting a single controlling source. But, my people have never been able to break into that locked circle."

"Think this 'Man' could be the King Pin?"

"I think all day, beloved brother, but it doesn't mean shit."

"What about this rat nest we found?"

"First I've heard of it."

"I sent you the photos."

"Very helpful. I'll take these to my Minister tomorrow."

"I'm staying here in Alexandria."

"Why?"

"My worst nightmare has unfolded."

"What do you mean?"

"The man who killed my wife and son kidnapped the woman I'm in love with."

More Troops Land

El Nouzha International Airport, Alexandria, Egypt
Next day, 6:27 AM

Buzzed, jet-lagged from two sleepless nights, Ara Agajanian stumbled from the plane's door through the landing pod behind two heavy-set Egyptian women, one grasping an armful of shopping bags, blankets, toys, the other clutching a sleeping child who had screamed all during the flight. Blocked by the two women in the narrow passageway, Ara choked back a scream.

Behind him, the long queue of disembarking passengers pushed through the confined opening of a single glass door into the customs landing portal area where uniformed agents in peaked caps lurked in tall glass-encased booths, demanding passports, landing papers, declaration sheets.

Ara dodged up to an empty station. A mustached agent took Ara's blue passport, opened, glanced through it.

"The purpose of your visit to Egypt?" he said.

"Business," Ara said.

"What kind of business?"

"Official business."

The agent shrugged, stamped the passport, shoved it back to Ara, turned his gaze the next person on line.

Ara pushed into the customs clearance area. More uniformed agents hovered behind low inspection counters.

An agent that looked like the one in the booth asked for his baggage stubs, passed them to an attendant who retrieved two pieces of luggage, a case for electronic equipment which he placed on the inspection table. The agent went through each piece, poked under the foam insulation in the electronics case.

"What is for all this equipment?" he said.

Ara thrust a document into the agent's hand.

"Here's my clearances," he said.

The agent signaled a supervisor who looked at the documents, nodded, mumbled. The agent made a check mark on Ara's luggage with blue chalk.

Ara scooped up the cases, rolled out into the reception area, rode the escalator down to the ground floor.

People greeting friends and relatives fanned out over the reception area. Ara scanned for familiar faces.

A voice behind him, made him turn.

"I'll relieve you of that weapons case."

The speaker was a thin man in plain clothes. He flashed an ID written in Arabic in Ara's face.

"This isn't a weapons case," Ara said. "It's just a tracking device."

"I'm confiscating it," the man said.

"Like hell, you are!"

A big man in khaki shirt and shorts stepped in front of the Egyptian plainclothesman.

"Who are you?" the plainclothesman said.

"Someone who knows that you're full of bullshit."

"I'm an official of the Egyptian government..."

"You're a fucking liar and a crook," the big man said. "Get out before I arrange it so they'll be removing your dead ass from here."

The self-declared plainclothesman turned around, disappeared into the crowd.

The big man grinned at Ara. Two men appeared at his side, took Ara's luggage.

"You look like shit, me boy-o," the big man said.

"That good, Dan?" Ara said.

Standing 6'3", Dan Doyle's blue eyes under bushy reddish blond eyebrows flickered, reflecting flashes of light. Short, curly reddish blond hair cropped short on top, buzzed close to the skull on the sides, a long thin scar marked his face racing from his left forehead to below his cheekbone.

Doyle indicated a tall thin man with short, dark brown hair, deep-set blue eyes standing next to him.

"You remember Jamie O'Naill, Galway lad, but can't help it."

"Grand to see you again, Doc," O'Naill said.

Doyle pointed to the man on his right.

"Dr. Hatim al Atar, our marine biologist." Doyle said.

Ara shook hands with a giant Egyptian gnome, his thick neck erupted from broad, muscular shoulders that supported a wrinkled broad face with a thick moustache spread in a wide grin. Short black curly hair crowned the dome of his head like inked moss on an ancient oak log. The arms poking out of the gold polo shirt covering his thick 5' 4" body were knotted, defined like a weight lifter's.

"Charming to meet you, Dr. Agajanian," Hatim said.

Doyle and Hatim picked up Ara's luggage, moved to the exit as O'Naill rushed off to get the van.

"We'll head out to the boat," Doyle said.

After they stowed the luggage in the rear of a blue VW van, O'Naill drove off with Doyle beside him, Ara and Hatim in the back.

"The rest of the lads will get here later today," Doyle said.

"I want to set up as soon as we get there," Ara said.

On the way, Ara sat back, drew a deep breath, stared out the window at the passing traffic, street scenes, people, colors, noise–until it all blurred. He dropped his head, dozed off.

Ara woke with a start. They were driving up to a docking area station. The guards on duty smiled, waved them through.

"Amazing what a wee bit of change'll buy," O'Naill said.

He drove the van down to the end of the slip, then stopped in front of a 125' red and black boat with the hull name, *Gael Lass*. A big man came down the gangway to greet them. Doyle got out, slapped him on the arm.

"Ara," Doyle said. "Our engineer, Gibby Owens. Welshman—but hardly ever talks."

Standing 6'5", broad chested, thick armed, dark brown eyes in an unsmiling face, pointed prominent nose, under dark brown hair cut in a buzz cut, Owens took Ara's hand in a gentle touch, nodded.

O'Naill and Hatim unloaded Ara's baggage. O'Naill lifted the case with electronic gear.

"Well now, look at what the Doc brought," he said.

"Let's get that set up right away," Ara said.

"Take a rest first," Doyle said.

"I'm OK," Ara said. "I napped on the way here."

"We can argue after we've had a drink," Doyle said.

Coming aboard, Ara looked over the large salvage boat. The afterdeck was overlaid with bamboo parquet tiles running aft to a drop-off fantail. Passageways ran along both sides. The sleek all-weather foredeck thrust out in front of the craft, the glassed-in bridge topped by an open conning station.

Ara followed the others into a wardroom below the bridge level.

"Let's get the tracker going," he said.

Ara took an electronic device the size of a small computer tower out of the case, plopped it on the table, plugged it in, fired it up, set up his laptop next to it.

"I've read about this kind of a tracker," O'Naill said.

"How's it work?" Doyle said.

"It's a transmitter that seeks a chip which sends a feedback signal to my laptop."

"A chip?" O'Naill said.

"A microchip, thin as a small postage stamp will echo a signature signal from the tracker's impulse within a 25 to 30 mile radius," Ara said.

"Where's the chip?" Jamie said.

Ara hesitated, cleared his throat.

"Embedded in Colene's buttocks," he said.

A pause. Silence.

Ara looked up, four sets of eyes fixed on his face.

"It's stuck to her arse?" Doyle said.

"I slipped it below the skin," Ara said.

The four men burst into laughter.

"Ah, the luck of that wee chippie," Doyle said.

"Better so if it works," O'Naill said.

Ara pecked at the keyboard of his laptop.

A black graduated reticle appeared centered in a red screen. Ara brought up a city map of Alexandria divided into sectors, superimposed the reticle over the map, moved the image from region to region.

A green blip appeared.

Ara zoomed the city map showing the streets.

"Hatim," Doyle said, "Do you know that area of the city?"

"Move it a bit to the right," Hatim said.

Ara moved it.

"The Jazeera in the Old Port District," Hatim said. "Many abandoned buildings there."

"Can you get us there?" Ara said.

"Yes. It's about a half-hour from here."

"When can we go?" Ara said.

"As soon as the rest of the lads get here," Doyle said.

"Davy's only about an hour away," O'Naill said.

"That'll give us a bit of planning time." Doyle said.

~*~~*~

From the bridge, Ara saw the hull name of the sister boat, *Gael Lad*, as she pulled alongside the end of the slip next to them. O'Naill, Owen and two more crewmen, secured the bow and stern lines on the dock. The gangplank dropped, a uniformed Egyptian customs officer climbed up ahead of O'Naill and Owen.

Doyle, at Ara's side pointed to a tall, sandy-haired man in khaki shorts, shirt with a red beret shaking hands with the custom agent.

"That hard-headed Scot's Davy Munroe," Doyle said. "We were in the same Royal Navy commando unit during the Falklands and Iraq."

Ara spotted a short, attractive blond woman in khaki pants, her hair cut in a short bob, step up to join Davy and the inspector.

"Who's she?"

"Mara, Davy's wife– the only human being on earth who can tell him what to do."

"When can we go after Colene?" Ara said.

"About twenty minutes," Doyle said. "Hatim and two of the lads are getting us another van and a truck."

"How many of us will there be?"

"An even dozen."

"Arms?"

"Yes."

The Egyptian custom agent left.

Munroe, his wife, Mara, and four crewmen came down and boarded the *Gael Lass*.

Mara shook Ara's hand,

"So," she said. "You're the lad who saved old Danny's arse."

"Dunno what for," Munroe said.

Mara punched her husband in the arm.

"Be nice," she said.

Monroe looked over at Doyle.

"Where do we stand?" he said.

"Hatim's on his way here with vehicles. We'll gear up, deploy and see what the site offers us."

"Right," Munroe said. "Mara and Tony will watch the boats."

"That'll give the buggers at least a bit of a sporting chance," Doyle said

Al Atar drove up in a VW van like the one parked on the dock. Another crewman drove an old, battered Land Rover pickup behind him. While Ara set up his laptop, Doyle and Munroe organized their crews. The men geared up, checked out weapons, tools, equipment, stowed them in green canvas duffle-bags, then moved them down to the vehicles.

"Load the duffels into the vans and the truck, then we'll go see what's at the other end of line," Doyle said.

Without a word, the men loaded the weapon-filled canvas bags in the backs of the three vehicles, climbed in, then took off.

Hatim drove the lead van, Doyle sitting next to him in front with Ara in the back seat. O'Naill sat behind the wheel in the following van with Munroe seated beside him. Two other crewmen tailed in the pickup.

Ara opened his laptop, zoomed in on the spot in the old waterfront. Hatim rolled down the window, hummed an Arabic song, lit a small cigar.

"The old waterfront's maybe 20 minutes away," he said.

"You know the street?" Ara said.

"The old Jazeera. Many old abandoned buildings, lots of contraband."

"What about the police?" Ara said.

Hatim smiled.

"Ah, yes, the police," he said.

They didn't speak again until Hatim drove down a long street lined by dilapidated abandoned buildings. Ara zoomed in on the computer screen, enlarging the picture.

"This is it," he said.

Hatim drove past the building, parked a block away. Doyle turned, looked over the scene.

"Time to punch in on the time clock." he said.

Double-take

Kom Ishu, outside of Alexandria, Egypt
same day, 11:32 AM

In levis, Israeli paratrooper boots, khaki shirt under a knit collar canvas jacket, black wool beret pulled forward over his brow, dark shades covering his eyes, Orhan kept his eyes on the house across the street.

Hamid ad Din had given him the address of Gamaal, the nasty-tempered police sergeant. An hour deep in his wait, Orhan saw movement. The door opened, Gamaal– short, dark, thick black mustache and eyebrows, cased the street, then with a glance back over his shoulder, got into a washed-out blue Simca, drove off.

Giving the Simca plenty of distance, Orhan followed from the outlying urban center into the old port district, noting that the Simca did not slow or give any sign that Gamaal was aware of a tail. Orhan's rented Honda, a faded, dust-covered gray, looked like thousands of other rentals in the city. He lagged far behind, just keeping the Simca in sight.

Coming into the Old Port area, the Simca turned down the Jazeera, a long road across a bridge that ran down into a spit of land that formed a peninsula thrust out into the waterfront.

A bridge covered a drainage trench hacking off the base of the finger of land connecting the road to the waterfront roadway which unfolded into a street lined with worn-out warehouses, vacant lots, storage areas, dumpsters, abandoned boats.

Orhan watched the Simca turn down a side road, pull to a stop alongside a bleached-brown wooden warehouse. Driving past the building, Orhan parked the Honda near a fenced-off area full of parked rusting tractors. Checking around, he snatched up a small day pack, got out, moved back toward the faded warehouse.

The wooden building sat back a hundred meters off the road. The main door was on the side, a small parking area in front. The windows were boarded up with narrow, 1X6" planking with gaps showing through.

On the far side of the building about a hundred meters away, Orhan saw a raised area on pilings, the remains of an abandoned jetty, its top, littered with the carcasses of a number of beached, worn-out boats, equipment, rusting car frames, some small weathered storage containers, that gave a good view of the nearby building.

The jetty connected to the warehouse by a rock, cement block, gravel and junk-strewn pile waterfront. Orhan saw he could cross over, then come up on the rear of the building.

Bent over, Orhan moved along the jetty's rim around to a spot where he could drop down to the crossing. He paused, looked across at the side door and boarded windows of the warehouse for signs of anyone watching.

A tap at his ear made him freeze.

A voice behind him said in English, "Don't move."

Orhan peeked over his shoulder, saw the gun barrel, raised his hands.

"Back up. Slowly. Hands raised."

Two men gripped his arms, dragged him backwards, twisted his arms, seized his wrists with a nylon restraint. Orhan turned to see them, in light green fatigues, faces smeared with face camo paint, maroon berets with no insignia.

"Brits?" he said,

The two men glanced at each other, pulled Orhan to his feet.

"Walk," one said.

They shoved him in front of them, pointed to a spot behind a corroded, corrugated tank.

A large man crouched there, decked out like the others, looked up at Orhan with blue eyes.

"Who're you?" he said.

Before Orhan could open his mouth, he heard a familiar loud whisper call his name,

"Orhan!"

Orhan turned, looked into the wide-eyed stare of Ara Agajanian.

"You know him, Doc?" Doyle, the big blue-eyed man said.

"Yes," Ara said. "He's on our side."

The big man nodded to the two men. Orhan felt his hands snipped free.

Ara gripped both of Orhan's hands.

"We're pretty sure Colene's in that building over there." he said.

"So am I," Orhan said.

Ara introduced Orhan to Doyle and the others. Orhan turned back to look at the old warehouse.

"Palestinians," he said. "They killed this guy Colene went to see."

"We know that," Ara said. "What they don't know is I planted a tracking device on Colene before she left."

"How did you manage that?" Orhan said.

"We'll have to discuss that another time," Doyle said. "Look. More company arriving."

Three gray SUVs sped down the road, thumped over the bridge, tore down the street, pulled up in front of the warehouse. Four men, dressed in desert fatigues, body armor, gray balaclavas, automatic weapons at high port, poured out of each car.

They formed into two teams, fanned out– one swept around to the side door– the other to the front. One member of each team slung his weapon, swung a 12 pound sledgehammer to the doors– both of the rickety wooden doors splintered at the impact.

The men kicked them open, entered the building firing their weapons.

The sputtered see-see reports of suppressed discharges along with three or four gunshots reached Orhan and the others hidden behind the trash on the facing jetty. They saw, smelled, heard rounds ripping through the wooden walls of the building.

Ara cried out,

"They're killing everyone in there!"

He lurched forward. Doyle and Orhan both caught, hauled him down, held him.

Orhan's face was pale. His eyes blazed. He choked,

"We can do nothing."

"Getting ourselves killed solves nothing, Doc," Doyle said.

Ara groaned, gripped Orhan's arm.

"We can't just let them kill Colene," he said.

The firing stopped.

"Easy, Doc," Doyle said. "Let's see what's up."

Orhan pulled a set of binoculars from his backpack, focused on the building.

Now, noise spilled out– voices, a man screaming.

"Someone's alive in there," Doyle said.

Then, silence.

More voices in muddled conversation, scuffling sounds leaked out of the building. Then, a woman's voice pierced out, "You sonofa..."

Orhan jerked his head back to Ara.

Ara's dark brown eyes widened, his mouth twisted into a tight grin.

"She's alive!" he said.

Orhan choked, nodded.

"Well, lads," Doyle said. "Let's see what else's on this evening's dance card."

Two men limped out of the building, propping up two more with blood on their fatigues. They eased into the rear van, backed around, took off down the street.

"Twelve in," Doyle said. "Four out. Three wounded."

Four more men piled out of the building, fanned out covering the exit of two more holding a man– an Arab, his mouth closed with duct tape, hands seized behind his back– between them. Two more came out with a woman– hands bound, mouth sealed with the gray tape. She kicked one of her holders in the leg.

"Colene," Ara said. "She's OK."

"Who's the Arab?" Doyle said.

"Abdi ibn Noor," Orhan said. "He kidnapped Colene."

The men pushed their two prisoners into the back seat of the vans, climbed in beside them. The four men covering their retreat, retreated back, climbed in the two vans. Then, they backed around, took off, Colene in the back seat of the lead van.

"We can track them," Ara said.

"No worry," Orhan said. "I know where they're going."

Hope Springs Eternal

81 Jazeera, Old Port District, Alexandria, Egypt
same day, 10:20 AM

The smell of cigarette smoke from the next room bit Colene's nostrils. She gagged, then forced her lips apart under the cellophane tape they used to replace the rag covering her mouth. She stuck her tongue through the opening, licked at the glue on the inner surface.

It loosened. Running her tongue around her lips, she freed her mouth. Breathing was easier now.

Colene shivered at the thought of rats. Now, used to the dim light in the unlit room, she twisted against the rough sisal of the tight cords binding her wrists and ankles, looked around, saw musty smelling wooden boxes, discarded paper containers, piles of unclear detritus cluttering the other wall of the small room.

The sound of loud voices in Arabic from the outer room bled through the door. The light from under the door threw a shadow across the floor, reflecting on something shiny. Colene focused her eyes.

A glass jar.

She scooted across, rolled the jar to the other side of the room, raised her legs, brought them down on the jar. The heels of her shoes bumped it, sending it rolling against the wall. Her heel hurt from the impact.

Scooting again to the jar, she pushed into the angle where the wall meet the floor. Again, she smashed at it, this time kicking with the heel of her shoes. The jar jumped, moved with the impact without breaking. The wooden floor and wall absorbed too much of the force to shatter the jar.

Glancing around again, she spotted a rusty pipe elbow at one end of the room. Laying in a pile of rubbish, it was the size of a fist with a stopper plug screwed in on one end. Scooting over, she rolled it out with her shoe heels, pushed, tugged, rolled it to the jar, turned it so the pointed end of the plug faced the jar, then jammed it with her heel.

A satisfying shatter.

Then, she heard the voices in the next room stop. At the sound of the approaching footsteps, Colene pushed her back up to the broken glass jar, sweeping aside the rusty pipe elbow with her fingers.

The door opened. The short dark man with narrow, rat-like scowling eyes glared at her. He came in, looked around.

"What is here?" he said in English,

"Fuck you, asshole," Colene said from behind her mouth covering.

All the rat man heard was an angry grumble.

"Being quiet too much, stupid woman," he said.

He turned, left, slamming the door.

Colene heard him walk back. The loud conversation resumed.

She picked through the bits of broken glass with her finger tips, felt a long shard. Moving it away from the other shattered glass debris, she tilted it with her finger tip, worked into her fingers, turned it, began to saw at the tough sisal fibers of the cord.

A shout from the outer room made her stop. Their voices went high pitched, excited.

A bang. Then, a crashing sound.

Gunfire. A series of pop-crackling sounds.

Bullets popped through the walls, sang past her ears like angry wasps.

Colene threw herself flat on the floor.

She heard men, coming in the building, more of the snick-snick sound, a few more hornet-like buzzes through the dark room, thumps, breaking when the bullets hit the rummage along the wall.

Then, quiet.

Voices again, English, American English.

"Clear?"

"Clear."

"Clear."

Colene kicked her heels, licked at the tape, hollered,

"In here."

Footsteps, the door was kicked open. A red laser beam cut through the dark room, two men, dressed in desert fatigues, faces cloaked in light gray balaclavas thrust automatic weapons in front of them, stormed into the room, pointing at shadows.

A man reached down pulled Colene to her feet.

"Sarge," he said. "In here."

A tall man stepped in from the other room.

"What's up?" he said.

"Hostage."

The man called Sarge, stepped over, pulled the tape from Colene's mouth.

"Who're you?" he said.

"Colene Mooney. I was kidnapped by these assholes. I ..."

"Ain't got time for that now," Sarge said.

Colene heard a man scream in the outer room,

"You bastards. Sons of whores..."

His voice was cut off.

Sarge looked over at the man holding Colene.

"Bring her out," Sarge said.

"Shall I cut her loose?"

Command Sergeant Major Platt, US Army, retired, looked back at Colene.

"Naw," he said. "Just cut that piss-ass rope off and cuff her good for now."

"What?" Colene said. "You sonofa ..."

Another man slapped a strip of duct tape over her mouth. The first man cut the sisal cords, replaced them with a tough nylon slip-cuff, pulled it tight.

Platt turned his attention to three men bleeding from wounds, directed another to help them out.

Colene found herself in a surreal scene of bodies flung around the room like life-sized dolls. The bodies of her kidnappers were strewn around the room. At her feet, laying thrown back on the floor, she saw the short dark rat man who had kicked her in the car, his hand clutching a pistol, his eyes rolled back in death, his body lined by a string of bloody bullet holes.

A noise at the doorway startled her. She saw the man in the front seat– Abdi– now, just like her, a prisoner, hands tied behind, mouth taped being moved out the door between two men.

The man who taped her mouth pushed her from behind.

"Come along," he said.

Someone pushed her outside where another man moved to her side, held her arms, leered at her.

"Be a nice girl and I'll give you a kiss when we get home," he said.

Colene jerked away, kicked him along the shin.

"Bitch!" The man said. He raised his hand back to slap her.

Platt's voice erupted behind them,

"Enough of that shit!"

The man dropped his hand, grabbed her arm, shoved her into the back seat of the SUV, slid in beside her.

"Just you wait, bitch," he said.

Platt slid into the front seat, turned, snapped back at the man.

"Boy. What part of e-fucking nuff don't you understand?"

"Right, Sarge," the man said. He turned, glared out the window.

"Move it out," Platt said.

The driver ground the SUV into reverse, spun back in a circle, jammed the gear into drive, then peeled out onto the main road.

In the back seat, stuck between the two big men reeking of cordite, Colene clutched the long glass shard in the palm of her hand.

~*~~*~

Standing on the jetty across from the warehouse, Orhan watched the SUVs with Colene and Abdi tear down the street.

"Couldn't we have done something?" Ara said.

"We could have got our asses shot off," Doyle said.

"Well, we know she's alive," Orhan said.

"Let's go down and look at their handiwork," Doyle said.

The men stood up from behind the dunnage, junk, rubbish littering the top of the jetty. Doyle, Orhan led the way over to the warehouse.

Coming inside the building they walked around and through bodies strewn over the floor. Smells of cordite, blood, urine, excrement stung Orhan's nose.

Munroe stepped inside, looked around, sniffed the odor of cordite.

"Mercenary perfume," he said.

"Those lads are pros," Doyle said.

Seeing Gamaal's body, Orhan took the pistol from his hand, held it to his nose.

"Looks like he was one of the few to get off a shot," he said.

"Lot of good it did the poor sod," O'Naill said.

Orhan moved from body to body, walked toward the back room, paused, pointed to the cut rope and strip of cellophane tape on the floor.

"The Palestinians must have bound her with that rope and taped her mouth before they tossed her in that back room," he said.

"Why'd they take Colene," Ara said .

"Chance." Orhan said. "Just being in the wrong place at the wrong time."

He squat, looked around the floor.

"This whole bloody mess just doesn't add up," Orhan said.

"How so?" Doyle said.

"American mercenaries," Orhan said. "Rogue archaeologists. Art smugglers. Missing caches of arms."

He looked down again at Gamaal's body, added,

"Crooked cops."

“Should we pick up the arms?” O’Naill said .

Munroe looked at the empty cartridges strewn over the floor.

“Naw,” he said. “We’d be money ahead just gathering up the brass.”

“Once a Scot, always a Scot,” Doyle said.

Orhan glanced over at a corner of the room, rose up, walked over.

“What do we have here?” he said.

Orhan picked up a nickel-plated revolver, flipped out the magazine cylinder, then snapped it shut, looked at the others.

“Not fired,” he said.

He passed it to Doyle, handle first, righted an overturned chair.

“Abdi was probably sitting here when the mercs broke in.“ Orhan said. “They rushed him, knocked away the revolver, hosed down the rest in the room. From the positions of the bodies, Gamaal and that little guy were the only ones to get their pieces into play.”

“Sounds right to me,” Doyle said.

“So, all this leads where?” Munroe said.

“They took Abdi alive because he knows where their missing arms are hidden,” Orhan said.

“But, where’s that leave Colene?” Ara said.

Orhan looked at Doyle, Munroe, finally at Ara.

“With her ass sticking out,” he said.

Captivity, Still

Al 'ila, The Big House, outside of Alexandria, Egypt
The same day, 10:20 AM

Colene spotted the Big House through of the windshield of the SUV.

What's next?

Platt, the big man in front called "Sarge," looked back at her, then over at the goon on her left who had threatened her back at the warehouse. The turd avoided Platt's gaze by scowling out the window.

Try anything cute, shithead, I'll slam your face with my head.

The two cars sped through the gates. Guards snapped to attention. Colene glanced at them.

Just like visiting my brother on the Air Force base– the same spit, polish and bullshit.

When they pulled up in front of the house, Platt piled out of the front seat.

"Bring 'em in," he said.

The man on her right, helped her out, led her up the steps into the big house. When Platt opened the door, Colene saw Morris, a big man with a blond buzz cut, narrow-set big blue eyes, a tight-lipped smile.

"How'd it go, Platt?" he said.

"Ragland, Jakeson and Tunny caught a couple, Sir," Platt said. "Nothing serious."

Two men came in holding Abdi between them.

"Take this craphead up to interrogation," Morris said. "We'll deal with his ass later."

The men pushed Abdi over to the flight of stairs, shoved him up the steps.

"What about the girl?" Platt said.

"Put her on ice for the moment," Morris said.

Platt took Colene aside from her guard.

"Mabel, Honey," he called out. "Could you come here a minute?"

Colene saw a big woman come out of the other end of the hallway, her face expressionless, her dark brown narrow eyes fixed on Colene.

"Sugar," Platt said. "Could you take little Miss Meddle-mess up stairs and eyeball her?"

"Yes," Mabel said.

She reached for Colene's arm. Colene jerked it away. Mabel backhanded her across the face, grabbed her, pushed her forward.

"Do what the man says, toots," Mabel said.

Her face smarting from the blow, Colene kept quiet as she mounted the stairs.

Morris looked back at her.

"Pull her gag," he said.

Mabel ripped the duct tape from Colene's face.

"Ow," she said. "That fucking hurt."

"Dainty, ain't she?" Platt said.

"Who in the hell are you?" Morris said.

"Colene Mooney, professor of biblical studies at Yale."

"How in the hell did you get messed up with this fucking Abdi?"

"I came to talk to Sheffield, the archaeologist. Those assholes broke in, killed him and kidnapped me."

"Good," Morris said.

"Yeah?" Colene said. "Well, piss on you too."

"Where'd you meet Abdi?"

Colene struggled to keep her voice from trembling.

"I don't know any fucking Abdi," she said.

"You saying you don't know these towelheads?" Platt said.

"All I know is one of them got his head blown apart right in front of me in New London."

Morris blinked, stared at her, then nodded.

"Yale," he said. "Bible studies– now, I know. You're that trouble-making bitch I had tailed."

"What?" Colene said. "You had no fucking right to tail me."

Morris turned to Platt.

"I had Steele on her ass," he said. "He popped Abdi's brother in the states."

"He bragged about that great shot," Platt said.

"Take these cuffs off of me," Colene said.

Morris's adjutant, Rambeau came up.

"Sir," he said. "Kingpin's on his way in."

"Never fails," Morris said to Platt. "He shows up just when we don't need him."

Morris looked up at Mabel holding Colene's arm on the stairs.

"Carry on, Mrs. Platt," he said.

The Dark Castle

The Honey Bee Café, Columbia, SC
same day, 1:35 AM

"Well, good morning, Congressman Styles"

A woman in her 50s, holding an armful of menus, wearing a print dress over her chubby body, her hair coiffed in a mess of tight curls dyed golden brown, her face powdered like an Egyptian mummy with brushed on rouge spots over the cheeks grinned at Damian Styles.

"Good morning to you, Mrs. Almond," Damian Styles said.

"Your usual table?"

"Yes," Styles said, "The Reverend K.D. Rogers will be joining me shortly."

"Splendid," Mrs. Almond said. "Come this way, please."

She led Styles to a table near the kitchen, set apart from the other tables, booths, bussing stations. She set the menu in front of him, signaled a young African-American waiter in a white shirt, black bow-tie, wrap-around white apron walking around pouring coffee with two pots in his hands.

Mrs. Almond took one of the glass coffeepots from the waiter, then shooed him away, poured coffee into a mug, set it before Styles, then motioned a young black waitress wearing a white uniform with a red and white candy-striped short apron to come over.

Damian decided on ham and eggs, orange juice, looked out of the dusty window, spotted K.D. Rogers dressed in his usual plain black suit, white shirt, dark tie, get out of his car. Rogers frowned at a couple in shorts in the parking lot, then made his way into the restaurant.

Styles stood, shook Rogers's limp hand.

"Would you like some coffee, Reverend?" the waitress said.

"Hot cocoa, please," Rogers said.

After she left, Rogers leaned over toward Styles, spoke in a whisper.

"What's ...?"

Rogers stopped, snapped his head around. The waitress came up, set a plate of ham, fried eggs, hash brown potatoes, grits, with a biscuit in front of Styles, then placed a mug of hot cocoa in front of Rogers.

Rogers sipped his cocoa.

Styles fell to his breakfast. Between bites, he said,

"We got the Conservative Caucus allied with the Fife'n Drum wing of the party in line to support 'Operation Backfire.' "

"Oh?" Rogers said.

"Wasn't easy but they've agreed in principle– on the strength of our supporting their lower taxes and cutting more social programs."

"I don't trust them," Rogers said.

"How so?"

"The Fife'n Drum party's weak on abortion, climate change, gay marriage and other important Christian issues."

"Doesn't mean a thing, KD. They'll fall right into line with us."

"They're a passel of Godless secularists, just giving lip service to conservative issues," Rogers said "I suspect their motives."

Styles wiped his mouth with his napkin, took a sip of his coffee, looked over at Rogers.

"Once the Arabs line up behind the militants we're giving the arms to, the whole Middle East will catch on fire," he said. "Oil prices will jump. People will be reminded of 9-11. These are the concerns that will affect their constituents. They know it and we know it."

"Can you guarantee that, Damian?"

"Only death and taxes, KD. But in my heart of hearts, I know that once this happens, all the support we need will be there."

"Well, I would like more assurance than your 'heart of heart' feelings."

"All the pieces are falling into place," Styles said, "Morris is in Egypt right now getting those arms to the militants who'll start the grass fire that will burst into a Middle Eastern Conflagration."

"How long will that take?"

"Morris told me he can ship the arms immediately. So, it could start within 24 hours after the Moslem fundamentalists get the arms and start their jihad."

"That soon?"

"Yes,"

Styles smiled, leaned back as a white-aproned busboy took the dishes from the table. When the busboy left, Styles leaned again over to Rogers.

"Once that happens, gas prices will sky rocket," he said. "There'll be a general panic and we'll have martial law declared throughout the country within the week."

Above the Citadel

On a hill overlooking Al 'ila, The Big House, outside of Alexandria, Egypt
The same day, 8:20 PM

Orhan led them up into the rocky hills overlooking the Big House. Parking the vehicles behind the crest of the hill, Doyle deployed the men into the rocks around an outcrop of the hill. Munroe oversaw the unloading of equipment, field gear.

Orhan crawled to a vantage point behind a bush-covered boulder, checked out the small islet's structure with field glasses. Munroe crept up beside him.

"How many are they?" Munroe said.

"I count 20 or 22," Orhan said.

He lowered the binoculars, stared over the darkening area.

"I'm going to call someone I trust," Orhan said.

Ara handed Orhan his satellite phone.

"Use my phone," he said. "Better reception."

Orhan moved back, spoke in Arabic for a while, then rejoined the group.

"The State Egyptian authorities can get a SWAT team here," he said. "But it'll take at least two or three hours."

"Too long," Ara said. "Colene's life's at risk."

Orhan looked over at Doyle and Munroe.

"I'm willing to go in now," Orhan said.

Munroe looked down at the big house through his binoculars.

"Whadya think, Dannie?" he said.

"I say, let's hit 'em while they're taking a crap," Doyle said.

"Be serious," Ara said.

"They don't know we're here," Doyle said. "They'll be down after a firefight and not on high alert."

Munroe lowered the field glasses, grinned.

"So, let's kick their arses off the toilet," he said.

~*~~*~

Mabel opened a bedroom door on the second floor, pushed Colene into a chair, leaned over, stuck her face into Colene's.

"Let's keep it friendly, sweetie pie," she said. "Stay shut up and just don't fuck with me."

Colene struggled to keep from trembling at Mabel's adder-like stare, but just glared back saying nothing.

Mabel stepped back, plopped her butt in a chair next to a bed, took out a pack of cigarettes, lit one, inhaled, stared at Colene, blew smoke out of her mouth and nose.

Colene moved the glass shard in her hand around, tried to saw at the plastic cuffs binding her wrists. She felt the hardened plastic resist the sharp glass edge.

"I have to pee," Colene said.

"Be my guest."

"If I piss on myself, you'll wind up cleaning it up."

Mabel did not change expression, dropped her cigarette in an ashtray, come over, jerked Colene up, pushed her to the far side of the room, opened the door with one hand, moved Colene in front of the toilet bowl.

She undid Colene's slacks, pulled down her panties, pushed her down onto the stool seat.

"Go for it," she said, then took a step away, folded her arms, her beady eyes still on Colene.

Colene leaned forward, urinated, tried again to saw at the plastic handcuffs. Again, no gain– the glass slid off the cuff bands.

Colene worked the shard back into the palm of her hand, looked over, nodded at Mabel.

The big woman came over, pulled up Colene's panties and her slacks, zipped them shut, shoved Colene back into the chair in the other room, then knocked the ash off the cigarette, inhaled while still staring at Colene.

A rap at the door. Platt stuck his head in.

"Sugar," he said. "You wanna bring her down?"

Mabel ground out the cigarette, got up, yanked Colene to her feet, pushed her through the doorway. They followed Platt down the stairs, into the living room where Morris sat talking to his two aides.

"Have a seat," Mabel said.

She shoved Colene onto the couch then sat down next to her.

Morris looked over at Colene.

"So, what's your story?" he said.

"I've no fucking idea what you mean, Junior," Colene said.

"I don't know what your act is," Morris said. "But, you're way outta your league."

"I can arrange some attitude adjustment," Mabel said.

"It might come to that," Morris said.

"She knows a helluva lot more than she's letting on," Platt said.

"That's a given," Morris said.

He sat back, fixed his narrow blue green eyes on Colene.

"Now," Morris said. "I'm gonna ask you once to knock off the shit and tell us where you fit in all this."

Colene tightened her lips to keep from trembling.

"I'll return the courtesy," she said. "I'm a professor of biblical studies at Yale here in Egypt on research. I was talking to this archaeologist, Sheffield when these terrorists burst in, shot him. hauled me off ..."

"We know all that," Morris interrupted. "But this goes back to the States. My man saw you making some kinda deal with one of these hajjis in a bus station."

"I was just trying to get some information on a stolen biblical text. I still don't know who he was."

"We made him as a known terrorist," Morris said.

"My only interest was the text he was trying to sell."

"So, we're up to our assholes and eyeballs in towelhead jihadis," Morris said. "You're hanging around a bunch of them and now you tell us it's got to do with the bible."

"I'm a biblical scholar, asshole," Colene said.

"Watch your mouth," Mabel said.

"OK, OK. Let's keep it on the ground," Morris said. "A lot of things just don't add up here."

"I can shake a few things loose from her," Mabel said.

A guard opened the glass door leading to the patio at the rear of the house, stuck his head into the room.

"Helicopter coming in, sir," he said to Morris.

"Looks like the Big Guy's arriving," Platt said.

Morris, his two aides, Platt stood up. Mabel gripped Colene's shoulder, pushed her into the corner of the couch.

"Don't move," Mabel said.

The lights, noise of the landing helicopter filled the patio. Morris, the other men stepped outside. A few moments later, Colene heard them greeting someone.

Someone important. Must be the boss.

Colene heard talking, laughing. Then, a voice, familiar, came through.

I know that voice. From where?

The glass patio doors opened. A tall, gray-haired man in a light beige suit holding a briefcase stepped in. Morris, the others followed him in.

The tall man looked over at Colene, stopped, blinked. His mouth opened.

"Colene?" he said.

She recognized him.

He was the man she had a one-night affair with years before, a man she thought at one time she might be in love with.

"Lane Daniels!" Colene said.

~*~~*~

Sliding his field glasses back into the hard plastic case, Orhan looked over at Munroe.

"Tell me what to do," he said.

Munroe swung his arm in an arc, signaled the men in over the crest of the hill. They squat down in a circle around him by the vehicles.

"There are no barracks," Munroe said. "These blokes are billeted in the big house. Our best in is to hit on all sides, pick them off as they come out."

"What about the guards, the fence?" Ara said.

"We'll split into four teams," Munroe said. "Three men on each flank. Two at the front and the rear. Two outside on support, bringing in the cavalry."

"Cavalry?" Ara said.

"You and Hatim, Laddie," Munroe said, "You'll be handling comms with the incoming SWAT force."

Doyle switched on a red LED light. Monroe drew a circle in the rough dirt.

"Two teams of three will come in on the flacks, two from the boat docks and two in the pickup will smash in the gate for a diversion."

"The Turk and I will come in from the rear, go in and get the lass," Doyle said.

"Their attention should be on the intrusion," Orhan said.

"Colene's still inside," Ara said "I don't like this."

"None of us do, Doc," Doyle said.

At Monroe's signal, four men unloaded two inflatable rafts from the pickup, loaded them into the back of the two vans. Then Doyle opened a trunk from the back of the pickup, fished out some flat cans of camouflage face paint, passed it to the men who smeared it over their faces.

Big, quiet Owen oversaw the unloading, distribution of the duffels with weapons, body armor, night vision devices, spare clips of ammo.

The men geared up, checked weapons. Doyle and Orhan smeared on the green, black, brown face paint.

"You do swim, doncha Turkish?" he said.

"I do," Orhan said.

Doyle handed Orhan a long combat knife in a hard plastic case. Orhan strapped it to his leg, picked up a Beretta 12S 9mm machine gun, slipped it into a waterproof nylon case, slung it with two extra banana clips over his back.

Munroe called the men into a tight cluster again. Doyle shined the red light over the spot on the ground where Munroe sketched an outline of the islet.

"Owen and his three lads will embark in the CRRCs over at the east point," Munroe said.

"CRRCs?" Ara said.

"Combat rubber raiding craft," Orhan said.

Munroe pointed to Doyle and Orhan.

"Paddy and the Turk will embark with me and my two lads to the west side, then go in the water over to the boat dock into the house."

"What about us," Ara said.

"You and Hatim will stay up here," Munroe said. "This gives you the best view to contact the SWAT force. Hatim's on the radio in Arabic. You on the phone to the guy in Cairo."

"How do we come in," O'Naill said.

"You and your mate, Sean Dunn will crash the front gate in the pickup," Munroe said.

"When do we hit?" Owen said.

"After the Mick and Turk get the ass, Paddy'll shoot a white chute flare," Munroe said. "Blow the wire and go in then."

Wearing headphones, speaking into a microphone, Hatim said,

"The National police are coming in by helicopter. They're about an hour and a half away."

"Should we wait for them?" Ara said.

"They could harm the lass if they hear the choppers," Doyle said.

Munroe stood, looked at faces of the men surrounding him.

"Ladies," he said. "Let's dance."

~*~~*~

Doyle drove the white van down about 400 meters west of the compound. The men offloaded the raft, lugged it down to the edge of the estuary, inflated it, climbed in.

Munroe, two others paddled from the sides toward the edge of the boat dock. Orhan sat ahead of Doyle who paddled, guided from the stern.

Orhan and Doyle slipped over the side from the stern of the boat about 20 meters from the boat dock. The water was cool as Orhan and Doyle breast stroked up to the speedboat tied to the side of the slip.

Doyle eased himself up into the gunwale of the boat, helped Orhan up. They unpacked, slipped night vision devices over their heads, looked over the side down the deserted dock.

"Strange," Doyle said. "No boat crew."

They slid down from the boat, crept their way down the slip toward the boat house.

The door was open. A light was on. Sounds of Heavy Metal music poured out pounding their ears, smells of cannabis tickled their noses.

Inside the boat house, Orhan saw two men, feet up on a table, passing a joint between them. Both wore sleeveless desert cameo undershirts, their weapons lay on the table.

Doyle motioned to move forward. Orhan followed him to the door, crouched down below the window. Doyle moved to the side, stepped through the door, struck the man taking a deep drag from the joint along the side of the head before he could react.

The other man grabbed for an Uzi machine pistol on the table. Orhan sprang like a cat, brought the butt of the Beretta down on the man's outstretched reaching hand, then cracked him under his chin with the barrel. Both men were down.

Spotting a roll of duct tape on the work bench, Orhan and Doyle lashed the men's hands together behind them, bound their feet at the ankles, taped their mouths, dragged them back into the dark work area of the shop, taped them back to back, tagged to the metal leg of a large lathe.

"Hold onto that roll of tape," Doyle said.

They slipped out of the boat house, moved through the dark shadows towards the edge of the big house. Spotting another guard posted outside a set of glass doors leading to the brick laid patio, Orhan pointed his fingers at his eyes, then at the sentry. Doyle nodded, acknowledging.

They skirted away from the wide patio, darted across an exposed area, crouched behind a row of potted palm trees, then made their way to the east side of the house.

Doyle tapped Orhan, pointed to an exterior fire escape ladder built onto the side of the house going up past three landings to the roof. Coming under the ladder, Doyle stopped, set his weapon down, motioned for Orhan to come.

Slinging the machine gun over his back, Orhan stepped in Doyle's cupped hands, put hands on his shoulders, sprang up, grabbed the lower rung of the ladder, came down with it. Doyle followed Orhan up the ladder onto the fire escape.

Leading the way up to the second floor, Orhan glanced through the window from the landing, caught a glimpse of motion through a half open door.

Peering in from the angle on the landing through the ajar door, Orhan saw what looked like the foot of a man tied into a chair. He motioned Doyle to look.

"That could be Abdi," Orhan whispered.

~*~~*~

Colene stared at the same gray eyes, the same handsome, rugged face of the man she knew as "Lane Daniels," who stood staring at her.

"Who in the hell is Lane Daniel?" Morris said.

The man came over to Colene, saw her hands were bound, looked back at Morris.

"Get those goddam cuffs off her," he said.

"Wait a minute..." Morris said.

"NOW!"

"OK, OK," Morris said. "Mabel, cut her free."

Mabel stood, pulled a pair of diagonal cutter from her tunic pocket, snipped the plastic cuffs from Colene's wrists.

The man she knew as Lane Daniels knelt on one knee in front of Colene, taking her hand.

"My name is Lawrence Darryl," he said.

"Why all the bullshit?" Colene said.

Darryl got up, took a seat beside her, Colene scooted back, glared at him, rubbed her wrists.

"It's complicated," Daryl said.

"Lawrence Darryl, Lane Daniels...?" Colene said.

"It solved the problem with monogram luggage, other things," Darryl said.

Colene repeated the name, the alias under her breath.

LD, she recalled. *Jim Corbett's notes!*

"What was your connection to Jim Corbett?" she said.

"I grew up with Jim and JR Hammond," Darryl said.

Colene looked over at Morris.

"What's your connection to John Wayne here?" she said.

"Pap Hammond's my wife's father," Morris said.

"We've been working on a project together," Darryl said.

Colene looked from Darryl to Morris.

Orhan was close. Darryl's the Hydra!

"You're in this shitty deal together," she said.

"Look," Darryl said. "I only wanted you to have access to the codex."

"Is it real?" Colene said.

Darryl rose, went to the desk, opened a drawer, came back, thrust some color photocopies of the codex into Colene's hands.

"It is," he said.

Morris broke in.

"I remind you we got three containers of missing assets we need to put in play in the next two days," he said

Colene looked up from the photocopies at Darryl.

"What's he talking about?" she said.

Darryl took a deep breath, sat down next to Colene.

"We're putting an action in motion that will have global consequences," he said.

"What action?" Colene said.

"We call it "Operation Backfire," Darryl said.

"More bullshit," Colene said.

"Getting arms to the right bunch of radical jihadis will start a pan-Arab revolt," Darryl said. "That will drive up oil prices that will create the conditions at home to launch an armed response."

"You're nuts," Colene said.

"No way," Morris said, "There's enough support now in Congress to impose martial law under the National Security Act."

"None of this will affect you," Darryl said. "You'll be back safe at Yale with the exclusive use of this codex."

"Our Christian Rapture pals ain't gonna like that," Morris said.

"I don't care," Darryl said.

He turned back to Colene.

"All you have to do, Colene," he said, "is wait here until everything blows over, then go home with the codex."

"I think that's a big mistake, LD." Morris said.

"I don't give a fuck what you think," Darryl said.

"So," Colene said. "All I got to do is wait here until the world turns to shit, then go home with all the goodies?"

"That's about it," Darryl said.

Colene looked over at Morris. His narrow-set, green-blue eyes blazed, his mouth pulled into a knot, in a red face, his arms folded across his chest.

She glanced at Darryl. He sat, hands folded in front, looking at her like a dog waiting for a treat.

She took a deep breath, handed the photocopies back to Darryl.

"I need to think," she said.

Darryl nodded.

"Mabel," Morris said. "Take her back upstairs."

Mabel stood, took Colene's arm.

Darryl raised his eyes, sought Mabel's face.

"Gently, Mrs. Platt," he said.

"Yes sir," Mabel said.

~*~~*~

Orhan pushed his nose up against the window, stared at the sight through the crack of the open door, then turned to Doyle.

"I'm sure that's bloody Abdi," Orhan said.

Doyle glanced at his watch.

"We got time," he said, "Let's look in."

Doyle looked at the window latch, took out a long flat wire from his pack.

"A piece off an old windshield wiper blade," he said. "Very handy."

Doyle thrust the flat wire through the jamb between the window panes, jimmied the slide of the catch, slid the window open.

Slipping through the window like a pair of tom cats, the two men moved to the open door. Peeking in through the opening, Orhan saw Abdi bound in a chair, arms lashed behind him by zip cuffs on his wrists. Two guards spoke in low voices standing to one side.

Doyle rapped on the door. One of guards stepped over, pushed the door open.

Doyle busted him on the chin with an upward whip of the butt of the stock of his Beretta. The man slumped to the floor.

The other guard dropped his hand to his holster. Moving in like a dancer on the balls of his feet, Orhan struck the guard on the side of the head before he cleared the pistol.

Doyle pulled out the roll of duct tape, ripped off two pieces, passed them to Orhan, then wound the roll, seizing the hands and covering the mouth of the man on the floor in front of him.

Orhan wrapped the wrists of the unconscious guard, pulled the guard's pistol from his holster, slipped in his own belt. After Orhan taped the guard's mouth, he dragged him over to a corner where Doyle had pulled his man. They placed them back to back, wrapped them with duct tape.

Orhan pulled the tape from Abdi's mouth, spoke in Arabic,

"Scream and we let your American friends torture you," Orhan said.

"I know you," Abdi choked out.

"Where's the girl?" Orhan said.

"Downstairs."

"How many are they?"

"Maybe 20, 25."

"Sounds like the lass is safe for the moment," Doyle said. "Let's get to the roof and get the show started."

"Let me go," Abdi said.

Doyle tore off a strip of tape, stuck it over Abdi's mouth.

"Not now, laddie," Doyle said.

From down the hall, Orhan heard voices.

A noise. A soft cry, then a falling, thumping sound.

Orhan glanced at Doyle, then went over to the door.

~*~~*~

Dazed. Images, emotions, new information plowed through Colene's head.

She started up the stairs. Then a shove from behind made her stumble.

"You ain't out of the woods yet, pussycat," Mabel said.

Colene blinked– aware of the long glass shard in her hand. Moving her hands to the front, she shifted the shard from her palm to her fingers, sharp edge out.

Mabel pushed her again.

Seeing the landing at the top of the stairs a few steps away, Colene spun around, slashed Mabel across the face, then kicked her in the gut.

Shocked, Mabel's hand went to her face. She gave a little cry, slipped, losing her footing, fell backwards. Her head twisted, hit the edge of a step. An inaudible soft snap. Her eyes glazed, dilated, her body slid head first to the bottom of the stairs.

Colene didn't look back. She dashed up the stairs to the landing, turned, sprint down toward the open window at the end of the hall.

Closing the Net

Teller Hotel, East Yonkers, NY
same day, 3:20 PM

The old hotel on the corner of West and Vane with its square Art Deco style, dark and light brown brick structure from the 30s, struck Mary Rich as a throwback to an earlier era. She loved the old structure. It reminded her of the old hotel where her widowed grandfather, Judge Herman Blackstone spent his final years after retiring from the bench of the New Jersey Supreme Court.

Rich turned into the alley behind the building, drove down into an underground parking lot. At the steel-bar barrier, an armed guard stepped out of a cement ante room, flashed a light in her car, looked from her ID to her face.

"Proceed, Agent Rich," he said. "You're expected."

She parked, took an elevator down into an underground structure below the old hotel. At the door, another armed guard went through the same ID procedure, then snapped a badge with her picture on her lapel, opened another steel door to admit her.

Rich went down a long hall of closed doors marked only with numbers, stopped, knocked at one.

Willie Johnson's voice came through, "Come on in, Mar."

Johnson sat at his terminal, pecking keys, scrolling pictures, charts, lists of numbers, names, addresses, tables, maps.

"I should have my ass kicked," Johnson said.

"I'll agree to that," Rich said. "Now, what for?"

Johnson turned in his chair, faced her.

"Ara, your pal Colene's buddy sent me an encrypted file, then sent me the keys on a separate line."

"That's handy."

"Well, I got busy and just opened it last night."

"And?"

"This guy has hacked files from the Rapture network and Congressman Styles. He's got names, dates, places, memos, emails, communiques, maps– all kind of crap you won't believe."

Rich gawked at the documents, files, displays on the monitor.

"He's given us enough on that megaturd gumball Reverend head of the Rapture Capture for you to get subpoenas," Johnson said.

Rich scrolled through a long file with logs, dates and receipts.

"Holy shit!" she said.

"Yep," Johnson said. "They're acting as a clearinghouse for offshore gambling houses, Native American casinos, on-line gambling– all channeled through their organization as charitable contributions."

"How does the money circulate back to them?" Rich said.

Johnson pulled up another ledger document.

"The Rapture Network has offshore accounts used to service their overseas "missionary" services," he said.

"How did he get this?"

"Dr. Agajanian has been a very busy man," Johnson said. "I'm copying you all this, but I wanted you to see it here first."

Rich scrolled though the files, shook her head.

"I can get warrants on these Rapture guys, but we still can't touch that scumbag Styles."

Johnson opened up another file on the screen.

"Our friend Styles has been leading a double life."

He pointed to a list of numbers.

"These are popular male homoerotic porno sites. See how Styles's email address shows up. Every time he logged in is recorded."

He opened another file.

"There's more."

He brought up a series of pictures along with a video.

"These photos and videoe are downloaded from a security camera at a gay club and strip tease place in Rosslyn, outside of DC. Look who's the star of the show?"

"Disgusting."

"There's more. Lots more."

Rich sat back, folded her arms.

"We can come down legally on the links to money laundering and gambling the Rapture Network's involved in, but the smut on Styles's not much," she said.

Willy grinned.

"Not so."

"What do you mean?"

"How will the people who surround him view these performances?"

"Point taken," Rich said. "But, the FBI doesn't deal in blackmail, Willy."

Johnson leaned back in the chair, stretched out his long legs, put his hands behind his head, grinned again.

"We do," he said.

Things fall Apart

Al 'ila, The Big House, outside of Alexandria, Egypt
The same day, 8:22 PM

Morris followed Platt and Darryl back into the front room.

"You're making a big mistake, LD," Morris said. "We've got too much riding on things falling into place and this twat could screw it up."

"What do you suggest?" Darryl said.

"Eliminate her."

Darryl glared at Morris.

"Out of the question," Darryl said.

A tumbling, thumping noise from the stairway near the entrance hall made Morris and the two men turn their heads.

"What the fuck..." Platt said.

They ran back to the staircase.

At the landing at the base of the stairs, Morris saw Mabel, head twisted back by her shoulder, legs crumpled, arms splayed out to her sides.

Platt ran to her side, knelt, cradled her head into his lap.

"Sugar," he said, "What happened?"

Darryl put his fingers to her throat, touching the carotid artery, then looked at Morris, shook his head.

"Baby," Platt said. "They cut your face!"

The slice across Mabel's face had stopped oozing blood– her dilated, open eyes were rolled back, her mouth open.

Darryl put his hand on Platt's shoulder.

“I’m so sorry, Sarge,” Darryl said

Platt lowered his head, drew his dead wife’s body to his breast, broke into loud sobbing.

“Oh, baby,” he said. “They killed you.”

Morris touched Platt’s shoulder.

“Let’s move her into the front room,” Morris said.

The two big men picked up Mabel’s body, carried her into the living room, set her on the couch. Platt fell to his knees, buried his face on her breast.

Platt‘s body convulsed with grief, sobbing. Then, he stopped, snapped his head around, snarled at the two men.

“That bitch murdered my baby,” he said.

“Take it easy, Platt,” Morris said. “She ain’t going nowhere.”

“It could have been an accident,” Darryl said.

Platt grit his teeth.

“T’weren’t no goddam accident,” he said. “Look at her face.”

Platt scrambled to his feet, his face beet red, his eyes blazing. He shoved Darryl back into Morris, ran for the stairs.

“Platt,” Darryl cried. “Wait!”

Morris held onto the struggling Darryl.

“Let him go,” Morris said. “In his frame of mind he could shoot us both.”

Rambeau, Morris’s aide, ran in from the hallway, stopped, stared at Mabel’s body on the couch. He swallowed hard then looked over at Morris.

“Sir,” Rambeau said. “We just got word from one of our informants in the local police that there’s a National Police SWAT unit mobilized that may be headed this way.”

“Shit,” Morris said.

Morris let go of Darryl, put his hand to his head for an instant, then signaled Rambeau to follow him. He took two steps, stopped, spun around, glared back at Darryl.

“You stay put, LD,” Morris said. “I gotta deal with this.”

He led Rambeau out of the room.

~*~~*~

Darryl waited until Morris left the room, turned to the large desk at the end of the room, grabbed a corner, scooted it to one side. He pushed up a square of the carpet exposing a rectangular cut out in the parquet floor. He lifted it, exposing the combination dial of an embedded safe, spun the tumblers to the opening combination, took out a leather covered case.

After he closed the safe, he dragged the desk back, picked up the phone, punched in a number.

"Get the bird fired up, Skip," Darryl said. "We're leaving right now."

~*~~*~

Orhan eased the door to the hall open—Colene dashed past him toward the window.

Orhan called out, "Colene!"

She spun around, the shard in her hand raised. Seeing Orhan, she dropped it, ran to him, fell into his arms.

Pent-up emotions–anger, fear, relief burst in a flood of tears.

"It's OK," Orhan said. "I'm here."

"How?" she said.

"Never mind. You're safe."

Clinging to him, Colene caught her breath.

"I think I killed that woman."

"What woman?"

"She was pushing me up the stairs. I turned and cut her, then I kicked her—she fell backwards."

She buried her face in the pit of Orhan's shoulder.

Doyle stuck his head out of the door.

"We have to move," he said.

"Give us a second," Orhan said.

Colene stopped crying, put her hands to her face.

"OK," she said. "I'm all right."

"This is Dan Doyle," Orhan said. "He's a friend of Ara's."

Doyle smiled, saluted from his brow.

"Ara? Here too?" Colene said.

"O, we're having a helluva party," Doyle said.

Orhan heard a thumping noise– someone running up the stairs. Doyle stepped back into the room.

Platt ran down the hall towards Orhan and Colene, his Colt .45 leveled at them.

His red, tear-streaked eyes focused on Colene, his teeth grit in a snarl showed in his drawn mouth.

"You killed my baby," he said.

Platt thrust the pistol at Colene.

Orhan moved in front of her.

"It was an accident,." he said.

"Fuck you," Platt said. He leapt forward, hammering the pistol at Orhan's head.

Doyle sprang from the doorway like a cougar, knocked the pistol from Platt's hand. Platt recovered from the impact, spun, struck Doyle in the face with a sweeping left hook.

Doyle jerked back, rolling with the force of the blow that grazed his jaw. He grabbed Platt's left wrist. Platt jerked his left hand free, jabbed Doyle hard in the ribs with his right hand.

Grunting at the hit, Doyle spun with it, shifted his shoulders, twisted his hips, brought his right hand up, struck the heel of his hand against Platt's chin.

Platt staggered back from the blow, flailed with his right fist at Doyle. The Irishman blocked the blow, stepped behind the big man, cupped Platt's chin against the heel of his right hand, grabbed the left side of Platt's head with his left, then lurched back with a violent jerk and twist..

A snap. Platt's body trembled—his eyes widened, dilated, glazed. His body went limp, then slumped to the floor.

Doyle knelt, touched Platt's throat for a few seconds, then swept his hand over Platt's face, closing his staring eyes.

"One tough sonofabitch," Doyle said.

"We've got to move," Orhan said. "Let's get Abdi up to the roof."

"Where are we going?" Colene said.

"Help's on the way," Doyle said.

Orhan, Dan went back into the room, hauled the kicking, squirming Abdi to the window. Grabbing his hands and arms, they shoved him through onto the landing, then pushed him up the fire-escape ladder to the roof. They moved him next to a tall vertical vent pipe. Orhan lifted Abdi's body up, Doyle raised Abdi's arms, slid them down the pipe to the roofing plane, flattened him on the floor of the roof. Orhan wrapped his ankles with the duct tape.

When Orhan finished, he looked around.

"Colene?" he said.

She wasn't there.

~*~~*~

Colene stepped to the side while Orhan and Doyle worked to get the struggling Abdi through the window. She watched them move him up the ladder to the roof.

She started forward– then hesitated, looked back at Platt's body, then spotted Platt's pistol laying on the floor.

An old Colt Army .45—her father had one just like it—in fact, he had shown her and her brothers how to shoot with it.

She picked it up, pulled the slide back, made sure a round was in the receiver chamber, the safety clicked off.

Making her way downstairs, she paused at the bottom of the stair. Sounds of confusion, men's voices rattled through the house.

She ducked back into the angle of the stair landing. Morris and his adjutant, Rambeau walked past her, hurrying down the opposite hall way.

Colene shifted the pistol in her hand, went into the front room.

She saw Darryl, throwing things into a brief case. When he closed and reached for the handle brief case, Colene stepped in, leveled the pistol at him.

"Where do you think you're going, asshole," Colene said.

Startled, Darryl's head snapped up at the sound of her voice. He smiled.

"Colene," he said. "Thank God, you're OK.

~*~~*~

"She's gone!" Orhan said.

"We can't delay any longer," Doyle said.

"Right."

Doyle pulled the flare pistol from his backpack, slammed in a shell, fired it aloft. The dot of orange light ascended about 300 meters, burst into a bright white light, floated down suspended by a parachute.

Orhan's cell phone went off.

"Orhan."

"Any news on Colene?" Ara said.

"She was with us until a few seconds ago," Orhan said.

"'Was?' " Ara said.

"I don't know where she's gone," Orhan said.

"Shit."

"I'll find her," Orhan said.

"The SWAT team's about a half hour out," Ara said.

Orhan heard the sound of the front gate crashing in, gunfire.

"It's happening!" Doyle said.

~*~~*~

With the headlights off, Jamey O'Naill drove the faded, rusted old, tan Land Rover pickup to the edge of the road leading onto the spit of land connecting the islet to the shore. Cutting off the engine, he let it roll to a stop right at the edge of the entrance.

He whispered to Sean, the man sitting beside him.

"Now, let's give this old beast a Dublin quick start."

They stacked their arms, backpacks on the open end of the truck bed. Switching on a red LED flashlight, O'Naill checked the two packs of C4 explosive with protruding contact fuses stuck to the truck's massive steel front bumper.

O'Naill and Sean pushed the pick-up ahead over the gravel covered surface from the driver's side. O'Naill steered it to the middle of the narrow road pushing on the driver's open window frame while Sean pushed against the tail gate.

The spotlight over the front gate cast a shadow extending some 12 yards down the road. The two men let the pickup roll to a stop just outside the ring of light.

O'Naill and Sean removed their gear from the truck bed, set it on the ground a few yards just behind the pickup.

O'Naill saw the orange flare go up, heard the whoosh of the flare pistol, slipped into the cab, started the engine, revved it twice, put it in gear.

Ignoring voices from behind the gate, he jammed down on the accelerator, running the engine to full throttle, snapped a clamp on the accelerator lever, turned on the lights, jumped out releasing the clutch. The pickup screeched forward, throwing a whirl of gravel, lurching forward toward the gate.

O'Naill dived flat, cheek down in the ground just before the pickup crashed into the gate. He saw the pickup's windshield shatter into shards, chunks, pieces, the cab ripped apart with bullet holes from automatic weapons just before it hit the gate. He buried his face in the gravel at the moment of impact when the front end of the pickup exploded.

As soon as the burning truck, gate, debris, settled, O'Naill and Sean grabbed their automatic weapons, skirted the burning pickup, then dashed into the compound.

Inside, two guards stood, their weapons trained on the burning pickup. O'Naill and his partner emerged from the fire and smoke on the other side, already firing. Both guards fell.

~*~~*~

After dropping off Orhan and Doyle near the boat dock, Munroe with his two partners paddled to the west side of the compound. Landing on the rocky edge, Munroe had the men place charges around a section of the cyclone fence, then take up positions outside on the slope of the estuary.

At the sight of the flare, Munroe pressed a charge key setting off 4 wads of C4 explosive. They exploded, tearing off a section of fence leaving a hole 8 feet in diameter.

Munroe yelled, "Go!"

All three men sprinted through the opening into the compound just after the gate exploded. Munroe saw the two guards fall in the light from the burning pickup, followed by the silhouettes of O'Naill and Sean.

Fanning out at the side of the big house, Munroe and the two men took cover behind three vehicles covering the side entrance to the building.

Two guards fired on them from one side of the house. Munroe's partner to his right took both out of them with a spray of automatic gunfire.

Four men came pouring out from the side door. Munroe dropped the first two. The two behind hesitated, then dropped to the ground.

"Toss your weapons and live," Munroe shouted.

Seconds later, the two men chucked their guns, lay flat on the ground, hands placed on top of their heads.

~*~~*~

Colene kept the pistol on Darryl without wavering.

"Thank God?" she said. "Thought we biblical bookers didn't do God."

Darryl smiled.

"O, I still believe, Colene," he said. "It was that boy-loving Jimmie Corbett that didn't."

"Jim Corbett was a great man," Colene said.

"You don't need that pistol," Darryl said.

"I'll decide that."

He held up the leather case.

"It's here."

Colene didn't move.

"I don't care," she said.

"Yes, you do," Darryl said. "That's why you came back."

He sauntered over, sat on the edge of the desk.

"You know I wanted you to have this," he said.

"You got a piss-poor way of showing it," Colene said.

"I sent Isaak to give it to you."

"He tried to sell it to me."

"That, I didn't know about," Darryl said. He shook his head. "Poor stupid, greedy boy."

"He got his head blown apart right in front of me."

Darryl shook his head.

"That was the CIA," he said.

"Bullshit," Colene said. "It was Morris and his boys."

Darryl started. "How in the..?"

He turned his face, scowled, looked back at Colene, took a deep breath.

"Come with me," Darryl said.

"No way."

Darryl picked the leather case, gazed down at it in his hands for a second. Then, he pitched it to Colene and lunged.

She grabbed for the flying case.

Darryl snatched the pistol from her hand.

At that moment, the windows, the doors to the patio rattled with vibrations from the shock of an explosion.

"What in the hell was that?" Darryl said.

~*~~*~

Owen's team deployed to the shoreline on the east side of the compound, inflated the raft, paddled about a hundred meters to the edge of the fence. The tall Welshman and his two partners fixed the charges to the fence, took up positions on the rocky shoreline, then crouched down waiting with weapons in their hands.

Seeing the flare mount skyward, Owen blasted the fence, led his two men in through the hole, just as the front gate blew.

They ran forward, towards a row of Dracena palms lined up in large ceramic pots. Owen, spotting three men coming up from a cellar exit, dropped to one knee, fired a burst hitting the first man. The other two ducked behind a metal shed, then returned fire from either side.

Owen signaled his team with a wig-wag motion over his head. They fanned out, came at the men behind the shed from both flanks.

Owen stepped forward, past a stone bench. Three shots rang from behind him, two hitting on the side of his body armor, one going through his throat.

Owen wheeled, fired back, stitching three holes through the red beret on the bald head of the black man lying prone under the bench. He convulsed, pitched his M14 forward, fell forward dead.

One of Owen's team ran to him. Owen fell to one knee, pointed to his bleeding throat, dropped his weapon, collapsed onto the ground.

~*~~*~

Darryl stuck Platt's pistol inside the waistband of his pants, picked up the leather case from the floor in front of Colene.

"Come with me," he said to her again. "It's all here—and it's all yours."

"No," she said.

Morris ran into the room, a rifle-grenade launcher in his hand.

Seeing Darryl and Colene near the door, he lowered the grenade launcher, rested it on a chair, came over to Darryl.

"What the fuck's going on here?" Morris said.

"It's over, Morris," Darryl said.

"Like hell," Morris said. "The assets aren't here. They ain't got shit on us."

"They got me, Tarzan," Colene said.

Morris looked from Darryl to Colene.

"Shoot the bitch," Morris said.

"No way, Morris," Darryl said.

"She knows too much, LD. She'll talk."

"Doesn't matter," Darryl said. "No one's shooting her."

"Fuck that shit," Morris said.

He jerked out the pistol at his side.

Darryl pulled Platt's .45 from his waist band, shot Morris through the throat.

Morris dropped the revolver, gurgled, fell to the floor clutching at his throat.

Colene gasped, stared at the bleeding Morris on the floor.

"He'd have shot you," Darryl said.
Colene glared at him.
"Come with me," Darryl said.
"No," she said
"For the last time, Colene. Come with me"
"Get the fuck outta my life."
Darryl shook his head, put the pistol back in his waistband, strode out the glass door to the waiting helicopter.

~*~~*~

Orhan spotted the helicopter when it lit up, took off, and approached the patio before the explosion at the gate.
At the sound of gunfire, he turned to Doyle,
"I've got to go find her," Orhan said.
"Wait. The good guys are on their way," Doyle said.
"I can't wait," Orhan said.
Starting for the ladder, Orhan stopped at the report of a .45 from the rear of the house.
He turned to Doyle.
"That came from inside," Orhan said.
He ran to the rear of the building, leaned over, looked down at the opening.
The helicopter settled on the patio, blades turning.
Orhan called out,
"Colene!

~*~~*~

Colene stepped over the groaning Morris, picked up his dropped revolver. She hefted the firm, heavy .41 magnum in her hand, ran to the open door.
Outside, she saw the stooping Darryl reach for the handle on the helicopter door.
She brought the revolver up in both hands, pulled the hammer back with her thumb, sighted the shortened barrel onto Darryl.
Colene screamed,
"Stop!"

Darryl snapped his head around. Seeing Colene with the pistol in her hand, he shouted,

"You won't shoot me, Colene."

Colene yanked the trigger. The big gun bucked in her hand.

The shatterproof Plexiglas of the helicopter blinked– a pit, a spider web appeared next to Darryl's face. He jerked the handle, dived into the open door.

Colene took a step forward, the revolver raised in her two hands, the hammer cocked back.

Darryl slammed the door. The chopper revved up for lift-off.

Colene aimed– this time squeezed the trigger, fired. When the revolver settled, she cocked it, fired again.

The two bullets hit the aircraft, dented the bullet proof cowling. The chopper rose, lifted from the brickwork patio.

~*~~*~

Looking over the edge of the roof, Orhan saw a tall man clutching something to his chest, run out, bent down, duck under the churning blades to the door of the waiting helicopter.

The man stopped, looked back. A second later, Orhan saw Colene step out, a revolver in her outstretched hands.

The man at the chopper door said something to her.

Colene fired, the revolver jumped. The man jerked back unhurt, then scrambled into the cab of the turning chopper.

Colene took a step forward, fired again.

Orhan pushed back off the edge of the building, ran to the fire escape, leapt onto it, his feet on either side of the side rails, slid down to the landing below, pounced through the railing opening onto the ladder below that, on to the landing below.

He looked up to see Doyle following right behind him, his Beretta machine gun strapped to his back.

~*~~*~

Colene leaned forward, squeezed off another round that ricocheted off the armored bullet-proof cowling of the rising helicopter. When it ascended overhead, Colene fired again into its underbelly with the same glancing effect.

She felt someone shove her aside, knock her to her knees.

Looking back, she saw Morris, his throat a bloody mess. He glared up at the rising helicopter, raised the rifle grenade launcher, fired twice, an armor piercing round followed by a rifle grenade just as the chopper whipped its tail around to reverse course.

Colene saw a hole appear, enlarge where the armor piercer and grenade hit, heard the whomp of the impact, then scrambled to her feet, ran toward the house.

The chopper burst into flames, exploded.

~*~~*~

Hitting the ground in a run, Orhan sprinted to the corner of the building. He saw the bleeding Morris stagger out, rifle grenade launcher in hand, swing it, knock Colene to her knees, raise the weapon to fire.

Orhan hesitated.

Doyle grabbed Orhan just as Morris fired throwing himself backwards yanking Orhan back around the edge of the building as the chopper exploded.

~*~~*~

After lurching to her feet, Colene ran to the open patio door when the chopper exploded. The force of the blast hurled her face first through the open double patio doors of the big house.

She sprawled flat on the carpet, spread out with face and hands down.

Outside, the burning chopper's fuselage crashed down on the outer edge of the patio in a rain of burning, flaming parts.

Seconds later, Colene raised her head. The room filled with smoke, stank from the explosion. Around her, little fires burned on the floor, the curtains, the furniture.

Her eyes adjusted. Some movement through the haze caught her attention.

She saw Morris thrown over by the desk at the end of the room. He rose up, glared at her, then crawled to the rifle a few feet away, grasped for, fumbled it, pulled it to him.

At her right, near the burning, overturned couch, Colene spotted Morris's Ruger .41 magnum revolver where she dropped it after the helicopter exploded.

She rolled, scooped it up, brought it to bear on Morris now raising, sighting the rifle at her.

In one motion, Colene pulled back the hammer, squeezed—the gun fired, jumped in her hand.

Morris flew back from the impact of the .41 magnum. The grenade launcher fell from his hands.

He slammed back against the desk, the new patch of red on his chest spreading redder than that on his throat. His head slumped to his chest, his eyes staring, seeing nothing.

Colene let the empty pistol drop from her hand.

She heard her name.

She looked up.

She felt Orhan take her into his arms.

She closed her eyes.

~*~~*~

Hearing that Owen was down, Ara piled in the VW van with Hatim holding a hand on his earphones, chattering in Arabic into the mouthpiece. Ara rolled down the hill, stopped at the gate of the compound, got out, ran past the burning pickup blocking the way to the front of the house.

Owens lay on a make-shift stretcher, his throat compressed, wrapped in gauze. Ara checked for vital signs, looked up at Munroe.

"Gone," Ara said.

Munroe nodded, tightened his mouth, looked away toward the flap-flap noise of six military helicopters flying straight in, thumping down, men spilling out, guns at the high port, then spreading out over the compound's grounds.

Hatim signaled, called out to a pair of policemen. One, a medical corpsman ran over to the stretcher, looked at Owen's body, looked up to Ara, shook his head. The other, an officer came up to Munroe, saluted.

"Major Farouk Hassan, National Police," he said. "Are you Col. Mehmet of Interpol?"

The front door of the house opened. Orhan, Doyle stepped through supporting Colene between them.

"Colene!" Ara said.

He ran to her as they eased her down on the edge of the stoop.

Colene looked up, her face scratched, soot and smoke stained, her eyes red, her hair singed– sticking out like a tramped-on fox-tail awn.

"I must look a mess," she said.

Ara motioned the corpsman over. He and Ara treated her cuts, bruises, cleaned her face.

The Major introduced himself to Orhan and Doyle, then received a call on his intercom.

"We're dunging out the craphouse," he said. "Those in the rat's nest inside aren't resisting."

Munroe called his men in.

"Retain your arms," Major Hassan said. "I assume you're under Col. Mehmet."

The Major turned away, to supervise his men.

Ara and the corpsman, Orhan helped Colene to her feet.

"Couldn't you have been a little quieter getting in here?" Colene said to him.

"Hey," Ara said. "You're always telling me how messy I am."

Orhan, Ara and the corpsman helped Colene into a helicopter. The corpsman climbed in, strapped her into a stretcher mount, set up an IV.

"I'm coming too," Orhan said.

"You're needed here," Ara said. "I'll be with her until you can get there."

Orhan stepped back, fought back tears as they took off.

Airlift

University of Alexandria Medical Center Hospital, Alexandria, Egypt
The same day, 1:20 AM

Ara followed the gurney bearing Colene into the emergency room. The corpsman attached the IV drip in her arm to a wheeled pole standard, stepped back as a nurse in green scrubs took over.

Ara started to go into the emergency room, a female doctor in a white lab coat over her scrubs, held her arm out, stopped him.

"Where do you think you're going?" she said in English.

"With my patient," Ara said. "I'm a doctor."

"Not here," the doctor said.

She frowned at him, stepped back, closed the sliding curtain around her.

Ara snorted, stood, glared at the curtain.

"Shit," he said.

Ara felt the corpsman touch his arm.

"Let's get some tea," the corpsman said.

Taking Ara's arm, the corpsman led him down the hall into a canteen, threw his medical pack on a table.

Ara plopped down in a chair, put his chin in his hand, scowled.

The corpsmen went to the serving area, came back with two glasses of tea, set one in front of Ara.

"Thanks," Ara mumbled.

They drank the tea in silence. When they finished, Ara jumped up, strode back to the nurse's station.

He saw the doctor at the desk writing down clinical orders in a chart.

She looked up at him when he walked up.

"Are you her husband?" she said.

"Just a friend."

"I've sedated her and moved her to a private room."

Ara drew a deep breath, looked the doctor in the eye, nodded.

"Come," the doctor said. "You can stay near her as long as you want."

~*~~*~

Orhan walked back to where the National Police rounded up the 4Sinc men. He noticed one of them that stepped forward, hands raised, to speak to Major Hassan.

"I'm Carl Rambeau, adjutant to our company's CEO, the late Col. Morris," he said. "As he's dead, I've ordered all our men to stand down."

"You and your men are under arrest for possessing and using lethal weapons in Egypt," Major Hassan said.

The SWAT team troops bound the hands of Rambeau and the other men with plastic zip-cuffs, then led them off under guard.

Orhan looked over the police collecting, arranging the bodies of the 4Sinc men, then said to Major Hassan,

"There's one more on the roof."

"Is he armed?" Major Hassan said.

"No," Doyle said. "He's wrapped nice and grand like a Christmas toy."

Orhan caught the attention of the Egyptian Police Major.

"Can you give me a ride to the hospital where they took the girl?"

The Major saluted.

"Of course, Colonel. You're well known as a friend of Egypt."

Awake

University of Alexandria Medical Center Hospital, Alexandria, Egypt
The same day, 4:33 AM

Zipping along on a kaleidoscope roller coaster, Colene sat holding onto the seat bar with both hands confronted by grinning demons with faces painted with purple eyes with black pupils. She chased away screaming gnat-sized, white-faced, red-wigged clowns dressed in military fatigues.

The man in the seat next to her was her father when the ride started. Now he wore a red spandex body suit exposing only his face with a long nose, beady, rat-like eyes with a whip-like mustache that reminded her of Faust's Mephistopheles.

The red shape-shifter grinned, leaned over to her, breath like cat dung, his brown yellow teeth pointed and gleaming.

"Dance with me," he whispered. "Now!"

She looked around her for an escape.

The tilting gondolas around her held only bloody bodies. Then, a dead woman in the seat in front of her raised up, turned around, glared at her.

It was Mabel.

Colene woke up.

She was in a room, in a bed.

She hurt.

Her face was cut, bruised, her left hand plugged with an IV tube.

She adjusted her eyes to light streaming from a night-lamp.

Someone was in the room with her.

Orhan.

He sat in a chair at the edge of her bed, asleep, his forehead bent, his arms crossed, his breathing wheezing with soft murmurs.

She touched him.

He stirred.

"Where am I?" she said.

He sat up, drew near, touched her face.

"Hospital."

"What happened....?"

He touched his finger to his lips.

"Shh. Later."

"Where's Ara?"

A snore snorted from the corner. In the dark, Colene saw Ara asleep in a chair, head down, arms folded over his chest, his glasses pushed back on his forehead.

"He came in with you," Orhan said. "I got here less than an hour ago."

"I don't ... I mean..." she stammered.

"You're safe," he said. "Rest."

"I ..."

She slept.

~*~~*~

In the rear of a narrow boat–a canoe, Colene struggled to keep her eyes open. She floated on a mist covered lake–no, a river. Moss, twigs, leaves drifted by, branches on the trees on the shore waved. She stroked the greenish water with a two headed paddle. The boat slugged along through the fog like the water was molasses.

Her eyes kept shutting. She rubbed them with one hand, gripped the paddle with the other.

She saw a man sitting in the bow of the boat. He raised his eyes, looked back at her, smiled.

Her eyelids closed, again and again.

The mist, her vision blurred his face.

"Ara?" she said.

No reply.

The smiling man—a silhouette with no features.

"Daddy?" she said.

The man laughed.

Then, a voice.

"Colene?"

The vision stirred, swirled, the face turned into a spinning circle.

She dropped the paddle, grabbed for the edge of the boat.

"Colene!"

Awake!

Orhan– leaning over the edge of the bed, looking at her, Ara at his side.

"Can you hear me?" Orhan said.

"Yes," she said.

Her mouth felt full of cotton balls.

"We have to go for a bit."

"Go? Where?" she said.

"Unfinished business. They need us both."

"Ara?"

Ara leaned in, put his hand on her forehead.

"You need to rest," Ara said. "We'll be back as soon ..."

Ara's voice—soft, like the whisper of wind blowing through an open screen door.

"Rest," he said.

She faded again into the shadows of sleep.

The Hydra's Hide

Coming up to Al 'ila, The Big House, outside of Alexandria, Egypt
The next day, 10:42 AM

Orhan jerked awake in the front seat of the van bumping over the chuckhole pocked road. Looking out, he took in the big house that Ara had dubbed the 'Hydra's Hide,' then glanced over at Ara dozing next to him in the middle.

Jamey O'Naill hit a bump. Ara snapped awake, rubbed sleep from his eyes, stifled a yawn, looked over at Orhan.

"Are we there yet?" Ara said.

Coming up to the blasted-open front gate, Orhan saw that the burnt hulk of the pickup had been hauled off. O'Naill drove up to the front of the house where a group of men were standing and talking.

When the van pulled to a stop, Hamid ad Din stepped over, opened the door. After Orhan got out, shook hands, made introductions, ad Din took him aside.

"Lots of questions to be answered," ad Din said.

"That's why we dragged Ara along," Orhan said. "If it's here, he can squeeze it out of their computers."

Ad Din led Orhan and the others through the hallway into the burnt-out living room. Ara pulled a laptop out from the rubble near the toppled desk. When Doyle and O'Naill set the desk upright, Ara jerked up a chair, set up his laptop, took out some small tools. Pulling the hard drive out of the damaged computer, he plugged it into his own, looked at the files scrolling across his monitor.

"Very organized—and, in English," Ara said.

One of the SWAT policemen came up, conferred with ad Din.

"We found what may be his main office upstairs," Ad Din said.

Orhan, Ara and the others followed the SWAT officer up to a room sealed with a steel door. A pair of SWAT techs brought up an acetylene torch, fired it up.

After they burned a circle around the lock and the door jamb, they smashed the door open with a nine pound sledge hammer.

Looking into the office, Orhan saw the massive black wooden desk near the window.

Ara pushed past the others, strode straight to the desk, found the desk top computer in a roll-out drawer. He removed the tower shell, pulled the hard drive, snapped it into a frame along with the drive from the recovered laptop, plugged his own into the outlet, then logged on.

Stepping to his side, Orhan went through the drawers on the left and ad Din on the right.

Ad Din took out the pistol, papers, files, folders, piled them on one end of the desk.

Ara motioned for Orhan to look at the monitor.

"You know what this is?" Ara said.

"Arabic," Orhan said. "But, it makes no sense."

Ad Din looked over at the screen from the other side.

"Encrypted files," he said.

Ara stared at the rows of cursive characters, rubbed his chin, then snapped his fingers.

"Give me a minute," he said.

Ara thumped the laptop keys. He muttered,

"Dang Arabic alphabet."

Across the room, Doyle stood staring at the 5' X 4' painting of a woman on the wall across from the desk. Then he peered behind the polished brass frame.

"Strong box back here," he said.

Doyle chose a narrow pic from Ara's tools, stepped back to the painting, jimmied the lock on one side of the heavy hinged brass frame until it popped open. Swinging the painting to one side, he exposed a built-in wall safe with split doors with two sets of tumblers.

"This one's for Jamey," Doyle said

He turned, hurried out of the room.

Orhan heard the tack-tacking rasp of a printer, paper spitting out from below the desk into a tray.

"Got it!" Ara said.

Ad Din scooped up the printed-out copies, read each one over, then looked over at Orhan, a grin spreading over his face.

"We've got Al Mehandi's ass cold," he said.

Coming back into the room, Doyle with O'Naill, Doyle showed him the safe.

"Got an enlargement glass, Doc?" O'Naill said to Ara.

Ara took out a square folding loupe, tossed it to O'Naill who caught it, unfolded it in one motion, turned, scanned the surface, the tumblers, then snapped the glass shut.

"Piece of cake," he said.

O'Naill rotated both tumblers– one clockwise, the other counter. He stopped twice, then eased the dials in the opposite direction. Orhan heard a noisy click, a squeak as O'Naill swung open the safe's double doors.

Doyle and O'Naill dug out papers, rolls of money from the safe, hauled them over to the coffee table.

"This will pay for dinner tonight," ad Din said.

Orhan looked through each folder of invoices, then compared them again.

"This is all one-sided, " he said. "Dozens of purchase records but no sales."

Ad Din looked through the folders, nodded in agreement.

"So, where are the goods?" he said.

Rest & Revelations

University of Alexandria Medical Center Hospital, Alexandria, Egypt,
The same day, 3:33 PM.

With a great spasm of her whole body, Colene came to. She looked around.

Light through a window lit the hospital room.

She saw a man– Egyptian, in dark fatigues dozing in a chair at the foot of her bed. He came to with a twitch, smiled at her.

"You're awake," he said in English.

"Where..." she started to speak.

He stood, stepped to her bedside.

"I'll call the doctor," he said.

He pressed a buzzer on a cord by her bedside.

A nurse looked in the door.

He spoke to her in Arabic. The nurse disappeared.

Two minutes later, an attractive dark-eyed woman in blue scrubs wearing a white lab coat with a stethoscope looped over her neck came in, walked over to Colene, looked into her eyes.

"I'm Dr. Sukkary," the woman said. "You're looking better."

"How did I get here?" Colene said.

"It's a long story and a long ride,"

"Where are my friends?"

"They'll be back soon," Dr. Sukkary said.

"I feel abandoned."

"The Turkish policeman and the Armenian doctor were called away on emergency."

"When will they get back?"

"Soon. I'm sure."

Colene lay back against the pillow.

Dr. Sukkary took the stethoscope, pressed it to Colene chest, looked into her eyes, then stepped back

"You're doing fine. You just need to rest."

Colene put her hand to her face.

"I feel burnt," she said.

"You were exposed to an explosion."

Colene looked up at the doctor.

"I only remember bits and pieces of last night."

"Just rest."

"I feel like I need a drink."

Dr. Sukkary laughed, walked to the door, turned, looked at Colene.

"A man from the American Embassy's here," Dr. Sukkary said. "He's been waiting for several hours to see you– but only if you feel up to it."

"I'll talk to him."

Dr. Sukkary motioned outside, a tall thin man in a suit came in. After cautioning him in a low voice, the doctor stepped out.

The man came over to her bedside, introduced himself with an ID folder, slid into a chair.

"Clarence Wilborn, US Embassy Security, Cairo," he said. "How are you feeling, Dr. Mooney?"

"Like shit."

"Are you up for a few questions?"

"Shoot."

Wilborn took a hard-bound notebook and pen from his pocket, then looked over at her.

"Did you hear your captors say anything about a load of missing military arms?" he said.

"Missing arms?"

"Shipping containers of guns."

"No."

"Did you hear any other information?"

Colene turned, looked Wilborn in the eye.

"Yeah, but you'll think I'm nuts when I tell you."

"Try me," he said.

Colene laid out the whole scheme for him, how Darryl told her he had involved Morris into feeding an armed uprising in the Arab petroleum nations to drive up gas prices to prompt a military invasion which would in turn provoke an imposition of martial law by right-wing political groups.

Colene looked over at the man next to her. She saw that Wilborn had stopped writing, his pen and notebook in his lap. He just stared at her now.

"This one man was going to do all this by himself?" Wilborn said.

"No. He was being helped by this John Wayne type, Morris."

"Morris was an ODS, overseas defense and security provider," Wilborn said. "Where's the connection getting the US government involved?"

"They have congressional connections and support from right wing political groups."

Wilborn didn't change his facial expression.

"It's been a tough time for you, Dr. Mooney."

"Told you, you'd think I'm nuts," Colene said.

Wilborn stood, eyes still staring, looked down at her, his lips moving into a tight smile.

"We'll talk more later," he said. "You've been very helpful."

He patted her left hand with the IV, turned and left the room.

Colene noticed the man in fatigues had stayed in the room.

"You a cop?" Colene said.

He grinned at her.

"Police corpsman."

"When's Ara coming?"

"He was here all night with you. When I relieved him this morning, he went off with the Turkish Interpol officer."

"What a fucking mess," Colene said.

She leaned her head back against the pillow, then fell asleep.

Hydra's Cave

The Big House, outside of Alexandria, Egypt
The next day, 12:32 PM

Orhan looked up at Ara who sat staring at his laptop screen, looking like a teenager ogling a girlie magazine.

Orhan wondered, *What's going on in that busy mind?*

"What's up, Ara?" he said,

"Look at this," Ara replied. "This guy was a control and neat freak."

Orhan and ad Din got up from the couch, went to the desk to look at the screen, standing at Ara's shoulder.

"This is a layout of this house," Ara said.

He zoomed in on an interactive image of a blueprint diagram of the house, opened detail boxes at different sections showing specific features of the interior of the house.

"He had this house refitted," Ara said. "The original construction has been modified in ... What's this?"

Doyle and O'Naill joined Orhan and ad Din, at the laptop screen.

Ara popped open a detail of the cellar.

"This is bizarre," Ara said. "Most of the original cellar has been sectioned off."

"What's so strange about that?" ad Din said.

"They've left only a small walled-off section," Ara said.

"Why's that strange?" ad Din said.

"According to the specs, this new section is constructed from reinforced concrete."

"Let's go down and take a look at it," ad Din said.

~*~~*~

Orhan and the others followed ad Din out to the cellar which was set in a recessed area directly beneath the fire escape. The door was locked with a flimsy clasp that O'Naill snapped off with a small crow bar.

Stepping inside, Orhan flicked on the light revealing a 4X3 meter anteroom for storing gardening and landscaping tools.

"Look at this," Ara said. "The back wall is made of meter thick reinforced concrete."

He pointed to the exterior wall of the cellar.

"This wall which is part of the original foundation is made of cheap, poured concrete, no more than 3" thick," Ara said. "The surface is rough and unfinished. Here, you can see settling cracks in it."

Ara stepped over to the interior wall, ran his hand over its smooth surface.

"This interior wall is made of a higher grade cement—likely imported," he said. "Notice the seams. They're made in sections which according to the specs are reinforced with rebar."

"That's a lot of concrete to protect garden tools from rats," O'Naill said.

"Exactly," Ara said. "There's something valuable behind this wall."

Ara took out a black Minimag flash light, shined it along the linoleum tile covered floor. Coming to a seam in the interior concrete wall that ran from the deck to the overhead, he focused the light along the angles, then tapped the wall with the end of the flashlight.

"Mr. O'Naill," he said. "Would you put your crowbar in the crack of this seam and give it a pry."

O'Naill jimmied the flat bent blade of the crowbar into the crack, pried it back. A thin cover of the wall popped loose. O'Naill and Ara pulled it back showing a wide locked steel door built into the wall.

O'Naill squatted down, examined the lock.

"A wee bit of C3 and this sassy lad will come off nicely," he said.

"Do it," ad Din said.

It took O'Naill and Doyle 5 minutes to blow the lock out of the door. After the blast when the smoke cleared and the debris settled, ad Din led the rest into the cellar.

The door stood in place, a torn hole gaped where the lock had been blown. O'Naill stuck the crowbar in the jamb cover of the door, leaned back on the handle, sprung the door open.

Ad Din went in first, found a light switch, clicked it on.

Orhan saw a deep chamber filled with crates and pallets laden with wooden and cardboard boxes, covered artifacts.

"*Ya sallaam*," ad Din said.

Orhan and the others walked through the array, looking in boxes, peeking beneath covers, popping open some crates.

"How much do you think this is worth?" Doyle said.

Orhan shook his head, looked over at ad Din.

"Off hand,"ad Din said. "Over 100 million US dollars."

~*~~*~

Outside, Orhan looked over at the burned hulk of the downed helicopter.

The National Police forensic team dressed in coveralls, faces covered, wearing rubber gloves, buzzed around the wreckage like huge white Arabic buzzing bees. Orhan spoke to the inspector in charge.

"Anything on the occupants?"

The inspector looked up from his clipboard at Orhan.

"There was only one body in the chopper," he said.

Orhan blinked.

"Only one?" he said.

"Just the pilot," the inspector said. "The headset was still on the body."

Orhan turned, walked past the boat house out to the boat dock. The yacht bobbed at its moorings in the flow of the receding tide.

The speedboat was gone.

Huddle Up

University of Alexandria Medical Center Hospital, Alexandria, Egypt
The same day, 7:13 PM

Brushing past orderlies pushing gurneys, patients in wheel chairs, doctors talking to nurses, Orhan, Ara and ad Din strode down the hospital hall to Colene's room. Coming inside, Orhan saw Dr. Sukkary and a nurse removing the IV from Colene's left hand. Seeing them come in, Colene looked over, grinned at them.

"So, you didn't abandon me," she said.

Dr. Sukkary stepped back as Orhan and Ara hugged and kissed her.

"You're looking better," Orhan said.

"Sorry, we had to go," Ara said.

Colene looked up at ad Din and said,

"I see you brought Omar Sharif."

Ad Din stepped forward, took her hand and kissed it.

Looking back at Orhan, Colene said,

"What happened?"

Orhan told her how Ara found the lock-away storage under the house.

"So, the guy I knew as Daniels, was a total crook?" Colene said.

"Still is," Orhan said.

"No way," Colene said. "I saw that helicopter blow up."

"So did I," Orhan said. "But, they only found the pilot's corpse in the wreckage."

"And, the speedboat that was docked at the pier is gone," Ara said.

Colene smiled.

"What's so funny?" Ara said.

"The codex's probably still intact," Colene said.

Orhan looked at Ara who shrugged and laughed.

"Now, that's dedication," Ara said.

~*~~*~

Ad Din arranged to have Colene's personal things picked up and brought to her from the Royal Hilton Hotel. While she was getting dressed, Ara stood outside in the hallway talking to Dr. Sukkary.

Standing a few feet away, Orhan saw a tall, thin American in a dark suit come up to ad Din, shake his hand.

"Orhan," ad Din said. "Clarence Wilborn from the US Embassy."

"Col. Mehmet," Wilborn said. "It's a privilege."

"What's your interest in Dr. Mooney?" Orhan said.

"We're concerned about three missing containers of stolen Ukrainian arms and ammo that was stolen in the States and transported here," Wilborn said.

"I doubt she'd know much about that," Orhan said.

"I'd hoped she might've heard something from her captors, but all I got was a rather fantastic tale."

"How so?"

"Don't take me wrong," Wilborn said. "I'm sure she was still under strong medication, but what she told me didn't make much sense."

"Now, I'm curious," ad Din said.

Wilborn told them Colene's story about a plot to start an uprising in the Middle East that would push fuel prices up, provoke the US to military intervention and thus enable conservatives to impose a theocracy through martial law.

When he finished, Orhan said to ad Din,

"Hamid, use your Omar Sharif charm to get that doctor to find us a room where all of us can talk."

~*~~*~

Dr. Sukkary showed Orhan and the others into a conference room, said she'd have some tea sent up, closed the door.

Orhan turned to Colene.

"Tell us what you heard from Darryl while you were held captive," he said.

She told again of the connections between Darryl with his smuggling network, Morris with his security contractors and connections with the politicians.

Wilborn's face did not change. He shot an expressionless glance at ad Din, then at Orhan.

"This is a pretty fantastic story," Wilborn said.

"It's true, though," Ara said.

Wilborn stared at Ara without changing expression.

Ara took out his satellite phone, slid it across the table to Wilborn.

"Call Ralph Samuelson," Ara said.

Wilborn's eyes snapped up from the phone in front of him. He glared at Ara, looked back down at the phone.

"OK," Wilborn said. "Let's go with what you're saying. We've still got the problem of three containers of Ukrainian arms getting into the hands of a bunch of nutcases who can launch a shit-storm."

"We can cover that," Orhan said.

"How so?" Wilborn said.

"We've got the man who knows where the weapons are," ad Din said. "We just don't know where they are right now."

Orhan tuned to ad Din.

"I can get it out of him." Orhan said.

Wilborn drew a deep breath, looked at ad Din then at Colene and Ara.

"We don't condone torture," Wilborn said to Orhan.

"I don't either," Orhan said. "It just doesn't work."

Confession and Absolution

Outside Burg al Arab District Prison, Alexandria, Egypt
two days later, 6:20 PM

The gnarled, pot-holed road snaked through the old industrial district on the way to the prison compound. Orhan took in the hodge-podge of old, dilapidated, abandoned buildings and structures. One new structure, shiny with paint, poked up like a green weed in a thatch of brown, dead brush.

Approaching the fenced area surrounding the prison facility, the road smoothed out the bumpy ride with a facelift of new tarmac. Orhan drove up to the security gate, showed his Interpol ID to the guard who waved him through.

Coming into the main office, Orhan surrendered his sidearm, signed into a log, then permitted himself to be patted down. He strung an identity badge around his neck, walked up to an iron door, then waited for it to be rolled back.

He stepped out onto a bare cement 18 meters wide alleyway that ran between the inner wall of the prison building separating it from the outer surrounding walled compound. Looking up, he saw guards with rifles monitoring his every step as he walked to the inner prison building between two parallel red lines 2 meters wide.

When he came to the prison building, a steel bar door opened, admitting him into a closed area 2 meters square. The steel barred door behind him banged shut, caging him until the iron door into the prison opened.

An armed guard motioned for him to enter, then patted him down again, checked his badge, then led him to an interior office.

Inside, a man in a green uniform marking him as a Lieutenant in the Egyptian National Police sat at a desk. When Orhan came in, he looked up, scowled.

"Who are you," he said. "And, what do you want."

"I'm here to talk to one of your prisoners," Orhan said.

"Impossible!" the Lieutenant said.

Orhan took a letter from his pocket, handed it to the Lieutenant seated in front of him. The Lieutenant snatched it from his hand, opened and read it.

He raised his eyes to Orhan. "You know General Abdulaziz Hakeem Rashad?"

"For a very long time." Orhan said.

The Lieutenant lowered his eyes, stood, bowed, offered his hand to Orhan.

"What do you require?" the Lieutenant said.

"Only a quiet room and privacy."

~*~~*~

Orhan sat at a plain wooden table at one end of the plastered brown 8 X 6 meter room with an old tape recorder against the wall. There was no furniture except for the table and two chairs.

Light from the late afternoon sun streamed in from a window on one side of the wall augmenting the dim light in the room from a single bulb in the center of the ceiling. Orhan sat with his back to the sunlight, a yellow notepad and pen lay on the desk in front of him along with an ovoid topless sardine can with burn stains and ash.

The barred door opened, a green uniformed guard shoved Abdi ibn Nur into the room. When he stumbled inside catching his balance, his manacles and leg irons rattled.

"Remove everything," Orhan said.

The guard unlocked the manacles, removed the leg irons.

"You may leave," Orhan said.

The guard left, closed the door.

"Sit down, please," Orhan said

Rubbing his wrists, Abdi strolled to the table, sat down across from Orhan, scooted the chair to keep the sunlight out of his eyes, leaned against the wall, resting one arm on the table, stared at Orhan.

Orhan set a pack of Marlboros with a pack of paper matches in front of Abdi.

"Smoke?" Orhan said.

Abdi glared, tightened his lips, shook his head.

"Go on," Orhan said.

Abdi stared at the pack of cigarettes in front of him, looked back, then reached down, picked up the pack, broke the cellophane seal, took out a cigarette, lit it, inhaled long and deep, then sat back, blew out the smoke.

"Let's talk about the guns you took from the Americans," Orhan said.

"What guns?" Abdi said.

"You didn't kill that American for the guns did you?"

Abdi glared at Orhan.

"What do you know?" he said.

"He killed your brother."

Abdi looked away, took another deep drag on the cigarette.

"It wasn't the Israelis," Orhan said. "It was Americans."

Abdi crushed the cigarette into the sardine can.

"You lie," he said.

"Darryl deceived you," Orhan said.

"I know no Darryl!"

"You know him as 'The Man.' "

Abdi's mouth tightened, his eyes snapped, glowed like dark coals.

Orhan went on.

"The Man, Darryl, sent Isaak to the States."

Abdi's hand on the table doubled into a fist.

Orhan watched him smoke for a minute or two, then spoke.

"You know," Orhan said. "South American drug dealers use poor, uneducated, needy people to smuggle dope into the States. They call these people, 'mules.'"

"So?"

"Do you know what a 'mule' is?"

"I don't fucking care!"

"It's an infertile cross between a horse and an ass."

Abdi glared, stared off into a corner.

"That's what you and Isaak were to this Man," Orhan said. "Mules."

"Why do you do this?"

"Because it's the truth."

Abdi screamed, "THE TRUTH IS DEAD!"

"Your brother is," Orhan said. "But, The Man still lives."

Abdi's head snapped around, his eyes narrowed. He stared at Orhan.

"You're lying," he said.

"They found only the pilot's body in the burnt-out helicopter. The speedboat was gone. What does that tell you?"

Abdi clenched his jaw, doubled his fist, his eyes fixed on Orhan.

"He has money stashed away," Orhan said. "When he wants, he'll find the guns. Then, he'll find another Palestinian mule like you and Isaak to do the dirty work and die for him."

"You don't know how it is for us," Abdi said.

"I've been in the camps in Lebanon," Orhan said.

Abdi's face contorted. He spat on the table.

"You call yourself a Moslem?" he said.

"I gave up believing in fairy tales the day you killed my wife and son."

Abdi stopped, straightened up, his eyes widened, his mouth opened. He choked, caught his breath.

"That's why you're here," Abdi said.

Orhan's face lost all expression. He sat, without moving, hands in front of him.

"Haven't enough people died to satisfy your illusions spawned from hatred?" Orhan said.

"Fuck you, Turk."

Orhan slapped both hands down on the table, leaned over, stuck his face into Abdi's.

"You serve the ones you hate," Orhan said. "They use you, they profit. People– your family, your friends, innocent people– die."

Orhan grit his teeth in cold anger.

"The rich oil sheikhs fatten themselves, your people bleed– those that do survive live in poverty and squalor."

Orhan drew his hand back. Abdi raised his hand, covered his face.

Orhan blew out his breath, let his arm fall, plopped down into his chair.

"I didn't blow up the car," Abdi said.

Orhan looked up at him, eyebrow knit, eyes blazing.

"I don't believe you."

"My car wouldn't start that night," Abdi said. "When I got to our safe house your narcotics people were taking away my four comrades. I slipped out of Istanbul with a Palestinian Greek fisherman."

"Go on."

"The Man sent Isaak. When he got to Istanbul a few days later, someone told him you'd had me killed."

"None of those men were harmed," Orhan said.

"He didn't know that."

"So, he killed my wife and son for revenge."

Abdi turned and yelled.

"He didn't know your wife was using your car that day!"

Orhan buried his face in his hands. He didn't move for a long time. Then, he raised his head, tears in his eyes.

"Our son was sick that morning," he said. "She used my car to take him to the doctor."

Abdi sat at the table, his head lowered. He spoke without looking at Orhan.

"For what it matters," Abdi said. "Isaak never forgave himself."

Orhan pushed back from the table, paced to the other side of the room. He hammered on the plastered wall with the heels of his fists, once, twice– a dozen times.

Then, he stopped, leaned on the wall with outstretched arms, dropped his head, stared at the floor.

He came back to the table, leaned over, looked Abdi in the eyes.

"How many more of us have to die in acts of supreme stupidity?"

Abdi leaned back against the wall, stared into Orhan's gaze. They sat like that for several minutes.

Then, Abdi dropped his head again, reached for the pack of Marlboros, shook out one, lit it, picked up the pen, turned the yellow pad in front of him.

"Here's a map to where we hid the containers," he said.

Interesting Dirt

FBI Office, Federal Building, Yonkers, NY
two days later, 9:45 AM

The receptionist looked up from her computer screen just as Ara walked through the doorway.

"Can I help you?" she said.

"Ara Agajanian," he said. "Agent Rich's expecting me."

At that moment, Mary Rich wearing a navy blue pinstriped pant suit, stepped out, took Ara's hand, led him into her office.

Coming in, Ara saw a tall, browned-haired, large brown eyed young man, his face in a broad grin. He stood, greeted Ara.

"Will Johnson," he said.

Ara declined coffee, took a seat on a couch next to Johnson as Rich pulled up a chair.

"Your files are very informative," Johnson said.

"And, mostly inadmissible," Rich said.

Ara opened the briefcase he had brought with him, took out two thick manila envelopes, handed one to each of them.

"Merry Christmas," he said.

"What's all this?" Rich said.

"The photos identify the deceased, Hamilton Morris, former CEO of 4Sinc, along with some other interesting items."

He handed Rich a letter.

"This is a notarized statement from Carl Rambeau, the acting CEO of 4Sinc permitting access to their all computers and communication files. Also, he's willing to make a statement about the complicity of his former boss in the assassination of the late Senator Sam Northridge and his staff."

"Holy shit," Rich said.

"How did you swing this?" Johnson said.

"Faced with doing hard time in an Egyptian prison," Ara said. "The former Major Rambeau was thrilled to cooperate."

Rich and Johnson picked through the papers, documents, photos and found the flash drives in the envelope.

"How's Colene?" Rich said.

"A bit banged up but back at Yale," Ara said. "We flew in night before last."

Ara stood and Rich and Johnson rose.

"I'll leave you to your chores," Ara said. "Nice to meet you both face to face."

Rich hugged him, kissed him on the cheek. Johnson pumped his hand.

"What can we say?" Johnson said.

"How about 'Let's go kick some ass,'" Ara said.

Unexpected Visit

Congressman Damian Styles Office, Capitol Office Building, Washington, DC
Two weeks later, 9:33 AM

Congressman Damian Style's office administrator glanced up at the tall young man standing in front of her with a pleasant face, big brown eyes, a college boy grin, dressed in brown slacks, a brown crew neck sweater, cordovan brown penny loafers.

He pulled out a flat billfold identifying him as CIA. He spoke in a low voice,

"I'm here to see Congressman Styles on a matter of national and state urgency."

She rang.

"Send him in," Styles said on the intercom.

Johnson stepped into the office, showed his ID.

"To what do I owe the honor of a visit from a spy?" Styles said.

"Not a spy, Congressman," Johnson said. "Just another cubicle dweller."

Styles indicated the chairs and coffee table.

"Coffee?" he said. "A drink, perhaps?"

"Nothing, thank you, Sir."

Johnson took out a manila envelope from his brief case, handed it to Styles.

Styles took out some photos, scanned through them.

He turned pale, caught his breath, looked up at Johnson.

"What in the hell is this?" he gasped.

"You tell me, Congressman," Johnson said.

"This is outrageous!" Styles said. "Where did you get this ... garbage?"

His face now red, Styles slammed the photos and envelope on the table, glared, spoke to Johnson in a growl,

"How much?"

His smile never wavering, Johnson swept up the photos, slipped them back in the envelope, looked over at Styles.

"We want you to resign, Congressman," he said.

"Fuck you," Styles said. "Your lurid shit won't stand up in court and you know it."

Johnson did not change his relaxed, smiling facial expression. "Your constituency will be most unforgiving when these photos appear in the public view," he said.

"You wouldn't dare," Styles said.

Johnson smiled, nodded.

"Yes. We would."

"This is blackmail!"

"We are a agency of the Federal government mandated to safeguard the public interest. That's hardly blackmail."

"You obtained this information illegally!"

"That's why I'm talking to you instead of the FBI."

"FBI?"

Johnson nodded.

"I can fight this in court," Styles said. "I've got some damn good lawyers ..."

"And I've got a former classmate who works with the liberal Columbia, SC, Slate," Johnson said. "My girlfriend works with the Washington Post..."

Styles's chest heaved. He covered his face with his hand, dabbed his handkerchief to his teary eyes.

"Why're you doing this to me?" he said.

"Operation Backfire."

Styles choked. He stared at Johnson.

"We knew," Johnson said.

Goodbye, Mr. Chips

FBI Office, Federal Building, Yonkers, NY
5:20 PM, the next day

After setting up the 27" flat-screen TV on the short table in the front of her office, Mary Rich arranged the plastic wine glasses alongside matching paper plates and napkins decorated with red, yellow, green, blue and purple balloons, then placed flat plates of cookies, cut veggies, sausages, in symmetrical array on the long table around two paper bowls of salsa, ranch dressing. Her secretary had brought in extra chairs, her office administrator had opened bottles of white and rosé wine.

The door opened, her supervisor, five other agents filed in, hugged, congratulated her, then turned their attention to the hors d'oeuvres, took seats in front of the TV.

Willy Johnson came in, gave her a big hug.

"Showtime!" Rich said and switched on the TV.

A banner with the logo of the Christian Television Network flashed across the TV screen. The strains of the hymn "Rally 'round the banner of Christ," blared as a voice announced, "Welcome to the Christian Family Hour."

The camera scanned the interior of a huge indoor arena, homed in on the stage where a chorus of singers in different colored choir robes stood in tiers above a small orchestra of players in white jackets.

A Master of Ceremonies with a combed stack of wavy gray hair in a dark blue suit strode out to loud applause, greeted everyone, invoked God's blessing on everyone, then introduced their host, the televangelist, JR Hammond.

A standing ovation greeted the big man in a Western cut dark blue pinstripe suit over a white Western shirt with small blue polka-dots, silver bolo tie with a turquoise cross, a red carnation pinned to his lapel.

Hammond quieted them down, telling how he once got caught by his mother sneaking off to go fishing when he was supposed to be in Sunday school. Then, he stopped talking.

He pursed his lips, folded his hands behind his back, dropped his head, stared at the stage floor in front of him.

After a short time, murmurs bled from the crowd like crickets.

"Here it comes," Rich said.

"I've made a tough decision," Hammond said on the screen. "As of tonight, I'm retiring from my ministry to spend more time in Christian reflection with my family."

Rich and her friends in the office broke into clapping and cheering.

"As you know," Hammond went on. "We suffered a tragic loss with the death of my son-in-law, former Lt. Col. Hamilton Morris, who died defending our freedom in a foreign land. I've decided to be there for my daughter and grandchildren in their time of need...."

Hammond went on about his decision, his commitment to God, Country and Family,

Rich leaned over to whisper in Johnson's ear.

"Morris's computer gave us a birthday present to deliver to the Reverend KD Rogers," she said.

New Horizons

Ara Agajanian's House, New Haven, CT
2 days later, 6:43 PM

Dinner was nearly finished. Colene poured some more red wine from the decanter. Ara herded grains of pilaf with a scrap of bread against his fork. Orhan took his third stuffed bell pepper.

"I salute the chef," Orhan said. "These peppers are like the one my mother makes."

"No kidding," Ara said. "It's my mother's recipe"

"I'm very good at opening packages and cans," Colene said.

"There's homemade ice cream with pistachios and black cherries," Ara said.

Orhan gobbled down the last of the stuffed pepper, wiped his mouth, stood up.

"Let me clear," he said to Ara. "You cooked."

"I'll just stack them in the sink," Ara said. "My cleaning lady's here tomorrow."

Colene drained her glass, sat it down on the table, tapped its side, then looked across the table at Ara.

"I read that Damian Styles resigned from Congress." she said.

"He'll be sorely missed," Ara said.

"The article also said Damian's going to be a consultant to the Rapture Network," Colene said.

"Life's tough for everybody," Ara said.

Happy Birthday

The Parsonage of Rev. Dr. K.D. Rogers, Columbia, South Carolina
2 days later, 3:27 PM

Wrapped up in a blue nylon jacket emblazoned with a badge, the bold gold letters FBI, Mary Rich stepped down from the lead of three black SUVs with federal license plates. Followed by two other FBI agents in the same jackets and four federal marshals, she strode across the well-groomed lawn, up the front door, pushed the doorbell.

A heavy-set woman in her 50s dressed in a pink and white print dress with her coiffed gray hair pulled back into an elegant French twist with bangs just below her eyebrows opened the door and scowled at Rich.

"Yes?" the woman said.

"This is Mr. K.D. Rogers's residence?" Rich said.

"I'm his wife," the woman said. "What do you want?"

Rich flashed her FBI ID.

"Agent Mary Rich, FBI. Mrs. Rogers. I have a warrant for K.D. Rogers."

"You'll have to come back tomorrow," Mrs. Rogers said. "Today's his birthday."

She started to close the door when Rich pushed her way inside.

"What do you think you're doing?" Mrs. Rogers said.

"Serving a warrant, Ma'am," Rich said.

"Leave. Now. Or, I shall call the police."

Rich pointed to the two federal marshals.

"Call them," she said. "They're right here."

K.D. Rogers stepped into the front room dressed in his dark blue suit, white shirt, thin black tie, with a red, yellow and green striped conical party hat on his head secured by an elastic band under his chin.

"What's going on here, Mother," he said.

"You are K.D. Rogers?" Rich said.

"I am the Reverend Dr. K.D. Rogers," he said.

Rich thrust the warrant into his hands,

"K.D. Rogers," she said. "I'm arresting you for money laundering, misuse of funds of a registered non-profit Christian charity agency and other conditions listed in this warrant."

"This is insane," Rogers said.

Rich pulled a card from her pocket, read Rogers his rights as another agent handcuffed his hands behind his back.

"I'm calling the police!" his wife screamed.

She ran to a phone on a stand in the hall way, punched in 911, screamed they were kidnaping her husband.

Rogers struggled in the grip of the two marshals who took him out the door.

"You can't do this to me!" he yelled.

Rich led them outside to the front SUV just as two blue police cars with lights flashing, sirens screaming pulled up. Two officers bailed out of each car, reaching for their side arms. Then, seeing the jackets of the FBI agents and Federal Marshals, they stopped.

Mrs. Rogers ran up to the first two policemen standing with their mouths open, staring at the federal officers loading Rogers into the back seat of the SUV.

"Stop them! Arrest them!" she screamed.

One of the policemen shook his head.

"Be kinda hard to do that, Ma'am," he said.

Rich helped the two agents get the struggling Rogers into the back seat.

"Try not to knock his hat off," Rich said.

Red's run done

Corkey's Coffee Corner, Seat Pleasant, MD
the next day, 10:26 AM

Leonard "Red" Bax slid into the booth at the end of the counter, signaled the waitress, then lit his 10th cigarette of the morning off his 9th.

The waitress, a tall, buxom woman in her early 50s wearing a pink and white uniform walked over and plopped the menu in front of Bax.

"Don't need no menu, Arlene," Bax said. "I always have the same damn thing."

"I was in hopes you'd realize you're not supposed to be smoking in here, Red."

Bax pushed the menu back toward Arlene, shifted his eyes away from her gaze.

"Just bring me some goddam coffee and my eggs. Spare me the goddam sermon."

Arlene swept up the menu and walked back to the kitchen area behind the counter.

Bax dumped a package of creamers in round little containers on the table from a small round bowl, then tapped out the butt of his 9th cigarette in it. Arlene set a mug of coffee in front of him. Bax took the sugar dispenser when she stepped away, shook in two tablespoons of the white crystals, stirred it with a fork from the set-up rolled in a paper napkin in front of him.

Taking a newspaper out of the side pocket of his jacket, Bax turned to the sports page.

"May I sit down?"

Bax looked up to see an African-American woman in a blue pants suit standing beside his table. He glanced around the diner, then turned to her with a scowl.

"Lots of empty seats. Why do you wanna sit here?"

She slid in the other side of the booth, opposite from him.

"Just wanted to be up close and personal with you, Mr. Bax."

"Do I know you?" he said.

"No," she said. "But, you soon will."

She took her ID billfold from the inside pocket of her jacket, opening it with a snap.

"Mary Rich. FBI."

Bax blinked, stared at the ID. His hand holding the cigarette trembled. His eyes rolled. Beads of sweat popped out on his brow, above his moustache on his upper lip. He took a deep drag on number 10 cigarette, then choked,

"What do you want?"

"First," Rich said. "I want to know if you're carrying a side arm."

"I am."

Two men in suits stepped up, stood by Bax on both sides at the end of the booth, their jackets open. Bax could see their side arms exposed.

"Please stand up and make no move toward your piece," Rich said.

"Why?" Bax said. "Am I under arrest?"

Rich looked up at the nearest of the two men.

"Read him his rights, Charlie," she said.

While the man named Charlie took out a card from his pocket, read Bax his rights, the other man helped Bax slip out of the booth, then removed Bax's pistol from the shoulder holster under his arm, leaned over, slipped out a snub-nose revolver from an ankle holster. Pocketing the two weapons in his jacket, the agent eased Bax's arms behind him, snapped on a pair of hand cuffs.

When Mary Rich slid out of the booth, Bax leaned forward, sticking his reddening face into hers.

"I ain't saying a fucking word until my lawyer gets here."

Rich smiled.

"You don't have to, Mr. Bax. But, your counsel will be joining our chat down at the Federal Building."

Bax lowered his eyes, as the three FBI agents ushered him towards the door.

Seeing Bax being escorted outside, Arlene, the waitress leaned inside the opening into the kitchen.

"Bill!" she said. "Cancel that order of fried eggs and white toast."

Hit and Run

Two blocks from the Rapture Network, Charleston, SC
the next day, 9:16 AM

Singing along to the old hymn pouring out of his radio, Damian Styles tapped time on the steering wheel as he waited for the light to change.

The light turned green, he took his foot off the brake, stepped on the gas, entered the intersection.

He was in the middle, when he glanced to his left, saw the red Hummer run the red light.

Then, there was noise, pain, darkness.

~*~~*~

A policeman was talking to an eye witness, an elderly African American woman in a pillbox hat on the curb beside the intersection where pieces, parts of the smashed car littered the street.

"So, you saw this van run the red light?" he said.

"Yessir, that's what I saw."

"Can you describe the van?"

"I can. It was one of them vans you see our soldier's driving."

"Like a Humvee?"

"Yessir. My nephew's in Iraq and drives one of them."

"Color?"

"It was red."

"Did you see the driver?"

"Yessir. White man, blond hair in a ponytail."

"Can you tell me some more what he looked like?"

"Wore a bill cap."

"See anything else he was wearing?"

"Hmm. Looked like a vest."

"Color?"

"Black. Leather, I think. Had a white tee shirt on underneath."

"Other features– facial hair?"

"Bushy mustache. Maybe a goat beard. Can't be sure."

"Eyes?"

"Can't say. Had on dark sunglasses."

"Anything else about the vehicle or driver."

"Well, he did have a bumper sticker."

"What did it say?"

"Well, it was a large fish eating a smaller fish with feet. Couldn't see what the fish with feet said but the big fish had 'Truth,' written on its side."

"Thank you, Ma'am."

"What about that man that got hit?"

"He was dead when the ambulance got here, Ma'am."

The Holy Grail

Bedroom, Colene's house, New Haven, CT
5 days later, 5:15 AM

Colene laid her head on the pillow watching the man she wanted to stay packing his suitcase. She fought back emotions as she watched Orhan's slow deliberate motions as he finished packing.

He looked back at her, smiled.

"No," he said. "I don't want to leave either."

Colene swallowed, choked back the urge to cry.

He came over, sat on the edge of the bed, stroked her hair. She took his hand, looked down, pouted.

"I'm not a cat," she said.

Orhan grinned at her.

"I've never thought of you as anything other than you," he said.

"Goddam it," Colene said. "Can't you see how I'm hurting?"

"Yes. But, it doesn't end here, Colene."

"What do you want?" Colene said.

"To be with you again as soon and as often as I can."

"We live in two worlds, Orhan," she said.

"We have two lives," he said.

"I'm confused—where does my life with you go from here?"

"It goes where we can take it," he said. "We accept the limits on what we can do, look for solutions and know we love each other."

She sat up, took him in her arms, pulled him to her, his head resting on her breast.

"What do we want, Orhan?"

"You want a book. I want the man who has it."

She let him go, scooted back, put her face in her hands.

"Damn it, damn it, damn it," she said. "It's never hurt like this before."

He took her in his arms.

"You're not alone. I've known pain—terrible pain. Right now, I'm wandering down the same path as you."

She clung to him.

"Did we fail somewhere?" she said.

"Not in the least," he said. "I found you."

"I meant do you feel we failed, because Darryl got away?"

"More amazed than any feeling of failure—I still wonder how he got out of that chopper."

"That dirty sonofabitch made a fool of me."

"He made fools of all of us, Colene."

Colene pulled her knees up to her chest under the sheet, leaned forward wrapping her arms around them, resting her chin on top.

"What happens to us now?" she said.

Orhan tilted her face to his, looked into her eyes.

"I'm not losing you," he said.

She reached for him, pulled him to her, her face next to his.

"Why are we wearing all these clothes?" she said.

~*~~*~

Tweed-New Haven Airport, New Haven, CT
11:51 AM, same day

Orhan held on to Colene's hand as they walked to the escalator to the departure area. He stopped in front of the landing, turned to her.

"Professor Fahir Casamlı at Ankara University has invited you to come and look through Foucault's notes," Orhan said.

"I sent him my agreement earlier this week," Colene said.

"You'll come to Turkey this summer?" Orhan said.

"I shall."

"That pleases me."

She wrinkled her brow, looked into his face.

"You're sure you're not disappointed that Darryl got away?"

"He's out there somewhere, but, now I know he's the Hydra when he tries something."

"Any ideas?" she said.

"Damn few right now."

"How about feelings?"

"To me, feelings are ideas."

"Now, that's a man's point of view."

Orhan shook his head.

"He's lost his network. He'll try to build a new one– and now, the trail is littered with traps. One slip and I got him."

"But, he has connections– corrupt people in important places."

"The fact remains– Hydra uses people as mere pawns."

"Is that how he saw me? A pawn?"

"No. He wanted to please you– you reminded him of his lost wife."

"Do I remind you of your lost wife?"

"Not in the least."

Colene grabbed him, kissed him, held him.

"I don't want to let you go," she said.

"I know."

Orhan picked up his carry-on bag, put his arm around her shoulder, walked with her to the escalator landing.

She kissed him.

He stepped onto the escalator, then looked back at her as he ascended to the next floor.

Hydra Redux

Hotel Daphni, Bari, (outside of Athens), Greece
the same day, 5:15 PM

The balcony of the hotel on the 6th floor looked out over the surrounding rooftops to the rolling hills beyond the town. The curtains of the double windows leading out to the narrow balustrade fluttered in the breeze blowing in from the sea.

Dressed in a long-sleeved white and blue striped tee shirt over blue jeans, Hydra sat on the edge of the narrow balcony rail, smoking a Cuban cigar, holding a glass of 7 Star Metaxa with chipped ice in his right hand. He gazed out to the southwest towards the road to Piraeus that ran through the brown hills.

Lost in thought, he perched on the edge of the railing for about 15 minutes. He finished the cigar, hurled the stub into the gutter of the street below, drained the glass, tossed the ice in a shower over the empty street, stepped back inside.

The room was large by rural Greek standards, 15 X 22 meters, an enameled iron-stead bed sat in the corner, a small table stood in the kitchenette, a chest of drawers, an armoire hunkered in the corner, a small desk sat tucked under a window.

He stepped over to a metal briefcase beside the desk, rolled the tumblers, snapped it open. He took out the codex, set it in front of him, ran his hand over its dried-out, rough leather binder.

He remembered a time in high school—a poetry class.

He had copied a poem that Jim Corbett had written from Corbett's notebook. Darryl then submitted the poem as his own—it won the senior class literary prize that year.

Corbett never said a word to him about it afterwards. He had just looked at him with eyes full of disbelief, disappointment, betrayal.

Hydra sat back in the painted wooden desk chair, tried to recall the poem—only part of it came back.

He murmured it aloud,

"Bum, in the hot dusty road–
vanished visions of springtime castles,
there..."

ABOUT THE AUTHOR

Frank P. Araujo

Anthropologist, linguist, advisor to pastoral nomads in the Third World, Frank P. Araujo has a lifetime of experience in the intrigue of international politics. A musician, he knows by heart the scores to a dozen operas. He plays bagpipes. He's a sabre fencer who speaks Basque, Russian, Japanese, Arabic and holds a black belt in martial arts. This is his first novel.

Made in the USA
Lexington, KY
29 April 2012